THE ELBE RESOLUTION

LLOYD HOLM, IN ADDITION TO BEING AN AUTHOR, is a board certified obstetrician in the Twin Cities. His writings have appeared in the *Omaha World-Herald*, *The Female Patient*, *Iowa Medicine*, *Contemporary OB/GYN*, *Hospital Drive*, the *American Journal of Obstetrics and Gynecology*, and *Obstetrics and Gynecology*. He lives in Cottage Grove, Minnesota with his wife, Gretchen.

ALSO BY LLOYD HOLM

The Ledger

Praise for *The Ledger*

"This wonderful book is authentic and detail oriented … whether you read as a historian, a romantic, or a war buff, you will find it satisfying on all accounts, and I dare you to put it down once you start."
—*GPS World*

"Skillfully written and historically correct with a smooth flow and relatable characters who stay true to form. Five stars for this uplifting read."
—*Terraverum Book Reviews*

"Take the time to read this incredible story of two young lovers who overcome all for the sake of love … Five stars."
—*Romantic Historical Lovers Book Reviews*

Lloyd Holm

The Elbe Resolution

A Novel

Fox Farm Press

FOX FARM PRESS

This book is a work of fiction, set against the background of actual events. The characters, however, are entirely fictional and are products of the author's imagination. Any resemblance to persons, living or dead, is entirely coincidental. The author's characterization of General Dwight David Eisenhower in this book is entirely fictional.

ISBN: 978-0-9847564-3-8

Cover design by the Fast Fingers Book Formatting Service
www.thefastfingers.com
Front cover images:
http://upload.wikimedia.org/wikipedia/commons/f/f0/Sinzig_enclosure.jpg

www.lloydholmbooks.com

Printed in the United States of America

To the memories of 17033669 and 35812931

"War settles nothing."

Dwight D. Eisenhower

THE ELBE RESOLUTION

prologue

Berlin, Germany
22 February 1943

SEPARATED BY THEIR OWN THOUGHTS, DORTHEA BECK and her husband sat in the first row of an empty courtroom. Since Hitler's appointment as Chancellor in 1933, all vestiges of due process within the Third Reich had been cut out like a cancerous growth, all glimmers of hope ruthlessly and methodically excised. Dorthea strained to hear any murmurs of justice that might assist her daughter—she only heard the hollow sound of Nazi boot heels echoing on the marble floors of the cavernous hallway just beyond the excessively ornate, tall oak doors. A stack of files sat on the polished table next to five empty glasses and a pitcher of water. From a frame on the wall above the judge's bench, Adolph Hitler glared down upon the People's Court with a look that guaranteed only *his* justice would be served.

In the silence she'd grown to expect, forty-five-year-old Dorthea Beck contemplated her only child's fate as well as her own. The daughter of a baron—a displaced baron at that since Hitler took power—Dorthea had always gotten her way. It wasn't until after she married Karl Beck that her subjugation began. Not only did he deprive her of that which she was accustomed, he took perverse pleasure doing so. She'd long since learned to steel herself even to remain in the same room with the sadistic bastard. Seated

11

to her right, her husband, Oberst Karl Beck, kept his hands in his lap and looked the other way as she opened her purse and removed her compact. With a quick glance in the mirror, the once beautiful woman confirmed the makeup touched-up an hour earlier success-fully disguised puffy eyes but did little to provide color to a pale, tired face. Before closing the purse, a fresh handkerchief replaced one stained with tears. Her head bowed, she no longer questioned why her daughter had been arrested; instead, yet another silent prayer was offered. *Dear God, please spare my Katrin, please dear God, I beg only this, please.*

Dorthea looked up, shocked to see every seat in the courtroom filled. *Who are all these people, when did they come in?* Several heads were tilted together, most with a hand over their mouths. *Probably whispering about me. Well, let them.* She stared straight ahead, trying not to feel those hundreds of eyes.

Safe in the knowledge he would remain silent, she continued to ignore her husband. It had been weeks since he'd said anything civil, years since anything loving. Finally she dared to look at him. *And to think I used to tell Katrin you're not one of them. How could I have been so foolish?*

She gasped the instant the door beneath the Führer opened and her twenty-one-year-old daughter emerged in handcuffs. A somber and disheveled prisoner stood before the bench, her face devoid of emotion, the spring gone from her step. Her once shiny hair, fashionably cut and trimmed, hadn't been soothed by a comb in days. Dorthea noticed the curious spectators gape at the young woman, then at Karl Beck. *Do they know he's her father, this Nazi? Do they even care?*

Her gaze followed the judges as they filed into the courtroom and stood behind their chairs, waiting for Roland Freisler, the presiding judge to take his seat. She focused on her daughter's back and silently voiced one last prayer.

Seated, the President of the People's Court turned his head

and nodded at the two judges on his left and did same to the two on his right. He no more than glanced at the contents of the file before he spoke. "Katrin Anneliese Beck, you are charged with being a member of the White Rose and you are hereby charged with high treason."

The girl's back stiffened as she stood straight. "I do not recognize your court as the true arbitrator of justice in Germany."

Dorthea Beck startled when Roland Freisler jumped to his feet and screamed.

"Jezebel!"

The other four members of the Nazi's People's Court exchanged knowing glances, then looked down at their motionless hands as Freisler's rant reached a crescendo. "You and your scoundrel scum do not even deserve to be considered Germans!" He slammed his fist down and shouted, "How do you plead?"

She remained unmoved.

"I will consider your silence a plea of not guilty." Without consulting his notes, he glared, malevolent, straight into her eyes. "Katrin Anneliese Beck, you willingly and knowingly associated yourself with elements of the White Rose, the most vile and treacherous organization in all of Germany."

She stood mute.

"What do you have to say for yourself, you worthless harlot?" His voice reverberated to the ceiling. "Are you, or are you not a member of the White Rose?"

"Are you asking me or telling me?"

Again he jumped to his feet, reddened cheeks aflame. He removed a single sheet from the file in front of him and waved it menacingly. "These are the lies you distributed at the University of Munich on 18 February 1943. Furthermore"—he leaned over the bench and shook the leaflet in her face—"this is what the Gestapo discovered in your apartment." The hushed courtroom rang with his voice. " 'Honest Germans, you must recognize what is happening around you. How many murdered Jews will it take for you to take action? The time to act is now. The time to revolt is now. The time to redeem ourselves before the world is now. Honest Germans, you must stand up and fight.'"

Dorthea Beck, nearly spellbound, watched Roland Freisler, in slow deliberate motions, rip the sheet into dozens of pieces, extend his arm and let the shreds float, back and forth, to the floor.

"Do you deny writing these despicable lies?"

"No."

Through a smirk he said, "You wrote them with the other scoundrels?"

Katrin Beck thrust her shoulders back. "They had nothing to do with it." She stared him down. "I wrote them myself."

For only the second time since arriving an hour earlier, Dorthea looked at her husband—not for support—but rather for affirmation. *I hope you're satisfied. And this is the honor you Nazis are so proud of.* With her handkerchief, she dabbed the corner of her right eye. Her husband looked straight ahead. *You son-of-a-bitch, I hope you rot in Hell.*

The two judges on both sides of the bench leaned toward the middle and conferred with Roland Freisler. After a few seconds, the resounding crack of his gavel shattered the silence. "Katrin Anneliese Beck, I see no remorse in your cowardly eyes. Furthermore, in delivering your sentence, I am compelled to consider the fact that you are the daughter of a Nazi officer."

With this announcement, all eyes turned to her father.

"An example must be made of you and your treasonous vermin. The President of the People's Court announces the verdict." With a final, forceful blow of the gavel on the bench, Roland Freisler issued his decree. "For the crime of high treason, the accused is sentenced to death by hanging. Take her away."

▪ ▪ ▪ ▪ ▪

Karl Beck ignored the sobs and heaving shoulders of his wife. When his daughter turned and looked only at her mother, he stood, adjusted his tunic, and walked out of the courtroom.

chapter 1

German Battalion Headquarters
Belgian village, near the German border
1600 hours
24 December 1944

THE COMING DARKNESS HELD THE PROMISE OF a quiet Christmas. Fierce fighting in what would later be known as the Battle of the Bulge subsided briefly as Hitler's desperate gamble to throw the Allied advance on its heels and force a peace in the West stalled. Frigid weather raged from the north and embraced all of Europe with a vengeance not seen since the Viking invasions. A cold, heavy fog straddled the entire eighty-mile Belgium-German frontier, aiding the German advance. After a week of stubborn fighting, tens of thousands of soldiers—German and American—had either been wounded or killed, an additional twenty thousand captured or missing.

A weary Major Hans Krüger descended fifteen wooden steps leading to the darkened cellar. He long ago stopped caring his uniform hadn't been cleaned or pressed in weeks. Uncombed blond hair clashed with handsome and distinct facial features. Five years of waging war had dulled his once engaging hazel eyes. At the bottom of the stairs an unteroffizier stood guard. Hans ignored the salute then stepped aside as the key turned in the lock. Upon entering the room, the unteroffizier set a lamp on the table. Hans looked around. At the top of the wall a partially covered window leading to the alley failed to keep out the cold. Remnants of a broken pane could be seen between two boards, frost painted the shards of glass. On the floor next to a damaged chest of drawers, a crumpled-up blanket filled the corner. In a chair by the table coated with dust sat a captured American soldier. Despite visible breaths, he didn't appear cold. Hans considered the man waiting to be interrogated. The insignia patches on his left shoulder confirmed a rank of sergeant with the American 99th Infantry Division. He had seen countless prisoners in the past but this one remained confident. In the diffused light the prisoner's blue eyes held none of the fear nor the defiance observed in other prisoners—they were soft and probing beneath a gentle wave of dark hair. Covered with stubble, his face suggested an age no different than the tens of thousands of soldiers in Europe at that moment in time.

Major Krüger glanced at his watch and turned toward the door. "Bring him upstairs."

chapter 2

DESPITE THE LULL IN FIGHTING, MAJOR KRÜGER emerged from the cellar to find the battalion headquarters a beehive of activity. Clerks rushed about filing dispatches, typewriters spit out precise German reports, and the whistles and whines of Morse code leaked from the headphones hugging the radioman's ears.

Hans motioned to his fellow officer. "Lars, what'd you find on him?"

"Only these." The man held out a letter and some photos.

"Anything helpful?"

"Nothing. It's from his wife in America, someplace called Iowa. She's pregnant, due any day."

"Does he speak German?"

"No, he just stood there the whole time with a stupid look on his face."

"Fine." Hans looked at his watch. *May as well get this over with.* He studied the photo of a beautiful young woman, perhaps twenty-one or twenty-two, standing confident next to the American. *If I didn't know better, I'd think she had German blood.* He studied the picture further. *Or French.* Her arm locked through the American's, a look of innocence complemented one of adoration and complete love. After scanning the back of the photo, he flipped it over and slowly ran his fingers along its worn edges.

Lars cleared his throat. "Ahem."

19

Hans looked up. "Sorry, I was daydreaming."

"Someone as pretty as her?"

A smile eventually crossed his face. "To be sure."

"How long's it been?"

"Too long. August. The 29ᵗʰ to be exact." He took one last look at the photo. "The sooner we start, the sooner we finish."

▪   ▪   ▪   ▪   ▪

Hans entered the room, sat at the table across from the prisoner and handed back the man's personal effects. As he spoke, Lars translated. "I'm Major Hans Krüger." When there was no response, he said, "I assure you, this is to be a friendly conversation. After all, it *is* Christmas Eve." When he noticed the prisoner glance at Lars, then rub the worn furrow of skin where his wedding band had been, he added, "Who's Irma?"

The prisoner turned abruptly and glanced back at Hans, then looked down at the photo. "My wife."

Hans' eyes were drawn back to the American's left hand. "Did you misplace your wedding band?"

"Yeah, something like that."

Major Krüger looked at the letter the prisoner held. "Your wife's with child, you look too young to be a father. Do you have other children?"

"No."

Silence.

Lars nudged Hans' knee under the table.

"Excuse me Sergeant, your last name, Veit, that's German."

The prisoner sat a bit straighter. "So."

"Ever been to Germany?"

"No."

Hans noticed the prisoner's calloused hands. "Tell me Sergeant Veit, do you hope to farm after the war?" He detected a hint of

20

surprise, then nodded toward the photo. "There's a barn in the background."

The American hesitated. "Yes."

"When did you see her last?"

More silence.

You're a cagey one, Sergeant Veit from Iowa. Can't you talk? "Sergeant, we already know the 99th Infantry Division arrived in England this past October, that you crossed the Channel at Le Harve in November." He pointed to the photo. "Answer my question, when did you see her last?"

"September."

"And, in America what did you and your *fräu* do?"

The prisoner looked at Hans. Both corners of his mouth seemed to resist the full upturn of a complete smile. "Dance."

"Is it not a shame about your Glenn Miller?" Hans shook his head side to side. "Needless casualties of war."

As he waited for an answer, the door flew open. The blast of cold air caused the lamplight to flicker.

"Damnation, shut the door."

"My apologies, Major." Anton stomped the snow off his feet, pulled off his gloves, and rubbed his hands together. "Just got off the line."

▪ ▪ ▪ ▪ ▪

Anton removed his fogged-over glasses and wiped the lenses free of moisture. After replacing them he looked about, approached a fellow office in the corner of the room and poured himself a cup of coffee. "The regiment's in position—"

"Do you mind? We're trying to interrogate this prisoner," Hans said from across the room.

Anton ignored his friend. "It's quiet for a change, and there's no report of enemy buildup along the line." Finally, he glanced over at Hans who still appeared annoyed. "Can't this wait? Come, let's celebrate your birthday."

■ ■ ■ ■ ■

The American prisoner looked to the translator as if to wonder what had been said. Hans shook his head, No.

"Forgive me Sergeant, I must know—is your unit expecting replacements?"

"Veit, Daniel J., Sergeant. 35812931."

Hans ignored the prisoner's refusal to cooperate. "Your comrades, they're tough men. Not the untested soldiers we expected." He scanned the prisoner for a reaction. "Has your company sustained many casualties?"

"Veit, Daniel J., Sergeant. 35812931."

Hans snapped his fingers. The unteroffizier standing by the door stepped forward. "I'm through with him. Put him back in the cellar."

Sergeant Veit made it a point to look directly at Hans. "*Vielleicht, Herr Major, werden Sie und mein Kind denselben Geburtstag feiern.*"

Hans recoiled. After an exchange of surprised glances with Anton and Lars he replied, "Yes, perhaps your child and I will share the same birthday." As an afterthought, he added, "Sergeant Veit, you didn't tell us you spoke perfect German."

"*Herr Major, fragten Sie nicht.*" You didn't ask.

chapter 3

Featherstone POW Camp #18, Northeast England
1700 hours
24 December 1944

A COLD WIND PLAYED OFF THE IRISH Sea and rattled the shutters of a barren assembly hall before slicing across Northeast England in search of the North Sea. Peter Krüger sat alone in the empty room huddled next to a pot-bellied stove ignoring the smoke seeping into his sweater. The bone-chilling walk from his barrack and the stinging sleet descending from persistent grey skies worsened his mood on this, his twenty-fourth Christmas Eve. In many ways, his captivity in the English prisoner-of-war camp mimicked his existence on the U-357. He continued staring at the floor. *What the hell did I do to deserve this? Two goddamned years and nobody knows I'm even alive.*

He finally looked up at the decorated fir tree sitting on the table and tried not to think of Christmas as a child or his brother Hans'birthday. Ignoring the sound of the opening door, he thought again of Berlin. The rush of cold air reminded him of the injuries his brother sustained in the Battle of Moscow. *Where are you now Hans, are you still alive? And Mother, how many tears have you spilled thinking I'm dead? Fucking Limeys anyway.*

Wilhelm slapped him on the shoulder. "Cheer up Peter, it's Christmas Eve."

"Why?" This is the second one for me in this God-forsaken hellhole. "There's nothing to be cheerful about." He squeezed his arms around his chest to warm himself. "I swear, it was warmer in that damned U-boat in December than it is here in the middle of June."

Initially, Peter convinced himself Wilhelm was a British agent. After all, he arrived in the camp only days after his own arrival with a story of having served with the Afrika Korps prior to his capture. Besides, not only was his hair blonder than Peter's, his build more solid, he even looked more German. Things seemed too contrived, his recollections of living in Bonn lacked specifics. He knew Wilhelm was planted in his barrack to learn the secrets of the Enigma machine, but as the months dragged on, Wilhelm never asked a single question about his duties on the U-357.

"I never thought I'd want to be back in the desert, but a winter here'll do that. The desert's better than freezing," Wilhelm said.

Peter glanced at his fellow prisoner. How can you always be so damned happy? "Cold? You don't know what cold is 'til they pull you out of the North Atlantic. Another ten minutes and I'd been a goner."

"What's worse I wonder, dying in the ocean or dying in the desert?"

"The ocean. At least in the desert you have a chance of being buried," Peter said without hesitating.

"What's that give you? Dead's dead."

"True, but at least you have peace. Reminds me of the Sailor's Lament." Peter cleared his throat. "One of the verses goes like this: 'There are no roses on a sailor's grave, no lilies on an ocean wave. The only tribute's the seagulls' sweeps, and the teardrops that a sweetheart weeps.' That's why the desert's a better place to die—a burial gives your soul peace."

Wilhelm nodded. "I see your point. But you were one of the lucky ones—"

"No, the dead, they're the lucky ones. Their suffering's over, mine was just beginning."

"How'd it happen?"

"Which, my surviving or the sinking?"

"Both."

Peter inhaled and closed his eyes. He didn't open them again until after he began to speak. "Just before Christmas I'd been on leave to visit Mother and Father in Berlin. Even my brother Hans was there. We were under orders to report no later than the 12th to assist in the outfitting of our boat. On time at 0600 hours on the 15th, we cleared the harbor alongside the U-525. Both diesel engines rumbled to life and we headed north toward the Norwegian coast. The first morning the crew whistled at their workstations. That ended when a patrol boat rammed our starboard side. No damage was done to our boat, only our mood."

Peter, for the first time, became aware others had entered the hall. "Our spirits rose again once our kapitänleutnant opened his operational orders, but then we encountered another mishap. We were yet to engage the enemy and while standing watch our quartermaster was swept overboard, lost at sea."

"Good God," Wilhelm said.

Peter persisted. "We then developed a threatening leak in one of the diesel engines. Because we were still along the coast, we stayed submerged during daylight hours. This only made the leak worse. Finally we cleared the coast and headed out into the North Atlantic. By this time, I *knew* we were jinxed."

"It must be terrifying being in a steel tube thrashing about."

"Five hundred tons of steel goes a long way in smoothing a rough sea, but it's actually calm submerged—and quiet—at least until the charges start going off."

Wilhelm's eyes widened. "I can't imagine. It must've been awful."

"*Ja.*" Peter straightened his back. "Once out into the North

Atlantic we remained on the surface running on one engine while the electric batteries charged. I exchanged radio traffic and played music for the men on the ship's loudspeakers. The kapitänleutnant had us sailing southwest to intercept a convoy. Meanwhile, the machinist mate repaired the leak." Peter could feel the corners of his mouth curve upward in a smile. "On the 24th the kapitänleutnant ordered that we submerge to lessen the heaving of the boat, then led the singing of Christmas carols. It had only been a week since we put out to sea so our food stores were not spoilt. The first few days' food is stored everywhere—bread, fresh meat, vegetables, and cheese. Each nook and cranny stuffed with canned goods. Bread hung from the piping, and of course, after each day, our supplies dwindled which made our passage more comfortable."

Peter scanned the faces gathered around. "Our cook did a wonderful job preparing our meal. We all laughed when he told us the Kriegsmarine couldn't have read his file since he was a chef before the war!" He leaned back, stretched his arms and shifted his weight on the hard bench. "My God, the odors on a U-boats are far from sweet—diesel fumes, urine, sweat and even semen. But he made us forget all these things. I swear, the smells coming from the galley magically transported all forty-three of us to our homes and our loved one's arms.

"After our meal we listened to recording discs on the gramophone, we read and re-read letters from home. Photos were passed back and forth, again and again. Finally, our kapitänleutnant reached behind him. With a grunt and a groan, he produced a duffel bag wedged into the storage area. We were surprised when he removed a package and said, 'My wife wrapped all these before we departed.' He then placed forty-two paper Christmas ornaments on the table like they were made of delicate crystal, one for each of us. 'Gretchen and I, we made these for you men.' Someone started humming. Within minutes, every one of us joined in the singing of *stille Nacht, heilige Nacht*, each staring off into their own world."

By this time, like metal filings drawn to a magnet, more prisoners gathered. A few sniffles could be heard. The prisoner across from Peter wiped his eyes and nodded, encouraging him to continue.

"Our Christmas celebration was not yet over. The kapitänleutnant waited to order the boat to periscope depth. He had another surprise—a special gift for the crew. He leaned back again, reached into the bottom of his duffel bag and carefully removed a record from its protective sleeve. His sly wink told me not to expect Christmas music. 'Play this for the crew. They deserve it.' I had no idea he liked jazz. Over the boat's loudspeakers the opening drum solo of Benny Goodman's *Sing, Sing, Sing* brought an exchange of nodding smiles to the crew. Feet tapped to the beat as our bodies swayed to the forbidden melody of American Swing. Both sides were played a second time. Only then did our kapitänleutnant order his elated crew to bring his boat to periscope depth.

"Rotating the periscope 360 degrees, he declared a clear horizon before we surfaced. Our ears popped from a cannon blast of stale air shooting out the hatch. Several men scampered to their posts and the 20mm gun was manned first upon surfacing in the event an enemy aircraft circled overhead.

"Once the 'All-clear' was announced other crewmen like myself were allowed to take in the fresh air. Always the last to go up top, it was my responsibility to receive and transmit messages to and from U-boat command in Lorient. Only after all the messages were encrypted and decoded did I handle the traffic from other boats. Then my turn would come. On deck one remained silent, for speaking to the men standing watch invited the wrath of our kapitänleutnant.

"We continued sailing southwest and by the 26th of December we were two hundred nautical miles west of the Scottish coast and two hundred and seventy north northwest of the Irish coast. Being that far out into the North Atlantic, I knew we would encounter the enemy. You see, when the kapitänleutnant plotted the convoy's deciphered co-ordinates on the chart he smiled as he compared our fix to their location. He tapped his finger not far from our position and said, 'Soon, two, maybe three hours.'"

"How fast were you sailing?" one of the other prisoners said.

"On the surface, sixteen to eighteen knots. Submerged, six to eight. Since we were ordered to engage the convoy, we were running full-bore—eighteen knots. About 1600 hours, we spotted them. The alarm sounded and we all rushed below. We hoped one of their escorts hadn't spotted us. The kapitänleutnant manned the periscope. He swore just as he ordered us to come about and ready the torpedoes—we'd been spotted. We *were* jinxed. My friend Martin, the hydrophone operator, said, 'I told you black cats were bad luck.'"

The prisoner standing next to Wilhelm looked confused. "Where'd the black cat come from?"

"On the pier shoving off, it darted out from behind some food crates, probably stalking a mouse." Peter arched his stiffened back. "The kapitänleutnant, still swearing, ordered two torpedoes to be launched before he ordered an immediate dive and course change. The officer with the stopwatch looked up after a minute and shrugged. Sixty seconds later we heard two muffled explosions. 'Well,' the kapitänleutnant said, 'we missed the destroyer, but we got lucky. We hit the convoy behind it.'

"The sound of engines on the surface stifled the cheer that shot through the boat. We feared what would follow. The kapitänleutnant, aware all eyes fixed on him, became the Rock of Gibraltar. He didn't flinch when the first depth charge erupted. He knew the blast was coming so he locked his elbows and knees. The second percussion knocked him into the bulkhead. He refused to reveal his pain. Or fear. Blood trickled from a gash in his scalp.

"None of us had ever seen such nerve. Cool and calm, he ordered the boat deeper, on a different course. We were the mouse, the destroyer the cat. His tactics worked as the noise of the destroyer faded, but our good fortune vanished at the sound of another propeller growing louder.

"The new leaks caused by the depth charges were rapidly repaired before the second blanket of charges rocked our boat. Some close, maybe three of them. The others were either too shallow or too deep. A few of the crewmen relaxed. I knew better. Watching Martin sitting at his hydrophone, the angle of his hunched back told me the stalking continued. He shouted out, 'Kapitänleutnant, two screws closing!'

"The kapitänleutnant ordered a change in speed and direction. This did little to fool the destroyers, I swear they could see us beneath the waves. Their kapitän anticipated our every maneuver. It's a funny thing about depth charges. We all looked to the surface as if we could watch them sink lower and lower through the black void. At least ten more depth charges jolted the boat from all sides, some even pushed us deeper. Again, our kapitänleutnant evaded the destroyers and we lived to withstand another punishing attack, then dove deep. Due to his nerves of steel, all the men remained calm.

"The bilge pumps were unable to keep up with the leaks caused by the depth charges. The boat was out of trim, and men had to hurry aft to counteract the accumulated water in the stern of the boat. We had been under constant siege for three hours by the time two more depth charge attacks took place. The first lacked accuracy, but the second found its target. By now, the auxiliary bilge pump failed, and after a total of nine attacks and countless explosions—with our batteries depleted—our options were limited. The kapitänleutnant must have thought we could out run the destroyers under the cover of darkness so he ordered the boat to the surface. Upon surfacing, we were only two hundred meters from the destroyers. They both raked the conning tower with gunfire.

"Then we were rammed by one of the destroyers. We six

survivors were the first to obey the order to abandon ship and were plucked out of the water."

Peter, unable to prevent the shaking chill that overtook him, continued his recollection. "Once they hauled me aboard the destroyer, I could hardly move. It's odd what you think about when you're doomed to die."

Several men nodded in unison.

"I thought about my brother Hans and what he felt after the Russian bullet slammed into his chest, or if I'd ever see him again."

"What about the other men?" someone said.

"All except the kapitänleutnant were instantly killed. He died after being washed overboard, wounded."

"How long were you in the water?"

"No more than ten minutes, but it seemed like hours. On the deck of the destroyer, standing was impossible. My muscles wouldn't support me and violent rigors racked my body despite the brandy I gulped."

"How'd they treat you?"

"I think because we failed to sink a single ship they didn't mistreat us. It was as if they took pity on us. We later learned the torpedoes we fired crippled a ship, but she still made ample steam to limp along with the convoy."

"You were on board how long?"

"Three weeks."

"*Three* weeks?"

"Well, they weren't about to alter their orders for six German sailors. They completed their escort duties, unloaded their booty, and we were brought here under the cover of darkness."

chapter 4

Sunday, early evening
24 December 1944

IN A FEEBLE ATTEMPT TO WARM HIMSELF as he walked, Hans adjusted the woolen cap over his head and snugged his collar. With every breath of frigid air his chest wall ached where the Russian bullet had been extracted three years earlier. Rubbing it helped, but in the cold it burned. He ignored the discomfort and gingerly stepped over the frozen, extended legs of a dead horse, its lifeless eyes blank and vacant. Pieces of cobblestone and brick covered its hoofs like a blanket. Along the street several buildings stood in ruins, their fractured walls defying gravity, a silent monument to destruction. The unmistakable odor of spent gunpowder—the perfume of war—permeated the air.

Hans opened, then quickly shut the front door of what was once the village café. Warm air flowing from the fireplace fueled a festive spirit. The assembled officers immediately began to sing. On one of the center tables sat a loaf of bread with a lighted candle stuck in its middle. Once the birthday song ceased, he gripped the table with both hands and blew out the candle. Uncorked wine bottles made the rounds to fill assorted glasses.

One of the officers shouted, "Major, tell us, how old are you?"

Hans sipped from his glass and raised it. "I was twenty-nine yesterday."

From a seat in the corner, his best friend, Anton spoke up. "Yeah, but tell them how old you are *today*." Hans grinned. "Thirty."

Laughter filled the room as the small but subdued celebration continued. Hans chose the seat next to Anton, a fellow officer since the Italian Campaign. Anton was the only one who knew of Aimée, and if asked, Hans would readily admit Anton saved him from the depression that threatened after Peter's U-boat was lost at sea.

"Hans," Anton's voice grew quiet. "Why so preoccupied? Trust me, there's no one else."

Hans looked warily to the side, relieved to see everyone else preoccupied. "What makes you so sure it's her?"

Anton smiled and nodded as if to say, Do you take me for a fool?

"How am I supposed to feel? Here it's Christmas Eve and I can't even post her a letter."

"I know you saw her in August." Anton gazed over Hans' shoulder to confirm no one was eavesdropping. "Your little ruse taking the dispatches to Sermaize-les-Bains may have fooled Oberst Beck, but it didn't fool me. Do you really expect me to believe you didn't see her while you were there?"

"Shhh, Anton. No one must know of that. Besides, I've already told you, once I arrived in Sermaize-les-Bains, she was at work." Under the circumstances he felt comfortable stretching the truth. Please Anton, just forget about it, there's no way I can tell you what really happen, even if you are my best friend. Hans refilled his glass as well as Anton's. "Do you think we need to send out a patrol this evening?"

Anton shrugged. "Fine, I get the hint. No patrols tonight."

"Good, the men deserve a rest. Once we're finished here I'll go to the line and assess our defenses. Until then, there's something I need to do."

"Not me, I think I'll write a letter to my mother. She'll be sad

32

not having me home. This is my fourth Christmas away."

"Sixth for me." Hans gazed into the distance. "Without a doubt, 1940 was the best."

"Why's that?"

Hans lowered his voice again. "This damn war wasn't over as fast as we'd been led to believe since England refused to die. In 1940, the division returned to Germany to prepare for the invasion of Russia, and most of us, especially those who had seen combat in Poland, were granted furloughs, so I spent Christmas with my family. It was glorious."

Anton raised his eyebrows. "And did you see Aimée?"

"No. I didn't see her again until the spring of 1942."

"After you were wounded?"

"Ja, not long afterward, before the division reformed in Lyon." He breathed deep, then let it out. "Yes, that Christmas was wonderful, but after the defeat at Stalingrad, none of the Christmases have much meaning, not like they used to."

Laughter erupted from a group of officers in the center of the room. The sight of one of them reminded Hans of a question he wanted answered. "Excuse me Anton, there's something I need to do."

He approached a junior officer and pulled him aside. "This afternoon I interrogated a prisoner from the American 99th Infantry Division—"

"Yes, Major, the sergeant and his driver who were lost in the fog?"

"Precisely. Who brought him in?"

The man hesitated. "Unteroffizier Meier. Is there a problem?"

"For *you*, no. Tell me, where can I find him?"

"Now?"

Hans leaned forward, locked his gaze onto the leutnant, and said, "Yes, *now*."

The officer pointed across the street.

"Thank you." Hans turned on his heels and walked toward Anton, grabbed him by the elbow, and whispered, "Carry on without me, I'll be right back."

"You're not going out to the line again are you? Send Lars or Dedric."

"I'll just be a minute, no one will know I'm gone."

Before he could leave several officers drifted over to wish him a happy birthday and to exchange Christmas greetings. Soon, the singing of songs they had all memorized as children could be heard.

Anton stood and looped his arm through Hans' elbow, and began to sing. Distracted, Hans kept looking to the door. Anton whispered in his ear. "Surely whatever it is can wait, after all, this is Christmas Eve."

The group of officers then formed a circle around a small fir tree trimmed with paper ornaments, arms draped over one another's shoulder. At the conclusion of the carol, Anton raised his glass. "To the Fatherland and our families. And to our loved ones back home."

One of the younger officers spoke up. "Major Krüger, we want to hear about your birth. I understand it's quite a story."

The room became still.

"I don't remember, it was a long time ago."

Several laughed. Another officer exclaimed, "Yes, Major, we all want to hear."

Hans looked to Anton for support and all he got in return was a nod. "Very well, if you insist. Remember, this is what I've been told." The assembled officers closed ranks as he began. "It was Christmas Eve, 1914. My father fought on the Western Front, in the trenches somewhere northeast of Paris. My mother lived with her parents outside Berlin. Father hadn't been home and Mother knew she could give birth at any time."

Someone behind Hans blurted out, "He must have been home

at some time, eh Major?"

Hans smiled, then sipped from his glass. "Well, as I said, Father was in the trenches. There wasn't much fighting and the entire front remained quiet. In the evening, several men dared to place fir trees trimmed with candles, much like this one, on the parapets above the trenches. Some of these German soldiers bravely ventured into No Man's Land mingling with one another and passed bottles around, sharing their favorite libation. Carols were sung and greetings exchanged. Soon, enemy soldiers—French to be sure—emerged from their trenches and joined the German soldiers in celebrating their shared Christmas Eve.

"The next day during this spontaneous truce a ceremony was held honoring the dead—both German and French. Afterwards, the men played soccer, others visited. My father met a Frenchmen, André. They exchanged addresses and to this day they're still friends."

"Was there ever such a thing in this war?" one of the younger officers said.

Arctic air burst into the room. Heads turned to the open door, then immediately back to Hans. Oberst Karl Beck, commander of the 29th Regiment, stood with knees locked, arms akimbo glaring at his regimental officers. "What is the meaning of this—this—this frivolity?"

Hans stepped forward. "The men wished to celebrate their Christmas—"

"Major," Oberst Beck scowled, "come with me."

He followed his oberst into the kitchen. The first time Hans had seen that reddened face, it was Robert-Espagne, four years earlier at the café. Just relax, don't let him goad you into something you'll regret.

"You know there's a battle going on all around you, don't you?"

"Sir, my men—"

"Do I need to remind you Krüger"—his voice had a sharp edge to it—"they're *my* men and I'll decide if and when we stop to ignore the Führer's orders?"

Hans looked straight ahead. "Yes, sir."

"Don't give me that smug attitude of yours." Karl Beck stepped towards Hans with his finger extended. "Not for"—poke—"one"—poke—"damn"—poke—"minute."

Hans' right hand clenched.

"Since August you've opposed me."

He could only think of thirteen men and women of Sermaize-les-Bains hanging from lampposts, their limp bodies bumping into a cold metal pole as they swayed, the vision a constant reminder of why he hated his commanding officer. Why murder them? They did nothing to you. He felt remorse despite knowing their deaths made it possible for his Aimée and her family to live, and six months later, the pain as intense as it was the following day. Hans grimaced. "I've done nothing of the sort—"

"Krüger, you're just as miserable a liar as you are a soldier. And human being for that matter."

He stood rigid, his face flushed. Don't say it. There's nothing he'd rather have than an excuse to shoot me. How convenient to have me out of the way. "Sir, what is it you wanted?" Hans dared not reveal his pleasure in seeing Beck's obvious disappointment.

"I want a patrol to probe the American lines."

"Now, sir?"

"No, not now you idiot. After midnight."

The light from the lamp flickered when Beck stormed out of the kitchen. Hans tilted his head back and stared at the ceiling. "If anyone deserves to die, it's that man," he said to himself.

When he returned to the party, the room was empty. Only the decorated Christmas tree in the middle of the room remained.

chapter 5

IN SPITE OF THE CONFRONTATION WITH OBERST Beck, Hans smiled at the sound of pealing church bells in the distance. Must be summoning the faithful to Mass. Plunging temperatures brought the notes closer but without the wind, it was impossible to determine whether the sound came from the west, behind Allied lines, or the east behind German lines. He gazed up to the sky and thought of his father with André Ferrand in No Man's Land on Christmas Eve thirty years earlier. Suddenly, an unmistakable awareness that Aimée survived August 29th settled upon him. Dear God, I pray she still thinks of me.

As the last peaceful toll drifted away, he remembered the German-speaking American and his expectant wife. Daniel Veit, 35812931 does your Irma feel it, that the father of her baby has been captured? What's to become of him now? He inhaled the cold fresh air. Cursed war, what does it matter? I need to do what I need to do.

Hans turned at the sound of Anton's crunching footsteps. He had grown to appreciate his friend's honesty and willingness to speak his mind—even at the risk of his own safety. "I thought you were off to write a letter."

"Forget that. What crawled up Beck's ass?"

"Come on," Hans beckoned, starting back along the path. "What a bunch of cowards. When I came out of the kitchen, everybody'd gone."

"Are you kidding me, the way he hates you, we weren't about to stick around."

Anton shrugged. "I'll never know what goes through his mind. I have my suspicions, but when he referred to last August, we all looked at one another. Next thing I knew, the party's over."

"He mentioned it, I didn't," Hans protested.

"Did he say anything else?"

"He wants a patrol. Tonight."

"I mean about August?"

Hans slowed his pace and exhaled into his cupped hands. "Not exactly, but you and I both know I know more than I let on."

"What time?"

"After midnight."

Hans continued walking. "What'd you want to tell me anyway?"

"You were right, it's true, the rumor you heard." Anton fastened the top of his coat and doubled his step to catch up. "Even I can't believe it. An officer in the 8th Regiment told one of our officers—his cousin I think—that Panzer SS soldiers shot several dozen captured Americans outside Malmedy on the 17th."

"It's just another rumor."

"Not this one. Seems the officer's cousin told him a squad from 8th came across the dead bodies after the SS departed."

"I tell you Anton, you've got to be more careful."

"With Beck all over your ass, you're telling *me* to be careful? The way I look at it, as long as you're alive, I'm safe." Anton shook his head side to side. "But even this, I find hard to believe. Everyone knows the war's not going well. When this is over, these people will be held accountable. This makes no sense—it's murder—nothing less."

"True, but maybe there're some who still believe Hitler, that we'll be victorious and it won't matter. Maybe they really believe this offensive will change everything. After all, you did say SS was responsible."

Hans quickened his pace toward the mayor's office. "Anton, I'll catch up with you later. There are a few things I must do."

■   ■   ■   ■   ■

Hans glanced at the dangling sign as he entered the mayor's office. The unmistakable aroma of a recently prepared hot meal hung in the air. Several tables were arranged throughout the room. One of the enlisted men spotted the major, jumped to attention and saluted.

"Where's Meier?"

The enlisted man immediately pointed behind him.

Hans approached the back table. "Meier, come with me!"

"*Now*, sir?"

He found the man's question annoying. "Now!"

chapter 6

SINCE THE END OF AUGUST, THE FATE of the Ferrands consumed Hans' every thought. Surely Aimée must know my division's hasty retreat made it impossible to post a letter affirming my love and affection. She would understand, wouldn't she? The more he contemplated it, the closer he came to accepting his fate. The thought gave him courage. Yes, I will do what needs to be done. He looked at his watch, then settled into the desk chair. Good, still plenty of time.

He was as focused as a general on the eve of battle by the time he returned to his billet, a quaint cottage on the edge of the village. His senses renewed by the fresh air, Hans knew what must be done. In his heart he felt Aimée was safe. After all, the Allies swept through Sermaize-les-Bains just after the 3rd Panzer-Grenadier Division, perhaps by a matter of days if not hours. And the Gestapo memo said it was to be the final roundup. But what if one of those Americans—one that spoke French—came upon the telephone exchange and discovered my beautiful my Aimée? No, she would never betray our love.

He reached for his pen and paper and adjusted the lamp. Removing her photograph from his pocket and propping it up against the books, he studied it closely in the flickering light. For the first time he realized she wore the same blouse she'd worn the first time they'd kissed. Recalling that summer's walk brought a smile. Her stunning black hair—tied with a blue ribbon—rested on her white blouse, the one with the blue print. He wished he could once again gently push the small tuft of hair away from her ear and kiss the soft tender skin beneath it. The first time he'd done so, she shivered, stood on tiptoes to kiss his lips and said, "I love you Hans Krüger." Her smile always transported him to a place and time when sacrifice and falling in love meant everything—a love he'd foolishly abandoned. He remembered lifting her onto the stone fence and his hand brushing against her soft breast. When he helped her down she'd clung to his side just a moment longer than necessary. Gazing intently at the photo, he followed the outline of her body with the end of his pen. With renewed confidence, he began to write:

Sunday
24 December 1944

My dearest love,

I write to you from a Belgian village along the German border. Like every day since we met, I steal a few moments to pray for your safety. Finally I have seized the opportunity for you to receive word I continue to survive and persist in my total and absolute love for you.

After the events of last August, have you forgiven me? It was the only way to save you and your family.

I remain safe despite this terrible war. For the life of me, I don't know why, but from time to time I've been touched by divine intervention. I was wounded—what is it, three years now—yet I survived. And fighting in Italy—some of the fiercest we have encountered—I was afraid, more so than I ever have been, but again I survived. This doesn't make me careless, but it does cause me to wonder.

Forgive me if what I am about to tell you sounds morbid,

but it's true. On the 16th of December this senseless campaign started with intense shelling prior to our advance against the Americans. Our initial progress was rapid, intoxicating for many. I'm sure there were some who thought we would be victorious in days and by the end of January we would be back in Paris. Stalled at a crossroad outside a village, I was about to walk to the front of the line of vehicles. For reasons I can't explain, I sat back down and waited. Moments later a blast erupted from the lead vehicle exactly where I would have been standing. As it burned, a second shell from an American tank ripped into the next vehicle, destroying it as well. Something or someone is protecting me, I'm convinced of it. There have been other instances, but in spite of this, please rest assured I continue to exercise caution.

I think of your family often. Please inform your father my parents have moved to Dresden and that they are well despite the privations this war brings.

Aimée, I don't know if this letter will find its way to you, but something tells me it will. I've written it countless times in my head, but now, sitting here, I seem so addle-brained.

I remember one of your first letters to me that wonderful summer of 1940. Do you recall telling me how you'd opened my letters to you and immediately look at how I began my letter and how I signed it? It made me smile because I, too, would do exactly the same. The first time you signed 'my sincere good wishes' my heart leapt with joy. Your closing, 'with my heartfelt affections' gave me the courage to tell you I love you. But please do not be distressed once you see—if you have not already seen—that I have not signed this letter. I believe you know why I take this precaution.

Aimée, my love for you is steadfast and strong as ever. Thoughts of you occupy me constantly, and it is because of the promise of your love that I persist in my desire to survive so one day I can stand next to you before your priest.

Aimée, will you marry me?

This is not how I wanted it to be, to ask you such a question in a letter. If something should happen, you must know this was my desire—that we be united forever. But what of your mother? Would it be bold of me to say I now know she will approve? And André? He will understand why I didn't properly ask for your hand first, wouldn't he? After all, he, too, was a soldier once.

One day soon I hope to tell you in person of the events that make it possible for you to read this letter.

I will pray for you tonight as I do every night. On this special Christmas Eve I give thanks that you may very well receive my sincere words of love and adoration. Please give my warmest regards to all.

Merry Christmas darling.

chapter 7

HANS SEALED THE ENVELOPE, KISSED IT, AND slipped it into his pocket as he stood to leave. On the street he slid both gloves on and with determined strides, found himself at the darkened café where his birthday celebration and confrontation with Oberst Beck had taken place. On a table in the center of the now empty café sat the small fir tree. The faint aroma of pine needles lingered in the air. He located a chair and seated in front of the tree, began to hum. After the melody ended he glanced at his watch and said, "I'd better get at it while it's still Christmas Eve." Entering the kitchen he struck a match. Once the kerosene lamp flickered to life, he looked about. Good, everything's in order. With his hand cupped over the chimney of the glass lamp, he blew out the flame.

■　■　■　■　■

As the door to the field hospital closed, the leutnant seated at the desk looked up from his papers. "May I help you Major?"

Twenty occupied and three unoccupied cots filled the room. Several bottles of plasma hung from the wall, each dripping into the arm of a wounded German soldier. Hans nodded at the American soldier recovering from his wounds in the cot closest to the door. I bet you're Veit's driver.

Finally, Hans answered the leutnant's question. "Yes, I need an ambulance."

A frown settled on the man's face. "Of course, Herr Major, but I have my orders—"

"I, too, have orders."

The leutnant looked confused. "Herr Major—"

"Leutnant, I need to reconnoiter the front line. An ambulance will allow me to do so safely and unmolested."

"But Herr Major—"

Hans remained calm. "The oberst has ordered a patrol for later tonight. I won't be gone but an hour."

"In that case, it's parked in the alley, but Herr Major, if there's an artillery barrage, return immediately or my hauptmann will have me shot."

"Certainly."

When he lingered a moment longer the leutnant looked up. "Is there anything else, Major?"

"Yes, a lamp."

Hans took the lamp, switched it on and off to confirm it worked and departed. Outside he peered into the ambulance's narrow storage compartment. Beneath the jack he discovered the pry bar he'd hoped to find. He removed it and let the lid fall. Once seated in the front seat, he laid the pry bar down, started the engine and drove immediately to the café. Relieved by the absence of activity on the street, he re-entered the building, grasped the Christmas tree and carried it outside as gently as he would a wounded comrade and placed it in the rear of the ambulance all the way to the right.

Back in the darkened café he pushed through the swinging doors to the kitchen. Into an empty wooden crate he placed the leftover bread, cheese, and candies; into a second crate went two bottles of unopened wine. There, this should do. After a final sweep of the lamp's beam, confident nothing was left behind, he set one crate atop the other. Carrying both, he left the café as quietly as he had entered. Through the opened back door of the ambulance he carefully positioned both crates next to the Christmas tree, propping it upright. With the aid of the lamp, he located a blanket and covered the tree and crates, then gently latched the rear door before driving off. In the alley, as the ambulance came to a stop, he grabbed the pry bar off the passenger seat, slipped it under his coat and walked to the street. Again he scanned both directions, then entered battalion headquarters. He kicked his boots against the threshold, as much to announce his presence as to dislodge the snow.

The obergrenadier immediately stood and saluted.

"At ease. I wish to see the prisoner." Hans opened the door to the cellar. At the bottom of the stairs another guard came to attention. "Leave us. I'll summon you when I'm finished." After the door shut, he listened for footsteps ascending the stairs.

When he set a kerosene lamp on the table Sergeant Daniel Veit rose from his blanket on the floor in the corner and stood. Hans remembered the American to be taller. In the flickering light, the prisoner's blue eyes widened as Hans removed the pry bar from his coat and set it next to the lamp.

"Sergeant, your driver's recovering in the field hospital from his wounds. Our surgeon's taking good care of him."

The prisoner retreated further into the corner. Hans persisted despite the lack of response. "Come now Sergeant, we both know you speak German. I'm not here to interrogate you further, we've learned all we need to know."

Again Sergeant Veit looked at the pry bar. "My driver doesn't know anything."

"It wasn't him. We have other sources." Hans realized what the prisoner was thinking and raised his hand as if to block the thought. "This isn't for you."

The prisoner shrugged. "What am I supposed to think? Just get it over with—"

"As you wish." Hans lifted the pry bar off the table and walked over to the boarded-up window. When he pried the bottom board free, the loud squeak arrested his efforts in an instant. He stepped over to the door, opened it and listened. The discussion at the top of the stairs hadn't changed. He returned to the window and finished removing the board, then gently placed it to the side. The second board loosened without a sound.

The prisoner remained in the corner. "What's going on?"

Hans removed an extra pair of gloves from his coat pocket and tossed them to the prisoner. "There's an ambulance parked outside in the alley. Crawl out this window and get into the back of it."

"No thanks, Major. I ain't interested in getting shot in the back of the head for attempting to escape."

Hans brought his palm to his forehead in frustration. "We hear rumors, too. We're Wehrmacht, *not* SS." He watched the prisoner purse his lips and look to the ceiling. "Sergeant, please, time is wasting."

Sergeant Veit remained in the corner, arms crossed.

"My patience is growing thin. Please. Believe me, I'm trying to help you escape."

"And you expect me to believe a Nazi officer?"

"We have more in common than you realize, Sergeant."

"Such as?"

"Perhaps you haven't yet realized the futility of this war, but like you, I miss my home and my family. Like you I'm in love with the daughter of a farmer. Like you, I'm separated from the woman I love and we're both powerless to do anything about it." He watched closely, hoping the words would sink in. "You've only been fighting a few months. This is my sixth Christmas away from those I love and I'm tired of the senseless killing. I loathe what I've been forced to do and what I fear I've become." He observed the sergeant's arms were no longer crossed. "Trust me. I promise— now help me move this table beneath the window."

Hans shut the door and locked it, then hid the pry bar under

47

his coat. At the top of the stairs he lingered a moment. As he approached the guard warming himself by the fire he said, "Here's the key. I'm through for now, but I may return tomorrow to interrogate him further."

"*Jawohl*, Herr Major."

chapter 8

SERGEANT VEIT CONSIDERED HIS OPTIONS—HE DIDN'T CARE for any of them. So what if he's not SS, he's still a Nazi. He grabbed one of the boards on the floor, climbed upon the table and peered out the cellar window. I'd rather have my baseball bat, but this will do. Two tires were clearly visible. Leaning forward, he strained to see more. Good, no feet. He pushed the board into the alley and squeezed out the window.

The instant he opened the rear door of the ambulance the clutch engaged. As the ambulance rolled forward, the door shut. He crouched low. With a tight grip on the board, he crept toward the driver. I'm a dead man if this isn't Major Krüger. The ambulance turned onto the street. What do I do if it's not him? Hell's bells, what am I supposed to do if it *is?* From behind the driver's seat he could see Hans Krüger's profile. Poised to strike, he tightened his grip on the board. "Major Krüger, where you taking me?"

"To the front."

"I thought we're at the front?"

Hans laughed. "We are. Trust me, you're going to the front of the front!"

Just what the hell is that supposed to mean? Sergeant Veit clung to the board even tighter.

West of the village the road curved, then headed into an intersection. As they came out of the curve, Hans turned his head to the side and said, "Sergeant, lie down on the stretcher, there's a sentry." When he stopped the ambulance the sentry snapped to attention.

"Herr Major." The man's breath condensed instantly in the cold air.

"At ease. Thank you for not saluting. I'm going on up to the line."

"Sir, there have been reports of enemy patrols. There's a camouflaged American machine gun emplacement at the edge of the forest."

"Thank you." As an afterthought, he said, "Merry Christmas." Slowly he inched toward the bank of trees illuminated by a full moon hanging in the sky.

After a few seconds, Sergeant Veit worked his way to the seat next to Hans. "Major, may I ask what in tarnation you're up to?"

"It's a long story. Let's just say that if I survive this war, I want to have something to tell my children, and maybe something for you to tell yours."

"That's a big *if*, Major."

▪ ▪ ▪ ▪ ▪

"Shhh," Corporal Grant Paulsen leaned his head to one side, his breath a cloud in the icy air. "You hear that?"

"What?" A second cloud lingered in the air.

"Could be one of ours." Paulsen signaled for Private First Class Sam Resnick to hold his fire. Both men in the concealed foxhole waited, tense, on edge. Resnick engaged the cocking handle of his machine gun. After a second pull, the metallic click confirmed the .30 caliber bullet chambered. A gentle squeeze of the trigger was all it would take to dispatch bullets to the intended target at over 2,800 feet per second.

"I'll be damned. Don't shoot, it's a German ambulance."

"Grant, what if it's a trap?"

"What if it is, we have them zeroed in don't we?"

In the crisp winter air, the loud crunching of snow beneath the tires of the ambulance made fifty meters seem as if was right next to them. When the noise ceased, Private Resnick's finger flexed on the trigger.

▪　▪　▪　▪　▪

Hans shut the engine off, drew in a deep breath, and closed his eyes. For the moment, the stillness of the night remained an illusion. Finally, he opened his eyes. Along the tree line nothing looked out of place. He knew the Americans were there and by now, it was obvious they weren't going to fire. He turned and looked at Sergeant Veit. "Before I get out there are two things—besides your freedom—I wish to give you." He ignored the skepticism and removed an envelope from his tunic. "Sergeant, I need you to post this letter. I can't since we're no longer in France. It's to the woman I love—"

"The farmer's daughter?"

Hans smiled. "Yes, she lives in the French village of Sermaize-les-Bains, west of here. Will you do this for me?"

"I'll do my best, Major." Sergeant Veit slipped his gloves off and stuffed the envelope into his jacket pocket. "And the second thing?"

Hans removed his right glove, leaned back into the driver's seat trying to reach into his pocket. "Damn, I'll have to let my hands warm up." After exhaling on his bare fingers, he put his gloves back on and signaled the American to get out and follow him to the back of the ambulance. Both looked warily at the trees. Hans opened the ambulance door, lifted the blanket off the crates and tossed it aside. He grabbed the Christmas tree by the stand and ran with it to a flat area beyond the ambulance and set it on the ground. Behind him, Sergeant Veit carried the crates and placed them next to the tree.

Removing his glove, Hans reached into his pocket and found what had eluded him. He rescanned the tree line in both directions. Assured they remained safe for the moment, he extended his hand, palm up. "I believe this belongs to you."

In the moonlight, made brighter by the snow's reflection, Sergeant Veit recognized his wedding band. Carefully picking it up, he said, "I—I—I don't know what to say."

"Let's just leave it at Merry Christmas." Hans saluted and within seconds the ambulance was backing away from the stunned sergeant.

▪　▪　▪　▪　▪

Private Resnick maintained a steady grip on his machine gun and watched two soldiers exit the ambulance. He didn't take his finger off the trigger until one of them—a German officer—proceeded to the back of the ambulance and removed a Christmas tree, only to set it down in the clearing. His face contorted in disbelief to see an American GI carry two wooden crates directly behind the German officer and place them next to the tree. Mesmerized, the men in the foxhole watched the German, his back directly to them, speak with the American, then salute.

Neither machine gunner comprehended the words in German they'd both clearly heard.

Private Resnick loosened his grip on his gun the instant Corporal Paulsen looked over and said, "What the fuck?"

chapter 9

Sunday
24 December 1944

Dear Mother and Father,

It has been too long since my last letter, but I dare not let such an important day pass without writing. I sincerely hope the two of you are able to celebrate a quiet Christmas together and perhaps exchange a special gift in the morning.

We are engaged in a very difficult struggle against the Americans in the Ardennes. The battle has been raging for a week but they refuse to yield to our more experienced troops. I am afraid if the German army does not prevail, we will be unable to drive a wedge between the Allies and hope for a negotiated peace.

Father, I enjoyed reading your last letter and learning of your work in the munitions factory. Did I read correctly that you report to the factory only two days per week? You didn't mention how long you've been required to do such work. Here on the front, we hear little of life at home so any details are a welcome change from the monotony of war. How many days a week are you able to work at the publishing house?

Mother, are you still at the hospital preparing bandages? It seems such a waste to have one of you making the bullets that will require the use of the bandages made by the other! Rest assured I don't think your bandages will be for me. Since word of Peter's death, I have the sense that he is protecting me and will ensure I am able to return home.

The officers of our regiment had a celebration of my birthday this evening. It was nice to get away from the war, even if for a few minutes. In the distance we hear an occasional artillery shell, but for now they are only a nuisance. There are those of us that feel it is a positive thing, that the Americans are low on ammunition.

Father, today I have thought often of your Christmas Eve thirty years ago in No Man's Land. Despite the numerous times I heard the story growing up, and André's recollection of the same, I never grow tired of it. Earlier tonight, a fellow officer asked to hear the story again!

I look forward to the day I can tell you what transpired on our front lines this evening and about my letter to the daughter of your friend, the poultry farmer. I have no way of knowing if she will receive it, but I pray she does.

Before I close, I wish to thank you for the wonderful Christmas memories I hold. How exciting it was for Peter and me on December 6th—St. Nicholas Day. We would put our shoes at the door for St. Nick to leave his treats. Do you recall how upset Peter became after I left a large boot and all he had was a shoe? And how he squealed with joy in the morning to see my boot filled with twigs and his shoe filled with nuts and candies?

As I drift off to sleep tonight I will think of you both. I look forward to the day we are all able to return home for good. This is my Christmas wish.

Your loving son,
Hans

chapter 10

Corporal Paulsen, in a firm voice commanded, "Halt. Arms up!" Eyeing the bedraggled man up and down, he barked, "St. Louis."

Sergeant Dan Veit thrust his hands above his head. "I don't know, Missouri?"

His index finger on the trigger of his carbine, he studied their unusual visitor. Looking at the man's feet, he brought his inspection upwards to his field jacket covered with filth. "Wrong—"

"Cheese?" Sergeant Veit quickly said.

"That was yesterday." The American corporal confirmed the safety on his carbine was off and moved the barrel twice in the direction of the trees behind the foxhole. "Sam, you stay. I'm taking this supposed American sergeant to the command post. I'll send someone back here pronto."

"Corporal," Dan Veit pleaded, "the Germans captured me yesterday. There's no way I'd know today's password."

"Move along. Don't tell me, tell Captain Briggs."

"You're making a mistake. I'm from Iowa."

"Right, you're from Iowa and you know General Eisenhower."

"Ike's from Kansas. My name's Daniel Veit, serial number 35812931." He pointed to the blue and white checkerboard insignia patch of the 99th Infantry Division on his left shoulder. "See, I'm with the 99th."

"Veit sure sounds German to me."

"Holy balls of manure, you think if I was a lousy Kraut, I'd use a German name?"

He nudged the prisoner with the barrel of his weapon. Sergeant Veit threw his right shoulder back then moved forward past the trees branches hugging the ground, laden with snow. Fifty yards ahead, a voice challenged them from a camouflaged foxhole.

"St. Louis."

"Browns," Corporal Paulsen replied immediately.

"Whatcha got there, Grant?"

"Not sure what to think. This German ambulance pulls right up to our foxhole and drops off a Christmas tree, a couple bottles of wine, some chocolates, and a loaf of bread—and this soldier. Says he's with the 99th, that he's from Iowa."

As they passed, one of the men eased out of a foxhole and looked him over. "I kinda think he looks familiar. Maybe I've seen him hangin' around the motor pool."

"Can't be. I heard him and the Kraut officer speaking German, plain as day." He jabbed the prisoner with the gun barrel. "Yeah, you *sprechen Sie* English pretty good for a Kraut."

Another soldier in the foxhole called out, "You leave the loot with Resnick? Mind if I give him a hand with it?"

"Fine. You take my position up front and I'll send someone." After a moment he turned and said, "Stay outta the wine."

▪ ▪ ▪ ▪ ▪

On their way to the company command post, beyond another clearing and across a traveled path, Corporal Paulsen broke the silence. "Motor pool, eh?"

"Yes, Corporal. I'm telling you, I'm not a German. My driver and I were captured after we made a wrong turn. I thought we were headed west but we must have been headed east."

"Like I said, tell that to the captain and keep your hands up."

Ahead, a small farmhouse bustled with activity, smoke flowing out the chimney. A line of pockmarks across the front of the house attested to a recent strafing of machinegun bullets. The lower corner of the roof, above where the corner stones used to rest, revealed a gaping hole stuffed with hay. Just as they were about to enter Baker Company command post, the door opened. A haggard looking soldier exited, but held the door. The aroma, a mixture of freshly brewed coffee and warmed fireplace air, assaulted their senses. Corporal Paulsen shoved his prisoner through the doorway.

Captain Robert Briggs, seated at a desk in front of a battle map, did not look up. While studying his company's position, he demanded, "Yes, what is it?"

Corporal Paulsen snapped off a salute. "Sir, out on the line, this sergeant here was dropped off by a German ambulance, right in front of our foxhole—I think he's a Kraut."

The captain finally looked up to see Corporal Paulsen standing to the side of his prisoner, his rifle half raised. He immediately stood. "Corporal, put that damn gun away. Veit, where have you been for Christ's sake?"

Dan Veit brought his hands down. "Sir, can I get some of that coffee?"

"Here, sit down and tell me what happened to you. Corporal, get the Sergeant some coffee."

▪ ▪ ▪ ▪ ▪

"Well Captain, my driver, too close to the front, made the wrong turn. Just about the time I say, 'Let's turn it around,' this German soldier jumps in front of our jeep and sprays the ground with his submachine gun. Unfortunately, Private Kane took one in the shoulder."

"Lucky for you they were looking for prisoners."

Sergeant Veit nodded in agreement. "So we stop and a squad

of Krauts come out of nowhere. Next thing I know, our hands are in the air and we're searched. This Kraut lieutenant helped himself to my watch and ring."

Captain Briggs looked instinctively at Dan's left hand. "I thought you said he took your wedding ring?"

"He did, but I'll get to that, Captain." Sergeant Veit sipped his coffee and set the tin cup down. "Kane went to a Kraut field hospital. They kept me in a cellar until my interrogations, both of us were in the same village."

"They interrogated you more than once? Which village?"

"Not sure, the signs were down. They questioned me twice, once by a captain, the second time by a major."

"Did either of them mistreat you? You heard what happened at Malmedy?"

"These were Wehrmacht, 3rd Panzer-Grenadier Division, 29th Regiment, not SS. They'd bring me upstairs and sit me at this table, then forget about me for a while so I sat there lookin' dumb. I've never seen so much commotion, action reports coming and going. Like I said, I just sat there like I don't know nothin'. About 14:00 hours this sergeant comes in all flustered about our defenses between here and Rocherath. Two officers, one a major and the other a captain, look over their map. This major—the one who interrogated me—says, 'Division is supposed to be pulling out of St.-Vith moving toward Elsenborn at dawn.'"

Captain Briggs looked at his watch. "You mean in the morning?"

"Yes sir."

"Are you certain? Weren't they speaking German?"

"They were, but I'm fluent in German."

"Sergeant Veit, we've got to get you to regimental headquarters. G2's going to want to hear about this."

"Yes, sir but there's more. The officers were—"

"But nothing." The captain raised his hand to cut him off. "I heard this evening that HQ is rattled, not sure what the Krauts are up to. Take my jeep. We'll radio ahead and let them know you're on your way. After you get back, I want to hear how you escaped."

Sergeant Veit saluted. "Yes, sir."

"And Sergeant, one more thing before you leave … don't get lost."

Sergeant Veit's blue eyes twinkled. "Yes sir. And Merry Christmas, sir."

chapter 11

Haute Desnié, Belgium
2300 hours
December 24, 1944

AT 394TH REGIMENTAL HEADQUARTERS SERGEANT VEIT ENTERED such a maelstrom of activity he had to step out of the way. Couriers distributing messages came and went. Near the communications desk an officer paced the floor like an expectant father. Bet that's Captain Renshaw. Sergeant Veit stood in front of the man and saluted.

"You must be the soldier that escaped. Captain Briggs said you had some intel for us."

"Yes sir. I'm to tell you what I overheard."

"First off, how can you be sure they didn't tell you what they *wanted* you to hear, then let you escape?" Captain Renshaw said.

Sergeant Veit looked at the floor. He's sure to think I'm lying.

"You did escape on your own, didn't you?"

"*Not exactly*, sir."

"What's that supposed to mean, Sergeant?"

"Sir, I'm sure it wasn't done to feed me false information."

"And how do you know that?"

"Sir, they had no idea I could speak German."

"You absolutely certain?"

"Sir, as sure as I'm standing here. They had no idea." He shook his head back and forth. "None."

"Okay Sergeant, tell me what you overheard and *how* you overheard it?"

"I'm sittin' in their command post waiting to be interrogated the first time. My driver got us lost outside Wirtzfelt when a German patrol ambushed us. My driver gets wounded and we're both taken prisoner. They took him to their field hospital and like I said, I was taken to their command post—"

"Where?"

"A village near Rocherath."

The captain looked at the map spread out before him and nodded.

"They sat me by a desk not far from the officers—a major and a couple of captains. The place buzzed with activity—"

"Chaos or activity?"

"Activity. Dispatches and reports came and went. I just sat there not lettin' on a thing."

"You take German in school, Sergeant?"

"Yes sir, but that's not where I learned it. My grandparents are German. It's all they spoke at home. Ever since I can remember, if I wanted anything, I had to ask for it in German. By the time I was twelve, I was fluent. High school classes taught me the grammar part."

"Got it. So tell me what you overheard."

"They're only sending out one patrol this evening. Apparently to probe our defenses." Sergeant Veit pointed at the map and tapped it with his index finger. "And, a company sized contingent with Panzers has been ordered to this intersection here while they move from St.-Vith to Elsenborn."

"Anything else?"

"Yes. I could have sworn I overheard one of the officers refer to an air offensive."

Captain Renshaw looked at his executive officer with raised eyebrows. "Air offensive? What makes you say this, Sergeant?"

"One of the officers commented about visibility and another said they had been expecting the attack as soon as the skies cleared. I heard them mention '*fallschirmjäger.*' That's German for paratrooper."

"Anything else?"

"Maybe." Sergeant Veit looked to make sure the captain was listening. "I picked up the phrase '*Bodenplatte.*' They lowered their voices like it was some kind of secret operation or something."

"What's it mean?"

"I don't know. I've never heard the word before. *Platte* means plate or flat surface." He shrugged his shoulders in defeat. "I have no idea what *boden* means. Sorry, sir, I can't help you any more than that."

"Forget it." Captain Renshaw turned to his executive officer as he finished scribbling. "Type this up immediately and get it to division HQ." He then looked back at Sergeant Veit. "Now, tell us how you escaped ... ."

He concluded relating the unusual specifics of his release and rubbed his chest to confirm the letter still resided in his pocket. Neither officer noticed the smile.

"And you're convinced the only reason this German major let you go is because it was his birthday"—he looked at his watch—"and it's Christmas Eve?" Captain Renshaw grimaced and said, "I don't know Sergeant—"

"Sir, begging the Captain's pardon, they didn't know I spoke German and I could see it in his eyes, he was totally wrapped up in this being Christmas Eve."

The officer smiled. "*Wrapped up*, eh, Sergeant?"

After one of the regimental commanders whispered into his ear, Captain Renshaw said, "Sergeant, how would you like to spend the rest of the war with us?"

"With you, sir?"

"Yes, with us. Now that we're about to cross the border into

Germany, we need a good translator. I'll call your C.O. and square it with him."

"When, sir?"

"Now. You get your gear together, tell your buddies and report back here at 0700."

Sergeant Veit looked skeptical.

"I'll see to it that you get an extra stripe."

The new company translator grinned, then saluted. "Yes, sir. 0700 sharp."

chapter 12

Sermaize-les-Bains
12 January 1945

IN THE CORNER OF THE CAFÉ CLOSEST to the window, Aimée found it difficult to concentrate on the newspaper, even the article about the successful Allied victory over the German army in the Battle of the Ardennes failed to capture her attention. Animated conversations spilled from nearby tables, all centered on the fighting to the east. One predicted the war would be over in weeks, another that Hitler would never surrender. She set the paper aside, eased out of the chair, and embraced her childhood friend, Marjorie, as she approached.

When seated, the waiter returned. Marjorie spoke first without looking up. "Coffee and a croissant."

"You, *Ma'm'selle?*"

"Coffee, *s'il vous plaît*," Aimée replied.

Marjorie looked around the room, then nodded toward the opposite corner. "Did you notice who's over there?"

Aimée lowered her head and leaned into the center of the table. "Shhh. Keep your voice down."

"Look at him. Just who does he think he is?"

Aimée couldn't resist the temptation to peek. "Well, I must admit he does seem to think—"

"What? That he's special. He's nothing but filth. The way

he aided the Nazis, he should be shot. One bullet. Doesn't even deserve two."

And what about me? I'm in love with a German, what's that make me?

"And he calls himself a communist. Communists aren't cowards and he's nothing but a coward." Marjorie took a sip of coffee and bit into her croissant. After swallowing, she finally focused on Aimée. "You're quiet. As usual, your eyes speak more than you do."

Aimée felt relief when she smiled. "Then my eyes need to quit talking so much."

"Why so glum?"

"I'm not glum, just preoccupied."

"It's Hans, isn't it?"

"Of course it's Hans. It's been almost five months and not a word. For all I know—"

"None of that. My Henri tells me the war will be over soon. Very soon. Before you know it, he'll be here in Sermaize-les-Bains chasing you around the barn."

Aimée, too preoccupied to blush, demurred. "But what do I do if he's not? Or worse, what if he's maimed. I just couldn't bear it."

"Be positive, it's only a matter of time. Look, aren't you the one who told me your mother's a new person since the Nazis—"

"Germans," Aimée corrected.

"Okay, since the *Germans* left. Doesn't that tell you something?"

"Well, it doesn't tell me Hans is alive."

"Fine, but you're the one always sensing things?"

"Not always. Besides, you know I haven't heard a word in months."

"Aimée, don't you see?" With a dismissive wave of her hand, Marjorie continued. "It's right in front of you. The fact that it's been since August and you haven't had one of your feelings—or whatever it is you call it—should tell you something."

Aimée felt the gloom lift like a blanket. "There's a reason you're such a dear friend." She reached over and squeezed Marjorie's hand. "What would I do without you?"

Marjorie raised her coffee cup when the waiter walked by. As he poured she said, "Half is fine."

"I'm serious. Just what would I have done without having you to talk to, especially when Maman was so cross?"

"You? What about me? Why do you think I'm so sassy? I'll tell you why, because you're always there to laugh or give me support." Marjorie's grin widened. "Do you remember the time in school when we stole Madame Bissett's purse—"

"*We?* I had nothing to do with it."

"That may be, but you knew about it. And I'll always remember you never said a word. I still laugh when I think of you shrugging with that innocent look of yours when the old cow asked if you knew who took her purse. I swear you're more like your papa than anyone realizes."

Aimée noticed the immediate change in her friend's color. "I've never seen you blush before."

"You never heard what I found in her purse, did you?"

Aimée leaned forward. "Tell me."

"A book."

"A book could embarrass you so?"

"It wasn't just any book. It was the *Kama Sutra*."

"The *what?*"

"*Kama Sutra*. I'd only heard about it from some of the older girls, and then just whispered bits and pieces."

When Aimée asked, "What is it?" her friend's cheeks continued their glow.

"It was a German translation of a Hindu book, but you didn't need to read German to understand the pictures." She leaned closer still. "It's a book about making love, drawings and all. I never knew there were so many ways."

66

Aimée could feel her own face flush. "Actual drawings of two people—"

Marjorie nodded. "That sometimes looked like one."

"Oh my. At fifteen, if I'd seen that, I might have fainted just thinking about Maman and Papa"—Aimée glanced at her watch, then stood and began to slip on her coat—"Goodness, it's nearly four o'clock. I promised Maman I'd be home soon."

On the street, the two friends hugged. "We should do this more often," Marjorie said.

"Promise?"

"I'll call you at work next week between classes, promise."

"Good, I want to hear more about your book and how Madame Bissett got her book back."

Marjorie winked. "What makes you think she got it back?"

chapter 13

Featherstone POW Camp #18, Northeast England
0800 hours
15 January 1945

MAJOR BLAINE HEATHRIDGE'S FIRST ASSIGNMENT IN HIS
Majesty's Army had nothing to do with guarding German
prisoners. Rather, 1939—the first year of the war—found him on
South Uist Island in the Outer Hebrides off the coast of Scotland
collecting meteorological data to be used by those actually engaged
in fighting. After three years of the most boring assignment
imaginable, Blaine Heathridge applied for transfer to a combat
regiment, not a prisoner-of-war camp. At least once a day, if not
more, he thought to himself, I don't care if I look like a scientist, I
should be killing Germans, not babysitting them.

He reached for the telephone before the second ring, held it
to his ear only a moment, then slammed it down. "Bugger it all.
Lieutenant! Get in here."

Lieutenant Reginald Morris burst through the door and
snapped to attention. "Hughes just rang me up. We've got a
kerfuffle on our hands. The damned Red Cross is here for a
surprise inspection. Quick, load the six U-boat prisoners from
barrack 15 into a lorry and send them off on a bit of a jaunt in
the country." He called out after him, "Be sure to pack up and
hide their bloody belongings., then get back here." Once the door

closed, Major Heathridge stood and walked over to the mirror. He leaned forward and tilted his head to one side, then the other. Confident his mustache was properly trimmed and hair neatly combed, he backed away and removed his glasses. After scrubbing the lenses clean he held them up to the light before replacing them on the nose he incessantly picked.

▪   ▪   ▪   ▪   ▪

Peter Krüger was the first prisoner from barrack 15 ordered onto the truck followed by five others. He watched two British guards hoist themselves into the truck. One reached up and dropped the tarp covering the back while the other slipped his hand beneath the tarp and struck the side of the truck twice. The instant they lunged forward the six German prisoners began to chatter—as the truck accelerated, the volume increased. The guards, devoid of emotion, ignored the prisoners' banter. Even though neither guard spoke German, both could interpret anxiety without assistance.

"*Wo nehmen sie uns?*" Steffen said. Where they taking us?

Peter shrugged. "I have no idea. It all happened so fast. That Limey corporal ran into the barrack shouting. Next thing I know, they stuffed us into this truck."

Five minutes later the guard seated beside the driver poked his head into the back and announced the rear tarp could be hoisted. Added light and fresh air brought sighs of relief.

The older British guard ignored Steffen when he asked in perfect English, "Hey mate, where we headed?" The younger guard moved the barrel of his Sten gun toward the prisoners but said nothing.

Reverting to German, Steffen said, "*Was denken Sie?*" What do you think?

"Why raise the rear flap *after* we passed the guard house?" Peter looked directly at the guards. "I know. We're being relocated to another camp where the weather's colder."

Six prisoners and two guards rode on in silence. Eventually the countryside gave way to a village. Steffen nudged Peter. With his hand covering his mouth he said, "This is Brampton. We must be headed west."

The information spread from prisoner to prisoner with a similar nudge and veiled announcement.

Without warning the clanging of an emergency vehicle could be heard. Seconds later the prisoners' truck drove off the side of the road and stopped just as a fire truck shot past. As both guards hopped out, Gregor said to Peter, "What are they pointing at?"

Peter lifted up the front edge of the tarp and peered out. A crowd of people gathered along the side of the road. "Must be a fire. There's smoke pouring out of a house."

chapter 14

Featherstone POW Camp #18, Northeast England
1045 hours
15 January 1945

IN SILENCE, DR. ARTUR HEGG EYED THE tapestry on the wall behind the major's desk and nodded. Centuries old, rich solid walnut paneling stretched to the ceiling. This office looks more like it belongs in a hunting lodge than a prisoner-of-war camp. The two other International Red Cross delegates from Geneva, Switzerland, led by Dr. Hegg, sat quietly waiting for Major Heathridge. Dr. Hegg scribbled on a pad. One of the delegates leaned over and looked at the big question mark and nodded in agreement. Barrack 15 had been underlined twice.

As the door opened, all three delegates stood.

"Gentlemen, sorry to have kept you waiting." The man offered his hand. "Major Blaine Heathridge."

Dr. Hegg responded first as he shook the major's hand. "Major Heathridge, thank you for meeting with us on such short notice. These are my colleagues, Marc Bryner and Linus Raio."

The major shook the hands of the other two delegates vigorously. "Welcome gentlemen. Tea?" He picked up the phone after all three nodded. "Sergeant, four cups of tea." He turned to Dr. Hegg. "Shall we get started while we wait?"

"Thank you, that would be kind." Dr. Hegg placed the notepad on his knee and flipped the pages back to the beginning. "First of all, I must commend you. Overall, the prisoners look entirely fit. The two I examined show no signs of malnutrition and voiced no concerns about their treatment. Prisoner #42, with the broken arm, is doing remarkably well."

"Splendid," Major Heathridge said, "we're doing our best."

Conversation ceased with a knock at the door. "Thank you Sergeant, that'll be all." A serving tray with four cups, a pot of tea, and four biscuits was set on the desk. "As I was saying, with the limited resources we have at our disposal, the prisoners, at least for now, seem content. Most, I dare say, realize they're the lucky ones and will survive this war."

Dr. Hegg sipped his tea then set the fragile cup on its saucer. "But Major, we do have one question." He glanced at his notepad. "We couldn't help but notice that barrack 15 had six empty beds. We inquired, but the prisoners seemed reluctant to tell us anything." He paused to give the other delegates the opportunity to assess the major's reaction. "Where are the six prisoners from barrack 15?"

The delegation did not anticipate such a quick response. "Gentlemen, you must be mistaken." Major Heathridge lifted a clipboard off his desktop and glanced at it. "Today's roll call indicated eighty-seven prisoners and eighty-seven matches the number of prisoners available."

"Yes, Major, but how do you account for the six empty bunks?"

"Quite simple, Dr. Hegg." Major Heathridge opened a drawer and began searching. "Ah yes, here it is."

Dr. Hegg grasped the memo offered to him and began to read.

POSTAGRAM

Date: 12/1/45

To: Major Patrick Heathridge, Commandant Featherstone POW Camp #18

From: Prisoners' of War Department, St. James Palace, London, S.W.1.

Please anticipate the arrival of six (6) additional German prisoners on or before 18/1/45.

Your resource allotment will be corrected accordingly beginning in February.

Time of origin: 3:30 p.m.

Dr. Hegg passed the note to his left. "I see." The other two delegates nodded. "Well then, Major. I would like to thank you for the tea. We must be off."

Major Heathridge stood and shook the hands of the delegates. "I guess there's no need to chat things up a bit more. If I can be of any future assistance to you, let me know."

▪　▪　▪　▪　▪

Lieutenant Morris watched each of the delegates descend the granite steps leading to the gravel auto path. When the car eased forward, he turned and bounded up the spiral stairs. Without knocking he entered the major's office.

"Have they left?"

The lieutenant walked over to the window. "They're just clearing the front gate now. May I ask sir, how'd it go?"

"It was a picnic in the park, a regular Sunday make and mends."

"The memo worked?"

"Didn't raise an eyebrow. The only thing we have to worry about is if they went directly to St. James Palace to look for the original, which I doubt very much will happen." Major Heathridge eased into his chair, lifted both feet onto the desk, and clasped his hands behind his neck. "Nope, didn't suspect a thing."

chapter 15

Brampton, Northeast England
1100 hours
15 January 1945

THE YOUNGER GUARD STOOD AT THE BACK of the truck and motioned the barrel of his Sten gun toward the ground. Dutifully, the German prisoners jumped down, one at a time.

A young woman, not much more than twenty, ran up to the emergency vehicle and cried, "Please, someone save my children." An old baggy sweater covered an ill-fitting print dress, her face—smudged with soot—a picture of terror.

The older guard ran toward the house to offer assistance while the prisoners leaned up against the truck. The crowd of gawkers didn't know whether to stare at the German prisoners-of-war or the house about to be consumed by fire. No flames were visible, but no one could mistake the fire's roar. The instant one of the rescuers opened the front door fresh air sucked into the house causing the fire to escalate into an inferno. Those watching shielded their faces with a forearm.

The rescuer slammed the door shut.

Screams from the distraught mother carried over the noise of the fire. "Please save my baby!"

No one dared enter the house. A man on a bicycle shouted, "Why don't you do something?" The older guard declared, "They're waiting for the hose and ladder brigade."

Steffen translated for his fellow prisoners.

Peter, without hesitation, dashed to the rescuer standing helpless at the front door just beyond the roof overhanging the porch. The guard with the Sten gun brought its barrel up but didn't shoot as Peter rushed past.

"*Sprechen Sie Deutsch?*" Peter said. The man shook his head, No. Peter intertwined the fingers of both hands, palms up, indicating that the man should do the same. Seeing this, one of the other German prisoners ran over. With both men's help Peter made it onto the roof in one bound. He reached for the window ledge to lift himself higher, paused to pull off his sweater, and used it to protect his elbow as he smashed the window. Unable to avoid being engulfed by the thick smoke bellowing out the window, Peter coughed uncontrollably. By the time he could breathe again, the smoke had dissipated. He looked down toward the assembled crowd. The young mother's terrified eyes urged him on. Instantly, he brought the sweater to his face, took a deep breath, held it, and dove through the window onto the floor. His eyes stung. Relieved to find the air close to the floor free of smoke, he crawled toward the opposite wall, forcing himself to take shallow breaths along the floor. The sound of a barking dog drew him deeper into the hallway. The red glow from flames crackling at the bottom of the stairs provided the only light. He rested but a moment and wiped the tears from his burning eyes. At the end of the hall he felt a doorjamb—rapid scratching and whimpering confirmed the animal's location.

He knew what he had to do. Using his sweater as a breathing mask, he stood and groped for the doorknob. Not finding it, he fell back to the floor. Renewed spasms of cough hindered his breathing. Seconds later he inhaled again and rose to his feet. He found the knob on the opposite side of the door higher than expected. Turning it, he fell through the doorway. Good, no flames. A terrier licked his face. On the floor a child, maybe three years of age, lay motionless. Peter rolled the boy over; at the sight of shallow respirations he gave a silent prayer of thanks.

Placing his sweater over the boy's face, he took another deep breath, scooped the dark headed child and dog up in one arm and felt his way along the wall. In the hallway, the roar of the fire told him it was climbing the stairs. With only three strides Peter reached the window. He placed the dog onto the roof and climbed out with the boy's limp body under his arm. In the fresh air Peter hacked and sputtered. He lowered the child and dog down to the men waiting below, then hung from the roof and dropped the few feet to ground. The boy's mother rushed over and squeezed her son to her breasts. The crowd let out a collective shout when the boy coughed and started to cry.

The young mother surged forward and pointed to the window. "My baby, she's still in her crib. Save her, she's in her crib." Stephan ran over and repeated her words in German.

Peter ran to the porch and without a moment's hesitation was catapulted onto the roof a second time and dove through the open window. While still on the floor, the fire crackled and roared to his left. He inhaled, stood, and bolted through the door, down the hallway. At the closed door, he opened it. Relieved to see little smoke had accumulated, he found the crib along the wall. He grabbed the flaccid infant and ran back through the smoke toward the window. Without his sweater, both eyes burned worse than before, smoke refilled his lungs. Stepping through the window he snagged his leg on a shard of glass. The assembled crowd gasped as he fell. He instinctively rotated onto his back and simultaneously clutched the baby tighter in his arm. When the fire brigade had arrived, they leaned a ladder against the porch roof. As the rescuers reached the top of the ladder, they caught Peter by the arm, arresting his descent before toppling off. In an instant the baby was transferred to another rescuer who slid down the ladder where the baby's mother waited. The baby began to whimper when her mother scooped her up and began kissing her about the head. Tears streaked the woman's soot stained face.

A second shout erupted from the crowd. On the ground, Peter stood straight. His eyes focused on the sharp pain in his left calf. Sunlight glinting off a long sliver of glass protruding past his pant leg like an arrow captured his attention. Seeing blood pooling on the top of his boot, he fainted.

chapter 16

Monday morning
29 January 1945
Dresden, Germany

Dear Hans,

Mother and I are overcome with joy to learn you are well and that your birthday and Christmas Eve was a safe and happy one.

Since the loss of Peter's U-boat it has been most difficult, especially for your mother. I thought at first our move from Berlin would do her good not being constantly reminded of Peter's room. But this was replaced by her not letting go of his letters. There are times I come home and I find her asleep in the chair with both arms clasped around her chest as if protecting them from an unseen thief. It's difficult for me to console her, however, your letter brought a glimmer of hope. Thank you for the joy it provided.

I must tell you how I smiled to learn of your letter to Aimée. It has been many months since my last letter to André and I fear it will be even more since our soldiers are no longer in France.

Mother does get out and accomplish her assigned work at the hospital, but as the war rages her work has become even more difficult. We are thankful we have been spared the air raids that so many cities must endure. No one seems to know why this is so, but we do not question it. What I do question—I know I am forbidden to write of what I am about to tell you, but I feel it is useless to keep such things to myself—is why this war has gone on for so long. We were told after Hitler conquered France that England was the enemy, then war is declared on America. After this we're told the Russians are the source of all evil and must be wiped from the face of the earth, yet no one stands up to this madness. Now, Germany is retreating west from the east, and east from the west. It is sheer lunacy. Rationing has reduced our allotment of food and all the refugees—they are everywhere it seems—only make it worse. But who am I to complain? I must remind myself that we have it easier than many for at least we are not being fired upon.

I almost wish my letter is discovered and I am arrested and taken away. It would be a welcome change to what we have to endure and the future surely provides little hope for us. One cannot help but be amused by the slogans that fail to inspire. The first year of the war, their slogan was "Strength Through Joy." If I close my eyes, it is not hard to envision Dr. Goebbels shouting "Total War!" while he shakes his upraised fist in the air. At the theatre, the newsreels cajole us to "Fight On To Victory!" And for what? It truly saddens me my pledge to André thirty years ago is broken by these evil men.

But alas, these are the musings of a tired old soldier who wishes for there only to be peace.

We wish you Godspeed and think of you always.

Your loving Father

chapter 17

Featherstone POW Camp #18, Northeast England
1330 hours
30 January 1945

THE BLACK ROLLS ROYCE STOPPED AT THE barricade guarding the entrance of the camp. A soldier stepped in front of the car and signaled the passenger window to be lowered. "Excuse me sir, do you—"

"Worthington. *Lord* Worthington."

"Excuse me Lord Worthington, sir, are you expected?"

"I most assuredly am not." He glanced at the soldier's rank insignia before his eyes bore into him. "Nonetheless Corporal, I demand to see the Commandant."

■　■　■　■　■

The soldier did not yield. "Wait right here." As an afterthought, he added, "Sir."

Back in the guardhouse, he dialed a number. "Sergeant, I have some gentry bloke out here demanding to see the major. You'd think he was King George hisself. Says he's a Lord Worthington, whoever that is."

"Scar beneath the left eye?"

"Why yes sir."

"Let him in. I'll notify the lieutenant."

▪ ▪ ▪ ▪ ▪

"Alistair, put up here by the front where you used to let me out." William Worthington took in as much as he could while his driver hurried to the back of the car. *My God, what have they done?* By the time he stepped out onto the gravel the reasons to shake his head had multiplied. "They haven't a farthing of respect for Worthington Manor and what she's done for the Crown. None, absolutely none."

Immediately another soldier approached. The once familiar sound of gravel crunching beneath the man's steps did nothing to improve Lord Worthington's mood.

"Young man, where might one find the Commandant?"

"Lieutenant Hughes, sir. I've been instructed to ask that you follow me."

"*You* can follow me." William Worthington ascended the steps generations of Worthington's had ascended before him, wearing furrows in the granite, indentations where water would pool like individual ponds after a rain. A frown settled on his face at seeing the scuff marks on the doorframe and the dent in the two hundred-year-old door his great-great-great grandfather had commissioned during the reign of King George II. Once in the entryway he no longer detected the soothing odor of linseed oil and polished wood that had defined his home for generations.

A short, yet energetic man in his early forties approached. "Lord Worthington, Major Heathridge. I am at your service and I must say, it's a pleasure to meet the man who owned such a wonderful home."

"*Owns*, Major." The man ignored the major's outstretched hand. "Need I remind you, I still own Worthington Manor?"

"Yes, Lord Worthington, my humblest apology. I meant no offense."

The major's words made little impression.

81

"Now what is it we can do for you?"

"I require some information."

Major Heathridge led the way to his office in what used to be the billiard room. "May I offer you a brandy?"

"That would be kind of you." While the major poured the drinks, William Worthington looked about the room. *I wonder where they've stored my table? And the portraits, where are they off to?*

"Sir, we've tried not to disturb things too much. The lot of your possessions are in storage. The men wanted to move your billiard table to the recreation hall. I told them I wouldn't hear of it, sir."

For the first time since arriving, he smiled. "Thank you Major. Now let me get to the point. As you probably know, there was a fire recently in Brampton—I've business dealings with the family, caretaker's daughter actually, and I wish to make inquires about a certain German prisoner-of-war who saved the life of her children." Lord Worthington studied the blank expression on Major Heathridge's face. "However, previous inquiries have led me nowhere. I'm told no such person is a prisoner at Worthington Manor."

Silence.

"Major, is this man a prisoner here?"

"Lord Worthington, I'm sorry, but without a name, I don't know how I can be of assistance."

"I surmised as much." Lord Worthington set his drink down. "Major, do you really wish to persist with such tomfoolery? Answer me that, will you? Mrs. Culbourn insists she recognized the guards, they were from this camp." He leaned forward. "All the same, with a mere telephone call I can have General Thompkins' aide here on the next train."

"That won't be necessary, but sir, this is highly irregular."

"I didn't consider it highly irregular that my home and property were appropriated for the war effort." He paused for effect. "I do, however, consider it highly irregular you appear to be hiding certain German prisoners-of-war in your camp."

"Sir, you don't understand—"

He reached toward Major Heathridge's desk. "Your phone?"

The major released the air in his lungs, his shoulders remained slumped. "As you wish."

He ignored the major fidgeting in his chair waiting for the call to be routed. "Clem, Willy here. Trust things are tip-top shape in London." After a brief silence he said, "Fine, just fine. Yes, I'll give Millie your best. Say, old chap, I have a Major Heathridge here, commandant of Featherstone POW Camp at Worthington Manor. I'll pass the handset off, but can you please tell him it's perfectly safe to simply tell me what it is I need to know?" He took a step to the side and held out the handset. "It's Deputy Prime Minister Clement Richard Attlee. He wants to talk to you."

▪　▪　▪　▪　▪

Major Heathridge stood before he spoke. "Major Heathridge here, sir."

"Major, please be so kind as to tell him whatever it is he wishes to know," the voice on the other end said.

"But sir, it involves Operation Paragon."

"Hmmm … ."

"Sir, are you there?"

"Put him on the line."

Major Heathridge handed the phone off. "Lord Worthington, he wants you."

▪　▪　▪　▪　▪

William Worthington lifted the handset to his ear and nodded. "Clem, I appreciate it. I understand, I won't repeat any of it.

You have my word." After another nod he said, "You, too. Yes, not a word," then handed the phone back to the major.

▪ ▪ ▪ ▪ ▪

Major Heathridge set the handset on its cradle and cleared his throat. "Sir, all I am at liberty to tell you is the man you have inquired about is a German sailor captured at the end of 1942 off the coast of Scotland. Due to the most top secret nature of his work in the Kriegsmarine, no one knows he's here, not even the Red—"

"Major, that's a violation of the Geneva Convention!"

"Sir, it's not my decision. I'm simply following orders. I can only assume the Admiralty feels it justified to keep Jerry from knowing the man's whereabouts."

"That's of no concern to me. Now when can I see him?"

The major's eyes flew open. "*See* him, sir?"

"How else can I thank him, Major."

"But sir, it's unheard of for a prisoner to receive guests."

"Major, is it not unheard of for a German POW to save the lives of two children?" William Worthington set his drink down and glanced at the phone. "*British* children at that. Now, *when* can I see him?"

He shook his head in resignation. "Lord Worthington, you can be most persuasive."

"Thank you, Major. I'll take that as a compliment."

Major Heathridge looked at his watch. "I'll have him here half two."

▪ ▪ ▪ ▪ ▪

The prison camp guard whistled, then softly sang the words to *Waltzing Matilda* as he escorted Peter to the manor house. Even the chirping birds flitting about the bushes adorning the once manicured lawn sensed the coming of spring, yet the unseasonably warm weather and sunny sky did little to encourage Peter. He wondered why he was the only prisoner to be summoned and escorted to the commandant's office. *The last thing I need is for everyone to think I'm some kind of traitor, that I've sold out to these Limeys. The war's lost anyway, what would it matter? Damn tune, what I wouldn't give to grab* my *matilda and waltz right out of here.*

He noticed the guard look up. Just inside the window above the path stood an impeccably dressed man in his seventies. Peter kept walking and ignored the man's smile.

Inside the manor, the guard came to attention and saluted. "Thank you Corporal, I'll take him from here." At the top of the stairs Lieutenant Hughes stopped in front of the desk. "Please inform Major Heathridge the prisoner he requested is here."

The sergeant pushed a button, then picked up the phone. "Sir, he's arrived." The sergeant stood, stepped over to the door, opened it, and indicated with his hand for Peter to enter.

Fluent German wasn't what he was accustomed to hearing. Peter had long since ceased wondering why none of the guards made more of an effort to communicate with the prisoners, thus it came as a pleasant surprise to hear the man he'd seen at the window say, "*Sie müssen der Held sein?*" You must be the hero?

He didn't know how to respond.

In not so fluent German, Major Heathridge said, "Krüger, you're here at Lord Worthington's request."

He looked straight ahead. "*Ich tat nichts.*" I did nothing.

"Nothing indeed." Lord Worthington ignored Peter's reticence and grasped the file Major Heathridge handed him. "Please forgive my manners and allow me to introduce myself. I'm William Worthington. Long before this war, I called Featherstone my home."

"Lord Worthington's an MP—a Member of Parliament. And a personal friend of the Deputy Prime Minister," Major Heathridge said.

He ignored William Worthington's outstretched hand and remained standing. *What are they doing with my file?*

"I see you were a crew member—radio operator it seems—of the U-357." Lord Worthington laid the file on the table. "Beyond that we know nothing about you. It seems you risked your life— twice I'm told—to save the lives of two English children. And a dog if I'm not mistaken."

More silence.

"Mr. Krüger, Major Heathridge here has allowed me to see you—if only for a moment—to express my gratitude." He held Peter's gaze. "And to see in what way I can assist you."

Peter looked at the major. *Even if I'd plucked Churchill himself out of the fire, I doubt you'd be able to assist me.* He maintained his silence.

Lord Worthington reached down, grabbed the file and flipped through the pages again. He pointed to the chair. "Please, sit down."

"No thank you. Sir."

"Very well. Then tell me, what did you do before the war?"

He remained silent for several seconds before he responded. "Studied."

"You were born in 1920. You must have been at the university. What did you study?"

"Engineering."

"And was this something your father studied?"

"No."

"Do you have any brothers or sisters?"

"One brother."

"Is he older or younger?"

"Older."

"I see. When's the last time"—Lord Worthington caught himself—"I mean, prior to your capture, when's the last time you heard from him?"

"November, 1942."

"And your parents?"

"December of 42."

"Peter, the Deputy Prime Minister and Major Heathridge here have granted me permission to see you. As I've said, I'm in a position to assist. What you did to save the lives of those children is commendable. I have known the family for years and I wish to repay you for your actions."

He finally softened. "Sir, I have done nothing anyone else wouldn't have done."

"This may be, but you're the one who risked your life. I needn't point out that none of the other people there—Englishmen I might add—even attempted what you did."

"Thank you, sir. Can you at least inform my parents I am alive?"

Lord Worthington glanced at the major before he responded. "That I cannot do—a matter for the Admiralty I'm afraid. The war's not going well for Germany, some think it will be over by spring. The Russians are nigh on Berlin and General Montgomery's about to cross the Rhine."

"How does this help me?"

"What I'm trying to say is when the war's over all the prisoners will have to be released. What we don't know is *when*, but as you can imagine, it may be a long while." Lord Worthington looked him in the eye. "This is where I can be of assistance. Through my contacts I will expedite your release and get you on your way back home to your family."

The corners of Peter's mouth began to turn upward. "You would do this for me?"

"I would insist upon it."

"How—"

"You have my word as an Englishman. The minute the hostilities have ended, and an armistice is signed, I will make the necessary arrangements. Rest assured, my wishes will be fulfilled."

Major Heathridge nodded and made an entry into his file.

chapter 18

Sermaize-les-Bains, France
30 January 1945

AIMÉE FERRAND'S WORKDAY AT THE TELEPHONE EXCHANGE started out like all the others since the Allies liberated France. Frequent breaks did little to dispel the monotony. In the washroom, before returning to her chair, she gazed in the mirror and smoothed her favorite white and blue print blouse. Tilting her head to one side, she checked the matching ribbon tied around the tress of black hair resting between her shoulders. Her cheeks had retained their usual red tint from the walk to work. Content all was in order, she forced a smile and hurried to the tangle of wires and the blinking light of an incoming call.

The caller's German accent surprised her. The instant she unplugged the patch cord from the panel, a new premonition took hold. The numerous calls requiring her attention failed to dispel her intuition. Never actually feeling clairvoyant, her feelings usually meant something. Since the call and throughout the afternoon, she couldn't stop putting her eyes to the clock. *Why can't I just forget about that call?*

At the conclusion of a day made longer by nagging thoughts, she walked the familiar route home. Because it was the route she and Hans walked that summer they fell in love, her premonition intensified. Her pace quickened. After opening the front door Aimée glanced at the hall table. Her shoulders collapsed. I felt so sure there'd be a letter for me. In a monotone she announced, "Maman. Papa, I'm home."

Claire, her younger sister, called out in a tone she recognized, but hadn't heard in months. "Aimée, come quickly. We're in here!"

In the kitchen, André, her father hunched over. His hand covered his mouth as he coughed. His other hand clutched the back of the chair. She failed to notice his pale complexion or the look of concern on her mother's face. Claire, standing next to her mother, squirmed with excitement. When her father's coughing spell passed, she saw him look deliberately at the corner of the table, then ease into the chair out of breath.

Aimée screamed at the recognition of Hans' handwriting. "He's alive! Maman! Papa! Hans is alive!" With the letter firmly in her grasp, she embraced Claire and spun around in a quick circle. "He's alive! Maman, he's alive!"

Tears began to form in the corners of her eyes as she tore open the letter. Claire stepped away in response to her drawing the letter close to her chest. Elsie Ferrand stood next to her eldest daughter while André remained seated. She read the first page, laid it down, then snatched it up again before Claire could grab it. "Oh, no you don't!"

Her father, still short of breath, held out his hand. "How in the world could he have posted this letter? Aimée, may I inspect the envelope?"

She ceased her reading and read the envelope again, then glanced at its back before she handed it to her father.

"I just don't understand." André took another deep breath and coughed. "According to the wireless, the German army's retreating further east. Aimée, when was it written?"

Elsie Ferrand interjected. "Papa, let her read."

She stopped reading and squeezed the letter to her breasts. "Oh Maman, Papa, I can't believe it—"

"Aimée dear"—cough—cough—"*when* was it written?"

She turned to the first page. "On Christmas Eve. I knew it, I knew he was safe."

Elsie put her arm over her daughter's shoulder. "Yes, yes, I am sure you're right. Our Hans can take care of himself."

"What else does he write?" Claire said.

Aimée's eyebrows tented as she re-read the first page. "Papa, whatever does he mean? He asks that I forgive him for what he did before the Gestapo arrived."

André fought off the urge to cough before he shrugged, not knowing what to say.

As she carefully placed the first page behind the second she added, "He wishes that I tell you 'Hello' and to give his regards to Maman and Papa as well."

"Anything else?" her sister implored.

"Claire!" the girls' mother admonished. "Now leave Aimée alone. She has plenty to worry about without you pestering her."

"Maman, I don't mind." she then embraced each member of the Ferrand family once again and with regained composure, slipped her arm through Claire's and headed for the stairs.

▪ ▪ ▪ ▪ ▪

Elsie sat down with a heavy sigh. "I don't want to see her hurt any more than she has been. That winter Hans was wounded and she heard nothing for months, it almost killed her." She studied her husband closely and wondered why he didn't respond. "You're ill."

An unrelenting cough rooted deep in his chest thwarted his reply. Finally, he said, "I think so."

She put her hand on her husband's forehead. "You've taken a fever"—she looked at him suspiciously—"and a cough. How long have you had it?"

Another coughing spell took hold and this time, it proved more difficult to catch his breath. "I ... I ... seem to be getting worse. It"—deep breath—"it started Saturday"—another deep breath—"after I swept the barn."

Elsie, quick in her judgment, said, "You, off to bed. I'll prepare some soup and call the doctor, he'll know what to do."

▪　▪　▪　▪　▪

The moment both sisters ascended the stairs, Aimée squeezed Claire's arm and drew her into their bedroom. Behind the closed door, she sat on the bed with crossed legs, her younger sister directly across. Ever since Claire turned twenty in September, Aimée noticed how she was no longer an annoying younger sister but a beautiful young woman. She had become a true and loyal friend.

"You must promise not to tell a soul." Aimée searched her sister's eyes. She didn't have to say it, but she did anyway. "Promise?"

Claire leaned forward and nodded. "I swear."

"You can't tell Maman or Papa."

Her impatience began to show. "I *promise*."

"Hans wants to ask Papa for my hand, he wants to marry me."

Claire leaned toward her sister and they hugged. "Of course you'll accept." This was stated more as a fact, but after a short pause she added, "Won't you?"

Aimée sat on the bed without responding, her eyes fixed on a photo of Hans resting on the dresser beyond her sister's shoulder.

She felt her sister's touch on her arm. "I can't even begin to imagine what you must feel … he'll return … we all know he will."

Finally, Aimée's said, "I feel it, too. I don't know when, but he'll be here to ask Papa—"

"What would he ever say to Papa?"

"I can only guess." Aimée studied her sister's furrowed face. "Why the frown?"

"I wonder what a boy—a man really—says to Papa. He adores

Hans so, it's easy to picture him shaking Hans' hand." Claire looked away. "But what about me? Will there be someone to call on me and ask Papa for *my* hand?"

Aimée reached out both arms and surrounded her sister in a warm embrace. "The fighting will be over and the men will return. Soon they'll be buying eggs every day. It wouldn't surprise me if Papa sells them one at a time just to keep the right one coming back more often."

When their laughter subsided, they heard a call to dinner.

"Oh, this is such a joyous thing. And Maman, I know she'll approve," Claire said.

Aimée laughed. "Since August, to hear Maman talk, you'd think Hans hung the moon and the stars."

Halfway down the stairs Aimée felt she might burst with joy when her sister said, "Well he did, didn't he?"

■　■　■　■　■

The doctor turned before leaving. "Remember—"

"Yes, I'll take his temperature twice a day. If it's greater than 104, I'll call you immediately."

"He should be fine, but the next twenty-four hours are critical."

"Thank you, Doctor." Elsie closed the door and rested her bowed head against it for a moment. Her survey of the doctor's kindly eyes for hope had yielded little. Returning to the kitchen she noticed the worried looks on her daughters' faces. She set the stew down and took her usual seat next to her husband's empty chair.

Dinner conversations, since the Allied invasion of Normandy in June, had been increasingly animated, but with her husband sick in bed—in spite of the letter from Hans—the atmosphere remained solemn. Both daughters hadn't seen their mother so distraught since August and neither could recall a time when her hair wasn't just so or her brown eyes didn't sparkle. She looked toward the stairs when her husband's hacking persisted for most of a minute.

"Maman," Claire said, "will Papa be alright?"

"I'm not sure. On the phone with Dr. Ganthier, I simply answered a few questions and next thing I know, he came right over. He said Papa'll be fine." She was clearly having trouble concentrating. "What else can he say?"—her lower lip began to tremble—"But his eyes told a different story. And his temperature, it's so high."

"Maman, I can help with the chores. Before I leave in the morning I can gather the eggs and Claire can feed and water the chickens. Papa won't have to worry, we'll do the work while he's in bed."

She looked at both her daughters. "Dr. Ganthier listened to Papa's lungs twice. He said Papa's rapid breathing and fever is serious, said Papa has pneumonia." She remembered how her own mother had died so suddenly and realized the impact her statement had on her daughters and quickly added, "The doctor also thinks Papa should be back to normal in a week or two." She didn't tell them about the bloody sputum he'd coughed up earlier.

"*Should* be?" Aimée said. "Aren't you scared?"

She reached across the table with both hands and grasped a hand of each of her daughters before saying, "No, Papa's strong so *we* must be strong. He'll be fine." She swallowed hard. "Papa told me we should carry on just like we normally would."

No one said a word.

Finally, Elsie said, "Aimée, you should begin writing Hans."

"Oh Maman, how could you suggest such a thing with Papa so sick. Besides, it's impossible for a letter to reach him. Who'd deliver it?"

"Now, now, listen for a moment"—she held up her hand—"please hear what I have to say. You both know your papa fought in the trenches before we were married, but what you don't know is, he used to write me letters that were never sent—"

"Then how did you get them?" Claire said.

"I learned of them after the war. You see, he was afraid to express his feelings—I think out of fear of *my* papa." She was relieved for the distraction and for seeing both daughters so intent on her story. "It wasn't until after the war he gave me the letters. I think there were close to fifty."

"Fifty!" both daughters said in unison. "Do you still have them?" Claire said first.

"Dear me no, I burned them years ago."

"Burned them?" Aimée said, surprised at such an admission.

"Why yes, it would have embarrassed him so if anyone else had read them." A smile came to her slowly. "He was quite romantic, your papa."

Claire nudged her sister's knee under the table.

"I think it was for this reason I said 'Yes!' when your papa asked me to marry him." She then looked only at Aimée. "Write letters, seal the envelopes as if you were about to dispatch them to him, but hide them away and when Hans returns, after you two are through kissing"—at this point both daughters began to blush—"give him the letters. This will make you feel closer at a time when he's far away and there's nothing you can do about it."

Aimée sprang to her feet and from behind her mother, encircled both arms around her neck and kissed her on the cheek. "Oh Maman, you are the sweetest! Papa, too."

Elsie grinned as she called out to Aimée scurrying off to her room, "Sweeter than Hans?"

chapter 19

Sermaize-les-Bains, France
Tuesday
30 January 1945

My darling Hans,

The excitement I feel is impossible to express, nonetheless I shall try. Your wonderful letter arrived today and was waiting for me when I returned home from work, like all the others you've written. Unfortunately, this letter to you will have to wait until that wonderful day you walk up the lane and I can deliver it in person. That is after I have released you from my embrace. It was Maman's idea to write a letter I cannot post—yet no one could convince me it really wasn't Papa's. He is such a dear, almost as dear as you, but I worry for him. He has taken ill and the doctor fears it's pneumonia. For now, he's confined to bed and Claire and I—Maman, too—look after him.

Hans, my darling, of course I accept your proposal. Is it too much to dream that at 25 I'd be your wife? To be at your side forever is simply wonderful. You wouldn't think me a foolish schoolgirl if I practiced writing 'Madame Hans Krüger' would you? Do you remember the times we'd talk and wonder what the future would bring? After you were wounded, I remember being afraid to think of a future with you, and now that I know you are safe, I will think such thoughts every day for it gives me much comfort.

I have longed to write this letter for weeks. As I see or hear things, or even think things, I find myself saying, 'I need to remember to write Hans about this.' I shall try to relate many of the events since August.

The citizens of Sermaize-les-Bains were shocked by what the Nazis did in August. For weeks not a single day passed that we did not see someone dressed all in black. It wasn't long before everyone heard they—I say 'they' for I know it wasn't you—had taken thirteen citizens and strung them up to die. One of our local physicians, Dr. Fritsch was among them. A brave man known to have risked his life many times with the Maquis and in the Great War, he was decorated for his courage. Because he spoke German, he attempted to reason with the madman responsible for this, and instead, he was one of the first to die. And for what? No one could possibly know the reason for this senselessness. And my friend, Julie, the telephone operator from Robert-Espagne, she told me of what they did in her village that day. Many reported that 500 had been killed in Robert-Espagne, Couvonges, Mognéville, Beurey-sur-Saulx, and Sermaize-les-Bains. The telephone exchange had never been so busy. I swear for a week there were more people stopping to gather the news than there were calls to be routed. Before long, it was known that 100, maybe less, had died.

Fortunately, the pall of sadness that fell over Sermaize-les-Bains lifted miraculously after the Americans arrived a few days later. Celebrations were rampant. American flags hung from windows and flowers were thrown onto the vehicles as they paraded past. Our neighbor, Monsieur Pelletier, walked up and down the line of American vehicles pouring wine into canteens, toasting soldiers along his way. And before we knew it, they were gone. Our freedom had been won, and for that we are so very thankful.

Now that was the happy news.

Once the jubilation ended, the finger pointing began. I know I sound bitter, but it's hard for me not to be. If anyone understands, it will be you. When I pause from my writing with my thoughts drawn to that horrific day, I can still see—no, feel and hear—that frightful mob.

With eyes closed, Aimée gently set her pen down. In doing so, the memories spilled out ...

A band of men from the Maquis marched up rue Lombard waving French flags, pushing a group of women before them. "Crying's not going to help you now!" The crowd shook their fists and chanted, "Collaborator! Collaborator!"

"There's another one!" one of the men shouted as he pointed. The door of the telephone exchange burst open and Monsieur Vignon—his cousin, one of the twenty-six men gunned down in Couvonges—shouted, "Here she is!" He yanked Aimée from her chair. "Finally you're going to get what you deserve."

The frenzied group stopped in the street where some chairs were set up and one by one, they began to shave the heads of the women.

"Collaborator! Collaborator!"

Fear gripped the women as the throng spat at them. No one in the crowd dared object. Finally Father Feuillerat rushed over and shouted at the Maquis. "What you do is wrong!"

Their leader pushed him aside. "Get out of our way old man."

Father Feuillerat regained his footing and stepped forward. "No one argues the Nazis were vile. No one knows more than I the pain they inflicted. No one felt more sorrow than me at the site of the bodies of those thirteen men and women hanging from the lampposts. You all know I've been the priest in this village for over fifty years. I baptized most of those we cut down, and those I didn't baptize, I performed their sacrament of marriage."

All movement ceased. The leader of the Maquis said, "Father, you do not understand."

Father Feuillerat held his ground. He calmly responded, "What I understand Gilles is this wrong does not make up for what the Nazis did. Painting a swastika on the shorn heads of these women will not bring back the dead." He then leaned into Gilles, looked him right in the eye like he was the only person on the street and said, "I understand that you are not free of sin and have much to confess."

Neither would yield. "I also understand Aimée Ferrand does not deserve this." He paused for a breath. "What you, Gilles, do not understand is the man—the German officer she is in love with—has been a cherished friend of the Ferrand family since the day she was born."

Gilles' jaw muscles tightened when Father Feuillerat continued. "No, none of you understand that André Ferrand, the man who helped keep you alive these past five years by selling—yes, even sometimes giving—you his eggs and chickens, was a friend of the German soldier's father. They met in No Man's Land on Christmas Eve in 1914." Whispers and nods swept through the crowd.

Father Feuillerat raised his hand and said in a loud commanding voice, like he was ending a homily, "No, Gilles, what you don't understand is that Major Krüger is not a Nazi. He is an honorable man and he came to me on that terrible morning to recruit my assistance. If his commanding officer had known he had come to me he would have been shot as a traitor, of this I am certain. He already knew I was a friend of the family and with my assistance he was able to save the entire Ferrand family from the Gestapo who were on their way to arrest them."

Gilles' jaw muscles tighten even more. When he lunged with

outstretched hands poised to choke the priest, the crowd gasped. Father Feuillerat moved faster than anyone could have imagined. Like a prizefighter, he stepped aside, grabbed the man's arm, twisted it behind him, and yanked it upward. Before sending Gilles sprawling to the ground, he grunted through clenched teeth, "You're no different than the Nazis you despise!"

Gilles picked up the scissors and stepped back away from the crowd. Several men surged forward to protect their priest ...

The shiver running up her back broke Aimée's trance. She hadn't even realized she had set her pen down. Picking it back up, she stretched out her arm and resumed writing.

> Hans my dear, I don't wish to burden you with all my troubles in a letter. When I hold you in my arms I promise I will tell you everything about how the Maquis behaved. It will comfort you to know Father Feuillerat is truly a saint. Since the day he was my guardian angel, there has been no trouble with the Maquis. Even Papa has noticed many of his outstanding accounts have been settled, some he never thought would be paid. In the street and at work—people I once thought were rude—now smile and speak to me when I pass. But for now, I will let these silly wounds heal.
>
> Hans, you would not believe Maman. Remember how she was so harsh and inhospitable the last time you were on furlough? There was so much of what she said I did not share with you for fear of causing pain and perhaps driving you away. Now, Maman acts as if none of that ever happened. Why just the other day she remarked to Papa, "I don't know where you ever got the notion I was not in favor of Hans." Papa was so perplexed. He looked at me and winked. How I kept from laughing I'll never know. Now Maman asks what meals she should fix for you after the war!

And Papa, he has taken to his sick bed—Maman says it's pneumonia. This evening after supper he looked so weak lying in bed, and because he labors just to breath, the twinkle is gone from his eyes. We already miss his silly little jokes and constant teasing. Maman tells us to be strong, but please say a prayer for him.

Father Feuillerat just left, he came to visit as soon as he'd heard of Papa's illness—Dr. Ganthier must have told him. Ever since August, Father Feuillerat and Papa have become close friends, I'm sure it has to do with that August day. Father said he'd return every morning after Mass and pray for Papa. I told him of your letter and he said, "I am not surprised. He is a very resourceful man, this Hans Krüger."

Yes, Hans Krüger, we all wish to know, how did you ever post my letter? You must remember to tell us after your return.

Hans, I pray for your safety every minute I am awake. In bed, beneath the covers I place a pillow under my arm and dream it is you I am holding. With these thoughts I smile and drift off to sleep.

Je t'aime—I love you my darling. I want you to know the next time I hold you in my arms, I will never let you go for I have said goodbye too many times.

> With all my love and prayers
> for your safe return, I remain,
> Eternally yours,
> Aimée

She finished the letter, folded and sealed the envelope. On the corner of her desk rested a beautiful walnut keepsake box, a gift from her parents. She smiled—and recited yet another prayer for her father—then thought of what he'd said when she had unwrapped the gift. "We don't know where it is you hide all those

letters from Hans—Lord knows Claire has tried to find them—
but your Maman and I think it's time they have a proper home."

She raised the necklace and small brass key up and out of
the soft delicate crevice between her breasts and removed the
chain from around her neck. She unlocked the box, lifted the
lid, withdrew Hans' last letter and read it slowly, savoring each
sentence like a delicate pastry. Finished, she kissed the letter she'd
just written, pressed it together with Hans' letter to her and placed
them both atop the others. A quick twist of her wrist locked the lid.
She studied the key as if it could yield even more secrets contained
within the walnut box, then replaced the chain around her neck,
letting the key fall to the warmth of its natural resting place.

"Please God, bring him back to me," she whispered softly.

chapter 20

Sermaize-les-Bains, France
23 February 1945

BASKING IN THE UNSEASONABLY WARM SUN, AIMÉE stood at the street corner next to the school building and waited for Marjorie. The familiar sound of the afternoon bell brought her eyes to the school's front door as two young girls darted out and scampered down the steps. Dozens more followed, spilling out onto the sidewalk.

"Hortense and Josette. Be careful! And don't forget your assignments." Neither heard their teacher call after them. Both girls skipped past Aimée—hand in hand—before they disappeared around the corner.

Aimée returned her friend's wave as they approached one another. Once they exchanged hugs Majorie said, "Thanks for waiting for me. After the week I've had, I need to get outside."

"I can see why." As they walked, Aimée looked up the street at all the schoolgirls. "Remember how much fun it was when we were only eight and school let out?"

"How could I forget? And remember Fridays? Your papa—"

"Waited for us with a bonbon?" Aimée said immediately.

"Every time." Marjorie's tone became serious. "And your papa, he's better?"

"Oh yes. Dr. Ganthier's certain it was pneumonia, but now he's back to his usual pranks."

At the intersection they paused to let a car turn, then crossed the street.

"Good, I can't imagine him any other way."

Back on the sidewalk a gentleman smiled, stepped aside, and doffed his cap before both women entered the café. The waiter escorted them to an empty table. Marjorie spoke first. "Two coffees." When the waiter left, she leaned forward. "Have you had a chance to think about our talk yesterday?"

Aimée focused on Majorie's twitching right eyelid. "I've known you for years and the only time your eyelid does that is when you're nervous. What is it?"

"It's nothing. Now, what about it? Do you want to go or not?"

"How could I do that to Hans? I'd never forgive myself."

"I'm not suggesting you do anything, only come to the celebration. Nothing more."

"Will *you* be there?" Aimée said.

"Of course. Cécile and Yvonne said they'd come. Some teachers from school, too."

"Anyone else?"

"Georges and Frédéric."

"Fréd Duval?" Aimée tossed her head back in disgust. "Not interested. I don't care whose birthday it is."

"Come on. You don't have to talk to him."

"He used to be a friend, not anymore. When the Maquis came that day to drag me away, he was one of them."

"I know. He told me how terrible he felt."

"That's only because Father Feuillerat was there."

"He's always been soft on you, even after he learned of Hans."

"Not once have I given him encouragement." Her tone became more defensive. "If I show up, he'll think I want him to walk me home. No thanks, I'm not going."

"Then bring Claire, she'll enjoy herself and she can walk with you."

Aimée softened. "I don't wish to spoil her fun. It seems she has more than a few admirers."

"She's not the obnoxious little sister she once was, is she?"

"Not any more. Papa says she good for business."

Marjorie finally smiled. "Any news of Hans?"

"I wish." Aimée looked up and thanked the waiter for her coffee. "It doesn't matter, I still write him letters." Seeing her friend's puzzled look, she continued. "Ones he can read when the war ends. Maman suggested I do it, but I know it was Papa's idea."

"Sounds like him. I'm sure it helps."

"It does, yet I still worry, especially with the news on the wireless. At night after the BBC broadcast I try to fall asleep, but it takes so long."

"I know."

Aimée reached over and touched Marjorie's arm. "You really don't seem yourself, you sure you're okay?"

"I'm not"—she waited for the patrons at the next table to leave—"not in the least."

"Is it Henri?"

Marjorie appeared lost, vacant. With words barely audible, she said, "Yes, it's Henri."

"What has he done?"

Her eyes looked as if they would mist over. "I fear I'm in a delicate condition—"

"How do you kn—"

"I just know." She paused while the waiter cleared the table next to them then whispered, "It's been five weeks since my monthly."

Aimée could feel the blood surge to her face. "You and Henri, have you been—been close?"

"Once. It was Christmas. For the Maquis, the fighting ended and he was home." Tears began to form. "It really wasn't his fault."

"Is it true what they say? Did it hurt?"

Marjorie nodded. "Only for a moment." She took Aimée's

handkerchief and dabbed both eyes. "I only thought it could happen if I was on my monthly."

Aimée leaned forward. "Have you felt ill in the mornings?"

"No."

"Your breasts, they tingle?"

Marjorie moved her head side to side. "No."

"Pains?"

"Two weeks ago, only for an hour—then they were gone, why?"

"And no blood?"

Marjorie's mood began to lift. "Just one spot, no more."

"I remember Maman discussing these things with my grand-mère. It was only a month before she passed. They were both so serious. I sat in the corner, acting like I was engrossed in my book. They thought I wasn't listening but I hung on every word. She told Maman, 'If your courses fail to arrive it means nothing, but if you tingle in the breast and you feel ill in the mornings, you're with child.' I had just had my first monthly—wouldn't you know it, on my thirteenth birthday." Finally, when Aimée saw the visible pallor of fear lift from her friend's face, she asked one more question. "Haven't you failed your monthly before?"

"Well yes, but we'd never—"

"If you ask me, I'd say you're concerned for no reason. If Grand-mère were alive, she'd say you weren't with child."

"You sure?"

"Absolutely."

When Marjorie smiled, Aimée smiled too. "Now that's more like it."

Marjorie reached over and squeezed Aimée hands. "How can I ever repay you?"

"No need. Your ear's always been there for me. I pray I won't be needing it for a long time."

The twinkle in Marjorie's eye returned. "What about you and Hans?"

"What about me and Hans?"

"Don't be coy with me. You know what?"

"No, if *that's* what you mean."

Marjorie raised one hand, her thumb and finger barely separated. "Not even—"

"No, not even," Aimée protested. "But … sometimes at night, I do wonder what it would be like. Then I convince myself something terrible will happen to Hans if I keep having such thoughts so I just roll over and try to fall asleep. Is that foolish?"

"Not in the least." Marjorie removed some coins from her purse and placed them on the table. "Since you and your grand-mère diagnosed my problem, let me pay."

On the street, the two friends hugged. "Give it some thought about the celebration. Claire will enjoy going."

chapter 21

Remagen, Germany
7 March 1945

THE LEUTNANT KEPT GLANCING AT HIS WATCH. "Major Krüger, the charge should have exploded by now." Moments later a spray of dust erupted like a geyser from the center of the structure and the entire bridge heaved upward as if it had received an electrical shock, then settled back down. A rumbling percussion rolled past two seconds later, then nothing more. The soldiers of Major Hans Krüger's battalion studied the Ludendorff Bridge—it looked the same. "Sir, the bridge still stands!"

Hans grabbed the binoculars and adjusted the focus. "I can't believe it. Americans are scurrying across and our troops do nothing! Get Lutz on the line. *Schnell!*"

Through a misty light rain, he surveyed all 325 meters of the Ludendorff Bridge protruding out of Remagen, its steel lattice a vivid contrast to the blue water of the Rhine. He knew the last remaining bridgehead to span the river stalled the inevitable and Hitler's miracle weapons weren't about to sweep the Allies out of the skies. The reality of the Allies pushing further into Germany solidified as the bridge defiantly ignored the exhortations of the German High Command. For months now the Führer's promises failed to evoke the pride and encouragement they once did, but in March of 1945, few dared verbalize such a thought.

Hans grabbed the handset. "Lutz, what the hell is going on there? The Americans are crossing." As he listened, he motioned for the map. "Fine, plug the leak and get some fire onto that bridge. Whatever you have available, use it." His posture stiffened. "I don't care what Major Behr said, the bridge didn't collapse. Yes, I realize I'm not in charge of the defense of the damn bridge, but for God's sake, I can see it from h—"

The leutnant looked at him after he threw the handset down. "Sir, what'd he say?"

"I don't know, the line went dead."

"Major, what are your orders?"

He took a moment to look at the map. "Simple. My orders are to follow orders. We proceed east at 1400 hours"—he traced a semi-circle on the map east of the Rhine—"and establish a defensive perimeter right here."

"But sir, the bridge, it's still intact—"

"Leutnant, I, for one, am not interested in getting shot for disobeying a direct order. Do you understand?"

"Yes, Herr Major."

"Good, then see to it that the battalion is assembled and on the move." For emphasis he added, "Before we're both shot."

▪ ▪ ▪ ▪ ▪

Hans returned to his command post, closed the door to his office and collapsed into the desk chair, closed both eyes, and rolled his head back. *What I wouldn't give to be in Sermaize-les-Bains.* He stood at the sound of footsteps and swept the papers on the desk into his satchel. Just as he was about to leave, the door swung open.

Anton, out of breath, entered. "We finally on the move?"

He didn't look up. "We have no choice—the Americans are crossing the bridge. Those damn fools didn't demolish it. Now the battalion needs to be in position before Beck starts breathing down my neck."

Anton followed Hans down the hall to the front door. "I'd hate to be the poor son-of-a-bitch that didn't get that bridge blown."

The two officers stepped into the waiting vehicle. "You can be sure heads will roll." Hans tapped the driver's shoulder. "East to Hargarten."

Anton looked over at his friend and said, "Why not Kasbach, its closer to Remagen?"

"That's precisely the reason. They have the bridge and we won't have the ability to deploy an immediate defensive position around Kasbach. Besides, the roads are better around Hargarten, not to mention the fact that it puts us closer to the autobahn."

Frequent stops punctuated the steady exodus of military vehicles. At each interruption heads turned upward to search the sky for American fighter planes. Hans leaned forward to address the driver, realizing they were moving amongst several fuel trucks. "Unteroffizier, pull off to the side and let these vehicles pass."

"Good thinking. That's exactly why you're the major and I'm the hauptmann," Anton said.

"You give me too much credit. I'm only trying to keep us alive." And how successful is that going to be? After several minutes of starting and stopping, Hans finally said, "Where were you in 1940? Remember, we all wondered why England didn't capitulate and end the war?"

"Me? I was a foolish twenty-two-year-old oberleutnant who still believed in the glory of the Third Reich and the Führer's victory." Anton removed his cap and smoothed his tousled hair. "It wasn't until so many died at Stalingrad that I began to realize we would never win this war."

Hans nodded in agreement. "Yeah, and then by 1943 'Will we win the war?' was the question no one had the courage to ask, especially me."

Resuming forward progress, both kept their own thoughts as

they rode on to Hargarten, neither one asking the question on every German soldier's mind since the failed Ardennes offensive: When—not *if*—will the Allies be victorious?

Anton broke the silence. "How long can we can hold out?"

"Four weeks, maybe six. The new American troops learn quickly. They grow stronger as we grow weaker. We're getting fewer and fewer supplies while our men must scrounge and steal from the farmers. At least in France the men had no concern for those they stole from."

"But still, it's better than having our fate decided by the Russians?"

Hans focused on the chaos around them. The Russians. Barbarians, every last one of them. Who's going to get to Berlin first anyway?—the Russians or Patton. Or maybe that egomaniacal Montgomery. "No, Anton, our days are numbered. Despite what Goebel says, since December the Wehrmacht hasn't been able to stage an offensive campaign. Our only role is a defensive one, nothing more. It's totally different now. We're fighting to *save* Germany, not like the early years when we fought for the *glory* of Germany."

Anton nodded. "Ja, did you see the last group of replacements? Old men and young boys. One of those lads couldn't have been more than thirteen, fourteen at the most."

Hans could only shake his head.

▪　▪　▪　▪　▪

The six kilometers retreat to Hargarten took three hours, the roadside littered with the burned out hulks of spent military vehicles, all headed eastward. A Panzer, its cannon defiantly pointed toward the enemy still smoldered, the victim of an aerial attack. The body of a once proud tank commander protruded out the hatch and slumped over the turret as if inspecting it one last time. Soldiers on foot, far outnumbering those in vehicles, streamed around the trucks, until the appearance of an Allied plane caused them to scatter like leaves in the wind. Only after the plane departed did the procession resume its deliberate trek east.

Compounding the frustration of the soldiers in the caravan, countless families and other nameless refugees clogged the road, their hand drawn carts piled with possessions. Neither group acknowledged the other as both struggled to stay ahead of the Allies. The morose travelers ignored the dead bodies along their route. The contorted faces of corpses fixated on the clouds; one pointed skyward at something none of the travelers could see.

The March sun failed to revive the battered souls of a defeated people. No one noticed the green grass or the buds beginning to show on the trees. A putrid mix of smoke, gunpowder, rotting flesh, and death smothered the usual aroma of early spring as soldiers joined the swelling number of refugees on foot. At a fork in the road, half the battalion headed north toward Lorscheid and the remaining half dispersed in and around Hargarten. Finally the line of vehicles came to a complete halt.

Hans stepped down from the car, spread a map across the hood and considered their location. He nodded in the direction of a grove of trees between the two tiny villages. "Leutnant, store the ammunition and fuel over there. Cover it with camouflage netting and post a guard at each corner."

Another fighter plane threatened to harass the column. Fear escaladed. A soldier looked up at the western horizon. "Here he comes again!"

Hans, annoyed at the distraction, scanned the horizon, then returned to studying his map. After several tense moments the terrifying drone of a swooping aircraft failed to materialize. One brave soldier hoisted himself to his feet and laughed. He pointed and said, "Wilhelm you dunce, that's a crow, nothing more."

Before the laughter could subside, a staff car swerved and

skidded to a stop in front of an old woman and two children pulling a cart. A dog, nothing more than a loyal mutt, stayed instinctively close to the children. The old woman, unable to pass, ignored the occupants of the car. With a terrified look on his face, the soldier who had been laughing snapped to attention and saluted. A scowling Oberst Karl Beck emerged from his staff car and screamed, "You stupid imbeciles have time for games?"

"*Nein* sir, Herr Oberst."

"Then keep moving!"

Hans watched the old woman as she ignored the oberst and brushed past him with her cart. He whipped around, his scowl deeper than Hans had ever seen. Incensed by the woman's demeanor, Beck stepped directly in her path and grabbed the handle of her cart. The woman's dog positioned itself in front of the children and lowered its head; the hair on the ridge of its back bristled, a deep growl emanated from the dog's throat. Beck released his grip on the cart and removed his sidearm from its holster. One shot at point blank range and the dog fell dead with a whimper.

Hans' jaw went rigid and his fists clenched as Beck calmly re-holstered his sidearm. "Major Krüger, get this goddamn column moving. Schnell!"

chapter 22

Wehrmacht Regimental Headquarters
Notscheid, Germany
14 March 1945

THE STAFF CONFERENCE BETWEEN BATTALION COMMANDERS AND
their regimental commander ended as solemnly as it began; little
enthusiasm existed for Field Marshal Model's defensive battle to
save the Ruhr and Oberst Beck's attempt to inspire those present
ranked an undisputed failure. As the assembled officers filed out,
Beck signaled Hans to remain and close the door. Now what's that
asshole want?

"I tell you Major, Model's a fool. We should move south
toward Frankfurt, not north. The Ruhr is lost. Let the stinking
Allies have it."

Hans watched his commanding officer lean forward and
shake his finger as if lecturing a schoolboy. "The only thing Model
says that I agree with is, 'A man who no longer believes in victory
cannot fight with the necessary toughness and contempt for death.'
What about you, Major? I see no contempt in your eyes. Not sure
if I ever did, for that matter."

Hans knew now was not the time to disagree or interrupt.

"The 29th Regiment's always been the best in the division
despite what General Denkert thinks. Certainly the 8th and the
50th have seen their successes, but not like the 29th, and besides"—

Beck slammed his fist on the desk—"which regiment saved the 3rd Panzer-Grenadier Division in Italy? I'll tell you who, my 29th, that's who." Beck pointed to his neck and the Knight's Cross dangling below his collar. "See this? This isn't handed out to just any soldier who survives a battle."

I really think he's losing it this time. Again, Hans offered no response.

"How long have you been in my command, Major?" Beck leaned back in his chair and before Hans could answer, he said, "I recall our first briefing back in France. Two years, that's what it's been."

Hans simply nodded, then said, "How far north are we to proceed?"

Beck, still annoyed, took his time to respond. "Fifty kilometers." After several moments he added, "Look at me, what do you see?"

Hans didn't know what to say. I give, a raging maniac?

"You see a fifty-two-year-old oberst, that's what you see. Let me ask you, how many other fifty-two-year-old obersts have you seen? None, that's how many. Did you know the American air corps has thirty-year-old colonels?" Beck ignored Hans' obvious discomfort. "No, I didn't think so. I tell you, I should have been a general years ago! Hecker, he's two years younger and he's a Generalmajor. That measly, mousey Schlomer is a Generalluetnant. Even my Iron Cross from the first war means nothing."

Hans, growing impatient, finally stood. "If you will excuse me Herr Oberst, I must meet with my staff."

▪　▪　▪　▪　▪

Beck sat motionless. An artillery barrage erupted no more than five kilometers to the west. The last burst rattled the windowpanes, bringing him out of his trance. Finally aware Major Krüger had already departed, he simply waved his hand in a disdainful gesture and resumed staring out the window.

▪   ▪   ▪   ▪   ▪

"How'd your meeting with the asshole go?" Anton suppressed a smirk and continued packing.

"Interesting to say the least." Hans removed a bag from under the bed and began organizing his personal items. "We're headed north, set to depart at 0500 hours."

"Oh for Christ's sake, why north?"

"Model's convinced the Wehrmacht should be defending the Ruhr—Hilter's directive no doubt."

"How's his mood?"

Hans slipped folded shirts into his bag. "About what you'd expect. He went off on a tangent about not being a general by now."

"Let me guess, he told you about his Knight's Cross again?"

Hans smiled. "He even mentioned his Iron Cross from the first war, but mostly he ranted about still being an oberst."

"Yeah, I bet. Mean son-of-a-bitch probably thinks he should be a field marshal."

"He asked me why he wasn't a general."

Anton looked surprised. "You didn't tell him did you?"

"Are you kidding? I wouldn't have the nerve."

Anton stopped packing and sat on the edge of his bed. "You suppose he thinks no one knows about his daughter?"

Hans continued filling his bag. "Hard to say. You never know what people really believe or don't believe when it comes to family."

"That's true, but I have absolutely no doubt, nor does anyone else"—Anton lowered his voice—"their daughter's involvement in the White Rose didn't just stall his career, it *ruined* it."

"Not to mention his life," Hans added.

"Did she really hang?"

Hans zipped the bag shut and set it on the floor next to the door by his other bag. "February, last year. The bastards couldn't wait. She died within an hour of sentencing."

"Is it true they both were there?"

"That's what I'm told."

Anton stepped over to the door to listen. Hearing no one in the hall, he sat back down and whispered, "You know him better than most. Do you think last August was more to do with his daughter or his not being promoted?"

Hans lowered his voice as well. "Both. He certainly is obsessed about still being an oberst, but it wouldn't surprise me if it wasn't as much about his daughter."

"I don't know what you think, but I've never believed his friend's murder caused him to snap. It was just a convenient excuse."

Hans thought back to that August day just seven months earlier; the news of the ambush by the Maquis momentarily paralyzed the regiment. The Maquis had started as a nuisance, but after the Allied landing at Normandy, they'd become a mortal threat. He looked over at Anton. "You may be right. He says they were good friends, but did you ever see them together?" He didn't wait for a response. "I never did."

"Rumor is, his wife blames him for everything. I can almost begin to feel sorry for the arrogant ass-hole."

"Not me." Hans picked up both bags by the door and headed out. "Not in the least."

chapter 23

Notscheid, Germany
14 March 1945

KARL BECK'S TUNIC LAY CRUMPLED ACROSS THE chair, his pants and suspenders in a pile on the floor nearby. Clad only in a half buttoned uniform shirt and socks, he sat up and swept his arm across the bedside table and grasped the neck of the bottle fully in his outstretched palm. For the fifth time, he attempted to fill his glass with brandy. "Now get the fuck in there this time and stay there." With exaggerated movement, he leaned over and persisted in trying to replace the bottle in exactly the same location it had been on the corner of the table. He wiped away the spilt brandy with his hand, licked it, then flopped back onto the pillow. Even if he'd tried, he wouldn't have been able to remember the last time he'd gotten drunk—sober he might have recalled Sunday night. Once a rare occurrence, it now had him making excuses twice a week.

Next to the bottle of brandy sat a framed photograph of his daughter, Katrin Anneliese. Taken on a Bavarian summer holiday in 1936 at the age of fifteen, it survived as the only photograph of her he possessed. Watching the sunrise in the mountains had been her idea, so father and daughter set out before dawn. At the summit of an outcropping of rocks they rested and shared a biscuit and jam. She pointed to a tiny lantern flickering as it danced from house to barn like a firefly on a summer's night, a farmer no doubt setting out to milk his cows. He guessed there were at least a dozen to milk, she said fewer, or else the farmer would have been at it sooner. He never thought he would one day miss his daughter's love of debate. At the time it frustrated him to no end, but now he'd give anything to watch her launch into an argument armed with logic and passion that even he had to admit garnered respect.

He reached over and gently lifted the photograph, coursed his finger over the frame, then the outline of her face. He smiled remembering the day she'd come home from her friend's with defiantly short hair. Why were you always so rebellious? Couldn't you have accepted the Nazis? Didn't honor and duty mean anything to you? Why? You didn't have to do it. I might have been able to assist you but you wouldn't let me. I could have told you it would mean nothing in the end.

He shook his head and placed the photograph of the daughter he had loved more than anything in the world back on the table. He stood, finished undressing and added his shirt and socks to the clothes on the floor. With an exhausted groan, he flopped into bed, closed his eyes and tried not to think about the date—14 March—and what would have been his only child's twenty-third birthday.

Within seconds sleep consumed him.

▪　▪　▪　▪　▪

Beck awoke drenched in sweat. The last thing he remembered before bolting upright was the image of the woman he now despised. Exactly two years ago, like a viper, she hissed the last words she'd spoken to him. "You son-of-a-bitch, why did the only good thing in my life have to die? It should have been you."

He fumbled in the dark for his watch. The phosphorescent dial glowed soft, barely discernible. 3:00 AM. He rubbed his brow and smoothed back his moist greying hair. He looked at the unfinished glass of brandy on the bedside table but thought better of it. Another hour and I must be up.

He closed his eyes in hopes of slipping back into the only refuge he knew.

chapter 24

Thursday
15 March 1945
Sermaize-les-Bains, France

My dearest and darling Hans,

It is impossible to express how much I love and miss you! I read your letter every day. The amazing thing is, something new is revealed each time. Even though you can't receive my letters, I enjoy telling you I accept your marriage proposal.

Praise God Papa is recovered from pneumonia! He took to his bed all of February and the first week of this month. I've never seen anyone so pale since my grand-mère passed and the night Papa's breathing became shallow, then rapid—I swear his fever nearly broke the thermometer. Maman, beside herself with worry, wouldn't leave his side. Father Feuillerat came immediately and upon seeing Papa, knelt down and administered his last rites. We all prayed the Lord's Prayer and afterwards, Claire and I went to the church and lit a candle, not knowing what else to do. The next morning his fever broke and by that afternoon his smile reassured us all would be well. The following day he joked with everyone. Papa even sat up and said, 'Have I gotten any letters from Hans while I was away?'

I tell you, until now none of us realized how much work

Papa did. At first he would simply tell Claire and me what needed to be done, but when his rapid breaths made it impossible for him to talk, we figured it out on our own. Maman says it's a wonder there are any chickens left to lay eggs and now that Papa is up and around, he tells us how proud he is of his girls, that if he had sons, they wouldn't have taken such good care of things!

Now that I don't have to worry about him, I am back to worrying about you. Papa tells me not to, for he is convinced you are safe. Maman feels it too. Now that he's better, we all listen to the wireless at night for news, hoping it will be proclaimed the war is over, but the end does not appear to be near enough for me. I swear the new Papa thinks he is a soldier again—he fancies himself a general perhaps. He has a map of Europe and after listening to the broadcasts he marks upon it how far the Allies have pushed into Germany from the west and the Russians from the east.

I know I wrote this before—how I wish you knew it already—but Maman also talks of little else except your safe return. Sometimes I wonder if an enchanted fairy didn't put a spell on her! When we are alone she will comment about you and what a fine son-in-law you would be. She says these things in a way that I wonder how she knows. I just shrug my shoulders and sigh.

There is a young man, Vincent, who has taken a liking to Claire. He came over one evening to see her, but only after he asked Papa's permission. Papa thought it suspicious he came over three times one week to buy eggs. After the first time he came back, he said he dropped the eggs and they all broke. The second time he said he needed more. I can't tell if Papa likes him and Maman seems to only like you. Poor Vincent, there is no way she will ever like him as much as she does you, but the important thing is, Claire likes him and he seems quite taken by her.

My friend Marjorie asks that I give you her regards. One day you will meet her and discover why we are such friends. There's nothing she won't say, especially if she puts her mind to it. It's her honesty I find so appealing. Do you know, in January just before I received your letter, we were at the café—to visit like we do—and by the time we were through with our coffee, I was reassured you were safe.

We continue to worry about your parents after hearing on the wireless about the bombings in Dresden. Papa says that the last letter he received from your father gave few details. Perhaps your father will find a way to get word to us that he and your mother are well.

I am sick of this terrible war. Yes, we are thankful it is no longer in France, but when will it ever end? However long it takes, you must promise to come to Sermaize-les-Bains, gather me up in your arms and squeeze me until I can no longer breathe. With God as my witness, I promise I'll never let you go again. Never!

Goodnight my dearest. I will hold you in my dreams and think of nothing but you until your return.

For all eternity darling,
my love is yours and yours alone.
Aimée

chapter 25

Near Gummersbach, Germany
23 March 1945

THE TWENTY-FOUR TON PANZER ROLLED AHEAD, CUTTING off the approaching staff car. With nowhere to go, the vehicle slid into the mud. From the back seat, Generalleutnant Walter Denkert sprang onto the road, stood in front of the tank and commanded it to stop; the tank turned abruptly to the side and stalled.

A hauptmann popped up through the tank's turret, ripped the goggles off his head and screamed. "You dummkopf, what do you"—he momentarily froze, then saluted—"I am sorry sir, I didn't realize it was you. Sir."

"Hauptmann, I am searching for the 29th Regiment. I've been everywhere between here and goddamn Paris. Just where the hell are they?"

As the hauptmann answered, a motorcycle shot past, flinging mud. "Sir, we're attached to the 8th. The 29th is on our southern flank"—the hauptmann turned and pointed to the right—"no more than five kilometers that way."

"Where's the nearest passable road?"

"Back to our rear two kilometers, then east. That should lead you right to them."

The hauptmann looked at his watch then paused to listen. "The American 99th is fifteen, maybe twelve kilometers back." Before the generalleutnant turned to leave, he added, "First crossing, then east, not west, General Denkert, sir."

Generalleutnant Denkert returned the hautpmann's salute and climbed into his car. "Down this road to the first crossing, then east. Schnell."

The driver expertly wove the car between the vehicles of the retreating column on one side of the road and the foot soldiers on the other. The once proud Wehrmacht looked downtrodden, wounded, nearly defeated. Soldiers whose uniforms were covered with mud and filth hobbled along on crutches, others supported their wounded blood stained comrades. One soldier, unable to see—like a blind Napoleon headed back to France—sat atop a horse pulling a wagon filled with wounded. General Denkert ignored the fact that not a single soldier walked with his head held high; the bravado of a conquering army had been beaten out of them. At some point their strut had turned into a shuffle.

Within two kilometers of turning east, the staff car encountered a squad resting on the side of the road. Observing their general, the squad snapped to attention and saluted.

General Denkert saluted in return. "Where can I find the 29th Regiment?"

"That's us General," the unteroffizier said, confused.

"And Oberst Beck?"

"Yes sir. Regimental command's in Gummersbach." The unteroffizier pointed to the village in the distance. "Last I heard, it's still there."

The other soldiers nodded in agreement.

▪ ▪ ▪ ▪ ▪

Three transports filled with able-bodied soldiers drove away as the general's staff car arrived in front of the cottage serving as the regimental command post. A clerk had just removed the Nazi flag that hung from the eaves. Parked outside sat a kübelwagen with its motor running. Boxes of files and other regimental papers filled the back seat. Generalleutnant Denkert stepped out of his staff car and signaled his driver to remain.

The cottage's front door—off its hinges—stood against the wall to facilitate the rapid dismantling of the regimental head-quarters. He walked briskly through the open door.

An oberleutnant brought his heels together, then saluted. "Heil Hitler!"

He barely raised his hand in response. "Oberst Beck, where can I find him?"

▪ ▪ ▪ ▪ ▪

From an inner room, a nervous appearing Beck emerged. "Gen-eralleutnant, what a pleasant surprise. I thought I recognized your voice. Please come in and sit down." His visitor made it a point to close the door. Beck, in a feeble attempt to appear calm, extended his arm. "Walter, do have a seat"—as an after thought, he added—"I regret I have nothing to offer."

"Karl, that's perfectly fine. I understand."

He looked away. "Yes, I'm sure you do."

After an awkward pause, Denkert said, "You realize I'm powerless to increase your supplies. The division's nearly out of ammunition, petrol stores are critically low, I have no troop re-placements. Field Marshall Model is running out of miracles."

"I know." He appreciated his old friend's honesty. "Our patrols constantly encounter enemy elements. We keep moving northeast, deeper into the Ruhr. I told my battalion commanders as soon as we start encountering our own troops, we're finally surrounded, finished."

Denkert offered no objection. "Soon, two weeks, maybe three, there'll be no escape possible."

Beck sighed. "Walter, remember our war in the trenches? We were young and all we did was grumble about the generals and their inability to win a war." He looked off into the distance. "Now we—err, you are the one they grumble about."

Denkert considered the comment. "Yes, but you and I both know you should be one of them. No one has forgotten that you were the first of us to reach the rank of oberst."

Both remained silent. Well, apparently Walter, someone along the way forgot.

Denkert fidgeted in his chair. "We've had our differences, but we've always been friends, have we not?"

Beck took his time in responding. "Yes, Walter, what you say is true. But something tells me you didn't risk your life just to tell me this."

Their gazes locked. Denkert looked away first. "You're correct. What I've come for is—you must believe me when I tell you this—the hardest thing I've ever had to do."

Beck lifted his head. "Yes, Walter?" Fine. Now out with it. What can you possibly say that could be any worse than all of this?

"Karl, Field Marshal Model specifically asked me to—"

"To what? For Christ's sake, to what?"

Denkert moved his chair closer. "Karl, we received a cable this morning informing us your wife, Dorthea … a neighbor found her dead in your apartment this week."

"How?"

"She apparently hanged herself."

His body sagged under the weight of his shoulders, eyes closed. Finally, he looked up. "Did she leave a note?"

Walter's voice, now barely a whisper, continued. "Yes, and a photograph of Katrin Anneliese. Both were on the chair beneath her body."

"I see."

"Karl, Field Marshal Model has specifically stated that if you wish, you may leave to attend to these matters."

And just where the fuck would I go, Walter? Without considering the offer, he said, "There's no one left for me to console."

"Karl, if there's anything I can do—"

He settled his gaze onto the back of Katrin's photo. He could only see his daughter's free-falling body the instant before it jerked to a halt, recoiling at the end of the rope. "Yes Walter, there is one thing …"

Walter waited what seemed minutes.

"The note—was it dated the fourteenth of March?"

He didn't wait to hear Walter's affirmative response—he already knew the answer. Without another word, he abruptly rose from his seat and left the room.

chapter 26

Featherstone POW Camp #18, Northeast England
4 April 1945

"GET UP YOU GOD-DAMN LOUSY KRAUT BEFORE I make you regret your Nazi arse was ever born."

Peter refused to move. For the last ten minutes the only word he heard was "Nazi." He knew he didn't deserve the beating and if he resisted, it would only be worse. *How come you never kick me in the face? I know, you're afraid of too many questions, you useless Limey pig.*

The beatings started after his visit with Lord Worthington the end of January. Word that he was now a pet prisoner with special privileges spread amongst the guards, yet no one stopped to realize his routine had not altered since arriving a little over two years earlier or that he had never been summoned back to the manor house.

The guard nudged him with his boot. Upon seeing his eyes flicker, he kicked him again. "That's for Elizabeth and what you good for nothing Nazi scum did—"

"Corporal!"

Lieutenant Reginald Morris had entered the room unnoticed. The man staggered and halted his leg in mid-swing. "Corporal Shaw, what's the meaning of this? He's done nothing to you."

Peter knew better than to smile. He grabbed the lieutenant's outstretched hand and suppressed a moan. "*Danke*, Lieutenant. *Danke*."

As he stood, the lieutenant studied him a moment and said, "*Sie sind willkommen. Est tut mir leid, dass das geschehen musste. Ich werde darauf aufpassen, ich verspreche.*"

Peter said nothing.

▪ ▪ ▪ ▪ ▪

Lieutenant Morris turned toward the corporal. "Well, what do have to say for yourself?"

"May I ask what you just said to that Nazi?" Seeing the extent of the lieutenant's anger, he added, "Sir."

"No, you may not." He nodded to the door indicating Peter should leave. "But, I'll tell you anyway. I told him I regretted this had to happen and that I would see to it that it didn't happen again." His stare intensified. "This wasn't the first time, was it Corporal?"

"The lying Kraut tell you I've beaten him before, did he?"

"The *lying Kraut*—as you put it—didn't, you just did. What kind of sadistic sot are you?"

"Sir, the lot of them have it comin', if you ask me."

"Fortunately Shaw, I didn't ask you. I'm sorry you lost your family, but he had nothing to do with it. Christ man, give it a think, he wasn't even Luftwaffe."

"Sir, I—"

"Shaw! Put yourself on report and be in my office at 1600 hours"—he ignored the corporal's salute—"and get out of my sight."

The door slammed leaving the lieutenant to his thoughts. *Damn war. I'll be beating my own men before long.*

chapter 27

Featherstone POW Camp #18, Northeast England
13 April 1945

ALL MORNING A GREY MIST HOVERED OVER the camp like a cloud of poison gas. Not only did the mist block the sun and keep a rejuvenating spring at bay, sounds and voices echoed off the buildings. For this reason the animated conversations of the guards by the gate garnered the prisoners' attention. Steffen strained to hear as they walked past. It was obvious something had transpired. Soon several automobiles entered the camp, none were observed leaving. "I wonder what all the commotion's about?" Peter said.

"Don't know. It's unusual, even for a Friday."

"You don't suppose the war's over?"

"Hardly. If that were the case, they'd be celebrating."

"Are you kidding? These Limeys," Peter said, "won't celebrate until their precious King George tells them to. Much too stuffy to do that on their own."

The two friends approached the perimeter and looked towards the manor house. "Just the same, I doubt the war's ended."

Peter and Steffen lingered inside the wire where the gravel met grass. Another vehicle drove up the lane and three women— all dressed in black—got out. The sleeve of the driver bore a black armband. Before Steffen could ask one of the guards why all the activity, Gregor came running up, out of breath.

"Did you hear? Roosevelt's dead."

Peter looked at Gregor. "Are you certain?"

"Very. Warner was scrubbing floors in the manor house and he overheard talk about a funeral. He said Churchill, on the wireless, announced Roosevelt died yesterday."

Peter and Steffen stood and watched. Both said nothing for several moments until Peter spoke. "It won't make a bit of difference—the war's all but lost. If we're to believe what we're told, the Allies are totally across the Rhine and the Wehrmacht's on the run." Peter played the gravel back and forth with the toe of his shoe. "Ja, Steffen, it's only a matter of time."

Both turned away from the wire just as one of the guards approached from within the camp. Peter whispered to Steffen, "Let's go back to the barrack. Since he lost a stripe, he's even less fond of me."

Private Shaw scooted in front of them and said to Steffen, "Roosevelt ain't the only one who's brown bread." He then glared only at Peter. "Tell 'em his precious Lord Worthington's just as dead, deader than a door nail, he is. Tell 'em to put that up his arse and sit on it for another two years."

Steffen translated.

I'll be damned if I'll let that animal get an ounce of satisfaction. Without a hint of emotion, Peter said, "*C'est la guerre.*" That's war.

chapter 28

Sermaize-les-Bains
16 April 1945

A LARGE WINDOW DOMINATED THE FRONT OF the telephone
exchange situated between the hotel and the post office. It not
only allowed the citizens of Sermaize-les-Bains to wonder about
the blinking light of an incoming call and to see the tangle of
patch cords protruding out of the three terminals, it also allowed
Yvonne, Cécile, and Aimée to observe the comings and goings on
the street. Residents wishing to confirm the latest rumor had long
since worn the threshold thin before stopping at the post office.
Everyone knew within hours—if not minutes—that a newborn
baby had arrived, or a friend and neighbor had passed. Not a single
resident of Sermaize-les-Bains considered it an intrusion on their
privacy—rather they welcomed it as a necessity.

If the information was of a harmless, benign nature, it was
always associated with a name, usually Yvonne or Cécile. But if
the gossip about to be dispensed was salacious, a lowering of the
voice and two exculpatory words—"I heard"— preceded it. On
the other hand, for especially risqué gossip, the blame for passing
such prattle shifted away from the dispenser by first asking the
innocent question, "Have *you* heard … ?"

Within the office, Yvonne, though not much older, treated
her co-workers like a kind aunt. Since 1938, two years before the

133

Nazis arrived, she had managed the exchange's official and unoffi-cial business. So it came as no surprise when she said, "Aimée, you don't seem yourself today."

Aimée released the strand of hair she had been twirling and grabbed the patch cord to connect an incoming call. "*Oui, Monsieur*, I will put you through now."

Yvonne persisted. "*Ainsi?*" So?

She tried to smile. "I'm sorry, I'm not trying to be rude. I worry about Hans. I fear something has happened."

"Don't be silly. What could have happened to your Hans? I'm told on the Western Front there are only minor skirmishes. I'm sure he's safe."

"Yes, yes, I know, but still, something has happened."

Cécile piped up. "Yvonne, I wouldn't argue with her. Remember when he was in France? Whenever she *felt* there was a letter waiting—"

"So." Yvonne routed another call before continuing. "That's because everyday there *was* a letter waiting for her. Goodness, even I could have predicted that."

The laughter from Cécile and Yvonne did little to relieve her angst. "I feel it. Something's happened."

Cécile and Yvonne exchanged glances, not knowing what else to say.

Aimée looked at her watch. "It's almost four. Do you mind if I leave?"

"It's my day to stay late, I can handle it," Yvonne said.

Aimée grabbed her purse, slung it over her shoulder and kissed them both on the cheek. Before leaving she turned to wave and said, "Many thanks, how can I ever repay you?"

Yvonne suppressed a smile and said, "Quit having premonitions."

▪ ▪ ▪ ▪ ▪

How Aimée got home, no one could say. It was one of those afternoons in which if asked, she would never be able to recall anything along her route, yet she found her way, as if guided by an invisible hand. Budding leaves on the once dormant trees and broad patches of green grass went unnoticed. Nor did she observe, on the edge of town, a foal walking on rickety legs next to its mother who stood guard in a protective stance, her muzzle prodding new steps. Even the fresh air, warmed by the afternoon sun, failed to arouse her senses. Instead, she focused on the feeling gnawing at her. *I know he's alive. He is, isn't he? At least, I pray he is. Maybe he's wounded worse than before. What if he's lying in a field, helpless?*

The more she worried, the faster she walked. When Monsieur Pelletier rode past with his wagon her head never lifted.

▪   ▪   ▪   ▪   ▪

Elsie Ferrand heard the front door shut and called out, "Aimée, did you remember the flour?"

Aimée headed to the kitchen and focused on the corner of the table. No letter. "Maman, I'm sorry, it slipped my mind."

Elsie finished drying her hands. "You're home early. Are you ill?"

"No, I'm fine. I can return to the market, I don't mind."

She took Aimée into her embrace and squeezed both shoulders. "Don't be silly. Is it Hans?"

"I had another one of my feelings today"—she fought back the urge to cry—"I wish I knew what it meant."

Elsie set the pot of water on the counter. "It means you haven't heard anything and this has you worried, nothing more. Now come and give me a hand with dinner." She quietly observed her daughter ease into a chair at the table, move the cutting board towards her, and begin to peel the potatoes.

"Maman, what if something terrible has happened, how will I ever—"

"Now hush. You're just getting yourself worked up."

"No, I'm serious. How will I ever know what happened to him?"

She sat down next to her daughter and tried to comprehend the depth of her anguish. "I don't know Aimée. With the Great War, your papa and I didn't fall in love until after the after the fighting was over." She reached over and squeezed Aimée's hands. "I wish I knew how to help. It's the unknown that's always so terrible to deal with. You must dwell on the known."

Aimée's eyes brightened.

"You know from his letter he's not fighting the Russians." As Elsie said this she brought her hands together as if praying. "He's a good soldier and you know he loves you."

"Maman, you do feel he's alive, don't you?"

"Aimée darling, we all do. You must believe."

"Maman, I do try, but these feelings … it's just so hard."

She leaned over and hugged her daughter. "We'll get through this, one day at a time."

Aimée arranged, then rearranged the remaining potatoes. "Maman, how'd you do it, I mean, last August how'd you and Papa live every day knowing the Gestapo might come any moment and take us away."

"Just thinking about it gives me the shivers." She smoothed her hair with her hand and smiled. "Between that and Papa's pneumonia, it's no wonder I'm turning grey." Elsie picked up the knife and rotated the last potato in her hand, never watching the thin peel unwind towards the table. "I tell you, I lived in constant fear. My heart would race every time I heard a motor vehicle or loud noise. I guess we lived one day to the next. Papa and I— we never lost faith, we prayed every day for our safety." Finished, she set the knife down and smiled at her daughter. "We—or at least I—had no way of knowing Hans would be the answer to our prayers."

"Maman, can I ask you something?"

"Of course." She pushed the knife and bowl to the side. "Anything."

"How did you know?"

She didn't have to ask—like a scholar comprehends a book, Elsie understood her daughter's inquiry. "It's a funny thing, you just *know*. I guess the best way I can describe it is when you think of him, all you can think about is the last time he gathered you into his arms and kissed you." For the first time, such a topic failed to bring a rush of color to Aimée's cheeks. "And how wonderful you feel around him." Thinking of her own husband, she said, "Trust me, you know."

▪　▪　▪　▪　▪

The meal and dishes cleared from the table, André settled into his usual chair, a newspaper on his knee. From the table next to him he found his pipe and tobacco. Elsie sat on the divan after collecting her knitting supplies. Aimée and Claire sat on the floor in front of the radio, ready to listen. André lit his pipe, reached over and turned on the wireless. "Perhaps the BBC will have more good news tonight."

The announcer had just introduced the evening's final selection of the London Symphony Orchestra. Aimée and Claire began a gentle sway to the soothing timbre of Mozart's Piano Concerto Number 21.

André jerked to attention and adjusted the volume, "Shh. Listen!"

" ... We are interrupting our program to bring you a news flash ..."

Everyone focused on the wireless as if expecting the announcer to appear at any moment waving the dispatch in his hand.

" ... This is London calling. Here is a news flash. I repeat. Here is a news flash. Allied Supreme Command has just announced that an estimated two hundred thousand German soldiers surrendered to Allied forces in the Ruhr valley this afternoon. I repeat. Allied Supreme Command has just announced that an estimated two hundred thousand German soldiers surrendered to Allied forces in the Ruhr valley this afternoon. It is believed that half of Field Marshal Model's forces have surrendered, however, the Field Marshal's whereabouts are unknown at this time … ."

Aimée jumped to her feet. "Papa, the war's over, the war's over!"

"He announced no such thing—"

"Papa, what else can it mean? Hans is safe, I know it."

André turned the radio down, about to speak. Elsie looked at him and softly cleared her throat.

"You're correct, for Hans the war must finally be over."

chapter 29

Iserlohn, Germany
16 April 1945

SINCE THE SUCCESSFUL ALLIED LANDINGS ON FRENCH soil at
Normandy in June of 1944 and Marseilles in the South of France
two months later, the Allies had driven east in hopes of beating the
Russians to Berlin. By the end of March the Russians were poised
for their final thrust on Germany's capital fifty miles northeast of
Berlin, however, the American's race to capture Hitler's lair ended
15 April when Allied Supreme Commander General Dwight D.
Eisenhower abruptly and inexplicably ordered the Allied armies
to halt their eastward advance fifty miles west of Berlin at the
river Elbe. His resolve defied all military strategy and despite the
vigorous protestations of General George S. Patton, the leader of
the American Third Army and Field Marshall Bernard Montgomery, the British leader of 21st Army Group, Eisenhower remained
adamant, refusing to allow Allied troops beyond the river's edge,
thereby leaving all of Berlin and the bulk of Germany to Joseph
Stalin.

Approximately 270 kilometers to the west, in the heart of the
Ruhr Valley, Major Hans Krüger studied the map. Small arms
fire could be heard in all directions. *For two weeks we've been
surrounded.* With his index finger he drew an imaginary circle
around Field Marshal Model's Army Group B. *Now that the*

American First and Ninth Armies have converged—he tapped the map repetitively overlying the city of Hager—we're finished. Enemy artillery continued its relentless pounding of the German army. Rifle shots less than a kilometer away disrupted his thoughts. "Anton, where are my company commanders?"

"Steiner's dead, killed yesterday outside Oestrich."

"Hahn?"

"Dead."

"Buchholtz?"

"Missing. No one's seen him since Saturday."

Hans looked skyward. "Great. That leaves me one stinking company commander. Any word from him?"

"None."

"What about Oberst Beck?"

"He's got his hands full. The other two battalions are currently taking heavy fire, both are down to less than fifty percent complement. Only five field pieces remain, but they've been without shells for days. He refuses to abandon them."

"For God's sake, why?"

"Don't know, ammunition and fuel are non-existent. We've no more supplies to treat the wounded."

Of the seven hundred men under Hans' command, only two hundred were accounted for and fit for service—replacements, despite their enthusiasm, were inexperienced and useless. He appraised his options. I'm tired. I'm tired of running. I'm tired of seeing men die. I'm tired of this insanity. As he was about to speak, a motorcycle and sidecar slid through its turn and stopped abruptly. Oberst Beck stepped out of the sidecar.

Hans had never seen the man with his top buttons unfastened or a stained tunic; Beck's tired, bloodshot eyes darted to and fro. The man's unshaven, soiled face seethed with hostility.

Hans and Anton saluted. Beck spit out his words like bitter fruit. "Krüger, what do you suggest?"

Hans looked at Anton before responding. "Sir, it is not my decision to make."

Beck snapped. "Goddamn it Major. I didn't ask you whose decision it was, I asked what you suggest!"

"Sir, I see no options. We have no supplies, no medicines. We've little ammunition."

Without conviction, Oberst Beck said, "The Führer expects us to fight on."

"That may be, but with what? To continue is suicide." Hans paused before uttering the inevitable. "Sir, it's over."

Beck wiped his nose with the back of his hand. "Major, I'm stepping down as commander of the 29th Regiment. Everyone knows you've always wanted my command. Well, now it's yours. Do as you see fit."

chapter 30

Iserlohn, Germany
17 April 1945

HANS CLENCHED THE WHITE FLAG AND HELD it high hoping the Americans at the opposite end of the pasture would see it. He looked back at the 29th Regiment one last time. Not a rifle in sight. Good, they followed my orders to abandon their weapons. One hundred meters from a jeep parked in front of what could have been a skirmish line, his thoughts raced. Just treat us humanely, that's all I ask. We're Wehrmacht, not SS. He knew for most of the American standing before him, it was the first time they'd seen a German soldier up close—a living one at least. Hundreds of eyes scrutinized his every move.

He held his head high. I can't tell if they look more angry or tired. He scanned the uniforms of the Americans before him. In the front of the line of men, next to a jeep, stood an officer. That must be the company commander. Hans approached the man and saluted. My God, he's just a kid. "I'm Major Hans Krüger, I wish to surrender the 29th Regiment." He unfastened his sidearm and offered it to the man.

The officer returned the salute. "*Major, ich bin Leutnant Zimmerman.*" I'm *Second* Lieutenant Zimmerman."

I should have known, a second lieutenant. And a cocky one at that. "Do I have your assurance my men will be treated fairly?"

He didn't anticipate the lieutenant's response but instantly understood why he didn't require a translator. "As fairly as you Nazis treated my grandparents when they hauled them away in the middle of the night?"

Hans protested. "I can speak for the men in my command. We're not Nazis. We're soldiers, nothing more, nothing less."

"We'll see." The lieutenant tossed Hans' sidearm onto the seat of the jeep then pointed. "Lead your men that way."

chapter 31

American 99th Infantry Division Headquarters
Iserlohn, Germany
21 April 1945

THE RUHR POCKET CONTRACTED LIKE A LEAKY balloon. Despite isolated resistance, German soldiers from individual grenadiers to entire divisions ultimately saw the inherent wisdom of surrender and acted accordingly. The Wehrmacht, once the most feared army in the world, disintegrated into an impotent collection of humanity. From their individual points of capitulation, men were herded into enclosed pens to await processing, then ultimately on to larger enclosures in vast open fields containing thousands. There they waited for an Allied response to an overwhelming problem destined to deplete the resources of a conquering army.

The processing lines moved slowly. As Hans waited, he ignored the thirst crying out from his parched throat and looked about the expansive hall. On top of a table in each of the four corners of the room stood an American soldier with a Thompson submachine gun loosely cradled in his arms. At least five hundred recently surrendered Wehrmacht officers, all from the 3rd Panzer-Grenadier, the 277th Volksgrenadier, and the 9th Panzer Divisions were divided up into four groups, each forming a line. The front of each line ended at a table; at each table sat an American officer, a stenographer, an interpreter, a clerk, and a stack of empty files.

A steady dissonance rose from the German prisoners. Whenever the clamor increased in intensity, the four guards stood straight, more alert. At one point, the sergeant by the main door removed a whistle from his pocket and blew it forcefully. The instantaneous silence was soon followed by a gradual increase in the din while the work at each of the tables resumed.

Hans' turn arrived. He walked deliberately to the table and snapped off a crisp salute. The American officer, a captain, ignored the gesture and said with an edgy tone, "Sit down."

Hans guessed him to be thirty. The man was clean-shaven and the smooth texture of both hands indicated a privileged existence. His snide and temperamental attitude made it easy for Hans to conclude the man commanded little respect. For this, he did not need a translator. Bet you haven't seen a day of combat—ever.

Like those before him, Hans handed the clerk his papers and sat opposite the captain. The clerk turned the cover on a new file and stamped each page before handing the papers to the interpreter. He then handed the file to the captain.

"There are just a few questions." The sergeant seated at the table repeated everything in German.

Hans nodded.

"You are Hans Krüger, is this correct?"

He couldn't stop himself. "Yes, *Major* Hans Krüger." He extended his hand to shake the captain's and said, "Your name is?"

Hans noticed the clerk suppress a smile as the captain reluctantly shook hands. "Captain Hughes." Before continuing, the captain consulted Hans' file. "*Major* Krüger, are you now or have you ever been a member of the Nazi Party?"

He looked the captain in the eye. "Nein."

"And how is it you avoided this?"

Hans glanced to both sides, then behind. "I detest the Nazis."

"You never even attended a party rally?"

"Despite what you might think, officers were forbidden to be party members until after the failed plot to kill Hitler. I assure you, not all officers are or were members of the Nazi Party. The SS maybe, but not the Wehrmacht." The captain's puzzled look amused Hans.

"Why fight with such intensity?"

He didn't hesitate. "We didn't fight for Hitler—or the Nazis. We fought for the man next to us. We fought out of a sense of duty, out of loyalty to the men we knew would die for us." Hans lowered his head and sighed. "And too many of them did."

The captain wrote quickly, then flipped the page. "When did you enter the Wehrmacht?"

"1938."

"You were twenty-four?"

"Twenty-three. I entered before my birthday."

"Your occupation?"

"I studied at the University of Berlin to be an engineer and entered the Wehrmacht at the completion of my studies."

The captain then lifted a black folder off the table and opened it. Hans observed it contained several photos of soldiers in uniform, none that he recognized. The captain looked at Hans frequently as he perused the photos.

"Have you always been attached to the 3rd Panzer-Grenadier Division, Major?"

"Yes. I was initially assigned to the 3.Infanterie-Division. After the Battle of Stalingrad, it was reformed as the 3rd Panzer-Grenadier Division."

The captain raised his eyebrows. "You survived Stalingrad?"

Hans looked down. "I was in Berlin recovering from wounds received in the fighting outside Moscow. These wounds required several surgeries."

"But you fought in the Italian Campaign?"

"Yes, then France, then the Ardennes."

The captain returned to the black folder and held it up to inspect one of the photos more closely while looking at Hans. "How is it you were a major, yet *you* surrendered the entire 29ᵗʰ Regiment?"

"I was actually a battalion commander, the 341ˢᵗ. The commander of the 29ᵗʰ Regiment, Oberst Beck——'"

"First name?"

"Karl. Oberst Karl Beck. He came to me on Monday, the 16ᵗʰ, the day we surrendered and relinquished command of the 29ᵗʰ Regiment."

"Came to you? Why you? Did he give any reasons?"

"Nein. I have no idea." Hans paused. If you don't have that son-of-a-bitch's photo in that black folder of yours, you should.

"No reason at all? Surely Major, there must be a reason?"

Hans shook his head side to side. "None that I'm aware of. After he did, a fool could see continued struggle benefited no one. The next day, the 17ᵗʰ, a dispatch arrived from Generalleutnant Denkert ordering our surrender. I then organized the regiment and under a white flag we proceeded toward Iserlohn. After we encountered your troops I asked to be escorted to the commanding officer. A Lieutenant Zimmerman accepted my surrender on behalf of the regiment."

Captain Hughes entered some final notes in Hans' file then said, "Next."

Hans stood and saluted. Before departing, in his best English he said to the clerk, "Good luck."

▪ ▪ ▪ ▪ ▪

Periodically a clerk would replenish the dwindling supply of empty files and remove the processed ones from each of the four tables. By the time two stacks of completed files had been taken away from Captain Hughes' table, twenty-four more German officers had been interviewed and dismissed to join the expanding number of German prisoners held in the enclosed athletic field outside the gymnasium.

Captain Hughes signaled for the next captured officer to step forward.

Oberst Karl Beck handed his papers to the clerk. Neither officer saluted. After a cursory inspection, the clerk handed them to the translator while Karl Beck sat opposite the American officer. Captain Hughes opened the new file just handed him. Beck thought he detected a hint of recognition in the captain's face. His pulse increased as Captain Hughes leaned over to the stenographer and whispered behind his upheld hand. Beck fidgeted in his seat as he watched Captain Hughes nod to the stenographer's response then stand to summon a clerk walking past. After a quick salute, the clerk disappeared.

The translator and Beck spoke briefly before the translator said, "Captain, he doesn't speak English."

"Fine. Let's get started. Colonel Beck, are you a Nazi?"

"Nein."

"Have you ever attended a Party rally?"

Beck broke eye contact. "*Nie.*" Never. He watched the clerk re-enter the room, in his hand a single file. On it, he thought he saw the last name on the file—Krüger.

Captain Hughes thanked the clerk and took a moment to review the contents of the file before setting it down. "Colonel Beck, how long were you in command of the 29th Regiment?"

I'll kill him. "Since the reforming of the division in April of 1943."

"Before the Italian Campaign?"

"Yes."

"Where you never offered command of the division?"

"Nein."

"Why not?"

"I don't know." Just what did that coward tell you anyway? "You'll have to ask Generalleutnant Denkert."

"Yes, perhaps I will. Until then, can you tell me why you relinquished command to Major Krüger on the 16th?"

"I have my reasons."

"Colonel Beck, you seem a little preoccupied. Is something troubling you?"

Silence.

Before Beck answered, Captain Hughes opened and reviewed the photos in the black file. Hearing no answer, he persisted. "After the Italian Campaign, your regiment moved north into France?"

What are you waiting for, why don't you haul me away. "Yes, after the fall of Paris, we retreated across France, fought in the Ardennes, and now we're here."

"Let's get back to France. Where was your regiment in August?"

Beck froze. This is what you're after isn't it. Don't show any emotion. Act calm. Take a deep breath. "Without my daily action reports, I couldn't be sure. Why?" I'll kill him, first chance I get.

"We're following up on a few routine matters. General Bradley has ordered us to make inquiries about some incidents that took place in France last August, nothing more."

■ ■ ■ ■ ■

Captain Hughes paused and considered his next question. This fuckstick's hiding something, but what? He looked at the collection of suspected war criminal photos again. The longer he waited, the more uncomfortable Beck appeared. "Why did you turn over command to Major Krüger?"

■ ■ ■ ■ ■

Beck considered the question, his mind racing. With his answer, he leaned forward. Careful now, don't overplay it here. "I turned over command to Major Krüger"—choose your words wisely—"because he was ... blackmailing me."

Captain Hughes nodded as he scribbled. "Go on."

"I'm not proud of some of my actions, but I am a man nonetheless. You see, I had an illicit affair with the wife of one of my officers. Major Krüger discovered our romance and threatened to expose my indiscretion. If he had done so, I assure you, the consequences would have been dire. I tell you, Major Krüger is an evil man."

He smiled to himself as he observed Captain Hughes chuckle and make an entry in his file. "Colonel Beck, I hardly think this is as serious an offense as you make it out to be."

"No? You tell me then, the woman's husband is Reichsführer Heinrich Himmler's favorite nephew, his sister's boy. If it had come to his attention, I have little doubt I would be shot. And by being the one to surrender the regiment to the American, that dog hoped to curry the favor of the Americans." He leaned forward and looked the captain in the eye. "In the Wehrmacht, we don't tolerate such cowards."

Beck, joining the line of fellow officers as they filed out the door, thought of little else. Exactly what did you tell them? First chance, Hans Krüger, you're dead.

chapter 32

West of Iserlohn, Germany
22 April 1945

Spring heralded the end of war in Europe. Throughout the countryside flowers erupted in unusual places while birds in search of nesting materials ignored the mass of field grey coats and uniforms, four abreast, trudging west toward the Rhine. Small clouds of dust billowed out from beneath the feet of soldiers as they shuffled past persistent reminders of the carnage that had ravaged all of Europe. Kilometer after kilometer craters from exploded artillery shells carpeted the landscape. Dead cattle littered pastures, their legs protruding out of swollen bodies at grotesque angles. Pockmarked buildings looked infected like an insidious and deadly disease had eaten away at the stones.

The city of Schwerte was no different than the other cities and villages along their route, nothing more than an endless pile of rubble, each and every pile as tall and cold as drifted snow. Not a single house escaped destruction. An occasional lone chimney jutted out as a reminder of what used to be a home. A few dazed inhabitants wandered the streets. An old man hunched over a wheelbarrow, filled it with bricks. A string of burnt-out tanks—American and German—cluttered the roadside standing vigil, engaged in one last mortal battle. The prisoners ignored a German staff car resting on its side, a body trapped beneath it with one stiffened outstretched arm waiting to be freed.

Further down the road, fresh laundry suspended from a clothes-line flapped to and fro in the soft warm breeze. A demolished barn stood next to the farmhouse, its roof collapsed onto crumbled walls. A boy, perhaps five years of age, dressed in ragged pants with numerous patches about the knees, climbed out of the farmhouse through a four foot hole in the wall, ran back into the house through the door, then back again out the hole. As he observed the soldiers approaching, he ran to the front door, grabbed a stick propped up against the house, put it to his shoulder like he had fired his rifle and fell to the ground.

The noise of the soldiers filing past brought the boy's mother to the door. Her looked of concern turned to horror at the sight of her son's limp, motionless body on the ground. She glanced at the soldiers, then rushed to the boy's side. Realizing she had been fooled, she snatched him up by the arm, swatted him on the butt and escorted him into the house. The soldiers that smiled thought of their childhood, the ones with somber looks thought of their own children and when they might be reunited.

As he and Anton marched side-by-side, Hans thought of his mother. "We were never allowed to play soldiers. Mother would become cross if Peter pretended we were in the trenches like Father in the Great War."

The two friends trudged on. After several minutes Anton looked over. "And what will they call our war?"

"It's not like you to ask such questions. Not only are you a cynic, you're now a philosopher." Hans thought for a moment. "I don't know—Hitler's War? All I know is it's not *my* war."

"But it *is* our war, whether we like it or not."

"True, and the sooner it's over, the sooner we get our lives back."

Anton swept his arm in front of him, indicating the landscape. "Our lives may be restored, but all of this, will it ever be new again? It'll take years. Decades even."

"Ja, but the dead, they're gone forever."

Anton hesitated, then said, "You never heard anything official about your parents?"

"Nothing. After the bombing in February, I'm afraid there's little hope."

"Since 1943, hope has eluded us all. Those poor men at Stalingrad—didn't they die full of hope? They stormed into the heart of Russia with no winter clothing."

Hans kept marching and said nothing.

"I–I–I'm sorry Hans, I shouldn't have brought up such things."

"No, you haven't offended me, but there are times I wish I'd died with them, especially after Peter. If Mother and Father *are* dead, it comforts me to know they're finally together."

"You and Peter were close?"

"We were. He was five years younger, but as children growing up, everywhere I went, Peter went. I knew I had to look after him and I did. I can still feel him there, holding my hand as we walked down the street on our way to the market for Mother. He'd never complain or make a nuisance of himself like some brothers and when we were older and he got bigger, he could beat me in any race, regardless of the distance." Hans inhaled deeply while keeping one foot in front of the other. "It's as if God reached into my chest and ripped out my soul leaving me to fend for myself. The hardest thing is falling asleep at night. One can't even imagine how terrifying it must have been, trapped inside that U-boat. I wonder if it took hours to die or did they all drown in minutes."

Nothing passed between the two for at least a kilometer. Finally Anton said, "How far have we gone?"

Hans looked at his wrist where the watch he had received from his father had been and cursed under his breath. "Dortmund's just ahead." He then looked up at the sun. "That's about right, thirty kilometers in four hours."

"Any idea where they are taking us?"

"None—probably as far as the Rhine. The autobahn's ahead,

just beyond Dortmund. I suspect we'll follow it west."

▪　▪　▪　▪　▪

A whistle and barked orders directed prisoners toward a field a hundred meters from the road. At the edge of the field several trucks lined up next to a large open tent. A squad of American soldiers stood guard. Excitement grew amongst the prisoners when it became apparent where they were headed. Saliva flowed and stomachs churned. The aroma of recently prepared food revived their steps. A line naturally formed along the edge of the field kitchen and as each soldier passed the first of the trucks, he received a mess tin, cup, and spoon. The American soldier doling them out repeated every few men, "*Setzen Sie fort sich zu bewegen. Setzen Sie fort sich zu bewegen.*" Keep moving. Keep moving.

Prisoners grunted in approval as they watched the cooks ladle a helping of stew into their tins. Several prisoners uttered "*Danke,*" as they moved down the line. A second American soldier wearing a frown and a stained white apron dropped a hard biscuit onto the stew. Each man received a half cup of water.

The prisoners, directed to the open field, sat on the ground to devour their meager allotments. Some of the prisoners poured what water was left into their tins, swirled the mixture around, and finished it off. What tongues couldn't reach, fingers could.

Fifteen minutes later, grumbling followed the sound of the whistle. Prisoners groaned their way to an upright position, the older ones and those nursing wounds were the last to stand. Once their march resumed, the columns of prisoners kept to the outskirts of Dortmund. Several empty American transport trucks rumbled past. Coughing erupted from the prisoners as a long cloud of dust settled on the men. Five Sherman tanks followed, each with an American sergeant protruding out the hatch, shoulders thrust back as if General George S. Patton had put him there personally.

The other side of Dortmund a sculpted horizon—bare where the trees had been scooped off the face of the earth—revealed itself. "Anton, there's the autobahn." With another kilometer behind them, from a slightly elevated position, two strips of concrete stretched westward, undulating slightly, as if alive. Soon the source of the movement became obvious—the Allies were using both sides of the autobahn to advance east, toward the Russians closing in on Berlin. Between the two, the defeated German Wehrmacht marched west.

Two kilometers further, the prisoners came to a halt where they waited for a lull in the convoy traffic. Minutes passed before their turn came to cross. As the prisoners resumed their trek, drivers stepped down from their trucks and soldiers riding in the back dismounted. Along the line of vehicles, American soldiers studied the German prisoners; many simply ignored them and finished their cigarettes.

On both sides of the autobahn, Allied vehicles of all sizes continued their migration. Several pulled artillery pieces, many pulled trailers. Jeeps loaded with soldiers—at least two on every hood—kept pace. Twenty minutes later, as the last truck passed, the final American soldier waved.

Anton spoke first. "Hans, it's no wonder the war's lost. Did you count the number of trucks?"

"I lost track at seventy-five."

"Must be a hundred—and half as many artillery pieces. Probably two divisions."

Hans spit out the blade of grass between his teeth. "It's only a matter of time." Moments later an unusual movement of the column ahead of them captured their attention. The commotion flowed toward them like a wave. Heads huddled two-by-two, then turned to the rear to pass along what they'd heard and the process repeated itself. Finally a prisoner in front of them turned and said, "We're to stop in Essen. Our final destination's Rheinberg. Pass it on."

Anton looked at Hans. "Rheinberg?"

"Makes sense, it's just on the other side of the Rhine."

▪ ▪ ▪ ▪ ▪

The procession of German prisoners reached Essen, sixty-five kilometers west of Iserlohn as the sun settled into the horizon. They had been marching, mostly non-stop, for eleven hours. Without breakfast, their noon meal hardly sustained them. Into a pasture south of the autobahn, the men collapsed, most too tired to advance another step. Worse than the hunger that racked their abdomens, thirst dictated every thought.

"Hans, they're going to starve us, aren't they?" Anton's voice, by now reduced to a dry rasp, barely rose above a whisper.

Hans resisted the temptation to move. At the sound of diesel engines he rolled over and looked up. "No, not yet."

Fifty meters from the prisoners, two sets of headlights illuminated the exhausted and hungry men. From the back of one of the trucks, American soldiers jumped down and assumed their posts as sentries. Prisoners eagerly unloaded wooden crates and stacked them on the ground along with several dozen empty five-gallon cans. Sentries ordered twenty prisoners to collect the empty cans, two apiece, and walk to the Ruhr River several hundred meters to the south. Other prisoners began opening the crates.

Hungry men pushed and shoved like farm animals at a trough. Every German prisoner nursed one US Army K ration meal and waited for the cans of water to return. Men driven nearly insane by thirst, sprinted to the cans. Bullets sprayed skyward from a machine gun halted the stampede. Tin cups emerged from every direction as the five-gallon cans of water leaned to one side. Once empty, guarded prisoners returned to the river for more. It took three trips to satisfy the thirst of two thousand German prisoners-of-war.

▪ ▪ ▪ ▪ ▪

Karl Beck used the light of the full moon to aid his movement within the encampment. Every ten meters a group of men huddled together for protection against the brisk north wind. Those with long coats were on the periphery as a buffer against the frigid temperatures. Eventually, Beck discovered his prey. Without warning, he yanked Hans to his feet and pushed him backwards sending him tumbling to the ground. Grabbing him from behind, Beck wrapped his arm around Hans' neck and forced it back. Attempts at resistance were futile.

"Just what did you tell them, Krüger?"

"Have you gone mad? I have no idea what you're talking about," Hans gasped.

Beck tightened his hold. "Don't give me that. You told him something."

"Who?"

"The American captain. Yesterday at Iserlohn."

"I have no idea what you're talking about. I told him nothing."

"You lying piece of shit. As your commanding officer, I demand you tell me what you told him."

Hans wrenched one arm free. "If you'll recall, you relinquished command."

Beck barely relaxed his grip the instant several men stood close, ready to lend a hand. The muscles of his jaw quivered. Through gritted teeth, he said, "I'm warning you Krüger, first chance I get, I'll kill you. Do you understand that? You're dead."

chapter 33

Essen, Germany
23 April 1945

UNABLE TO SLEEP, HANS STRETCHED HIS STIFFENED joints. It only took a moment before he remembered why he was more sore than usual. Turning his head to the side, he could see the gathering light as the sun crept above the horizon. Countless columns of steam rose like campfire smoke from motionless German soldiers sleeping in huddled masses. Frost, that would be gone within the hour, covered the tips of grass as sentries silently paced the perimeter of the encampment knowing the ascending sun would soon warm their bodies. As the men stirred, the sound of frequent coughs momentarily silenced the chirping birds.

"FWEEEEEEEEEET!"

The American guard took the whistle from his mouth, stood on a crate and yelled, "*Wir ziehen aus! Zehn Minuten!*" On the move. Ten minutes.

Hans shook off the cold and struggled to his feet. "I'm going to shove that damn whistle down his throat."

Anton chuckled. "And ruin your image?"

He ignored the taunt and looked around for the trucks they had seen the day before. "Damn, I hate the thought of marching on an empty stomach."

Anton looked equally discouraged. "I'm beginning to wish

we'd surrendered to the Russians."

"Be careful what you wish for. It'd be a long walk to Siberia."

▪ ▪ ▪ ▪ ▪

After three hours of marching, the autobahn turned south to Düs-seldorf following the course of the Rhine. The prisoners marched west along a newly worn trail cut through the terrain. As they approached the river, their trail rose up out of nowhere.

Anton tried to see ahead. "There can't possibly be an intact bridge and it would take too long to ferry us across." Before Hans could respond, the Rhine came into view. Stretched end-to-end, a floating bridge of several pontoons strapped to one another, spanned the expansive blue waterway. On top rested a roadbed of planks. It appeared to be at least eight feet wide and capable of sustaining considerable weight.

Hans admired the bridge's simplicity, especially when he realized the strength of the current. Once on the structure, it only took a few strides to become accustomed to its motion, but before he could completely deduce the bridge's design, he stepped onto the muddy western shore. The slight incline—unlike the steep shore at Remagen—ensured easy access to the crest of the terrain overlooking the river. Looking back, the trailing edge of prisoners was just beginning to cross. Because everyone focused on where they had been, no one looked ahead. When they eventually did, a groan escaped from each and every parched throat.

As they approached their destination, the combined odor of musty wet soil and raw sewage assaulted them. A wide muddy trail that sucked boots off men led to a ten-foot high barbed wire enclosure measuring a mile and a half square. On the west side a rail line served as a natural border. A once placid grassy expanse overlooking the Rhine had been transformed into the Rheinberg Meadow Camp, now home to tens of thousands of German prisoners and all the pain and suffering of an entire generation.

No buildings were visible, not a single tent. Only evenly spaced guard towers, each containing a soldier manning his machine gun, broke the horizon. Two American sentries lifted the barbed-wire wooden gate and swung it open to admit the men of the 3rd Panzer-Grenadier Division. No flowers were thrown, no pretty girls ran to embrace and kiss the vanquished heroes of the Wehrmacht. All that greeted them were filthy field grey uniforms and dirty unshaven men with resigned, gaunt, and haggard faces—the faces of men who had fought gallantly, but lost.

A lunar landscape—now devoid of vegetation—had quickly formed within the perimeter. Earthen craters erupted everywhere. Dug with spoons, these holes afforded little shelter. After a rain, prisoners huddled in mud. At night, the men crouched low in their dugouts to avoid brisk winds and frigid temperatures. During the day little protected them from the sun.

# # # # #

The first day the meadow camp received prisoners—along the entire length of the enclosure's east side—men dug a continuous trench atop of which rested a row of thick long poles perched two feet above either side of the trench. This served as their latrine. Provided the winds blew from the west, the odors were tolerable; if the wind blew from the east, a sickening stench covered the camp like a shroud.

For two days, the men received no food. Water was not available until the end of the first day when two railroad tank cars were parked on the track outside the wire cage. The cars had been filled with water but the unmistakable taste of petrol suggested the car's former use. From each car two hoses ran under the wire and terminated at separate spigots. The lines to fill tin cups formed before dawn; during the day each of the four lines stretched fifty meters, never longer, seldom shorter.

On the third day, several trucks arrived. The mass of prisoners migrated to the gate and milled about. A dissonant murmur accompanied the unloading of countless cases of K rations. Sentries kept vigil, one finger on the trigger of their gun. American soldiers eyed the Germans inching toward them while watching the cases of K rations they were to distribute. Two hours later, just like the other crates before it, the final one evaporated. The discarded wood and cardboard disappeared into the interior of the camp faster than the K rations—wood to fuel small fires, cardboard to line dirt walls.

▪　▪　▪　▪　▪

Twenty-year-old Gottfried Mauer felt lucky but he wasn't sure why. Perhaps it was simple fact he survived three battle wounds with his handsome face unscarred. Regardless, in spite of the wounds and a crushing injury to his right foot, he ignored the pain and disabling limp. His dirty uniform blended with the thousands of others crammed into the camp. Like them, he relied on perseverance to survive.

With a strand of barbed wire he had sharpened the stub of pencil. On two small pieces of paper torn from his bible he wrote notes and for three days he stood at the edge of the wire and kept vigil, ready to release the missile. Both notes were carefully folded and wrapped around a rock the size of an egg, wrapped again with a piece of material torn from his shirt, then secured with thread. He gripped his future tightly in his right hand.

At first the only people to walk past the perimeter were soldiers, but by the second day, his anticipation grew as people from the countryside began to appear. Once the American soldiers realized that only curiosity brought them closer to the wire, the native Germans were allowed to linger. American guards intervened and began to force the curiosity seekers back only after several of the prisoners surged toward the wire and shouted, "Bread."

Working her way toward the edge of the assembled crowd, a

distraught middle-aged woman, puffy eyes darting back and forth, searched. Standing opposite Gottfried she cried, "Do you know my son, Franz Decker?"

He quickly looked up and down the wire for sentries. "What division?"

She shouted, "The 130th Panzer."

Gottfried cupped his hands. "I'm sorry, they're not here."

The woman looked as if she'd been told her son died that very morning. Before she turned away, he hurled the rock and cried, "Pick it up! Please, pick it up." He let out a sigh when the approaching sentry outside the wire failed to realize why she bent over. The woman stood upright, turned and waved half-heartedly before heading toward Rheinberg. Well away from the sentries, she reached into her pocket and withdrew the rock. While carefully unknotting the thread, the notes fell to the ground. She scooped them both up and scanned the outer, more soiled note first.

My name is Gottfried Mauer. Please take this message to Katja Richter. She lives in Rheinberg on Kanalstraße. Thank you. Gottfried Mauer

The woman looked over her shoulder before she read the second note.

My dear Katja,

I love you dearly and I want you to know I am alive. Conditions are terrible and we are all starved, some near death. Please bring food to throw over the wire tomorrow at midnight. I will be waiting at northwest corner.

Use caution. You must not let the guards discover you. I live to see you tomorrow.

Your loving Gottfried

The woman wiped her eyes dry, carefully refolded the notes, and put them with the cloth and thread in her pocket, then smiled. A renewed spirit propelled her to Kanalstraße.

▪ ▪ ▪ ▪ ▪

Daily, thousands more prisoners straggled through the wire gate of the crowded camp. By the beginning of the second week, illness prevailed. The handful of captured surgeons cordoned off a section of the camp for the ill and ministered to their needs as best they could. Pleas for medicines and supplies went unanswered. What bullets didn't kill, bacteria did. Every morning those that died during the night would be dragged from their earthen hovels to the gate. Disturbed mounds of earth, as if created by a giant mole, erupted in the open field beyond the meadow camp.

With every growl of his stomach, Gottfried feared he'd be forced to the latrine like the others. By the sixth day, those that trotted usually left a trail of bloody mucous and liquid stool leading to the edge of the logs lining the foul pit. For most of the men infected with dysentery, removing their pants before evacuating their bowels provided no benefit. Occasionally weakened men would topple into the cesspool and drown—he feared this the most.

Throughout the day he thought of nothing but food. Convinced his desire for food outweighed the need to see his darling Katja, guilt invaded every thought. He prayed she'd understand. After all, they were to be married and every letter she'd sent had expressed her undying love in ways he never knew existed.

In the dark, K ration cigarettes glowed like fireflies. Murmurs of subdued conversation could be heard before they eventually died away, extinguished by the night. Gottfried, again, rotated his watch to the precise angle needed to reflect light off the dial. "Finally," he muttered. In spite of the pain in his foot, he stood.

Guided by a rising half-moon in a cloudless sky, he quietly limped his way to the northwest corner of the camp. Stumbling, he barely maintained his balance.

"Watch where you're going."

"I beg your pardon, I—"

"You imbecile. The latrine's the other way."

He ignored the man's gesture to the opposite direction and kept picking his way across the camp. Exhausted, he arrived at the northwest corner and looked at his watch. Ten minutes. To avoid suspicion, he crouched low and looked around. Good, no sentries. Peering into the darkness beyond the wire, he whispered as loud as he dared, "Katja?"

No response.

From the path he had taken, something caught his eye. Motionless, he peered into the darkness. Finally, he shook his head. *No, I must be imagining things.* He looked at his watch one more time. Midnight. *Please Katja, you must come.*

He heard a woman's voice. "Gottfried? Gottfried, are you there?"

Gottfried searched both sides of the wire for sentries, then into the darkness. "Shhh. I'm here."

Drawn to the other's voice, both edged closer to the double strands of wire. Separated by inches, they extended their hands to one another but could not touch. Through tears Katja whispered, "Gottfried, I was delirious to receive your note. A woman brought it to me yesterday."

Gottfried's eyes tried to pierce the darkness. "Katja, I love you."

"I brought bread. And a potato. I'm sorry, it's all I could—"

"Shhh. That's plenty. Toss them over the wire."

She stepped away and hurled the loaf of bread. It cleared the wire and fell into his hands. The potato hit the top wire sending a reverberation up and down the perimeter, then fell to the ground with a thud. Gottfried stretched out on the ground, barely able to touch the potato. Only with contorted movement he swept it toward him. Once upright, he looked up and down the wire again. "Katja, you must go. Surely a sentry will come."

In vain, Katja extended her arm through the wire. "I will return tomorrow at the same time, I promise."

"Be careful." Gottfried stretched his arm out as well. "I love you my darling Katja. I love you."

He watched her disappear like a ship into the fog. He thought of the last time they were alone. He had kissed her neck gently, the first time he'd dare to kiss her shoulder and run his hands along the soft contour of her breasts. He longed to do it all again. How could anything look so firm yet be so soft. He smiled as he envisioned her squirm ever so slightly in his arms. Before Gottfried could continue the thoughts that would lead nowhere, he noticed the movement again, only closer. He instinctively stuffed the potato into his pant's pocket and dropped the loaf of bread down his shirt. Assured his treasures were safe, he limped his way into the middle of the camp toward the main path. Turning frequently, he remained vigilant. Eventually he found the crater he'd dug with his spoon and cup. He lowered his head and mumbled a prayer of thanks. Buried under his coat, he quietly held the bread in his hands, dug his thumbs through the crust and snapped it in two. Half of the loaf went into his coat pocket and the other half he placed in front of him. From his pants pocket he retrieved the potato and laid it next to the bread. As soon as the first portion of bread absorbed all the saliva his hunger had generated, he bit into the potato and ripped a portion free. What little moisture remained in the potato aided in cajoling the dry bread into his stomach. For the first time in days, his stomach ceased its gnawing rumble. Flinging the coat off his head brought a rush of spring air. Refreshed, Gottfried rolled it up and rested his head next to the bulge created by the remaining bread.

Within minutes he was asleep.

chapter 34

Rheinberg Meadow Camp
Rheinberg, Germany
29 April 1945

GOTTFRIED MAUER AWOKE AND STARED UP AT the cloudless sky. For the first time in days, his first thoughts weren't of food—they were of Katja. Physical desires had returned and thoughts of her played as free as a spring breeze. *If I were to escape we could be together forever.* His head shook side-to-side in response to his musings. *No, I'd be shot. Besides, if she brings me food, even twice a week, I won't need to risk it, at least for now.* After deciding against escape he remembered the bread in his pocket. A quick squeeze of his coat brought a smile. *Good, just where I left it.* Sitting upright, he yawned, then stretched his feet. Muscle spasms sent him back down as pain gripped his disfigured right foot like an electric shock. Rubbing did little to soften the knotted muscles, and it wasn't until he hobbled to an upright position and walked in a circle, that the pain subsided.

He bent over, scooped up his coat, and headed toward the stench. Unlike the lines for water, there were never lines at the latrine. Inhaling deeply, he stood before the log lining the pit. The fascination of watching a rivulet of urine course down the side of the pit helped overcome his urge to vomit. Finished, he turned away and released the stored air.

Along the perimeter, he limped toward the partitioned-off infirmary. Weakened soldiers never looked up. *And I thought I had it bad, they can't even stand.* At the front of what appeared to be a line, he approached the exhausted surgeon applying a dressing.

"You're in my light." The scowl on the surgeon's face deepened. "Unteroffizier, you must wait your turn."

Gottfried turned his back to the waiting patients and at the same time, extracted the remaining bread from the coat pocket.

The surgeon's mouth fell open. "Where in God's name did you get this?"

"You might say it fell out of the sky." He pointed to the pregnant woman shaded by a makeshift tent. He'd been surprised to see civilians in the camp. *I guess we're all refugees now.* "I want her to have it. She looks as if her confinement could arrive any day."

"Ja, soon." The surgeon smiled. "Very soon."

"I will try to bring more. She—no, both—will need it."

The surgeon fumbled for words. He finally said, "Unteroffizier, what is your surname?"

"Mauer. Gottfried Mauer."

"Gottfried, you are a godsend. I don't know what to say."

"Say nothing. One day my Katja will be pregnant and when she is, I pray people are kind to her."

Before Gottfried shuffled away, the surgeon took the bread to his patient with a cup of water. The woman's hands went to her mouth in disbelief. After the surgeon pointed to Gottfried, she smiled, waved, and patted her abdomen.

Back on the main path through the Rheinberg Meadow Camp, Gottfried, unaware of his limp for the first time in weeks, glided between groups of soldiers, each discussing the undeniable outcome of the war. He smiled and shook his head after someone said, "You wait, with Roosevelt dead, Truman will seek peace with the Führer." He turned to see who'd utter such nonsense. For the second time since leaving the infirmary, a sudden movement caught his attention. Gottfried waited until he'd passed an open area, then pivoted abruptly on his left leg.

▪ ▪ ▪ ▪ ▪

Hans and Anton stood waiting to fill their tin cups. A slow but steady flow of water ensured the lines were orderly, but the incessant thirst of the prisoners guaranteed the length of the lines would remain unchanged throughout the day.

"Shouldn't we at least boil this before we drink it?" Anton said.

Hans glanced over Anton's shoulder.

"Are you looking for someone?"

Hans lowered his voice, almost a whisper. "I saw Beck this morning, snaking through the camp. It's best to avoid him—so far I've been successful."

"The man's mad. Word is he cracked after his wife hanged herself."

He nodded. "Between you and me, the man was halfway there long before that."

"Too bad. First his daughter, then his wife." Anton raised his cup slightly. "What about the water? Have you heard it's poisoned?"

Hans scoffed. "I'd worry more about starvation than poisoning. Personally, I'd rather they poison us, it's faster." He shook his head as he surveyed their surroundings. "There's no way the Allies were prepared for this. I overheard an American major by the gate say the Allies expect more than a million prisoners once the war's over. Imagine, having to feed over a million men."

"Are the Allies really capable of starving thousands of German soldiers and innocent people?"

"Of course they're capable. They defeated our army, didn't they? Think about it. Do you see any effort to aid us?" He answered his own question. "None. Just yesterday, an American soldier—a sergeant—approached wanting to throw food over the wire. The sentry threatened to shoot him if he didn't step back."

"Did he?"

"Did he what?"

"Throw food over."

"When the sentry was out of sight, the sergeant ran back and tossed what food he had over the wire, then continued on his way."

Anton smiled. "It seems not every American wants to starve us."

"Yes, but once they discover what Hitler and his Nazis did to the Jews—if they haven't already—we'll be left to our own devices. The Americans will do nothing to assist us. Sure, there's water and K rations, but only what's needed to relieve their consciences." He looked around the camp. "We need shelter. We need medical attention. The Americans may not be intentionally killing us, but that's precisely what's happening."

"Now you're sounding like me," Anton said.

Hans continued. "Have you heard how many dead are hauled away every day? I've seen them. No less than ten each morning. That's three hundred a month. Sure you can say it's the sick ones, but the longer we're here, the more sick ones there'll be. And as the sun rises in the morning, they, too, will die."

Before Anton could respond, a series of shouts swept the camp. At the main entrance, three trucks arrived and crate after crate after crate of K rations were unloaded and brought inside. Two American guards slipped out through the gate before it closed and locked. Prisoners rushed the stacks of manna and ripped them apart, every man for himself. The sentries, indifferent to the melee, resumed their patrol.

▪ ▪ ▪ ▪ ▪

Like Christmas Eve as a child, minutes passed slowly for Gottfried, his own thoughts the only distraction. During the day he'd gazed at Katja's photograph or read his Bible. Following that he'd re-read her last letter yet another time. He knew it by heart and each time he slid it out of his pocket, he smiled. Passing the letter beneath his nostrils caused him to think of her embrace. For the second time in as many days, such thoughts aroused him. Oddly, he found the situation comforting, knowing his desire for her outweighed his desire for the food she would bring.

With a coat draped over his head, he lit a match and studied his watch. Good, it's time. He crawled to the edge of his crater and struggled to stand. Excitement bordering on exuberance drove away his pain. He carefully picked his way to the camp's northwest corner. At the main path crossing the center of the camp, he stopped and pivoted on his good leg—the sound behind him ceased. Continuing on, he arrived at the corner, fell to his knees, and looked again to his rear.

Seconds became hours. The sentry could be heard long before being seen. As he walked slowly past, Gottfried assumed a fetal position and feigned sleep. A second sentry approached and the two lingered at the corner, their muffled voices barely audible. One struck a match and the instantaneous flash of light became two glowing cigarettes. Come on, get it over with, I can't believe these Americans actually smoke on patrol. The unmistakable odor of burnt tobacco evaporated into the soft breeze once the glowing butts were discarded and ground into the earth. The erect shadows then separated and resumed their patrol.

He waited before he approached the wire. Finally he whispered as loud as he dared. "Katja?"

"Gottfried, over here."

Both stretched an arm toward the other, their fingertips inches apart.

"I was afraid they wouldn't leave." He considered lifting the wire, but thought better of it. Time, it's only a matter of time. "Katja, bless you for coming, you mustn't linger."

"I know. I know." She raised her other arm revealing a cloth sack, then whispered, "I brought you more food. There's a letter and a piece of peppermint."

He quickly glanced to his left, then his right. "Katja dear, you're an angel."

She stepped back, swung the sack upward and launched it over the wire. He snagged it in midair. "Katja, be careful. I love you."

"I will come tomorrow, I promise."

He watched her back away, wave, and turn toward Rheinberg before being absorbed by the night. Opening the sack, he groped the bottom of the bag to find a letter, another potato, two small loaves of bread, and a small piece of candy wrapped in paper. The letter went directly into his shirt pocket.

Less than fifteen meters from the wire and well away from the first inhabited crater, Gottfried was instantly lifted off the ground and thrown onto his back. A resounding thud accompanied the rush of air forced out both lungs. What the hell? His paralyzed ribs wouldn't yield to his brain's command to breathe. He instinctively squeezed the sack the instant he felt it being plucked free. With his other hand, he tried to knock his assailant to the ground.

"Give me that sack, you goddamned cripple!"

He released the sack and screamed in pain, his right foot angled further by the forceful thrust of a dirty boot. To the sound of Gottfried's cry, several men came running. He felt his shirt pocket and confirmed Katja's letter was safe.

Gottfried pointed after his assailant. "He attacked me. He stole my food."

One of the men hoisted him up. "Did you see who attacked you?"

"Ja, I saw," Gottfried said.

"Me, too," claimed another.

A third added, "I've heard stories about him, until now I never believed them."

chapter 35

Rheinberg Meadow Camp
1 May 1945

WORD OF THE THEFT SPREAD THROUGH THE camp like influenza. Hungry groups of prisoners devoured the news instantly, then wanted more.

" ... the shouting started at 12:30—I know because I looked at my watch. I tell you, Mauer never regained consciousness. He didn't die until later."

Another knew that wasn't true. "No, he didn't die, he just passed out from all the bleeding, nothing more than that."

Most everyone had an opinion, especially about Katja and the food. "He doesn't have a wife, but he got her pregnant. She's from Essen. No one knows how, but she found him here. The food was from a relative in Rheinberg."

One prisoner commanded the most attention. "Gottfried. Gottfried Mauer. Known him for years. He himself told me Beck attacked him—no doubt at all." The prisoner's voice became evangelical when his listeners started to drift away. "You know Beck murdered an entire Polish family back in '40"—heads nodded after he said—"and don't forget last August in France."

The next day after learning of the assault and theft, General Denkert conferred with Colonel Timothy Riley, the American commander of the Rheinberg Meadow Camp, and convened a prisoner-of-war military tribunal. Such stories of Beck's cruelty fueled speculation like gasoline on a fire; the fact that he stood accused of the attack surprised no one. Seven German senior staff officers from within the Rheinberg Camp sat in judgment on a makeshift bench of wooden planks. Gottfried sat at one end of the row, Beck on the other.

General Denkert cleared his throat before beginning. "As ranking commanding officer, it is my duty to initiate this hearing. Sadly, it has come to my attention that two nights ago, in this camp, Unteroffizier Gottfried Mauer was attacked and robbed. This unprovoked attack resulted in minor injuries and the food he'd recently received was stolen." General Denkert turned to his right and focused on the defendant who stood to face the charges. "Karl Beck, you are accused of assault and theft." The instant General Denkert uttered these words, he raised his hand to quell the murmurs. "How do you plead?"

Beck ignored the jeers and a hush gradually ensued. Even prisoners who didn't serve under him recognized his thin, menacing face. Impossible to determine if the rank, his threatening glare, or the fear of retribution silenced them, they nonetheless remained tempered. Perhaps it was the rumors of his ruthless acts and senseless murders during the war that silenced them. He glared at Denkert. "Not guilty."

A renewed cry from the spectators brought the general to his feet. "Enough!"

No one dared whisper, all idle movement ceased. Beck took his seat as General Denkert addressed Gottfried. "Unteroffizier Mauer, please stand and tell us, to the best of your recollection, the details of the evening in question."

Gottfried pushed off the bench with determination. Fifteen minutes later he sat back down, visibly relieved. General Denkert commanded the first witness to stand.

"Kurt Schröder, what did you observe that evening?"

"About midnight, I saw Oberst Beck following Unteroffizier Mauer."

"Anything else?"

"Unteroffizier Mauer—I knew it was Mauer by the limp—came to the northwest corner of the camp. I became suspicious when he fell to the ground as the patrolling guards met at the corner. I wondered if he was planning to escape. Next thing, I saw him"—he turned a pointed at Oberst Beck—"creeping along the ground, stalking Mauer."

General Denkert paced in front of the bench. "Very well, what did you observe next?"

The witness looked only at General Denkert. "I heard the soft whispering of a woman's voice coming from beyond the wire. In the moonlight I saw Mauer snatch a sack out of the air. He turned back toward the camp and before he got more than a few meters, Oberst Beck sprang up and tackled him. They tumbled to the ground. Then Oberst Beck stomped on Gottfried's foot." The spectators' response gave him the courage to finish. His voice a little louder, he said, "He called him a 'Goddamned cripple.'"

General Denkert warned the prisoners a second time. Finally, he nodded to the witness.

"That's it, sir. Then a lot of other prisoners came running and Beck—I mean Oberst Beck—disappeared."

"Thank you, you're dismissed." The witness stepped away without looking at Beck and slipped into the mass of prisoners.

Karl Beck stood as commanded.

"Oberst Beck, what do you have to say?"

"Generalleutnant, I have no idea what this man's talking about. I was sound asleep in my hole when all this was taking place." Beck stood erect and maintained eye contact with the judges, his voice solid without the hint of equivocation. "I wasn't anywhere near the wire last night."

"Is there anyone who can verify this?"

"I don't need a witness to verify anything." Beck looked to the judges again. "Besides, their search yielded nothing."

General Denkert addressed the judges. "Do any of you have questions?"

None were posed. General Denkert conferred quietly with his fellow judges then stood before the prisoners. "We'll consider the testimony we've heard and our decision will be announced tomorrow, the second of May at 0800 hours."

▪ ▪ ▪ ▪ ▪

Few of the prisoners dispersed after the proceedings ended, most stood in small groups discussing the testimony. No one doubted Beck's guilt—speculation centered not on the verdict, but rather, how harsh the sentence would be. Anton wasn't so sure. "Come on Hans, Denkert and Beck have been friends for years and the war's all but over. There's no way he'll get what he deserves."

"I know the Generalleutnant is an honorable man. He'll be just, on that you can be certain."

"Fine, but what can he decide? So Beck assaulted an enlisted man, big deal. The most he'll do is slap his wrist."

Hans stood and gazed out beyond the wire, squeezed his eyes shut, then opened them the instant his fleeting thought departed. "You're probably right. The more I think about it, the more I realize he'll *never* get what he really deserves. Once the war's over, he'll disappear into thin air."

"And you say I'm the cynic?"

"Well, now I am for a change," Hans said. "Mark my word, what he's done will force him into hiding, never to be seen or heard from again."

chapter 36

Rheinberg Meadow Camp
1 May 1945

Karl Beck's preoccupation with the pending verdict evaporated when he noticed the man standing in the food line. Discreetly studying his features, even before spotting the scar he'd know anywhere, Beck discerned the man's true identity.

Jonas Keller.

Recognition had come quickly. Grenadiers tended to be patient, especially after years of combat, but this man exuded a sense of entitlement. His uniform, that of a grenadier, didn't fool Beck for a minute. The Jonas Keller he knew was an officer. And how convenient to be the only soldier from the 13th Panzer Division, a division hundreds of kilometers from the Ruhr Pocket. Moreover, the filth on the uniform suggested months of fighting with little opportunity for cleaning, yet the skin of the man failed to reveal the rigors of combat. The pores on his neck were free of the embedded grime of a common soldier and his hands were smooth, his fingernails clean. The jagged scar on the back of his right hand confirmed what Beck suspected. He recalled the foolish escapade on Jonas' brother's bike that resulted in such a deep laceration. But what disguised him so successfully? Of course—the glasses. And not just any glasses. Jonas Keller wore the ill-fitting glasses of an enlisted man. How clever.

He sat along the wire with his K ration, away from the other men. Beck made it a point to sit next to him. For two minutes only the sound of the K rations being opened, consumed, then tossed aside could be heard. Finally, Beck leaned in and said, "Why the disguise, Jonas?"

He looked over both shoulders before responding. In a barely audible whisper, he said, "I knew it was you Karl, but I thought you already knew why." He looked his older brother's best friend in the eye. "I'm sorry, but I didn't want to make things any more difficult for you."

"Weren't you in the crowd? How could they be any more difficult?"

Jonas considered his words carefully. "I was there. I wish I could have testified on your behalf. I would have, you know. I would have lied for you."

His comment made no impact. "It's a shame about your brother. Was he really involved in that mess?"

"Worse than that. He was one of the leaders. At the time of Gerhard's arrest he had a copy of the assassination plans in his briefcase, hidden beneath a false lining. There wasn't even a trial—they shot him the next morning."

"Did the Gestapo suspect you?"

"Ja, they suspected everybody, but I knew nothing of my brother's activities. Nothing."

"Then why the disguise?"

Jonas looked at him intently. "Can you keep a secret?"

Beck lowered his voice. "Of course, you can trust me."

He looked over his shoulder again. "I was with the B-*dienst*—I cracked Russian codes and intercepted their traffic. Once I rose to the rank of major two years ago, all the de-coded Russian intercepts crossed my desk before being passed to Berlin—everything.

"And?"

Jonas hesitated. "I need to tell someone, someone I can trust."

Beck smiled. "Who would *I* tell? Better yet, who *could* I tell?"

He pointed to the obvious absence of fellow prisoners for at least a four-meter perimeter. "As you can plainly see, I have no friends."

"True." After a deep breath, Jonas continued. "We would occasionally crack the Russian codes, bits of a message here and there, then nothing. Had we cracked it before Stalingrad, we wouldn't be here today. But after our loss that winter, the Russians became careless and we finally broke through. We've been reading their traffic like the morning paper ever since; unfortunately it was too late—the Wehrmacht was already on the run."

With interest, Beck observed Jonas become even more anxious. "One day a message passed by one of our agents buried deep in the *Glavnoye Razvedyvatel'noye Upravleniye*—Russian secret police— caught my eye."

"What kind of message would force you to hide in this stink-hole?"

"It's not the message that has me here—it's what I did with it." Jonas glanced over Beck's shoulder before he continued. "Ironically, what I discovered *could* be my everlasting salvation." He paused yet again.

Come on you dunce, out with it.

"You see, beginning in 1943 there were rumors coming out of London—"

Beck swore under his breath as a group of three prisoners lingered nearby. Jonas stood abruptly and walked away. What a dimwit. Beck tried to comprehend what he'd just heard as he watched Keller disappear into the massive sea of prisoners. Damn them, why'd they have to come along? What was he going to tell me anyway? For now, despite not learning what Jonas so desperately wanted to share, the distraction of his trial and miserable existence in the Rheinberg Meadow Camp suddenly seemed endurable.

Beck continued to sit in solitude and rub the stubble on his chin as a crow winged its way across the sky. He'll tell me, sooner or later.

chapter 37

Rheinberg Meadow Camp
1 May 1945

THE OBVIOUS JUBILATION EVIDENT IN THE AMERICANS could not be found on any German faces at the news of Hitler's death. Though few prisoners openly mourned the loss of their Führer, all mourned the loss of their comrades and the Germany they thought they'd fought and sacrificed for. It was more than the latest war news wearing the prisoners down. Gradually—but decisively—the faces of the German prisoners thinned. Individual rations had been meager at best; most of the men lost weight at an alarming rate. No one could have guessed another sunset would have come and gone without sustenance. Like hungry tigers at the Berlin Zoo, men paced back and forth growling at one another. Normally rational men lashed out, incapable of maintaining a civilized conversation with friends they'd fought alongside for years; within this discontent and growing darkness, conversations turned to justice. Some thought Hitler got what he deserved, others thought he cheated the hangman; none mourned. When nothing else could be offered about their dead Führer, a new question surfaced. "Tomorrow, what about Gottfried, doesn't he deserve justice?"

One prisoner considered what he had heard. "Gottfried's a good man, we fought together for almost three years. Of course he deserves justice, but it won't happen. Nothing will happen.

Denkert won't have the courage to pass judgment on Beck, never in a million years. Nothing will come of it."

Another prisoner whispered, "Let's mete out a little of our own justice tonight, in case the General's feeling extra lenient tomorrow?"

The first prisoner cocked his head to the side, signaling his desire to continue the conversation in private, at a safe distance. "What did you have in mind?"

"Nothing special. Perhaps a coat over his head while he's sleeping—a thorough administration of *proper* justice, something for him to remember."

After a long moment, the silence was broken. "Fine, but no one else."

"Agreed." The two shook hands. "Water spigots at midnight."

▪ ▪ ▪ ▪ ▪

Sounds of activity rose from the camp like mist in the morning sun. Empty tin cups clinked as they filled with water. Prisoners stretched and yawned while others headed for the latrine. Karl Beck, unable to do either, remained motionless, one eye swollen shut. Every joint ached. A searing chest pain captured his immediate attention. Just after the attack had begun—before he lost consciousness—he remembered hearing the unmistakable cracking of ribs. This morning, the grinding sound of bones brought a sudden rush of nausea followed by a resurgence of pain with each shallow breath.

He refused to cry out for help. No one would come, besides it would only give his enemies a sense of satisfaction to know such a lasting wound had been inflicted. Swearing under his breath, Beck struggled to one elbow and observed the surrounding vacant craters. Goddamned bastards—fuck 'em all—every last one of them. Once upright, he fumbled for his belt. After exhaling on the brass buckle, he rubbed it on his pants. A reflection revealing one eye to be purple and completely swollen shut brought an immediate groan. Dried and crusted blood coated his upper lip. His index finger instinctively probed his front teeth, testing the integrity of each. None were loose.

Exhausted, he held his breath and eased back down, squirming until the position causing the least discomfort revealed itself. He tried to recall the voices before the pummeling began. There were two of them weren't there? I'd give anything to know who the hell did this to me. Once his ribs ceased grinding on one another and the intense pain dissipated, he rested.

chapter 38

Commander's office, Rheinberg Meadow Camp
3 May 1945

AN EXUBERANT DIN FILLED THE MEETING ROOM. One discussion would grow loud and more animated and the one next to it, not to be outdone, would intensify as if a competition had been engaged. These increasingly authoritative debates fixated on discharge points and the latest news concerning Berlin, a few talked about the war with Japan; everyone knew someone who knew something. At the point all the men were chattering and none were listening, Colonel Riley stood, cleared his throat and announced, "Gentlemen, thank y'all for being prompt."

The noise—now bordering on chaos—continued. The colonel, a native Texan, had risen through the ranks saddled to his desk. His repeated requests for a combat assignment had been ignored, but in spite of this, he took his job seriously. He nodded at Sergeant Hamlin standing, with folded arms, at the door. The sergeant placed two fingers in his mouth, inhaled deeply and released it. The loud whistle arrested all conversation and everyone looked incredulous that such a method was employed to insure their attention. Colonel Riley ignored the sergeant's smirk as he repeated himself.

"Gentlemen, this ain't no rodeo." Those that knew the colonel smiled. "Now, before we get started, as you've all heard, Hitler's dead." After the robust round of cheers and clapping subsided, he continued. "The latest news from the BBC World News confirmed Berlin is on the verge of capitulation and Hitler's body was discovered in a shallow grave outside the Reich Chancellery." A second cheer arose. Colonel Riley raised his hands. "We have no idea what the Germans will do. For now, we're still at war and until we're otherwise informed, there's a lot of steers to round up." A grumbling now moved through his staff. "Let me be perfectly clear. I don't want to hear anymore about discharge points and who's going home first. We have a job to do and we're going to do it."

"That's better." He scanned the faces. "Men, I don't like it any more than you do, but until we get different orders, I'm fixin' to assume once we're finished here, we'll break camp and head to the Far East and prepare for the invasion of Japan. Before we get on with the meeting, any questions?"

A brave first lieutenant stood. "Colonel, sir, with the war in Europe ending soon, do you have any idea about stateside leave, I mean, before we're sent elsewhere?"

"Fair enough. Short of getting yourself wounded—which is unlikely at this point—I would say there will be some provisions for extended leave, but the logistics have to be worked out. Something will be filtering down from division no doubt." Colonel Riley glanced at Sergeant Hamlin. "Now, if there are no other questions, let's get started. Accommodations. As you know, the German prisoners have done a wonderful job of constructing our barracks and offices. Monday we begin interrogating prisoners and processing them further. To that end, I need to have the prisoner work details prioritized and assigned." He looked out into the group. "Captain Avery, I'm putting you in charge of this. I expect all of the requests to be fulfilled pronto once the processing is completed."

Heads turned to Charles Avery sitting in the back row. He fidgeted in his seat and replied, "Yes, sir."

"Secondly, this comes directly from SHAEF—Ike himself no doubt. Our prisoners are officially known as DEF. Disarmed Enemy Forces. I'm sure Ike has his reasons, but as far as we're concerned, it makes our job easier. For one, we ain't tied to the rules of the Geneva Convention."

Muffled voices between several officers could be heard.

"I know what you're thinking. Just because the Red Cross won't be hanging around, this does *not* mean we treat the Germans inhumanely—"

"Like they treated the Jews?" someone offered from the rear.

Colonel Riley ignored the comment. "As you know, it's been a challenge to keep the prisoners fed. Yes, there have been a few days we didn't have the rations for two meals a day. Hell, there's been times there wasn't any food for two days in a row, but from now on we're supposed to supply each prisoner with at least fifteen hundred calories a day, hopefully eighteen hundred. This means two K rations each and every day. Once we get them processed and allocate their work-release assignments, it will take some of the burden off of us and put it where it belongs—the German people."

Several heads nodded in agreement, no one raised their hands to ask a question.

"All of you are aware of the deplorable conditions within the camp and many of you are no doubt impressed with how resourceful the Germans are at improvising shelters. Therefore, before we discard anything that might be of use to them, I want it placed outside the main gate and Sergeant Hamlin here will see to it that it's taken inside the compound."

One of the more serious officers raised his hand. "Sir, what about escape?"

"You or them?" Snickers could be heard throughout the room. "Seriously, I doubt escape is much of a threat. They have to know the war's all but over *and* they have to be thankful they're not in

Russian hands. No, I don't think escape is on their minds, at least not yet. Anymore questions?"

"Sir, what's your take on the disciplinary problem with the camp right now?"

"Good question Lieutenant. If you're referring to the tribunal decision about that Nazi colonel, I think the issue's closed." Colonel Riley paused. "Any of you get a look at that poor SOB today?" A few nods and chuckles were heard. "Well, after their Kraut general got a look at him yesterday morning, he figured justice had already been served."

"Any other questions?" Colonel Riley looked about the room. "Very well. Let me say one last thing—just because Hitler's dead don't mean we lose site of our task. *Never* underestimate the Hun. Look at the price we paid in December when we thought we'd just wait till spring, cross the Rhine and sashay right into Berlin."

Satisfied with his remarks, he looked over at Sergeant Hamlin who snapped to attention and ordered, "Dismissed!"

chapter 39

Rheinberg Meadow Camp
8 May 1945

"To Ike!" Colonel Riley hoisted his glass for yet another toast.

"To Ike!" echoed from every throat.

He picked up the extra release of *The Stars and Stripes*, scanned the headline and smiled. "I can't wait to see his photo. I'll bet he's got a grin a mile wide—like a jackass eatin' thistles."

Unbridled laughter erupted. Captain Avery pleaded, "Colonel, read the headline again."

He took another sip of champagne. "I'm not sure I can focus anymore. But before I try, another toast." Clearing his throat, everyone present turned to face him. "To our families back home, may we be with them soon."

Glasses raised in unison. "Here, here!"

"And to our brothers-in-arms, those who survived"—he could feel his face flush as he thought about his younger brother— "and those we leave behind."

"Here, here!"

An awkward silence filled the room. Before anyone could offer another toast, he adjusted his reading glasses, reached for the paper and held it aloft for his staff to see, then read the headline. "VICTORY! Nazis Reveal Surrender To Western Allies, Russia."

Everyone in the room inched closer. "The unconditional

surrender of Germany to the Western Allies and Soviet Russia was announced by the German high command yesterday morning."

He raised his hand to quell the outburst. "The official announcement from the Allied governments are expected to come simultaneously from Washington, London and Moscow today. The British Ministry of Information, proclaiming that today would be 'Victory in Europe Day,' said Prime Minister Churchill would make 'an official announcement' at 3 PM.

"President Truman said he had agreed with the British and Russian governments that no surrender proclamation would be made 'until simultaneous announcements could be made by the three governments.' King George VI of England sent General Eisenhower a cablegram last night congratulating him and his armies on the 'complete and crushing victory' in Europe."

When the print-type got smaller, he stopped and looked up. "We've got plenty of copies to go around." He handed the stack of papers to Sergeant Hamlin and stepped out of the way. "Pass 'em out. Any that's left, see that the rest of the men get one."

Captain Avery came along side. "What are your plans after the war, sir?"

"Me, the minute I get home, I'm gonna do nothin' for three months, then start mendin' some fences."

"*Oh?*"

Colonel Riley chuckled at seeing the man blush. "No, not those fences. I've got pastureland that needs lookin' after and miles of barbed wire to inspect. Got a little cowpoke to take along to boot. That's what *I* got planned. You?"

"Nothing that exciting, sir. Probably settle down, join the family business."

"Somehow I can't see you doin' that. Married, yes." He looked his captain in the eye. "Making metal gizmos for the rest of your life, no."

"Don't worry, sir, I won't be. Soon as I get home—whenever that is—Dad wants me on the road. Sales, that sort of thing. He's never had a salesman, but he predicts once the war's totally over, business will explode."

"Don't be chompin' at the bit, it may be awhile. Maybe a year or more."

"I won't, sir. I just hope they keep us here awhile longer before sending us to some island in the Pacific."

Colonel Riley motioned for the captain to follow him into the corner. "I'm told we'll be here babysitting these Krauts at least another six months. By then the Marines ought to have the Japs on their knees. Looks like we may be going home from right here."

chapter 40

Rheinberg Meadow Camp
18 May 1945

"Major, where are they taking us?"

Once outside the front gate Hans raised his head to look around and savored the fresh air. "I overheard Captain Avery mention Rheinberg, beyond that, I haven't a clue."

Not exactly the freedom he dreamed about, the four-kilometer march was a welcome change. Three weeks of captivity had seemed like three years. Since his interrogation in the new camp office, Hans wondered what would become of him. *I'm sure they believed me when I told them I had studied to be an engineer, but what's my religion got to do with anything?* Still perplexed, he looked around and counted nineteen other prisoners. The unteroffizier marching next to him didn't look familiar. Hans double-stepped to get back in cadence and said, "I'm sorry, I don't know your name?"

"Willy. Willy Baumann. 8th Regiment. You can't be expected to know everyone, sir."

Hans nodded and studied the man before extending his hand. "Hans Krüger." The firmness of Willy's grip and his solid physique impressed Hans. "Baumann? Your father a builder?"

Willy stood taller. "Of course, and his father before him. I followed in their footsteps."

"Then there will be much to do when you return home."

"Ja, much to do. Mother and Father will be happy to see me."

Hans blinked hard. "I'm afraid my parents weren't so lucky, they were in Dresden."

The group halted as the American sergeant in front raised his hand. They had marched well past the open spaces on the outskirts of Rheinberg and were now within the town itself. Rheinberg, and its 5,000 inhabitants had been spared the damage of aerial bombardment, nonetheless the tanks and artillery of the US 8th Armored Division in pursuit of the Wehrmacht's 130th Panzer Division inflicted severe damage. Most of the structures stood disfigured, some beyond recognition. In front of St. Peter's Church, two American soldiers serving as escorts stood to the side. The American sergeant began to speak. Hans leaned into Willy and whispered, "He should have paid more attention to his lessons when they tried to teach him German."

" ... first thing, clear everything surrounding the church. Some of the debris may be used again, that's for you to decide. As you can see, part of the roof is damaged. There will be scaffolding made available for repairs. The stained glass windows will be a challenge but one of you is a glassmaker. Do the best you can. We come every day until finished, then we move to another building in town."

The sergeant walked over and spoke directly to Hans. "Krüger, you're an engineer?"

"Yes, but only a design engineer."

"Just the same, you *are* an engineer. The colonel's concern is the roof. He assured the priest the necessary repairs will be made. Understood?"

Hans nodded, then stepped back to inspect the wounded structure. A gaping hole in the roof, approximately ten meters in width, allowed passersby to see the ornate woodwork adorning the ceiling. Indeed, birds had built nests in the exposed rafters. The granite block wall soared to the roof, mostly intact, but three, maybe four blocks had been dislodged and were missing. He rubbed his chin. They must weigh at least a ton each. The top of what used to be the belfry had been blown away. The church bell rested on a timber supported by the damaged walls. It will be a challenge, but we should be able to fix this.

Hans walked to the other side of the church in search of Willy. "I'd like you to serve as my foreman."

He grinned and nodded enthusiastically.

"See to it the men begin by clearing the debris away. Don't discard anything until you have personally inspected it. I'll be inside."

Hans pulled the heavy front door open to discover an enthusiastic man about to exit. The priest's receding hairline ended at the border of black hair splashed with grey, his dimpled chin made less obvious by a prominent nose. He thrust out his hand and said, "God Bless you my son, you must be Major Krüger? Colonel Riley said you'd be here. I'm Father Rentz."

Hans bowed, looked the priest in the eye and shook his outstretched hand. "I've been assigned to rebuild your church."

"Yes, yes, yes, so you have. Let me show you the damage. I fear it's much worse than it looks."

Inside, Hans instinctively looked to his right, dipped his finger in the Holy Water and made the sign of the cross. He reverently walked past the rear pews and looked up, astonished by the beauty of the sanctuary. As if by divine guidance, the granite blocks dislodged near the hole in the roof had fallen, missing the altar by less than a meter. Obviously, mechanical assistance would be needed to move them.

Father Rentz, with a sweeping motion of his arm, pointed to the ceiling and the heavens beyond. Gentle brown eyes affirmed a level of devotion his parishioners no doubt appreciated. "I wonder if the roof's starting to weaken. I need to know if it's safe to continue saying Mass. Half my prayers and supplications have gone for the roof, that it doesn't collapse on our parishioners."

"Father, do you have a ladder? I need to inspect the roof."

"No, but if you follow me, I can take you to the belfry—er, what's left of it. From there you will be able to determine your needs."

Halfway to the top, Hans said, "Father, may I ask, how is it the Americans agreed to repair your church before anything else?"

"Phew." Father Rentz leaned against the wall. "God's work, my son." After a slow, deep breath, he added, "The American commander, Colonel Riley actually sought me out." The priest continued to lean against the wall.

"You alright, Father?"

"Why yes, but it's been awhile since I've been to the top of these steps—awhile indeed. There was a time I didn't have to rest." When his breathing became regular, both resumed their ascent. "Colonel Riley and his translator came to me and told me his brother—a priest in America—made him promised he would lend assistance to the Church in any way he could." Father Rentz stepped aside. "If you don't mind Major, can you lift the trap door?"

Hans heaved his shoulder into the door; it swung open to the sound of pigeons taking flight before it slammed to the floor. Hans scrambled up the ladder and extended his hand to the priest who followed. Cigarette butts, no doubt left by an artillery observer, littered the floor of the belfry. Hans straddled the hip of the slate roof and inched his way toward the gaping hole. Within an arm's length of the abyss, he stopped to study the damage, then carefully returned to the safety of the belfry.

"Father, can you get me a pencil and some paper, and perhaps a slide rule. I'll need to make some calculations."

"We can go to my office and I'll find what you require. Is there anything else you can think of?"

"Oh my, there are many things I'll need." Hans shook his head. "It will be nearly impossible to repair the roof and walls without a derrick. And the materials—I can produce a list of what is required," he added, "but I'm afraid I can't produce a miracle."

"Ah my son, the miracle is not in having our church restored, the miracle is that even in the midst of all this devastation, there are those willing to make it happen. You must remember, I'm a simple man of faith. I believe the American colonel will supply what we need."

▪ ▪ ▪ ▪ ▪

Father Rentz opened the drawer of his desk and removed a ruler as well as paper and a pencil. "For now, you can use the desk in my office. As for the slide rule, I'll have to make some inquiries. I'm afraid I can't use one to calculate the wages of sin and the cost of forgiveness."

Hans smiled. "Thank you Father. This will be fine. Now before I get started, I must check on the men." Emerging into the sunlight, Hans was speechless. In the time it had taken to survey the damaged roof, the crew had cleared most of the debris surrounding the church. From nowhere wheelbarrows and tools had appeared and at least twenty additional townsmen—all old men—pitched in to assist.

"What the hell?" Hans looked around to see Willy approaching.

"Major, you should see this." He led Hans to the back of the buildings. "Scaffolding. All we could hope for."

"And you did this?"

Willy pointed to an organized pile of supplies. "Yes, Major. Much of what we moved can be reused, if not here, elsewhere."

Hans' eyes widened as he mumbled.

"I'm sorry, Major. I didn't hear you?"

"I said, 'it *is* a miracle,' that's all."

"Major, there's more."

"*More?*"

"While we were working a woman came over and promised to return with food. She said the priest sent her."

▪   ▪   ▪   ▪   ▪

At the end of the afternoon, from a blown-out window in his office, Father Rentz smiled. The exhausted but contented workmen sat on the grass rubbing their sore muscles, waiting for the truck that would return them to camp.

"May I wait in the church until the truck arrives?" Hans said.

The American sergeant nodded. "Sure."

Hans settled into the last pew, and bowed his head in prayer, his fingers intertwined. Not until he crossed himself and raised his head did Father Rentz sit alongside him.

"Forgive me Major—"

He looked over at the priest. "Hans. Father, please call me Hans."

Father Rentz smiled. "Very well Hans. Forgive me for disturbing you, but—"

"Oh no, you're not disturbing me. I was just … just—"

"Praying?"

"That too. Actually, I was thinking about my last confession."

Father Rentz paused, then nodded. "Reflection is good for the soul."

Hans' sigh was barely audible. "It was August 29th."

"You remember the date?"

Hans replied, "Father, I will *never* forget the date, for many reasons," then remained silent.

Father Rentz focused on Hans' creased forehead. "Is there something you wish to share?"

"Father, could you could do me a favor?"

"I don't see why not, if it's in my power to do so."

"Could you send a message on my behalf to France?"

"Where in France?"

Hans looked hopeful. "Are you familiar with the Saulx valley?"

"Alsace?"

Hans' voice piqued. "Yes, Sermaize-les-Bains. You know of it?"

"I assume this would be to a woman, a French woman?"

"Yes Father. I haven't seen her since August 29th. She must know I'm alive."

The priest sat quietly, before speaking. "I am sorry. This I'm unable to promise. It's not that I won't assist you, but it may be of no use. Presently, there's no guarantee I can post a letter to that region."

Hans looked defeated.

"Reims must be close to this town?"

"Maybe sixty kilometers to the north," Hans said.

Father Rentz rubbed his chin. "I have a parishioner traveling there to visit her sister, she departs at dawn. Perhaps she could assist."

Before he could tell Father Rentz all that he wished to say, Willy burst through the door.

"Major Krüger, the truck is here."

"Go. Now," Father Rentz commanded.

Hans stood. "Father, please. Write to Father Feuillerat in Sermaize-les-Bains. F-e-u-i-l-l-e-r-a-t. Tell him I'm at the Rheinberg Meadow Camp and that I survived the war. He'll know what to do."

Before he bounded out the door, Father Rentz reached out, squeezed Hans' hands and said, "I will do my best."

chapter 41

Featherstone POW Camp #18, Northeast England
15 June 1945

WHY IN GOD'S NAME AM I GOING to the manor house? Last time they dragged me here Lord Worthington promised his assistance after the war and just where is he now? Peter's chest fell. No one heard him say, "Six feet under, that's where."

With the war in Europe over, the Red Cross had abandoned Allied-held prisoners-of-war in the belief they would soon be returned to Germany; no one knew exactly how long that would take. The most repeated rumor had them back home in two years. Regardless, the attention of the world and the Red Cross now concentrated on the ghastly discovery of Holocaust victims. As for the remaining German prisoners-of-war, there were English crops to harvest and English factory quotas to fill.

With these thoughts Peter found himself back in the major's office. A well-dressed man in his forties, maybe early fifties—leaning on a cane—stood next to Major Heathridge. His narrow face beneath a receding hairline looked familiar.

"Peter, I'm Lord Worthington's son, Walter. I regret my German's not as good as Father's, but I shall endeavor to do my best." Walter Worthington extended his hand. Peter hesitated, then grasped it. "I understand you're the man my father spoke so highly of?"

Peter said nothing.

"I see." Walter Worthington looked at Major Heathridge who gave him an encouraging nod. "Well, be that as it may, before Father died he was very precise in his instructions. At the end of the war I was to get you back to Germany. It just so happens a steamer's departing tomorrow in the afternoon, bound for Bremerhaven with relief supplies. My secretary has booked your passage and I'm here to escort you to Portsmouth."

Peter didn't know what to say, but from a lifetime of experiences, one memory dominated his consciousness. Whether the memory was of the anticipation of the journey or of the trip itself, he couldn't say. Perhaps it was simply the reconstruction in his mind of the events told over and over again by a parent. Either way, images of his first train ride to visit grandparents in Bavaria played before him.

"Well, man, what do you have to say for yourself?" Major Heathridge prodded.

Peter snapped out of his trance. "Danke. Danke." He lunged for Walter Worthington's hand, released it, grabbed it again and shook it one more time. Finally Peter looked about, surprised at such a wide grin on Major Heathridge's face.

"Peter, Major Heathridge here assures me you can be ready to travel within the hour." Walter pointed to a small empty suitcase by the door. "Pack your belongings while I tidy things up here. Don't dally, we're to be in Haltwhistle in time for the 11:13 to Carlisle station."

▪ ▪ ▪ ▪ ▪

After a meal of bland kidney pie at the Carlisle pub, both travelers boarded the train. Passengers along the corridor nodded in recognition at Walter Worthington, most ignored Peter. As he followed behind, he assumed they wondered why a man of Walter's breeding would travel with such a man of lesser means. Peter entered their compartment and hoisted his suitcase onto the overhead rack. Walter crossed the threshold, reached into his breast pocket, and handed Peter his release papers. In a hushed tone, he said, "You may as well have these. I shan't need them further."

Two women seated in the compartment looked up.

"May we?" Walter said.

Neither woman spoke, both nodded.

Walter translated the conductor's announcement—they had boarded the train to Manchester and should arrive on schedule in three hours. Peter noticed the older woman watching the conductor beyond the glass as he worked his way down the corridor. She set her knitting down, stood and opened the compartment door. Once in the corridor, she motioned the conductor closer. Peter could see her finger wag. When the compartment door re-opened Walter offered the conductor Peter's ticket and his own. The conductor punched both tickets and handed them back to Walter.

"You got along at Carlisle, did you?"

Peter looked up and nodded, then glanced at Walter.

"I'm askin' a question—just where did you figure you was headed?"

Peter turned to Walter. "*Was fragt er?*" What does he ask?

The conductor grabbed both sides of the compartment doorway, bracing for battle. "We ain't transporting no lousy Nazi-buggars on my train. No, sir we ain't." The conductor reached for Peter's arm. "Now off with you."

Walter struggled to rise. "Wait just one minute. This man's traveling with me and we *will* travel to Manchester unmolested."

The conductor glared only at Peter as he replied. "And just who might you be?"

Walter remained standing. "I'm Walter Worthington and this man is a friend of my father's—*Lord* Worthington."

The conductor released his grip on Peter's arm and replied, "Begging your pardon, sir. I didn't realize—"

"No, you most certainly did not."

The door to the compartment slammed shut just as Walter said, "Are things always this exciting when you travel?"

Both women exchanged glances but kept knitting.

"Not usually."

Several minutes passed before Walter spoke again. "Tell me, do you have any family?"

"Yes, I have a brother, Hans. He's six years older. My parents live in Berlin."

"Your brother, did he serve in the Kriegsmarine as well?"

"Hans was—or at least I hope he still is—in the Wehrmacht, a major. I haven't seen him since just before Christmas, 1942. The year before he'd been wounded at the Battle of Moscow. When he recovered fully he hoped to be sent back to France, but that's all I know."

"And your parents?"

"Father's a book editor in Berlin. He and Mother married before World War One. His experiences in the trenches caused him to caution me about war. He tried to warn me about Hitler. Father despises him."

"And you?"

"In the beginning I was enthralled but eventually I came to see him for what he was." Peter paused before he continued. "I actually saw Hitler once, so close I could have shaken his hand."

"Oh?"

"It was the 1936 Olympics. I know you can't tell by looking at me, but I was a good athlete once—I excelled in the javelin throw. In a local competition I took first place and won tickets to the Olympics. As a sixteen-year-old I set a record with a toss of nearly 60 meters. But my record meant nothing compared to Gerhard Stöck who won the gold medal for Germany. You could not believe the excitement. Gerhard had been trailing throughout the competition and when Hitler entered the arena the crowd immediately rose to their feet. Gerhard, the next to throw, launched his spear an incredible seventy-one meters to win the gold. This stunned everyone. All of Germany swelled with pride as Gerhard received his medal. At the time people thought Hitler had done it, inspired Gerhard to excel." Peter finally paused to take a breath. "That's how foolish we were. We thought Hitler possessed the power and magic to made it happen. Not Father. He tried to tell me about Hitler. We argued about the 'Jews Forbidden' signs. He said they had been removed from the city prior to the games. I refused to believe what he told me, that Hitler only did this so the world would not see him for what Father knew him to be—an evil man. Even with the roundup of Jews two years later I refused to believe this about Hitler."

"How long did it take you to believe he was right?"

"My first doubts came on Christmas Eve, just before my capture."

"Christmas Eve? How is that, weren't you out to sea?"

"I was the radio operator on our U-boat—"

"At your age?"

"Yes, I've always had an interest in wireless sets. Father brought one home for me, a gift from a client. I couldn't have been much older than nine or ten. That sparked my interest and in the Boy Scouts I learned to communicate by code. The rest fell into place. When I joined the Kriegsmarine, they naturally selected me as a radio operator."

"What's that to do with Hitler on Christmas Eve?"

"Standing watch that afternoon I scanned the usual frequencies. I understand how radio waves travel and what is possible and not possible. On Christmas Eve, Berlin transmitted a Christmas message from the troops in Stalingrad. The message sounded as if it originated next door. Not even a hint of static. It's impossible for a message to be transmitted thousands of kilometers all the way to Berlin without one crash of static or variation in the voice pattern.

I knew it was faked." Peter smiled to see Walter so engrossed in his recollection. "The more I thought about it, the more I recalled things Father said. The war had begun to turn bad for Germany. I thought at first the guards were lying, trying to demoralize us. But as other prisoners joined us, it became clear. And after the war ended and we were allowed to receive newspapers, it all became obvious how evil they were."

Walter leaned into Peter to whisper the next question. "Do forgive me for asking, but did you join the Nazi party?"

As he spoke, Peter ignored the two women sitting across from him and looked Walter in the eye. "Never. Father would have disowned me. I'm not even sure I ever wanted to join the Nazis now that I think about it. Perhaps there was something I couldn't see that kept me from doing so. However, I was proud to join the Kriegsmarine."

"Why the Kriegsmarine?"

"I don't know. Silly as it seems, it sounded romantic."

"Ah, the notions of youth. Don't get me wrong, I was young once myself. How well I understand."

Peter focused on Walter's cane. "Did your limp come from service?"

Walter Worthington ran his fingers over the cane's worn head. Its shaft of polished walnut was topped by an inlaid ivory border beneath a brass knob in the shape of a dog's head. With it he tapped his wounded leg. "Dunkirk. I come from a long line of soldiers, but the first to serve with the 50th Infantry from Northumberland. During the Battle of Ypres-Comines Canal I was shot-up in the hip. If it hadn't been for the evacuation, I'd been like you, stuck in some prisoner-of-war camp in Germany, ready for the dustbin, or worse, dead."

The crimson flush on Walter's face surprised Peter. "I'm sorry old chap, I just realized your family knows nothing of your whereabouts these past two and a half years. I'm sure they'll be delighted to see you, simply delighted."

"Especially Mother. I remember how sick she appeared when Hans left for the Wehrmacht. Then me—it was almost unbearable to watch her as my train eased out of the station. She learned of Hans' wounds and it nearly killed her. I can only imagine the torment she must be going through not knowing of my fate, fearing the worst. Father will be strong, but Mother ... I don't know."

"Your brother, you said you two were close?"

Peter smiled. "Mother used to say if she didn't know better, she'd have thought we were twins. We were inseparable. Whatever Hans did, I did. Wherever Hans went, I went. As we got older, the mischievous pranks were usually my idea, not his."

"Which of you got in trouble?"

"Hans. Mother always said to me, 'Now you go to your room. I'll deal with Hans, I know he put you up to this.' Later—whatever it was we'd done—Hans would soften Mother up by telling her he made sure I remained safe." Peter gazed out the window, then said, "And you know, he never took it out on me."

"When's the last you've heard of him?"

"December '42. He had been wounded in Moscow at the end of '41 but his wounds didn't heal properly and he required more surgeries. He was in Berlin the same time I was on furlough. That turned out to be the last we saw each other." Peter's voiced trailed off, then continued. "He's alive, I can sense it. I don't know where, but I know he's alive."

Walter removed a pocket watch from his waistcoat, checked the time and looked out the window. "It amazes me how time flies. From the looks of it we should be into Manchester before long, then perhaps we'll have our own compartment."

Peter nodded and returned to studying the English landscape. County lanes with painted canopies of tree branches stretched from village to village. Several bicycles and horse-drawn carts hurried about, intent on their business. Small fenced green fields with one or two cows standing guard before a farmhouse came and went.

"Walter, I'm curious about all the villages. So many of the homes are made of rock and the roofs are thatched, made of straw. I'm not used to such a thing."

"I suspect not. We don't have the luxury of the forests you have in Germany. We've learned to use the resources at hand."

Within minutes open fields gave way to rows upon rows of crowded streets and homes. Motorized vehicles filled the streets and as the houses ended, factories came into view, smoke pouring out the chimneys. The conductor didn't bother to open the door to their compartment, but announced from the corridor, "Manchester Station, two minutes." Peter looked down to see several additional tracks, all running parallel. He counted five by the time their train slipped under the covered archways of Manchester station.

The two women watched Peter stand and pull his suitcase from the overhead rack as Walter stepped into the corridor. One of the women grabbed the other's finger and pushed it down when she began pointing. Peter lingered a moment before leaning over their travel companions and whispered, "*Auf Wiedersehen.*" Goodbye.

When both gasped, Walter turned around only to see Peter's expressionless face looking straight ahead.

chapter 42

ON THE HALF-EMPTY TRAIN TO MANCHESTER WALTER secured an unoccupied compartment. "I insist you enjoy the journey, you may not see the English countryside again."

The route south out of the city mirrored the route in, only reversed: factories, crowded streets and homes, open spaces, then occasional villages. Once the farm fields reappeared, they didn't let up for hours, a patchwork of greens interspersed amongst darker, newly planted fields.

"There's so much color, it's beautiful," Peter finally said. "I wish I could open the window and breathe it all in. I never realized before but that's the one thing I missed most, the smells. My God, the odors on a U-boat would turn your stomach and those damp and musty smells will never be missed. But the smells that remind you of something pleasant always bring a smile."

Walter nodded in agreement. "I know precisely what you mean. My grandmother favored a rather distinctive talc, one I seldom notice. At the ticket agent's window in Manchester the woman in front of me wore the very same talc. One whiff transported me to my grandmother's parlor and with my eyes closed, I could feel her hugging me after I arrived for a visit."

"I agree," Peter said. "It's amazing what the nose can do. Of all the senses, we think seeing or hearing is the most important, but I wonder if the sense of smell isn't the most powerful?"

Again, Walter nodded. "If someone laid a dish of eggs in front of you and they didn't look right, but they smelled like the best eggs ever, you'd eat them without a second thought. On the other hand, if they looked perfect, but had a foul odor, you'd turn away. On top of that, your taste buds would be totally put off, all because of your smeller. Yes, I would say the nose rules the roost."

With his eyes closed, Peter let his head settle back as he inhaled. "Lilacs."

"Lilacs?" Walter said.

With his eyes still closed, Peter said, "That's what I smelled earlier today. It took me right to Berlin before the war where Mother always had a vase with lilacs, their fragrance filled the room."

Walter looked over and studied his travel companion. Yes, I can see why Father felt so strong about giving him a boost. Not at all what I thought a German should be. Walter watched Peter's head rocked gently back and forth as the train rolled along. By the time the conductor entered the compartment, Peter was fast asleep. Walter offered the conductor their tickets and said in a low voice, "How long before Portsmouth?"

The conductor tugged on the fob hanging from his waist, flipped the cover open and whispered, "A little over three hours. We should be arriving on schedule at 11:23," then snapped it shut.

Walter attempted to look out the window but the moonless night made it impossible for him to see beyond the reflection staring back. He lifted his stiffened leg with both hands and massaged his sore thigh. I wonder what the bloody bloke who shot my leg would think if he could see Peter here and me riding on to Portsmouth? What if it was Hans? Could be, couldn't it? Walter realized the folly of the thought and turned his musings to the father he dearly missed. My God, you could be stubborn. Walter recalled the time, red as a beet, the man nearly exploded during one of their arguments before the war. He refused to ever admit Churchill might have been correct about Hitler—even after Hitler revealed himself to be an evil maniac. Walter smiled. I think you secretly admired Churchill. To only himself he mumbled the last words he remembered his father utter about the Prime Minister, "My, how the people love that man. They'd follow him down the river Styx, through the gates of Hades."

As they approached a small station an hour north of Portsmouth, the train's rhythm ceased. Peter stirred, stretched, and yawned while Walter removed a package from his briefcase and untied its strings. "Hungry?"

"Famished."

"I know. Rationing, it affects all of us. Before I left this morning, Mother had this wrapped."

By the time Walter undid the last of the paper wrapping, Peter had began to salivate. "I've forgotten the last time I've tasted chicken. And a hard-boiled egg. How?"

"Quite simple really. Chickens can't read the Ministry of Foods rationing orders and they produce as many eggs as they damn well please. Rationing only limits what we buy, not what we produce or consume. Don't get me wrong, we don't over-indulge, but before I left for the camp this morning, Mother insisted."

Peter devoured the chicken leg. With each successive bite it became increasingly difficult to keep his fingertips from his mouth. Several minutes after Walter had placed a chicken bone on the wrapper, Peter laid a shinier one next to it.

Walter enjoyed watching Peter pick up his hard-boiled egg and inspect it before he cracked the shell and began peeling it away. Peter added the bits of shell to the two leg bones on the wrapping then lifted the egg to study it further before rotating it in his hand as a jeweler might inspect a precious stone. From a small container on the seat between them, Peter removed a pinch of seasoning and sprinkled it on the indented portion on the top of the egg. "You do realize there is only one way to eat a hard-boiled egg don't you?" Peter said.

"No, actually I didn't, but obviously you do."

"There's always a flattened area at the top, everyone knows it's for the seasoning." Peter delicately bit off the top portion of the egg. "If you do it right, you should have a second flattened area, but not to the yolk yet. Never bite off so much you get right to the yolk." To this he added more seasoning. "Then you peel this part off by hand and the upper portion of the yolk is ready to be removed." After he set the remaining egg on his lap, he removed the yolk, sprinkled it with more seasoning, and popped it into his mouth. "It's like two snacks, the white and the yolk." He lifted the last of the egg and offered it up like a champagne toast before adding a final pinch of seasoning to the cavity left by the yolk. "Without a doubt, the best part." He then laid the treasure on his tongue, closed his eyes and slowly savored the gradual mixing of seasoning and firm egg white.

"I shan't look at another hard-boiled egg the same ever again," Walter said after Peter swallowed the last morsel.

"Best egg I've ever eaten."

Walter smiled. "Forgive me for asking, but is there a girl perhaps awaiting your return?"

"Me? No, not anymore."

Walter tried, without success, to keep his eyebrows from rising.

"Before I left Berlin for the last time—"

"December of '42?"

"Yes. While on leave the girl I thought was mine became engaged to an officer in the Wehrmacht." Peter continued without hesitation. "Actually, I was a bit relieved."

"Oh?"

"Her mother would have been more than a challenge and not the least bit handsome."

"Indeed." Walter grasped his leg and adjusted his position. "When I was your age Father used to warn me, 'If you want to see what a woman will be like in twenty-five years, simply observe her mother.'"

Peter could only smile.

▪   ▪   ▪   ▪   ▪

The two fatigued travelers rolled into Portsmouth station on time and without incident. After a short ride to their hotel, Peter insisted on carrying Walter's suitcase as well as his own. Walter stepped ahead and opened the door, then stood to the side. "Thank you, Peter." When no one appeared to register their arrival, Walter reached for the bell, but hesitated. "I think I hear someone in the next room."

Peter surveyed the lobby. The carpet appeared a bit threadbare, but clean. The bookcase behind a leather smoking chair would explain—if it could talk—how the war years have been kind to the inn and that the Englishmen, who sat in the chair and nursed their pipes, looked forward to a new prosperity. "These accommodations look wonderful."

"Oh yes. I've been here with Father. Last time we crossed the Channel, in fact."

At that moment a short gentleman of about fifty years stepped from an inner office into the doorway. His wide yawn accentuated a round face. "Forgive me, I didn't mean to keep you waiting."

"Two rooms, if you please," Walter said as he spun the register around to sign their names.

The clerk then looked at Peter. "I must say, it's been ages since I've heard German spoken in these parts. Before the war, all the time, but not since 1939. No sir, not at all, unless you count the wireless, that is."

Walter translated for Peter. Both smiled at the clerk.

"Will you gentlemen be needing anything else?"

"Nothing," Walter said, "excepting a hackney carriage in the morning to take us to the pier."

"Departing for the continent are you?"

"Just my friend here." Walter placed his hand on Peter's shoulder. "He's returning home."

■　■　■　■　■

At precisely 11:00 in the morning Walter and Peter stepped out of the cab onto pier number 8 into a cauldron of activity. Two derricks lifted, then swung crate after crate of dry goods onto the deck of the ship as men scampered about lashing them in place. A line of passengers steadily crept up the gangway before disappearing into the HMT Empire Halladale. Peter grabbed his suitcase and lifted it off the pavement to prevent it from being run over by a baggage cart as Walter asked the cabbie to wait. At the end of the line of passengers, the ship's steward held a clipboard and inspected tickets for those waiting to sail.

Walter looked at Peter. "It's a funny thing. I should think we'd have been best of friends if not for the war. Father most certainly would have approved." He then removed Peter's ticket and ten five-pound notes from his coat pocket.

Peter's eyes grew wide. "I don't know what to say. Never in my wildest dreams would I have thought I'd be headed home."

Walter smiled. "Above the water too, no less."

Peter set his suitcase down and grasped Walter's hand, shook it vigorously, and embraced him. "I'm ashamed to say, there was a time I could not have cared less about the English, hated them actually. I—"

Walter winked when he said, "You mean you had little use for a bunch of us Limeys?"

Peter embraced him again. "I will write and tell you all there is to tell. You have my word."

Walter's voice waivered. "Very well then. Off with you."

■　■　■　■　■

Peter turned and joined the end of the line. When the steward asked for his ticket in English, he shrugged "*Es tut mir leid. Ich spreche Englisch nicht.*" I'm sorry, I don't speak English.

The steward smiled and replied in German, "*Ihr Name?*" Your name?

"Peter Krüger."

The steward ran his finger down a list on his clipboard. "Welcome aboard, Mr. Krüger. You are on A deck, cabin twenty-five. Enjoy your voyage."

The last to board, Peter slowly ascended the bobbing gangway. Once on deck, he sought out a place at the railing. The loud ship's horn caused all the passengers to jump with fright. Seagulls sliced the air above, waiting to escort the HMT Empire Halladale to open waters. The cabbie hadn't moved, yet Walter was nowhere to be seen. Momentarily distracted by wharf hands releasing lines, Peter resumed the search for his benefactor. The moment a deep rumble from the churning propellers rose through the deck, Peter instinctively looked up at dense smoke billowing out the stack. Gradual forward motion quickened his walk to the stern. Leaning over the railing, he spotted what had eluded him. Walter, growing ever smaller, had claimed a spot at the end of the pier, his upraised cane waving like a pendulum.

chapter 43

Rheinberg Meadow Camp
20 June 1945

As HE WAITED AT THE SPIGOT FOR his cup to fill, Karl Beck whispered, "Last night—"

Jonas cut him off. "I knew you'd find me." His cup full, he added, "Come, let's go where we can talk."

Beck brushed past the looks of contempt to an area free of prisoners and stood next to Jonas. Both gazed out beyond the wire. Jonas turned back toward the center of the camp. "Like you, the longer I'm here the shorter I have to live. They're going to find me."

"Forget me. You, your disguise keeps you safe. Soon you'll be a free man. But, with what little you told me, your concern is warranted."

"Someone recognized me. Everywhere I go, the same man's close by."

Beck turned quickly but didn't notice anyone lingering.

"I haven't seen him this morning. Yet." Jonas waited until Beck's attention turned away from the other prisoners. "You still wish to hear my plight?"

"Of course."

"I did it for Gerhard. I knew—since we were losing the war— that I had to deprive them of it, the filthy scum."

"Deprive them of what?" Beck said in an interested tone.

"Can't say, not now at least. But I can tell you it's monumental. The German agent working inside the Russian secret police—the one I mentioned earlier—stole a top secret file before returning to Berlin."

Beck stepped a little closer, studying Keller's face as a fortune-teller reads a palm. "What file can be that important?"

Jonas wouldn't budge. "Not now."

"They know you have it, don't they?"

"Of course. My only chance of survival is that Berlin doesn't find me."

"How could they?"

"Think about it? What's to keep them from telling the Americans? If they do—which they surely will—the Gestapo will be the least of my worries."

Beck considered what he'd been told. "And I thought I had troubles."

Jonas pointed to the newly constructed buildings outside the wire. "For now I'm safe, I think. As soon as the Americans start sifting through the files of every one of us—looking for whatever it is they'll be looking for—then I'm not so sure."

"What are you going to do?"

"Should they track me down, my survival depends upon convincing them if anything happens to me, the file—the photos, the negatives and the tape—will be passed on, to you perhaps. Better yet, I can escape and acquire a new identity."

This was the first he'd heard Jonas talk of escape. "You don't really believe that would save you, do you?"

"Which?"

"Either. A new identity would be next to impossible to secure and when—not if—the Americans find you, they won't care what you claim to have. Anyone who threatens them, well, they'll shut them up, permanently"—he snapped his fingers—"just like that."

The furrow in Jonas' forehead and the lack of response to his comments didn't go unnoticed. "Jonas you're right—your concern *is* justified." Beck waited a moment longer. "Don't forget Gerhard was my best friend. At the academy we did everything together." Without pausing for breath, he added, "You're more likely to succeed with my help."

"You'd assist?"

"After what they did to my daughter?"

Jonas' face turned crimson. "I'm sorry Karl—"

"You're not the only one with a grudge."

"You mean it?"

He offered Jonas his hand. "Not only will I assist you, we can plan our revenge together, simple and sweet—the Nazis and the Americans."

"Securing a new identity is easy. All it takes is a name. Someone, preferably a civilian about your age who died—this part is vital—and is from a city that has been severely bombed." Jonas talked faster, hardly taking a breath. "I know for a fact Hamburg's records were destroyed by fire. Simply tour Ohlsdorf cemetery— it's on the northeastern edge of the city. Since birth records and death records aren't merged, find a marker for someone born the same year as you, but died young, say as an infant. Present yourself with that name to the authorities and explain all your belongings have been lost and you need to acquire new papers and identification. Give them whatever facts you create. Because they have no way to verify anything, you're provided new papers."

Beck whistled. "You've thought of everything."

"I have. For now my concern is survival."

"And Hamburg," Beck added.

"I must retrieve that file." Jonas lowered his voice even further. "I wrapped it in oilskin and buried it in the Ohlsdorf cemetery. I guess you could say Gerhard's keeping an eye on it."

"Brilliant. How fitting—beneath your brother's headstone."

"Yes, but if something happened to me you must know the

file's not beneath *his* headstone. The Gestapo—once they set their mind to it—can find anything. They'd no doubt discover such an obvious location, so I buried it beneath the stone directly to the west of his. The name on the marker is Gruen. Friedrich Gruen."

"Is there a landmark close by to guide me?" Beck was again relieved his question failed to raise suspicion.

"Very—a statue of a woman and child."

"How can you be sure the cemetery's not been bombed?"

"I'm not, but it's located away from the demolished part of the city to the northeast."

Beck nodded. "You certain it's still there?"

"Should be. The area where Gerhard's laid to rest is approximately two hundred meters due east of the main entrance on Fuhlsbüttler Straße, then a little north. Once we—"

We? You're more stupid than I thought.

"—pace off two hundred meters due east, there is a large marble monument twenty-five meters to the north—Oeling is the name engraved on it—it's the one of a woman and young child, a girl. Gerhard's grave is a little to the east of this, ten meters, no more."

Beck reflected on all Jonas had revealed and extended his hand. "I'll assist you. *I* may not have any friends, but you can sleep tonight knowing *you* do."

chapter 44

Berlin, Germany
21 June 1945

PETER, LIKE A BOXER WHO CAME TO the title fight exploding with hopes and dreams only to find himself lying on his back in the final round—bloodied and dazed—discovered himself on the outskirts of Germany's capital two days after arriving in Bremerhaven. Three years' anticipation quickly crumbled to dust at the sight of each and every building along the route to Berlin. The first day of his struggle from Bremerhaven confirmed how much he'd been sheltered at Featherstone. It wasn't until he'd arrived in Berlin that he fully realized the extent his city suffered from Allied bombing and the Russian siege. Street after street and block after block undulated in a confluence of desolation, mortar and brick skeletons picked clean by scavengers.

He encountered only two types of people—those swarming like ants over the demolished buildings in a futile attempt to raise civilization from ruins and those who never made eye contact, mindlessly wandering about waiting to be told they could return home. *This is not the Berlin I left three years ago.* Peter's eyes were drawn to several planes flying overhead—the clear blue summer sky a startling contrast to the grey demolished buildings. At an intersection on the western edge of the city next to what used to be an athletic field, stood a barricade. An American soldier standing guard stopped all traffic proceeding into Berlin with his outstretched hand. As Peter approached he was relieved to hear the guard speak German.

He cleared his throat. "Excuse me. I would like to pass."

"State your business."

"I'm returning home to my mother and father. Lottumstraße, just north of the heart of Berlin."

The American noticed the accumulated dust on Peter's shoes and his mismatched clothes, his disheveled appearance no different than the thousands of other refugees.

"Where are you traveling from?"

He set his suitcase down and offered the soldier his release papers. "An English prisoner-of-war camp."

"You've crossed into the Russian Occupation Zone. Effective Monday, they will take over control of this area."

"What does that mean?"

"Your guess is as good as mine, but chances are, it won't be good." He handed Peter his papers back and simply said, "Good luck."

▪   ▪   ▪   ▪   ▪

Each street he crossed, Peter tried to remember what the buildings looked like before the war. He scrutinized the people and wondered if they could be friends. Would I recognize them? Would they even recognize me? And Hans, I pray mother and father have news of him. As he crossed the streets of his youth, he became more concerned about what he might find at 285 Lottumstraße.

Near the corner of Lottumstraße and Choriner Straße he hesitated. A stooped-over man in pants that used to fit approached on the sidewalk. A few meters away he veered toward the street without looking up. Peter stepped to the side, then touch him on the shoulder. "Mr. Kappel? Mr. Kappel, is that you?"

The man looked up. The blank expression lacked recognition.

"Mr. Kappel, it's Peter. Peter Krüger."

A look he could not decipher replaced the old man's gaze. "Mr. Kappel, are you alright?"

"Peter … Oh my … Peter, you died years ago."

Peter reached over and steadied his old neighbor. "Mr. Kappel, my parents? Are they safe? And Hans, do you know of Hans?"

"This is quite a shock—a happy one to be sure—but quite a shock." The old man continued. "Oh yes, your parents, they moved to Dresden." The old man extended his arthritic arm as best he could. "You must come with me. Frieda will want to see you. I'm afraid we have little to offer but we can visit."

Peter picked up his suitcase and followed. People who looked vaguely familiar waved at Mr. Kappel as they made their way along the sidewalk. A line had formed at the corner in front of a Red Cross truck dispensing bread; no one smiled nor laughed as they inched closer to the small loaf that might sustain them until the truck returned the next day.

The grassy courtyard where Peter and Hans played, no longer existed. Determined workers emptied wheelbarrows, brick by brick, onto a growing pile of debris. From the second floor window that used to be Hans' room, sections of plastered wall were thrown to the ground causing clouds of dust to billow, then settle.

Mr. Kappel led his guest across the threshold of the apartment building, its door long since ripped away. Despite the destruction, Peter smiled at the recognition of the parquet floor. It didn't surprise him to see that the wooden stairs had been recently swept; the cloth doily resting on a small table beneath the bannister brought a second smile.

"Ah Peter, I remember you and Hans running up and down the stairs. Up and down. Up and down, all day long."

"We never stopped to think your apartment was right below. How could you stand it?"

"Frieda would tell me, 'Eduard, they're just boys. Let them

play, they mean no harm.' Back then I didn't like being the superintendent, having to live in the basement. But now I'm glad for none of our walls have holes in them." Mr. Kappel opened the door to his apartment and allowed Peter to enter first. "Frieda darling. Come see who I've found."

Mrs. Kappel looked the same. Her hair, a bit greyer, rested above her shoulders just as Peter remembered it. A faded baggy blue sweater, open in the front, concealed a body twenty to thirty pounds thinner. "Eduard, where"—her hands shot to her face—"My God, I thought I'd seen a ghost." Peter stepped toward her and she wrapped her arms around him. "It's you. I don't believe it."

Eduard Kappel ushered them both to the kitchen table. "Peter, sit. We must tell you about your parents." Frieda put her hand on Peter's. "I'm sorry I have no cookies like before when you were a boy." She looked at her husband, and then back at Peter. "Can you believe it?"

Peter smiled but said nothing.

"Oh please forgive me. Yes, your parents. Well now, they moved to Dresden in 1944, after they received word about your boat." Peter didn't notice the quick glance at her husband before she said, "We haven't heard of them since winter."

"Do you have their address?"

"It may be here somewhere." She got up and opened a drawer looking for something she knew didn't exist. "As you can see, we have few possessions. Before the Russians arrived in Berlin we went to the country to live with a cousin. Eduard hid his tools." She stepped over and patted her husband's shoulder. "Fortunately, the Russians never found them. Everything else was gone, but not his tools. If it hadn't have been for that he never would be able to make our apartment look so nice."

Peter looked about the room. "How do you survive?"

"Your father gave Eduard a kerosene stove before they moved—"

Peter sat straight. "A small stove about this big?" He separated his hands to indicate its size. "With a metal case?"

"Yes, do you remember it?"

"Do I? It's a Primus stove, a gift from Father."

"Well, it's kept us alive," Eduard said.

Frieda sat back down at the table. "Everyday my dear husband walks to the river to bring back water for me to boil. But Peter, if it was yours, you should have it back."

Eduard nodded enthusiastically.

Peter raised his hand in protest. "Nonsense. You need it more." They both laughed when Peter said, "Besides, I'm not going camping for a long time, you keep it."

With that Peter lifted his suitcase onto his lap and opened it. "On the ship—crossing the Channel—I purchased bread, tea and some potatoes." He handed two tea bags and three potatoes to Frieda. "Mother and Father would want it no other way."

Frieda stared in disbelief. "Peter, you always were the sweetest little boy! Hans—now he was clever—but you were always my favorite."

"Frieda, look what you've done. The boy's all embarrassed."

"I'm fine, really I am. But my parents, do you have their address?"

Frieda bit her lower lip. "I'm sorry, but upon our return last month little remained. We did exchange a few letters but all I remember is they lived in an apartment on ... on Dürerstraße, yes, that's it, 72 Dürerstraße."

"And Hans?"

Mr. Kappel put his hand on his wife's arm and said, "After he recovered from his wounds they sent him back to France."

"France?"

"Yes, I'm quite certain of it. Your father couldn't contain himself. I remember he beamed as he said, 'Hans is so glad to be back in France.' But that was before the Italian campaign—"

"Do you know where, what division?"

"Your father told me he was still a major, with the 3rd Panzer-Grenadier, a new division formed in Lyon. The only thing I can tell you is in April his division—along with most the others on the Western Front—surrendered in the Ruhr valley." Eduard bowed his head and said, "I'm sorry I can't tell you more."

Peter looked his old neighbor in the eye. "Don't worry, I'll find him."

chapter 45

Rheinberg Meadow Camp
21 June 1945

COLONEL RILEY SETTLED DOWN TO A BOTTOMLESS stack of paperwork. A photo of his wife and four children rested next to a small bronze statue of a cowboy branding a roped steer. At the sound of a knock he looked up. "Captain Avery, hear you got a burr under your saddle." He pointed to the chair across from his desk. "Have a seat."

"Thank you, sir. There's been some trouble with the prisoners."

Colonel Riley peered over the glasses settled on the end of his nose. "Yes?"

"Sergeant Hamlin reported the burial detail collected the bodies of the Germans that died overnight—"

"How many this time?"

"Eight—"

"Only eight? What's the concern then?"

"Sir, one of the Germans didn't die of natural causes. He'd been strangled. Doc took a look at the body. Said he's never seen a more obvious case of strangulation, probably a piece of wire."

"Any information about the dead man, had he been cleared yet?"

"That's the reason I'm here. He had no identity papers. No one knows who he is."

Colonel Riley corrected him. "*Was.*"

Captain Avery ignored the comment, his voice increasing with intensity. "And get this, the insignia on his uniform, 13th Panzer Division."

"Your point?"

"Colonel Riley, the 13th Panzer Division is attached to Army Group C. They capitulated in the south, near Bavaria."

"You sure?"

"Absolutely."

"So who was he?" Colonel Riley said. "Maybe one of the more zealous Nazis did him in."

"Sir, I have no idea, but I've ordered photos to be taken of the dead body and that they be passed along to G-2. It's possible he's being sought for war crimes."

"Really Avery, another dead German, regardless of how he died, is hardly a concern. Besides, he could have been on leave the week the Wehrmacht collapsed." Colonel Riley picked up another report to review. "File your paperwork, but if I were you, I'd forget about it."

"Yes, sir I will, but sir, this is the first one that's been murdered."

Colonel Riley ceased reading the report in his hand and let it fall. "Come now Avery, maybe he hung himself?"

"With all due respect Colonel—from what?"

"Fine." He tried not to appear frustrated. "Summon that Kraut general and I'll inform him of your suspicions. Now, if you don't mind, I'd like to get back to work."

chapter 46

Sermaize-les-Bains, France
21 June 1945

Notre-Dame de la Nativité—Our Lady of the Nativity—stood sentinel as Sermaize-les-Bains' church beside the gently flowing Saulx River for nearly eight hundred years and since its destruction in September of 1914 during the Battle of the Marne, it had been the home of only one priest. That summer, prior to the beginning of *la première guerre mondiale*—the First World War—the archbishop decreed Sermaize-les-Bains' priest would be sent to Reims the following January, but after the church was utterly demolished by the Germans that September, the good parishioners implored their archbishop to let the priest who helped rebuild their church and their souls stay; his Most Reverend relented, stating their priest would never leave. So it was that every morning Father François Feuillerat would look up at the steeple clock and tug at the coarse but ancient wooded door before entering the church to celebrate Mass.

Like most in Sermaize-les-Bains, André Ferrand, despite not being able to recall his priest without a full head of grey hair, did not believe Father Feuillerat could possibly be seventy-three years of age. If asked, he couldn't say exactly what year the good Father first came to their village or where he came from for that matter. All anyone in Sermaize-les-Bains knew was that he had been their priest longer than they could remember, certainly well before the first war. Indeed, Father Feuillerat performed the sacrament of marriage or baptism for virtually everyone in the village; it was commonly stated he'd performed the funeral Mass for half those in the cemetery nestled next to the church.

Everyone agreed the most recognizable feature about the man was his gait. He didn't walk like a stray dog that seldom seems to know where it's going, never in a hurry. No, wherever Father Feuillerat went, he zipped about with missionary zeal, always with a smile and a wave.

André knew no other priest. He considered the man his friend, even more so since his near fatal pneumonia and the priest's administration of last rites and daily visits. Despite this bond, he would never know the role his priest played in his wife's adoption as a child. He only knew what Elsie's father—Monsieur Blaisé—had told him, Elsie's parents were Jews and Elsie was two years of age at the time of her adoption.

The one thing about Father Feuillerat André did know is that on 29 August 1944, his priest risked his life to save his family. For that, he would be eternally grateful.

Seated next to the wooden desk in the church office, André waited patiently. After Father Feuillerat appeared, he said, "I apologize. My chores prevented me from coming sooner. The eggs, you know."

Father Feuillerat's agility in sliding behind his desk surprised him. "What I have is important. Once you see, you'll understand."

André shrugged, unable to divine the source of the urgency. "If it's eggs or chickens you need—"

"No, not this time." Father Feuillerat produced an envelope from the top drawer of his desk. "I've a letter here with wonderful news. It's from a Father Rentz in Germany and it concerns you."

"*Me*, Father?"

"Yes, you. It was posted a week ago."

"I don't know a Father Rentz." André's eyebrows raised as his eyes widened. "News of Hans?"

"Indeed, our Hans is very much alive—"

"Where?" he said, barely able to resist the temptation to grab the letter.

"Hans is being held by the Allies in a prisoner-of-war camp in Rheinberg, along the Rhine. He—"

"Is he safe?"

"André, please! Yes, he's safe, now allow me to read the letter." Father Feuillerat smoothed the creases out on the desktop and began:

"Father Feuillerat,

I entrusted this letter with a parishioner to post from Reims with every prayer it finds its way to your able hands and heart. I am Father Helmut Rentz, pastor of St. Peter's Catholic Church in Rheinberg, Germany. I write on behalf of a German officer, a man who has been assigned to a work detail repairing our church. This man's name is Hans Krüger. He has impressed me as a very earnest and industrious individual and has sought my assistance.

He simply wished that I write and inform you he is alive. He assured me you would want to know.

With warmest personal regards,
The Reverend Helmut Rentz, S.J."

André didn't know what to say. His mind struggled to absorb it all. "Aimée? Have you—"

"Certainly not, I wished to go to you first, not knowing what his true disposition is, especially at the camp. I've not heard good things about these camps, and your Aimée, she is beside herself with worry, is she not?"

"Father, we must assist him, it's the least we can do."

The priest stroked his chin. "Since I received this letter, I've given it much thought." He reached over to grab a packet from the bookcase and spread out two Michelin maps on his desk, one of France, the other of Germany. After a lengthy discussion, the co-conspirators sat back in their chairs. "I agree, four hundred kilometers isn't too far. With a little luck we could make it in a couple of days, but you mustn't breathe a word of it to Aimée."

André nodded eagerly. "*D'accord.*" Okay. "I like your plan. She's been through plenty. It's all we can do to keep her spirits up."

On their feet, the two hugged and kissed cheeks in the traditional French manner. "It's settled. We travel to Rheinberg. Elsie will approve. I can solicit my neighbor to assist with the chores." André looked his priest in the eye. "You're certain you can steal away?"

Father Feuillerat didn't hesitate. "Absolutely. I've not had a day's rest since before the Occupation. Five years is a long time."

chapter 47

Thursday
21 June 1945
Sermaize-les-Bains, France

My Dear Father Rentz,

Your letter created tremendous joy in Sermaize-les-Bains!
Major Krüger's father is an old friend of one of my parish-
ioners, a Monsieur André Ferrand, and this last August I met
Major Krüger for the first time under terrifying circumstances.
You may rest assured he is an honorable man and any courtesy
you extend him is justified.

M. Ferrand and I will to travel to Rheinberg. With our Lord's
guidance, we hope to leave on the 29th, a week from tomorrow. It
is impossible to say what day or time we shall arrive for we have
only heard of the travel woes. I will post this letter today and pray
it reaches you in advance of our arrival and that it finds you well.

Do not worry about our accommodations. We hope to
make suitable arrangements after we arrive. As for the duration
of stay, this will be determined by the success of our mission.
We trust it won't be but a few days.

Yours in Christ,
François Feuillerat, S.J.

P.S. M. Ferrand wishes me to ask that you inform Hans his letter of Christmas Eve was received.

chapter 48

Rheinberg, Germany
27 June 1945

A RENEWED SPIRIT EMBRACED FATHER RENTZ AS he stood in the shadows cast by the morning sun, looked up and admired the newly repaired roof and steeple. Like after committing a venial sin, a sense of guilt nibbled at him when he thought of the surrounding buildings. He knew they'd be rebuilt in time. *Patience, we must have patience. Just because it took our Lord only seven days to create the earth, only He can perform miracles.* Immediately chastising himself, he muttered, "Six, not seven."

Hans looked up from the drawings spread out on the table. "I'm sorry Father, did you say something?"

"It took our good Lord just six days to create the entire world, but *we* must be patient. Yes, all good things come with time." The priest looked back up at the roof. "But I must say, it amazes me what you and your men have accomplished."

Hans smiled and tossed his pencil onto the drawings. "Father, you aren't the only one who's amazed, but with what you have been feeding these men, it's no wonder they're so willing to work."

"Nonsense, it's not the power of food, but the power of the human spirit. My father used to say, 'Hard work feeds the spirit like prayer feeds the soul.'"

Hans offered nothing in response.

Father Rentz looked to see that no one was near. "I received a post from Father Feuillerat. You must be very special to him. It seems he and a Monsieur Ferrand are traveling from Sermaize-les-Bains." He observed several of the workers sit on the grass nearby to rest. "I believe we should go inside to my study."

Hans could hardly restrain himself, his excitement as obvious as a child on Christmas morning. Barely past the threshold, he whispered, "How soon?"

"Perhaps Saturday, maybe"—Father Rentz waited for the door to his study to close—"Sunday, and he did wish me to inform you your letter of Christmas Eve arrived."

"Did he mention Aimée?"

"This is the woman you told me of?"

Hans nodded. "She's the daughter of Monsieur Ferrand."

"I see." Father Rentz hesitated a bit. "Are you lovers?" When he saw Hans flush a bright red, he diverted his eyes and said, "I mean, are you two in love?" The priest then extended his arm for Hans to sit in the chair next to his desk.

"Since the day we met, the fifth of July, 1940."

Father Rentz, now seated across from Hans, leaned forward. "I'm not surprised you remember that date as well."

"Of course. It was a Friday. We were on furlough and my fellow officers dropped me off in Sermaize-les-Bains on their way to Paris. I intended to join them once I fulfilled a promise to my father to visit his old friend, Monsieur Ferrand. From the hotel it was a short walk to their farm. André recognized me immediately as my father's son. After a short visit he invited me for supper the next day and during the most memorable stroll with Aimée, we fell in love."

"Ah, I remember the first time I fell in love." The priest smiled when Hans fidgeted in his chair. "There's no need to be embarrassed. I assure you, you're not the first to be surprised at such a thing."

"But Father, I've never heard a priest—"

"What, you think we're not human, that we didn't live before our vows?"

"No, it's just I've never—well, I mean, I—"

"To survive, man must love and be loved in return." He was relieved to see Hans relax.

"Forgive me Father, but this is not something one is accustomed to discussing with a priest. I—"

"What people don't understand is, I loved the Lord more. It was not a conscious decision, but one I knew in my heart. Once I realized this, my path, fortunately, has been an easy one." He looked at Hans. "But the right path is not always the easiest. Look at the paths you've taken in your life—sometimes the right one is the hardest."

He allowed the silence to help formulate Hans' response. After several moments, Hans said, "Most of my choices have been out of my control, the killing and the fighting. But, there was a time I took the wrong path—the easiest one—and I broke my Aimée's heart."

"Oh?"

"Yes, I ended our romance. In doing so I convinced myself I did it to protect her. I'm ashamed to admit I did it to protect myself."

"And what could you possibly need protection from?"

"The Gestapo."

The priest's eyebrows shot upwards. "The Gestapo?"

"Aimée's mother is Jewish. The entire family was about to be arrested by the Gestapo. Last August I finally came to my senses and rescued them."

"And Father Feuillerat knows this?"

"Knows it? He was my accomplice."

Father Rentz only nodded as Hans related the entire story. Finally, after contemplating all he had been told, he said, "I think now I understand why Father Feuillerat and Monsieur Ferrand are traveling to Rheinberg."

chapter 49

Dresden, Germany
27 June 1945

THIRTY KILOMETERS SOUTH OF BERLIN THE AUTOBAHN stretched directly to Dresden. What had been a crater-avoiding, jostling ride on the outskirts of Berlin turned smooth once in the country. The faces of the passengers, somber as those in a funeral procession, dictated the mood throughout the bus. Even the bright smile of a three-year-old with springy curls couldn't coax coos and smiles from the passengers.

The river Elbe flowed through Dresden 190 kilometers south of Berlin. Once the undisputed center of Germanic culture, Dresden was now poised, in a few short weeks, to find itself—along with a large portion of Germany—under Russian dominance, a domination only the Russians anticipated. Because of their army's brutal and indiscriminate crimes against the women of Berlin, virtually all Germans wished to be in the British or American occupation zones to the west by the time summer ended.

Since leaving Germany's once proud capital, an uneasy feeling nagged Peter. Why Dresden? He grasped the suitcase sitting on his lap, never daring to leave it unattended on the rack overhead. Had the other passengers suspected it contained food, he would have feared for his life. *Thank God the captain of the boat warned me about the food shortages. I bet Walter arranged for me to* purchase some of the ship's stores with the money he'd given me. God only knows where I'd be if he hadn't.

■　■　■　■　■

He noted the passenger next to him. The man looked friendly, but since leaving Berlin, he sat mute. An overgrown moustache stretched to the corners of his mouth and smothered his upper lip. Like so many others, his eyes searched the faces looking for loved ones lost in the bombings.

Peter cleared his throat. "If we hadn't just left Berlin, you'd never suspect there'd been a war."

The man simply nodded.

Peter fought the continued silence. "Are you from Berlin?"

"The Allies were smart."

"Excuse me?"

Without looking at Peter the man said, "They didn't bomb the autobahn because it would be valuable to them after the war."

This time Peter nodded.

After a long moment the man turned his head to look at Peter's shoes, then his pants, and finally his shirt. "Did you serve?"

"Kriegsmarine. On a U-boat."

"Headed home?"

Peter thought for a moment before answering. "I don't know. My parents moved to Dresden while I was away. I don't know where, all I have is an address." Peter reached into his pocket and handed the man the piece of paper he had received from Mr. Kappel.

The man examined it, unaware how long it took him to respond. "When's the last time you've heard from them?"

"Christmas of '42. Since January of '43 I've been held in an English prisoner-of-war camp. After my released I came straight to Berlin only to learn my parents moved to Dresden."

The man took another long look at the piece of paper. "Ever been to Dresden?"

"Never." What's he wanting to say that he's not saying?

With a newfound animation in his voice, he said, "Forgive me, I've been rude." He offered his hand. "Norbert. Norbert Engel."

"Peter Krüger."

"Well Peter, I don't know how to tell you this, but Dürerstraße is in the center of the city, by the river Elbe."

"So?"

Norbert's moustache hardly moved when he swallowed. "Last February, Mardi Gras to be exact, the Allies fire-bombed Dresden."

Peter could feel his heart begin to race. "The entire city?"

"No, but there were two raids that night by the British, then one by the Americans the next day." In a monotone, he continued, "We lived on Hofmannstraße, also near the center of the city. Since Dresden had no industry few believed it would ever be bombed, but when the alarm sounded I went out into the street and looked to the northwest. Christmas trees were falling from the sky."

"*Christmas trees?*"

"Two British planes had dropped flares to guide the bombers. They looked like Christmas trees with candles all aglow. It all became so eerie and surreal as they descended without a sound. The clouds glowed as a warning of what would follow. People gathered in the streets and pointed. From the northwest, the relentless drone of bombers could be heard. As if they were all awakened simultaneously, the people in the streets ran for shelter. Just as Emma and I settled in the cellar, the earth shook like God Himself grabbed our building and moved it about. Then came deafening explosions. Dust erupted from every crack in the wall with each blast. People screamed, some prayed, all believed the end had come. The air was stale. The lights had long since gone out, all we had was a lantern. In its dim glimmer people's eyes reflected terror."

Peter tried to envision such a scene. Maybe they weren't even in Dresden, and if they were, I'm sure Father would be sure they were safe in the shelter.

"Next came the smoke followed by the roar of fire. We could see the amber glow through the cellar window. A bomb exploding in the street pulverized the window, shards of glass sprayed the wall. Air escaped out the cellar window just before our eardrums popped."

Stunned, Peter could only listen. *My God, it sounds like a depth charging.*

"An air raid warden had followed us into the cellar. He stood on a chair and pointed to the window and shouted, 'We have to get out of here before we suffocate!' He opened the cellar door only to find a blocked stairwell. We were trapped. It became impossible to breathe and the smoke only made it worse. In the corner a neighbor found a shovel and a pick. The men began to dig at the wall. Within minutes they broke through to the cellar next door. One of the men grabbed the lantern and poked his head through the hole. His face told us what we feared. 'Dead. They're all dead.' Emma trembled. The men attacked the other wall. Air rushed through a second hole the instant it opened. Our breathing became easier. One by one we crawled through the opening. Luckily, the people that had been in this cellar had survived. We followed their footsteps up the stairs. As we climbed we didn't know what to expect—nothing could have prepared us for what we saw."

He didn't feel Norbert's nudge. "Are you okay?"

Peter's trance finally broke. "My God, I had no idea."

"I can stop if you like—"

"No, I'll be fine. I need to know."

"Very well. Fire was everywhere, illuminating the street like the sun on a cloudless day. The putrid smell of burning flesh filled our nostrils. Not a single structure escaped destruction. The center of Dresden had become a massive, roiling fireball. Then without warning an invisible wall of air knocked us to the ground. If I hadn't been holding so tightly to Emma, she would have been swept away.

One of my neighbors stood the moment a second blast of air roared up the street, air summoned to the fireball. In front of our very eyes he was lifted off his feet and sucked into the flames at the end of the block." When Norbert finally took a moment to rest, his chest heaved as he exhaled. "The last thing I remember seeing is the look on his face as his outstretched arms reached for us. I told Emma, 'We must get to the river.' So we clung to the street and crawled over the debris. The winds were less forceful as we approached the river and finally we could stand, but even then, we had to lean forward."

Peter tried not to sound desperate. "But there were survivors, weren't there?"

"I'm sorry, I don't mean to frighten you so. Of course there were."

"What did you do to survive?" was all Peter could say.

"I had just said I should go back and see what's left of our apartment. Emma begged me not to go. She said we could go in the morning. I was about to argue when a second group of explosions shook the ground. The roar of the fires had been so loud we never heard the next group of bombers. The air-raid sirens failed to sound. The explosions grew close. We ran to a boat I remembered along the river's edge, flipped over onto the shore. On our way, we were joined a young mother, perhaps your age, clutching an infant.

"The bombs were getting closer. The instant I lifted the edge of the boat for the four of us to crawl under, the concussion of a bomb pushed us to the ground, slamming the boat down on top of us. In the darkness we huddled. We prayed for forgiveness, we prayed God would spare our lives. Emma had taken off her overcoat for us to lie upon and I removed mine to cover us all.

"The firestorm sounded like a train. Under the boat it echoed as if it had been routed through the dungeons of Hell before it found its way to the four of us. Finally, we were able to sleep but only in fits and starts. After several hours we could still hear the low dull roar of burning fires.

"At morning's light I pushed the boat off of us. The shock of what we beheld defies description. It was as if we woke up at the very gates of Hades. The Dresden we knew before darkness fell had been transformed. To the south, there appeared to be little damage, but toward the city, nothing but smoldering, collapsed buildings. Not a single structure stood where once majestic architecture stretched for blocks. Dazed, we walked along the river's edge before we turned toward the city. Those unlucky souls that couldn't find shelter lay dead, burned beyond recognition. As we approached what used to be our street, a few people in front of their apartments poked about hoping to find something salvageable, perhaps some food."

Peter finally spoke. "The survivors—where'd they go?"

Norbert finally realized how it must be to hear his story. "I feel terrible telling you such things."

"Don't. When I'd first heard Father and Mother moved to Dresden, I had a bad feeling—"

"*Aach*, you never know." Peter appreciated the lighter tone in his voice. "The stories we've heard about people that survived are astounding. Our friend's block was utterly flattened. That afternoon, sifting through what remained, their dog came out of nowhere to run circles about its master's feet. How he survived or where he went, no one knows. Another couple refused to come out of their cellar after the first bombing. Even after the second bombing they were still in the cellar clinging to each other under a blanket soaked in water." Norbert paused. "But when—"

"*There's more?*"

"Yes. Off in the distance, about mid-morning the sirens sounded again. We looked to the west. This time it was the Americans. Emma and I ran back to our boat to take refuge. Those that crossed the river and were away from the bombing were spared. But those that lingered or refused to believe there could be more, well … they paid the price for their foolishness."

Father would never be so foolish. Never. Peter began to relax. "The young mother and child?"

"Never saw them again, I can only pray they survived. She never told us her name. With our home destroyed, we journeyed to Dessau where my sister lives. We were fortunate. At the sound of the first alarm, I took my wallet with what little money we had."

"That *was* fortunate," Peter said.

"After we arrived in Dessau we were able to get word to our son Matthias that we survived. He served in the Wehrmacht, 3rd Panzer-Grenadier Division."

Peter sat erect. "That's my brother's division."

"My boy used to be with the 386th Infanterie-Division. After Stalingrad, it combined with the 3rd Infanterie-Division to form the 3rd Panzer-Grenadier Division. Maybe he knows your brother?"

"Perhaps. Hans was a major, but I know nothing of his whereabouts—or if he's alive for that matter."

Norbert placed his hand on Peter's arm and patted it. "This much I can tell you. The entire division surrendered in the Ruhr valley in April." The man clasped his hands together in supplication and looked upward. "Thank God, it was to the Americans, not the Russians. We've not heard from him but we've since learned the Americans are keeping thousands of our soldiers in prisoner-of-war camps up and down the Rhine."

"Where's the 3rd Panzer-Grenadier Division now?"

"Emma thought someone told her Büderich. I don't know though, there are several I'm told. We've also heard there are nearly one hundred thousand men in each of these camps. I can't believe it. One hundred thousand? Impossible."

"Büderich?" Peter said.

"North of Düsseldorf, along the Rhine."

Peter quickly computed the distances in his head. "That's at least six hundred kilometers to the west."

"True, but when you find your parents, the three of you can head west to find your brother."

"I can only pray for such good fortune."

The man again clasped his hands together in prayer. "Yes, and if you discover our Matthias you could tell him we are safe?"

▪   ▪   ▪   ▪   ▪

Peter clutched his suitcase and stepped off the bus into a throng of refugees, all pushing or pulling a cart or buggy overflowing with their only remaining possessions. Before the bus slipped from view he looked back at the window where Norbert sat. Peter held up the piece of paper with Matthias' military service number written on it. How am I going to find Hans, much less Matthias?

As the bus lurched forward Peter turned toward what used to be the center of Dresden. My God, it's amazing anyone survived. The extent of the destruction took his breath away. Berlin hardly compared to the unending rows of brick skeletons and unorganized piles of rubble that stretched block after block after block. Nothing could possibly have eased his nausea. Along a sidewalk five boys, no more than eight years of age sat, each with an outstretched hands begging for food, their gaunt narrow faces beneath sunken eyes. He stopped next to the last boy and held his gaze. He's wearing the same style shorts Hans and I wore. Peter stooped down to balance his suitcase onto his knee, opened it carefully and removed a loaf of stale bread. The boys smiled in unison. They jumped up and surrounded Peter as he broke the loaf into pieces. Each cupped their frail hands around the gift and sniffed it like a dog before shoving it into their mouths. Satisfied their stomachs might ache a little less, Peter stood to leave only to have ten hands reach out and touch his clothes, nothing more.

Armed with a map and an address he walked the middle of a wide street in search of 72 Dürerstraße. A pair of Russian soldiers with carbines slung over their shoulders casually walked along. He ignored the taller one who glared at him before spitting on the ground. In the middle of the street a man stacked bricks. He finally looked up, aware Peter wished to ask him a question.

"Sir, excuse me. Can you tell me where 72 Dürerstraße is located?"

The man, without making eye contact, raised his arm and pointed to the north. "It used to be one block over and two blocks down." Without waiting for a response, he resumed his work.

Head hanging, Peter picked his way in the direction indicated. The further into the destruction he ventured, the narrower the path became. By the time he found Dürerstraße, there wasn't room to accommodate a truck. Workers, like a trail of ants, grew out of a basement. Each handed off debris so rapidly it looked as if they were all holding hands. At the end of the line a pile of bricks swelled. He made his way along the line of workers until he saw the number 72. At the door's opening he asked the first worker who acknowledged him, "Is this 72 Dürerstraße?"

"Ja," was all he said.

"Were there survivors?"

Another worker answered. "If they went to the cellar they didn't survive, no one did."

"How would I know if any are still alive?"

The worker pointed. "Check that wall across the street, survivors leave notes for family and loved ones." He then took a brick to pass along. "You could inquire at the refugee center. They keep a list of all known survivors."

Peter wiped tears away with the sleeve of his shirt. "How many?"

"How many what?"

"How many died?"

"Tens of thousands, nobody knows."

chapter 50

Rheinberg, Germany
29 June 1945

Settled deep in the well-worn chair, Father Rentz dozed, his newspaper halfway to the floor. Reading glasses barely hung on the end of a long slender nose as his head slumped forward. He awoke with a start and readjusted his glasses. The second knock brought him to his feet. Stiffened joints impeded his rush to the door.

A kerosene lamp illuminated two exhausted travelers. Father Feuillerat, with a relieved look, said, "You must be Father Rentz? I'm François Feuillerat. May I present Monsieur André Ferrand?"

Father Rentz ushered the guests into the rectory. He appreciated the gesture of a German introduction but responded in French. "Thundering Disciples! Yes, but I insist you call me Helmut. I wasn't expecting you until Sunday, tomorrow at the earliest." After an exchange of greetings he added, "Do come in." He led his guests toward the sitting room. "My goodness, how did you manage to arrive so soon?"

Both men set their suitcases on the floor and immediately eased into chairs. "A tiring journey to be sure, but one we're glad we made," Father Feuillerat said.

Father Rentz estimated André to be fifty, fifty-three at the most. The other priest's age was another matter. His totally grey

241

hair didn't coincide with his spry and agile entrance. He looked for wrinkles on the back of his hands for a clue. Sixty-five, seventy-five? Remembering his manners, he said, "Can I offer you something to drink? A glass of wine perhaps?"

Father Feuillerat, again, spoke for both travelers. "Nothing for me, just a soft seat that doesn't rock back and forth."

André nodded in agreement.

Father Rentz smiled. "Despite your letter stating you'd arrange lodging, I insist you stay at the rectory. My housekeeper is always looking for things to do. After I received your letter she immediately prepared your room." The protestations didn't cease until he added, "Besides, there are no other accommodations."

"That's most gracious," Father Feuillerat said. "We worried perhaps we'd embarked too hastily. In Sermaize-les-Bains, unlike the last war, we have not suffered the destruction others have, but our passage from Köln brought me back to the first war. Along the tracks whole villages were destroyed. I'd forgotten what mankind could wreak upon God's earth. Perhaps it's a small miracle we made it."

"Yet we survive. Why? There are those here in Germany, as there are no doubt in France, who would say it is only to prepare for the next war." He looked heavenward as if to affirm the answer to his question. "And they would probably be correct."

Both guests nodded.

"You must be famished." Their host scurried off to the kitchen where he rummaged through the cupboards and called back to his guests, "I regret all I have to offer is cheese and bread with some wine, and a sausage I've been saving."

André spoke this time. "That would be perfect, but why don't we add a couple eggs to the menu?"

Father Rentz returned from the kitchen in an instant. "Did you say *eggs*?"

The French priest pointed toward his travel companion. "Indeed. André here is a poultry farmer."

"Yes, my Elsie insisted I bring eggs. She knew they'd come in handy." He reached down and lifted the smaller suitcase onto his lap, then smiled as he tapped it lovingly. When the clasps were released and the suitcase opened, Father Rentz inhaled sharply.

▪   ▪   ▪   ▪   ▪

After a meal of traditional German *spätzle*, Father Rentz patted his lips with his napkin. "It's been a long time since eggs have been put to such divine use."

Father Feuillerat looked to André and then at their host. "It's been very difficult in France, but we don't have the refugees Germany has. I can't imagine the hunger—"

"All of Europe is hungry. Few have hardly any food … except the Americans."

"Does that mean Hans is well cared for?" Father Feuillerat said.

André joined in. "Yes, what is his status?"

Father Rentz placed both elbows on the table as he explained. "Acceptable, but only because it's warmer now. It was more difficult in April for they had no shelter. There still isn't, just holes in the ground the men dig, but at least it's warmer." He noted his guests' reaction to the news of the camp and added, "He's lucky to be on a work detail where the men are better fed away from the camp."

Relieved, Father Feuillerat said, "Your letter, it spoke of repair work. Tell us more."

"In March, shelling did much damage. Major Krüger and his fellow prisoners have repaired the steeple and roof. One of the men repaired the stained glass window in the most expert manner. How, I'll never know. As for Major Krüger, he refuses to take any credit for the work." Father Rentz picked up his guests' plates and placed them atop his. "In the morning you must inspect his handiwork. I'm relieved to say in spite of the conditions at the camp, he retains a good disposition and sense of purpose."

André's forehead wrinkled with concern. "It is not so good at this camp?"

"It pains me to say the conditions are appalling. I'm not able to determine if the neglect is intentional or simply a result of war. Colonel Riley—the camp commander—is very firm with the prisoners, but he's a good man. He says the camp conditions are out of his hands and I believe him. I tell you, General Eisenhower has shamed the Americans. And the food shortages—they affect us all. At first we were able to visit the camp, but with the worsening shortages, because so many beg for food, the colonel sees no one without a just cause. But I have been lucky, Colonel Riley allows me to visit as often as I like. Still, he won't let me say Mass for the prisoners. Oh, I have offered, but so far it has not been permitted. No, I am only allowed to minister to the dead."

An even more concerned look settled upon André as Father Feuillerat said, "But you are permitted to pray over the dead prisoners?"

"Yes, before they're buried in the meadow beyond the camp." Father Rentz crossed himself before he continued. "The only comfort they have before they die is to know they will be buried on German soil."

Father Feuillerat nodded. "How many prisoners are there? What's to become of them?"

"Tens of thousands, perhaps one hundred thousand. No one knows what the Americans have planned. You will see for yourself, then you'll agree our biggest worry is that Hans not succumb to disease. He appears healthy now—just thin—but after he returns to the camp at night, God only knows what awaits him. I assure you, the rumors of prisoner's deaths are to be believed." He uttered this with a confidence neither guest doubted. "Yes, the sooner he's released, the better."

"Tomorrow—we'll see Hans and be able to meet with the camp commander?" Father Feuillerat said.

"Hans will be here tomorrow. The only day he's not is Sunday. As for Colonel Riley, we go to his office in the morning. His brother's a priest in America so he may be favorably disposed to assist us."

"Will he tell us anything?" Father Feuillerat said.

"Perhaps—"

"Would he even let Hans go free?" André added.

"I don't see how. After all, he must follow orders, but hearing Hans' story about your family, Monsieur Ferrand, I now understand your desire to assist."

André rubbed the two days' stubble on his chin, the dark growth a sharp contrast to his salt and pepper head of hair. "Then we must have a plan, one that cannot fail. With the conditions at the camp, it would be terrible for Hans to have survived all that he has endured only—"

"I agree. We're not returning empty handed." Father Feuillerat thought a moment before he continued. "Could we help him escape?"

"Too dangerous. The perimeter's patrolled and the guards are armed. Besides, you'd have to get him back to France unharmed."

"He's right, but there must be a way," André said. "Could we disguise him as a priest? He could return with us, no one would question a priest, especially now that the war's over."

Father Rentz shook his head side to side. "But he still wouldn't have release papers from the camp. Surely at some point he'd need them."

▪　▪　▪　▪　▪

André jumped to his feet, startling both priests. "I have it! I know this will work."

After he shared every detail of his plan, Father Rentz excused himself and returned with a decanter of cognac and three small glasses.

Father Feuillerat raised his glass and said, "Tomorrow the Allies will be no match for the French *and* the German Catholic Church." All three glasses were raised and all three heads tilted back. "And remember, Helmut will tell Hans of our plan first thing tomorrow. If we see Hans—hard as it will be—he must be ignored."

Of course, Father Feuillerat said this as much for himself as he did for André.

▪ ▪ ▪ ▪ ▪

Through his partially open office door, Colonel Riley eyed two priests and a layman. What do they want? Whatever they're selling, I'm not buying. The man seated between the two priests kept rotating the brim of his hat through his fingers. When the colonel pushed a buzzer, a clerk sprang to his feet and entered. Colonel Riley motioned him to close the door.

"Who's that with Father Rentz?"

"Some French priest and one of his parishioners."

"Great, just what I need, an international delegation. May as well show them in."

An American sergeant followed the three visitors into the office. Stepping from behind his desk, Colonel Riley smiled as he extended his hand. "Father, such a surprise. To what do I owe this honor?" The American sergeant translated.

"Colonel, I would like to introduce you to a colleague of mine, Father François Feuillerat and a friend of his, Monsieur André Ferrand." After handshakes were exchanged, Father Rentz continued. "Colonel, we would like your assistance and in particular, we hope you will be able to help Father Feuillerat and Monsieur Ferrand."

Colonel Riley opened the door to his office and snapped his fingers. "Corporal, bring in two extra chairs. Coffee, too." The three guests settled into their chairs. Okay, here it comes, this ought to be good. "Alright Father, shoot. What is it? The help getting' outta hand?" The translator did his best to make the colonel's question understood.

"Oh no, Colonel, the men are doing a splendid job. In fact, the majority of the work is almost complete." Father Rentz looked down, inhaled and continued. "No, we're here on another matter. You see, Father Feuillerat's parish is in France, Sermaize-les-Bains in the Marne region."

Colonel Riley failed to observe his translator steal a glance at the two Frenchmen. "And Monsieur Ferrand is from the same village?"

"Yes—"

"You know Father Feuillerat how?" the colonel said.

"Both of us are—are—are—"

"Are what?"

"Men of the cloth."

"Yes, yes, I can see that. Is that how you—"

"Yes, Colonel," Father Feuillerat interjected, "we have exchanged letters in the past."

Colonel Riley looked only at Father Rentz. The relief on the priest's face went unnoticed. "How can I possibly help?"

"We have come to learn that German soldiers held in Allied camps may be released for work details, much like your prisoners that have rebuilt our church."

Colonel Riley nodded. "Go on."

"Monsieur Ferrand is a poultry farmer in Sermaize-les-Bains. The region relies on his farm for eggs and chickens. Now that the war has ended, he needs to increase production but he has no one to assist him."

"And you want someone from our camp? Aren't there prisoner-of-war camps in France?"

"Colonel, this is true, but poultry production is specialized and since Father Feuillerat and I have been corresponding, I told him of one of your prisoners, one who has been assisting in the rebuilding of our church."

"Continue," the colonel said.

"As they rest, I have gotten to know the workers. I learned that a Major Hans Krüger has extensive experience with poultry farms. I told Father Feuillerat of Major Krüger in one of my letters and he traveled to Rheinberg in hopes that maybe you would allow Major Krüger to return to France with Father Feuillerat and Monsieur Ferrand—"

"Father Rentz, I'd like to assist you, but—"

"Colonel Riley, I personally assure you that Major Krüger will be treated well and will come to no harm."

"Father, that's not the issue. I can't just let prisoners go willy-nilly with anyone who needs someone to do their damn chores."

Father Rentz translated into French for André. A short but spirited exchange ensued. "Colonel, Monsieur Ferrand wants me to tell you there is more to running a poultry farm than chores."

At that moment, the translator spoke up. "Colonel Riley, might I suggest we summon this Major Krüger to your office and determine how much he really does know about poultry farming."

"Good idea Sergeant."

"Colonel Riley, since Major Krüger is with the work detail at church today, I propose we meet again Monday next to discuss this further."

"Agreed. Come Monday morning, I'll see to it that Krüger's available. I hate to send you back to the barn without any horses, but I warn you, that could happen. I'm not interested in making it any easier on these Nazis. Besides, that just ain't how we do things around here." Colonel Riley shook his head back and forth. "Monday morning it is. I'll expect you at 0800 hours."

chapter 51

Rheinberg, Germany
30 June 1945

As Hans worked, Father Rentz grabbed him by the arm. "I'm sorry I wasn't here when you arrived. I met with Colonel Riley."

"*Oh?*"

Father Rentz whispered, "You can't tell a soul what I'm about to share—"

"You received word from Sermaize-les-Bains?"

"Shhh, no one must hear us." The priest tugged at Hans' sleeve, ensuring they were well away from anyone. His voice quivered with excitement. "Father Feuillerat and Monsieur Ferrand arrived last night, the three of us met with the colonel."

"You what?"

The priest raised his hand. "Let me explain … ."

■　■　■　■　■

From around the corner, the workmen could hear a spirited conversation in French grow louder. Hans turned his back on the three men the moment they appeared. My God, they're actually here. I can hardly stand it. Strolling about, Father Rentz eagerly pointed out the many repairs. When they looked to the roof, Hans, unable to concentrate on his work, stole glances of André and Father

Feuillerat. With equal discretion, the two Frenchmen did the same while pretending to focus on the masonry work beneath a stained glass window.

Father Rentz extended an arm upward. "Most parishioners agree the glass is more colorful and vibrant now, especially when illuminated by the sun."

André nodded in approval. With hands behind his back and leaning forward, he admired the prisoners' handiwork. Not far from Hans, he began humming *Stille Nacht, Heilige Nacht* softly to himself. Hans focused on his task and ignored the mocking glances exchanged between his fellow workers behind André's back. For the remainder of the day, no one could have guessed his newfound exuberance was linked to the musical Frenchman.

chapter 52

Rheinberg, Germany
2 July 1945

MONDAY MORNING HANS CONTINUED TO PLAY HIS part, acting confused when told he wasn't going to accompany the work detail into Rheinberg, even more confused when brought before the camp commander. Sitting outside Colonel Riley's office, he attempted to eavesdrop beyond the closed door—without success. He squeezed his hands together as they lay in his lap, folded. Dear God, please make this work, please. I'll do anything. Anything. Moments later his shoulders stiffened and he winced, his thoughts raced to the image of the dead Polish woman lying on the floor. Impossible for him to blot out her imploring gaze, he squeezed his eyes shut yet another time. You know I was only following orders, surely You know that. Before Hans could chastise himself further, the office door opened.

"Major Krüger."

Hans caught himself before his mouth fell open. It can't be. Daniel Veit, what are you doing here?

Colonel Riley stood and said, "Thank you Sergeant." He then looked at Hans. "Major, I summoned you here to discuss your future."

Hans nodded meekly and ignored the translator as he repeated the colonel's statement in German.

"Major, you know Father Rentz." Hans looked at the priest and bowed slightly. "This is a colleague of his, Father François Feuillerat. He's from a village in France, Sermaize-les-Bains. With him is a parishioner of his, Monsieur André Ferrand. And, we've got a translator here to help us out." Hans could only stare at Daniel Veit as he translated before he abruptly held out his hand. The extra hard squeeze and shake from André went unnoticed by the others.

"Colonel, it's a pleasure to meet these gentlemen, but what's that to do with my future?" Hans noticed neither Father Feuillerat nor André so much as raise an eyebrow.

"Major"—the colonel cleared his throat—"how much do you know about poultry farming?"

▪   ▪   ▪   ▪   ▪

I sure as hell hope this works. Sergeant Veit saw a look of concern forming in Hans' eyes. Before Hans could say anything, the translator added in German, "Go along with this. Say something—anything."

Hans complied.

"He says he has spent endless hours on a poultry farm."

"Ask the major if he actually grew up on a poultry farm. Tell him his file indicates he's trained as an engineer."

The translator looked at Hans, then said in German, "I'm going to convince him you know all about poultry farming. Just start talking so I can make it work."

While Hans talked, Colonel Riley added, "Sergeant Veit, you grew up on a farm. Ask him something about farming."

Hans looked only at Colonel Riley as Sergeant Veit translated. "No, I didn't grow up on a poultry farm, but my uncle operated one and I spent many of my summers until the war assisting him in any way I could."

"Now hold on one damn minute," Colonel Riley blurted out.

Sergeant Veit remained calm.

"What's going on here? The only word besides *nein* I know in German is *ingenieur*—I remember it from this man's file—and I'm pretty damn sure I never heard the word ingenieur come out of either mouth." Colonel Riley pointed to Hans and added, "I said it, but neither of you did."

Sergeant Veit's response was immediate. "You're absolutely correct, sir. I never used the word ingenieur. I said, '*Ihre Studien an der Universität waren nicht Landwirtschaft, stimmt dass?*' Your studies at the university were not agriculture, were they?"

When Colonel Riley nodded, Sergeant Veit added, "Sir, if you ask me, even though he didn't grow up on a farm, he knows more than enough to serve this man's needs."

Colonel Riley sat in his chair, his fingertips pressed together. "I don't like it. No sir-ee, not one bit. I don't mind helping out St. Peter's—in fact it's my duty—but this, this smells like a pile of dung." With a wave of his hand, Colonel Riley said, "Don't go translating till I tell you to."

Colonel Riley either didn't see or chose to ignore the concerned looks being exchanged in the room. Nor did he notice the confused look on Father Rentz's face.

"Just why the hell should I let this"—he hesitated to say the word Kraut, or worse, Nazi—"this ... this ... man go? Can anyone give me a reason?"

When no one responded, he said, "Damn it Padre, you're supposed to dispense advice. Start dispensing."

Father Feuillerat looked at André, then Hans.

"Imagine that, a speechless priest—thought I'd never see the day." Colonel Riley regained his patience. "Well?"

"Obviously, the Lord has a plan. And that plan is for this man to assist Monsieur Ferrand in his poultry business. Clearly, Major Krüger has the skills to be of valuable assistance *and* it has been my impression he's diligent and honorable. Plus, the work at the church is all but completed." The priest smiled as much to himself as to Father Feuillerat and André. "Indeed, it appears to be part of His plan."

Colonel Riley considered all that had been said for several tense moments. "Well, it looks like your friends got themselves a hired hand. It's against my better judgment, but I trust you."

Father Rentz translated all into French after Sergeant Veit had repeated it in German.

"Major Krüger, I'm assigning you to a work detail on a poultry farm in France. To keep things simple, you will be listed as being under the supervision of Father Rentz here who will receive monthly updates from Father Feuillerat and Monsieur Ferrand. Do you understand?"

The moment Sergeant Veit finished talking, Hans looked straight ahead and nodded.

Colonel Riley turned to the priests. "I'll sign the necessary transit papers and passes. Come by this afternoon and he's all yours. I'll have my staff keep Father Rentz here appraised of the disposition of the prisoners in the event things change."

No one in the room heard the colonel's final admonition, "Don't make me regret this—I must warn you, it may be necessary to claim him at some time in the future."

▪   ▪   ▪   ▪   ▪

Hans quickly retrieved his personal items and sought out friends to bid them farewell. He gave little of the details regarding his 'transfer'—as he referred to it. Observing Anton approach, he walked toward him. "You've heard my news?"

Anton smiled. "I can't believe it! Released to work on a farm in a French village. I somehow knew it would be Sermaize-les-Bains. Just how did you arrange it?"

"I didn't. I simply asked the priest in Rheinberg to contact the priest in Sermaize-les-Bains. Next thing I know, I'm headed there to work on a poultry farm."

"And not just any poultry farm, I bet."

Hans ignored the comment. "Anton, you've been a true friend. I don't know how to thank you."

"I'm the one who should thank you. Few people would have put up with such a naysayer."

The two stood staring at one another. Hans reached into his pocket. "Before I leave, I want you to have this."

Anton recognized it immediately. "I can't, that belonged to your father. Hans, I can't accept it."

"Do you remember the time we were talking in our room, that April before we evacuated Rome?"

"Of course I do. I convinced you Aimée hadn't given up on your love."

"Your advice that day—everyday in fact—meant the world to me. It truly sustained me."

"That's what friends do. Besides, what's that to do with your pocketknife?"

"You mentioned you'd give anything to have the pocketknife your grandfather had given you. Maybe this can replace it."

Anton took the gift "I don't know what to say."

Hans embraced his friend. "Then say nothing. I must go. After you're released, you'll know where to find me."

Anton grasped Hans' hand and shook it. "Godspeed. You've been a dear friend, one I'll never forget."

▪　▪　▪　▪　▪

Hans felt a sense of hopelessness as he looked past the closed gate to observe Karl Beck approach Anton, lean in and poke him repeatedly in the chest with his finger. God am I glad to be through with him, may the fires in Hell never die. If he figures out where I'm headed, he just might come after me, but then again, if he's smart, he'll never set foot in Sermaize-les-Bains.

A familiar voice disrupted his concentration.

"Major Krüger, there you are, I wanted to find you before you left."

Unaware of being watched, Hans turned to the voice and smiled. "Sergeant Veit, I hoped I'd see you before leaving. I had no idea you were at this camp. How can I begin to thank you for what you did."

"For what *I* did. Are you kidding me? No, I'm the one who should thank you for setting me free. I'd shake your hand right now, but I don't want to raise any suspicions. Though I must admit, it took me a minute to figure out what your friends had cooked up."

"No, I mean Aimée received her letter. A thousand thanks."

Sergeant Veit blushed. "I take it Monsieur Ferrand is Aimée's father?"

"Yes, *and* the friend of our family."

Before anymore could be said, a jeep carrying the two priests and André arrived. "Private," Sergeant Veit said to the driver, "be sure to get them to the train depot safely."

As the jeep accelerated, Hans turned around from the front seat and called out, "Daniel, your Irma, did she have a boy or a girl?"

A grin erupted on Sergeant Veit's face, his blue eyes sparkled. Through cupped hands he yelled, "A boy. His name's Steven, born on Christmas Eve!"

▪ ▪ ▪ ▪ ▪

Little conversation passed during the ride to the train station—all kept their thoughts to themselves. André spent the entire fifteen minutes looking over his shoulder as if expecting Colonel Riley himself to drive along side and order Hans out of the jeep. Finally Father Rentz, seated in the middle of the back seat, spoke directly into André's ear, "Monsieur Ferrand, the colonel is an honest man. If he gave Hans permission to go, he won't change his mind."

André could only smile in return.

After the two priests, M. Ferrand and Hans had been dropped off and the driver well out of sight, André set his suitcase on the sidewalk and embraced Hans warmly and kissed both his cheeks. "I'm sorry Hans, the colonel might have gotten a little suspicious if I had greeted you in such a way this morning." André embraced him again, then held him at arm's length. "Tell me, what news do you have of your parents?"

Hans remained strong. "Nothing. My inquiry to the authorities in March all but confirmed they died in the bombing. The letter I received said there's little hope they survived the firestorm that engulfed Dresden. I only pray that they were together at the end."

André shook his head in sorrow before wiping away the moisture from the corner of his eye. "This cursed war. Perhaps your father knows we're together now."

Hans changed the subject. "I can't believe this is actually happening. How did you do it?"

André remained cautious. "I don't know, but after the translator said what he said, I got nervous. Why the colonel couldn't hear my heart pounding is a mystery. I thought he'd seen through our little ruse. But then I realized the sergeant was on our side." Relaxed, André smiled. "At the time, I'd swear you knew him and just now when you called out to him, I knew there was more."

"There is. He's the one who posted my letter to Aimée."

"How? How could an enemy soldier do such a thing?"

Hans raised his hand to shield his eyes from the sun. "He was a prisoner, captured during the Battle of the Ardennes. I interrogated him on Christmas Eve and after that he escaped."

"With a letter for Aimée in his pocket?"

Hans maintained his composure. "A miracle, wouldn't you say?"

André grinned. "A miracle indeed."

chapter 53

Rheinberg, Germany
2 July 1945

THE TRAIN STATION CONCOURSE BUSTLED WITH ACTIVITY, American GIs and civilians everywhere, but like vinegar and oil, the two groups refused to blend. The civilians, not sure what to believe after five long years of Joseph Goebbels' propaganda machine, stole furtive looks at the GIs while the Americans remained aloof.

André took in the travelers, soldiers and refugees alike. "The Americans, they're not as I remember them in Sermaize-les-Bains. They're more reserved."

Father Rentz finished scanning the crowd. "Perhaps it's because you're in Germany. We'd been led to believe the Americans are barbarians, just as bad as the Russians. After all, they're not the liberators here they were in France."

André turned back from studying the soldiers. "That's it, the American's haven't figured out how to respond to the Germans. And by the time they do, the new leaders will be telling everyone they started the war. Oh yes, in France the finger pointing has already begun." André took a breath and studied his audience. "Surely you remember what we were told after my war, and look what we learned. Nothing. This war will be analyzed just like the last, and in the end it will mean nothing. Of course, they'll blame it on Hitler—that he caused it—but aren't we all to blame? Didn't we let this happen?"

The two priests looked at one another as Hans responded. "He's right. There had to have been a time someone could have stopped Hitler. I don't know who or when, but someone could have."

Father Rentz glanced at his watch. "I agree but if we keep discussing this, you'll never get home." Several announcements came in quick succession. "I'm afraid it's time for me to go."

Father Feuillerat embraced his fellow priest, then held him at arm's length. "Thank you Helmut for what you've done. I'll write you often of Hans'—er, shall we say, *progress*."

André couldn't resist. "My Elsie will see to it that he doesn't learn too much from the chickens."

As both priests blushed, Hans said, "Father Rentz, I don't know how to thank you—"

"No, son, it's I that should thank you. You not only restored my faith, you help restore the faith of my parishioners. Now, no more of this. You must be off." Father Rentz waved as the three travelers headed toward their train. After yet another announcement ended, he called out, "Godspeed and safe travels."

▪ ▪ ▪ ▪ ▪

Hans settled into his seat and after what seemed an eternity, the train began to rock back and forth, gently at first, then in a soothing cadence. Countless memories surfaced, one by one as if waiting their turn. His parents running from a burning building. Jacob. The dead Polish woman and her doomed unborn child. The Battle of Moscow and the Russian bullet ripping into his chest. Letters. Peter. The Gestapo's last roundup. Aimée writing about the goslings and their mother. Irises. Lilacs. Walks. Stolen kisses. Karl Beck. Hans squeezed his eyes shut. Please God, grant me peace.

▪ ▪ ▪ ▪ ▪

The hours passed slowly and idle conversations did little to make the trip go faster. Distractions helped, but once underway, Hans could think of little besides Aimée and holding her in his arms. He smiled, thinking of André's intricate planning. But why did he have to agree to let her go to Reims?

Hans caught André looking his way. "Are you sure she'll be home tomorrow?"

"Yes, very sure. They were only going to Reims for two days. She assured me she and Marjorie would be home by 2:00."

"And she knows nothing—"

"Absolutely nothing. She thinks I accompanied the good Father to visit his brother."

▪ ▪ ▪ ▪ ▪

Difficult as it was, the three travelers waited until afternoon to share what Father Rentz had given them. With stomachs satiated by the loaf of bread and the wedge of cheese, drowsy nods punctuated the afternoon. Just before sunset, as their train eased through the village of Prüm before crossing the Belgian border, Hans yawned and looked out the window to see a young woman with a small child holding her hand as they walked. Both faces were drawn and sad, the very look of hunger. He pivoted in his seat to study them further as the train gathered speed. He didn't turn back around until her red headscarf slipped from view in dusk's fading light. The steel-wheeled metronome continued its persistent, rhythmic click, click, click.

Hans gave little thought to the conductor walking quickly through the car toward the front of the train, but when the train slowed and the conductor leaned over empty seats to determine what caused them to slow, Hans cupped his hand to the window.

In the darkness, the telltale lights of a town or city were not visible. He looked to André and Father Feuillerat, both shrugged as if to say, We have no idea. Most passengers accepted the delay. A man in the row ahead blurted out, "Must be a cow blocking the tracks." André agreed. "That's it, a cow." Another passenger from the front announced, "We're stopped at a road crossing."

A woman at the front of the car began pointing. Hans sat erect. In the passageway between cars the conductor talked with the two American soldiers and an officer who had just boarded. His pulse raced. André nudged Father Feuillerat and said, "Look, it's the Military Police."

Two MPs, followed closely by an officer, entered. The conductor whispered something to the officer. Immediately after pointing directly at Hans, the three Americans advanced. The officer held a file in his hand like the ones Hans remembered seeing at the processing center in Iserlohn. The man's red hair and freckled boyish face looked harmless, almost innocent. But the total lack of a smile was concerning. His uniform told nothing more than the fact that the man had attained the rank of captain. Hans noticed the closer they came, the less innocent the captain looked and the tighter he gripped the file, now safely tucked under his arm.

Before the American captain could speak, Father Feuillerat said, "*Pouvons-nous être utiles?*" May we be of assistance?

The captain frowned. "*Ich spreche Französisch nicht.*"

Hans translated for André and Father Feuillerat. "He said he doesn't speak French."

Upon realizing Hans spoke German, the captain opened the file and spoke directly to him. "*Ihre Identitätspapiere?*" Your identity papers.

The captain, confused by Hans' response directed to Father Feuillerat, was even more confused by Hans' papers being handed over by a priest.

"You were an officer in the Wehrmacht?"

Hans strived to remain calm. "Yes, a major with the 3ʳᵈ Pan-zer-Grenadier Division."

The captain scrutinized the file a moment longer before looking up. "Are you sure it wasn't the 3ʳᵈ Panzer *SS*?"

"Positive," was all Hans dared say.

"And you're traveling where?"

"Those papers"—he forced himself to take a deep breath—"should tell you what you need to know."

"Well, why don't you tell me anyway, *Major* Krüger?"

Hans could see Father Feuillerat begin a silent prayer as he placed his hand on André's knee. "I have been assigned to work on this man's—Monsieur André Ferrand—farm in Sermaize-les-Bains, France. Father Feuillerat has been entrusted to be my guardian." He looked directly at the captain. "It's all right there, signed by a Colonel Riley."

The captain stared hard at Hans. "Isn't Sermaize-les-Bains just north of Robert-Espagne?" Both his travel companions tensed upon hearing the familiar name.

"You know of it?" was all Hans could bring himself to say.

The captain paused. After several anxious moments spent perusing the file, he finally said, "Yes, we passed through Robert-Espagne in August."

Hans, like a grandmaster chess player waiting for his opponent to move, said nothing, his body language revealed less.

Immediately the captain said, "What division?"

"The 3ʳᵈ Panzer-*Grenadier*."

"Where did you cross the Rhine, Major?"

"Ludendorff Bridge. Remagen."

"What day?"

"7 March. 1944."

Captain Richard Jenks closed the file. "You're free to go. The man we're looking for is SS. I'm sorry to have troubled you." Before turning to leave, he handed Hans' papers back to Father Feuillerat.

▪ ▪ ▪ ▪ ▪

Father Feuillerat and André crossed themselves and let out simultaneous sighs. "Hans my boy, I thought he was about to haul you away," André said.

Father Feuillerat crossed himself a second time. "I don't know, for the life of me, how you stayed so calm. And did you notice how the one MP kept his hand on his weapon? My, I think I've used up a month of supplications and Hail Marys."

"I'm afraid their work won't be done for a very long time." Hans thought about Karl Beck and the thirteen lampposts in Sermaize-les-Bains. "A very long time indeed."

▪ ▪ ▪ ▪ ▪

A fitful night and numerous stops along the way, twenty-seven hours after leaving Rheinberg, their train arrived in Saint-Dizier, twenty kilometers south of Sermaize-les-Bains. At the ticket counter André appeared more confused than tired. "What do you mean the train no longer goes to Sermaize-les-Bains?"

The clerk looked up from his paperwork, first at the clock, then at André. "The first trestle north of Saint-Dizier is no longer safe."

"It *was* a few days ago," André argued.

"The Maquis sabotaged it in August. Yesterday one of the engineers declared it unsafe."

"Is there not someone who can provide us a ride to Sermaize-les-Bains?"

"Impossible."

Father Feuillerat stepped up to the window. "Surely someone would be willing. We've been traveling all night and all day. The only thing we desire is not to spend another night away from home. We've traveled this far and we're so close."

André hoisted his suitcase onto the counter and opened it. "Father, do you think these might help." He lifted the small pillow covering the six remaining eggs as if showing off a newborn baby. The clerk found it difficult to look at anything else.

Father Feuillerat said, "As we were saying, is there anyone who could drive us to Sermaize-les-Bains?"

The clerk rubbed his chin. "Sermaize-les-Bains isn't so far, twenty kilometers perhaps."

"These are for anyone who can do the *impossible*," André said as he closed his suitcase.

A Window Closed sign instantly appeared on the counter. "If you can wait a moment, I'll drive you myself. My truck won't be comfortable, but it'll get you there."

▪　▪　▪　▪　▪

Behind the station, the clerk apologized for having a vehicle propelled only by wood. Hans smiled, then helped load the splintered logs necessary for the forty-kilometer round-trip. He smiled again when the clerk insisted André and his suitcase ride in the front. Father Feuillerat and Hans balanced on crates as the truck sputtered north beyond the outskirts of Saint-Dizier towards Sermaize-les-Bains.

Reminders of war persisted. Trucks and tanks, long ago scorched by fire and abandoned, dotted the countryside like headstones. Only their shapes indicated who might have died defending them. Hans craned his neck as they passed. Where are those men now? And that tank, was it attached to my battalion?

"Does this look familiar?" Father Feuillerat said.

"I've traveled this very road before. Seems like eleven years since I'd been here, not eleven months." After a large bump, Hans adjusted his wooden crate. "We were bivouacked last August just five or six kilometers to the west in Saint-Eulien. In fact, the last time we passed through the rail station in Nancy it was sheer chaos. The Americans were right on our heels."

"Indeed they were," Father Feuillerat said. "It wasn't more than thirty-six hours after you left that the first Americans rode through Sermaize-les-Bains. Don't be offended, but we had such a celebration, French and American flags everywhere."

"Yes, they'd have been from the 80th Infantry Division. We had many skirmishes with them as they chased us across France into Belgium."

"Before we knew it, they were gone. A few stragglers perhaps, but nothing more."

After several minutes of silence Hans gazed at the aging priest. How could I ever repay him for what he has done? "Father, you know I'll never—"

"My son, you needn't say a word."

"But Father—"

Father Feuillerat raised his hand abruptly. "Not a word. Ever."

Beyond the open fields, wide swaths of green before a backdrop of solid blue dominated the passing countryside. The flat land north of Saint-Dizier gave way to a terrain of gently rolling hills and a roadway canopied by trees. Splashes of sunlight painted the road. It was a landscape harboring no threats. Gone were the apocalyptic scenes Hans witnessed throughout the battlefields of Belgium and Germany. When he looked up to the sky he marveled at the joy of his survival, not to search for marauding American fighter planes. Death no longer lingered in the air or waited around the next curve in the road.

As the truck slowly accelerated out of a turn the engine sputtered, then backfired. Hans fell to the bed of the truck, pulling Father Feuillerat along side him. Seconds later he raised his head. Embarrassed, he sat up and helped the priest back onto his seat atop the crate before brushing off his back. "I'm sorry Father—"

"Nonsense, think nothing of it. I suspect it will take some time before such noises seem normal."

Hans could only nod and smile meekly. After what seemed an eternity, he pointed at the shrubs lining the road where birds flitted from bush to bush, branch to branch. "Father, the birds—do they even know the fighting's over?"

"They must. Like you, they did what they had to do to survive. And to survive, one needs hope."

Hans pondered these words. "Do you know what I hope? I hope the nightmares come to an end."

Father Feuillerat, leaning forward, adjusted his seat. "Like the loud noises, it will take time."

"Is there enough time? Before I left for the Wehrmacht in 1939 my father told me, 'War is something you don't want to remember, but something you can't forget.' At the time it made little sense." Hans steadied himself as the truck's gears shifted. "Understanding commands a higher fee than I realized."

"Yes, it usually does."

Past a stand of trees, Hans looked west at the sun and guessed the time to be about five o'clock.

"Goodness, is that your stomach I hear?" Father Feuillerat said.

Hans shrugged. "I hardly notice it anymore. At first it wouldn't stop. Right after we surrendered we didn't eat for two days, then little after that." He patted his abdomen and smiled. "But there are better days ahead."

"As soon as we arrive at the rectory, Madame Dubois, my housekeeper, she will prepare a meal."

Hans nodded his approval as they rode on. Eventually, his thoughts, like they usually did, returned to Sermaize-les-Bains. I can't wait to see the look on her face and to hold her again. God, I pray she's forgiven me. He turned to assess their progress, then looked at the priest. "Father?"

"Yes?"

"Will you perform—I mean, if—"

"If she says yes, is that what you mean?"

"It's just that I worry—"

Father Feuillerat could only smile. "Of course she'll say yes."

■　■　■　■　■

On the outskirts of Sermaize-les-Bains André instructed their driver to stay off the main streets and approach the church in such a way to avoid anyone that might see them returning with Hans. On the road behind the rectory, as it crosses the Saulx River, André hopped out of the truck. Hans assisted Father Feuillerat in stepping down.

"Father," André said, "I'll have the driver leave you two here and take me home."

Hans picked up both suitcases and turned towards André. "You're sure Aimée's not due home until—"

"I told you, it will all work out. She'll be home tomorrow afternoon."

Hans sniffed the air. "Good, it may take me that long to clean up."

André laughed. "Maybe you don't have to. She could have caught cold while she's away."

All three hugged. André climbed back into the truck and pointed in the direction of his farm while Father Feuillerat led Hans into the rectory.

chapter 54

Rheinberg Meadow Camp
2 July 1945

THE GREENISH-YELLOW BRUISE ACCENTUATING KARL BECK'S
ENTIRE mandible and right eye persisted for weeks. A distracting
ache still lingered, and when he bent over, it was an unwelcomed
reminder of the vicious attack he'd suffered six weeks previously.
Most victims of such an attack would have withdrawn, remained
aloof and hidden. Not Beck. Defiant, he refused sympathy, instead,
he strutted around the camp like a stud bull at pasture.

Because of his obvious hatred for Hans and the generally
known threats against his life, the rumors of Hans' release dissem-
inated in the time it would take a strong wind to blow across the
camp. Since hearing the rumor, Beck loitered along the barbed-
wire fence at the gate waiting for Sergeant Hamlin to pass. Anyone
watching could see his lips move as he paced. "I must have been
hearing things, there's no goddamn way he would be sent to work
on a farm in Sermaize-les-Bains. Sermaize-les-Bains? It can't be."

He went over again and again in his mind the last time he'd
been there. The 29th of August, wasn't it? Now that I think of it,
Krüger showing up on the street that day was peculiar. Some dispatches, my ass. He showed up for a reason, now what was it?

Before he could consider it further, Sergeant Hamlin stepped
off the porch of the supply hut and began walking toward him.

"Sergeant Hamlin, *Kann ich eine Frage stellen?*" Can I ask a question?"

The sergeant looked at his watch. "Schnell."

"It's all over camp that Krüger's being released this afternoon."

"Not released. He's being assigned to a work detail."

"In Sermaize-les-Bains, France?" How convenient. "How'd this come about?"

"I have no idea. All I know is the old man approved it. He leaves this afternoon."

He ignored the sergeant's intent gaze and stepped forward. "I have information Colonel Riley might like to know."

"Such as?"

"Major Krüger's in danger. They only want to kill him."

"Wouldn't that save you the trouble?"

Hoping to seize the sergeant's attention, he continued. "Didn't anyone think it suspicious a farmer in France would want *him* and no one else? Sure, I admit I hate his guts"—I want him for myself. I don't want anyone else stealing my fun—"but what's wrong is wrong. Now Sergeant, can I see the colonel?"

"Tell me what's so damned urgent and I'll run it past the colonel. If it's important, he'll summon you. In the meantime, I've work to do."

Beck glanced at the sun. "No, don't go, there's little time. We'll do it your way." Before Sergeant Hamlin turned to leave, he inhaled deeply and looked him in the eye. "Last August 29th— just before you Americans arrived—Major Krüger left his post without orders and traveled to Sermaize-les-Bains. That afternoon thirteen citizens of the town, men and women, were strung up and hanged—murdered in cold blood. The French obviously suspect Krüger of this crime. They've discovered—don't ask me how— the Allies had him here in this camp. The Frenchman concocted whatever story he told the colonel to allow him to come to Ser- maize-les-Bains and he's playing right into it. Can't you just imagine his reception?"

"You know for a fact thirteen citizens were murdered?"

Beck nodded. "Absolutely—women, too."

Sergeant Hamlin looked back at the commander's office. "Wait here. You'll tell the colonel what you just told me?"

He suppressed a smile and nodded a second time.

▪ ▪ ▪ ▪ ▪

Sergeant Hamlin walked into Captain Ward's office and saluted. "Excuse me sir, the lieutenant told me to come to you."

"At ease Hamlin. What's on your mind?"

"It's about that prisoner the colonel authorized to be released to work on the poultry farm in France—"

"What about it?"

"Well sir, I think we may have been duped."

"How so?"

"The German colonel, the one—"

"For Christ's sake Hamlin, we've got close to a hundred thousand Germans out there."

"Sir, the one causing all the trouble—"

"Beck?"

"That's the one. He told me Krüger murdered thirteen Frenchmen—men *and* women—last August in the same village the priest comes from, if he even is a priest."

Captain Ward stood and walked over to the window. "That Beck over there by the gate?"

"Yes sir. I told him to wait there while I talked to Colonel Riley. Is he busy?"

Captain Ward looked at his watch. "He's leaving in a couple of hours for a meeting, won't be back until tomorrow. Let me check."

▪ ▪ ▪ ▪ ▪

270

Captain Ward reentered the room. "Okay, you've got two minutes."

Sergeant Hamlin followed him into the colonel's office. After he finished relating Beck's story, Colonel Riley said, "Where's he now?"

"Just outside. Should I get him?" Sergeant Hamlin said.

Captain Ward interrupted. "To tell us what? That a Nazi thief and suspected murderer just accused a fellow Nazi of murder?"

Leaning back in his chair, Colonel Riley gave his captain a disapproving look. "Now gentlemen, it would seem we have a possible problem on our hands."

Captain Ward ignored the silent reprimand. "Colonel, look at it this way, if he didn't do it, so what? If he did do it, the French will mete out what he's got coming a lot faster that we ever would. By now everyone must know what murderers the Nazis were. It's their business, not ours. Besides, it's one less mouth to feed and it saves us the trouble of hanging the son-of-a-bitch."

"But Colonel Riley," Sergeant Hamlin stood straighter, inhaled and said, "we can nab him before he leaves."

Colonel Riley rubbed his chin. "Let me think about it awhile before I leave for Düsseldorf." The colonel put both hands on his desk as he stood to end the meeting. "For now, if we have to, we can always radio ahead. One thing's for sure, I trust Father Rentz. "Besides, we know where this Krüger's going and that Nazi Beck sure ain't going anywhere."

chapter 55

Rheinberg Meadow Camp
2 July 1945

LIGHTNING SILHOUETTED TREETOPS BEYOND THE CAMP AS Karl Beck, both hands clasped behind his neck, lay motionless. His thoughts were of his conversation with Anton the day Hans departed. The man didn't deny Krüger had a woman in Sermaize-les-Bains. *It's the only thing that makes sense.*

Only when the storm closed did he grab the three-foot long plank he'd hoarded and set out for the camp's southern perimeter. Rolling thunder shook the ground. At the edge of the latrine he looked back twice before leaping across the open pit. Relieved he'd cleared its foul water, he crawled the last five meters. At the first of two wire fences he listened, then looked carefully in both directions. Convinced there were no guards, he slipped the plank under the wire and lifted it, barely able to squeeze beneath. He did the same with the second fence just as rain pelted the back of his neck. At the next flash of lightning he froze, then resumed his slithering advance toward the Rhine.

He thought about the conversation he'd heard along the wire Saturday. Lingering by the gate, one of the guards—in a voice laced with bravado—told of his *fräulein* and how he took her for a walk along the river. Beck's interest had peaked as the guard told of the rowboat along the shoreline and what they'd done in it; the graphic description of her hips had captivated more than just the other guard.

On open ground, well beyond the wire, Beck stood, then pressed on. The cool air indicated the river was near. At the crest of a slight rise, along a stand of trees, he smiled at the Rhine flowing before him. Gentle waves, raised by the wind, licked the shore. Confident in the knowledge of the rowboat's location, the dark expansive void that thwarted the Allies for so long was no longer of concern. He picked his way through the trees to the shoreline. I'm sure it's around here somewhere. To the north, the foliage ended, to the south trees crowded the water's edge. Beck went north. No more than a hundred meters, tied to a stump, he discovered the rowboat. He grinned thinking of the fräulein and her guard. Once up-righted, two oars spilled onto the ground. He tossed the plank into the water. With this current, I should set a course about forty-five degrees to the opposite shore.

Seated in the boat, oars in the water, Beck faced west and tugged on the left oar. In response the bow turned south, against the current. Satisfied, he worked both oars. Focused on the riverbank slipping away, he repeated, "… God … damn … Krüger …"—pull—" … God … damn … Krüger …"—pull—" …God … damn … Krüger …"—pull—" …God … damn … Krüger … ."

Twenty minutes later the boat's keel settled into the muddy shore. Beck jumped down off the bow, grabbed the line hanging over the gunwale and walked a few meters until the boat paralleled the shoreline. He grasped the stern and pointed the bow toward the middle of the river. Assisted by a hefty shove, the boat caught the swifter current and pointed north—within seconds it disappeared. Any luck at all, it'll be floating past Wesel by morning.

He looked back across the water. Good no search parties. To the east he strained to see any lights from Dinslaken four kilometers ahead. Convinced of his safety, he saw no advantage in proceeding further until morning. Entering a dense stand of poplar trees, he stripped several branches of leaves and fashioned a bed no less comfortable than the one he had escaped.

▪ ▪ ▪ ▪ ▪

Colonel Riley looked up as he set his reading glasses on the bottomless stack of reports. Captain Avery entered. "At ease, Captain, I hoped you'd be here soon. Any news on the shipments we're expecting."

The captain saluted. "No sir, that's not why I'm here. I think one of the prisoners escaped—"

"Just one?"

"Well, at this point we're not sure. A local farmer complained his rowboat's gone missing. I had the guards search the perimeter and behind the latrines the wire looks as if it's been disturbed—not cut, just lifted up and set back down. Because of the rain, there aren't any tracks."

"That's it, one prisoner?"

"Yes sir, but we're pretty sure it's that Kraut colonel, the one the rest of those Nazis put on trial."

"How could you possibly know?" Colonel Riley said.

"I took the liberty of asking General Denkert. He said he'd check into it. You can imagine his relief once he discovered no one had seen the crazy colonel since yesterday."

Riley snorted. "Yeah, I can just imagine how happy he is to be rid of that trouble maker—I'd swear he got into a patch of locoweed."

"Sir, shouldn't I at least alert the authorities?"

"For Christ's sake son, we *are* the authorities." He returned his glasses to their usual location and picked up the report he'd been reading. "Pass it along channels if you must, but beyond that, I wouldn't get too worked up."

"But sir, why escape? It's almost as bad on the outside as it is in there."

274

"Captain, if I knew what the Nazis were always thinking don't you suppose I'd be in Washington telling guys like me what to do?" He looked at his watch. "Now if you'll excuse me." Colonel Riley shook his head and muttered, "Must've been one big patch."

▪　▪　▪　▪　▪

Surprised by his uninterrupted sleep, a famished Karl Beck sat up, rubbed his sore arm and shoulder muscles and struggled to stand. Once upright, he picked his way to the edge of the trees where he detected a faint sound. Somebody's chopping wood. His eyes failed to penetrate the mist. He stopped to listen for voices from the opposite shore. Relieved, he ventured toward the familiar sound. Soon he found himself free of mist and warmed by the sun. He turned to see an elongated wall of fluffy cotton slowly drifting above the Rhine.

The rhythmic noise drew him closer. Smoke floated out the chimney of a stone farmhouse, nestled along the trees. His stomach churned in response to the aroma of baking bread. Crouched behind the low fence that separated him from his first real meal in weeks he waited. Satisfied it was safe, he stood. Once erect, he attempted to smooth his uniform as he walked toward the sound of the axe. The farmer's wife, her stout frame obliterating the doorway, summoned her husband. She started to call "Otto!" a second time, then froze as Beck approached. When she realized he wore a German uniform, she ran toward him, but halted at the sight of his bruised face and disheveled appearance. She regained her composure. "You come with news of my boy?"

Beck stopped, unsure how to respond. The farmer, holding a pitchfork menacingly, came and stood next to his wife. Resisting the urge to look back toward Rheinberg, he leveled his gaze on the farmer. "May I approach?"

The woman clasped her hands together. "Please, do you have news of my Lennard?"

The farmer said nothing.

Beck smiled. Neither the farmer nor his wife noticed the slight hesitation in his response. "I've come to tell you your son is fine, just fine."

She brought both hands to her mouth. "Oh, my prayers have been answered." Sunlight glinted off the tines of the raised pitchfork. Her husband didn't look convinced.

Finally the farmer spoke. "The last letter we received from my boy said he was east of here, yet you come from the west?"

Becks's mind raced. "Sir, I can explain, but I assure you, Lenny—"

"Otto, he calls him Lenny too," the woman said. "Please, how is my boy?"

"May we go inside?" Beck added, "*Bitte?*" Please.

The farmer refused to yield.

His wife pleaded, "Please Otto, he has information for us."

Beck relaxed once the pitchfork lowered and the farmer said, "You must understand, it has been hard on the boy's mother. My name is Otto. Otto Bachmeier. This is my wife Trudy."

Beck shook hands with them both and replied, "I'm Raynard Ostermann. Major Raynard Ostermann." He offered nothing more as he followed the couple into their home. Ostermann ignored the aroma of the freshly cooked breakfast as he looked about. Simple yet comfortable. He searched for a photo that would assist him in continuing his ruse. On the wooden mantel rested a photograph of a soldier, probably no more than eighteen. His youthful and eager appearance looked no different than the hundreds of thousands of German youth serving in the Wehrmacht. Ostermann replaced the photo on the mantel and sat in the chair Otto offered him. "When did you hear from him last?"

The farmer quickly retrieved a letter from a chest of drawers and handed it to their guest. "January. He was in Bitche, along the French border, but we hear nothing since."

"Please Herr Major, what can you tell us?" the woman said.

Ostermann placed the letter on the table after a cursory glance at the front of the envelope. "I assure you, Lenny is fine." Bitche? Must have been with the 25th Panzer-Grenadier division. Beck nodded at the photo and said, "Lenny's no longer a grenadier, he's an unteroffizier with the 36th Grenadier Division."

"But he fought with the 25th. Now you say he's been promoted?" the farmer wanted to know.

"An unteroffizier? How can this be?" his wife said. "That photo was taken only a year ago."

"You will be proud of your son. After a prolonged battle against the Americans at Bitche, additional Wehrmacht troops headed into battle. An American fighter began to strafe a Wehrmacht column the moment a staff car's engine stalled. The fighter circled back preparing for another run just as Lenny yanked the dead driver out of the car, started the engine, and drove the car, with the officer in it, into the ditch. Bullets from the fighter peppered the roadway where the staff car had been moments before. Lenny's quick thinking saved the life of one of the division commanders. This staff officer was attached to the 36th Grenadier Division and he insisted Lenny replace his dead driver." Raynard Ostermann couldn't resist the temptation to smile. "This is how my fellow officers and men got to know him."

The farmer nodded. "Ja, that's our Lenny."

Ostermann continued. "After the American's pushed us east, in April we surrendered near Iserlohn in the Ruhr valley. From there we marched to a prisoner camp in Büderich, to the north. We've been prisoners since the end of April."

The woman looked at her husband before she said, "If they've set you free, where is our Lenny?"

"I received word that my mother was dying in Essen. As an officer, I was released. Lenny inquired if I would follow the river south. I told him I would so he described your farm and told me where to cross the Rhine—"

At that the woman jumped up from the table. "Herr Major, please forgive me, we have been most rude," as she scurried about the kitchen. "I was just calling Otto for his breakfast when you arrived. Please join us."

After consuming a simple meal of bread with jam and fried eggs, the farmer said to his wife, "Trudy dear, gather some food for our guest. It will make his journey easier." While she accomplished this, Raynard Ostermann noticed the farmer wait for his wife to leave the room before saying anything further. "Thank you Herr Ostermann. Thank you for giving me my family back."

Ostermann said nothing.

Within a minute the woman returned carrying a cloth sack stuffed with provisions. "There are some apples we'd been saving, a few potatoes—they're old but still tasty—and some fresh bread."

Ostermann took the sack from the woman. "Herr Bachmeier, Frau Bachmeier. Thank you for your kindness."

"Would you like us to tell Lenny anything when we see him?" the woman said.

"No, just give him a hug and welcome him home. It's been a long struggle."

"Ja, too long," the farmer added, his wife nodding in agreement. Arm in arm in the doorway, they waved as Raynard Ostermann turned and headed east.

Several hundred meters away muttered to himself. "Beck, I can't believe you sometimes. Raynard Ostermann—where the hell did you come up with that?" He chuckled. "If Lenny boy does ever does come home, they'll spend hours trying to figure out who the fuck Raynard Ostermann is. And if he doesn't return, they'll think their precious little Lenny died a hero."

Out of sight, he turned toward Hamburg. Three hundred and fifty kilometers is a long way on foot, but if I keep at it and the roads are passable I should be able to put forty to sixty kilometers a day behind me. If that's the case I could be in Hamburg in a week, provided I find food along the way. Beck slipped his hand in the sack and tore off a piece of bread. This should keep me going for three days. He then opened it and looked inside. No, four.

chapter 56

Sermaize-les-Bains
4 July 1945

"Madame Dubois? Madame Dubois?" Father Feuillerat scratched his head. "I wonder where she's off to?"

While Father Feuillerat searched for his housekeeper, Hans stepped into the living room and looked about. Numerous small picture frames decorated every table in the room. Why on earth would a priest have so many photos?

Father Feuillerat walked back to his study and called out, "Madame Dubois?"

Hans leaned over to examine one of the images. When he heard footsteps, he set framed photo down.

"Those are my parents and the children are my brother's. Even though I don't have a wife, I'm still grateful to have a family."

Hans remained silent.

"Everyone's surprised when they see all the photos. Richard—my brother—he never travels to Sermaize-les-Bains. Before the war, if I wished to see my nieces and nephews, I had to go to them." The priest picked up a photograph of a child standing next to a wagon. "She's my favorite niece. They named her Françoise, after me." A broad smile settled on his face. "But she didn't inherit my disposition. I fear she's a bit temperamental."

Both turned in the direction of the cellar door as it opened. A slightly stooped woman emerged from the stairway, her hair tied in a neat bun that made her appear five centimeters taller.

"Ah, there you are Madame Dubois. You mustn't have heard me calling."

She set her broom down and leaned it against the wall. Her narrow, pursed lips curled downward at both corners. "I heard you alright, but I was busy in the cellar."

"Ah, very well then," Father Feuillerat said. "Madame Dubois, I would like you to meet Hans, the soldier I told you about."

"It's a pleasure to meet you, Madame Dubois."

The woman ignored Hans' hand. "So you're that German officer Father said to expect?"

Hans smiled nonetheless. "Yes, I've been a prisoner-of-war. Monsieur Ferrand and Father Feuillerat have arranged for my work-release to assist on the Ferrand farm."

"I'm sure they have," was all she said.

Hans looked at Father Feuillerat not sure how to respond.

"Well now," the priest said quickly, "can you prepare us a meal? We're both famished, not to mention exhausted from our journey."

Father Feuillerat picked up Hans' bag to escort him to his room. As they walked down the hall, the creaking floors reminded Hans of his parent's apartment in Berlin. Running his hand along the woodwork cemented the memory. Just before the end of the hall, he resisted the temptation to peer past the open door of the priest's room.

Father Feuillerat set his suitcase down inside the guest room. "It shouldn't take Madame Dubois more than an hour. See you then."

▪   ▪   ▪   ▪   ▪

Hans entered the dining room only to find his host uncorking a bottle of wine. Once seated, the priest poured two glasses and toasted his guest. "To a successful journey. And tomorrow."

Hans raised his glass and nodded. "And many thanks to you and Monsieur Ferrand."

When the door from the kitchen swung open, Father Feuillerat inhaled deeply. "Madame Dubois, your efforts in the kitchen smell wonderful."

The woman said nothing and placed a plate in front of Father Feuillerat followed by Hans' plate. Before leaving she said, "It's the best I could do on such short notice, I'm sure you understand."

Hans looked at both plates but said nothing. A portion of meat twice the size of his took up the center of Father Feuillerat's plate. A full potato with gravy sat next to the meat. His potato—half the size of the priest's—had no gravy.

"I must apologize for Madame's boorish behavior." Before he could respond, the priest exchanged plates. "I insist. After all, you're my guest ... "

Hans, unable to discern Father Feuillerat's mumblings, attempted to reassure him. "Father, I understand, believe me. The war has affected everyone."

Father Feuillerat pushed himself away from the table. "Thank you, now eat up and enjoy. *Bon appétit*! I'll see where Madame Dubois has hidden the cheese."

Hans sat at the table and finished his meal. Voices could be heard coming from the study. Their intensity compelled him to gather the tableware, plates, and glasses and return them to the kitchen. In silence, he returned to his room.

▪　▪　▪　▪　▪

" ... I've already told you, I'm not insisting that you like *all* Germans. All I'm asking is that you consider how rude you've been and what I've told you about *this* German." Father Feuillerat lifted both arms heavenward and sighed. "You've been my housekeeper how long? In all those forty-odd years I've never known you to act this way. I'm telling you, Lorraine, I know this man's heart." Not only was it the first time he had ever called her by her first name, it was the first time she'd ever heard him raise his voice in anger. "Consider this fact. If he were the devil you think he is, why did he risk his life to save Aimée and her family last August?"

Madame Dubois eased herself into a chair, nodded slowly but didn't reply. With her handkerchief, she dabbed at the corner of her eyes.

Father Feuillerat, before leaving the room, patted her kindly on the shoulder. From the doorway he looked back to see her staring out the window. He prayed her thoughts would soften by morning.

chapter 57

Rotenberg, Germany
4 July 1945

FINDING HAMBURG'S OHLSDORF CEMETERY GUIDED KARL BECK'S every step; finding food and freedom occupied his every thought. In the meadow camp he tolerated the hardships soldiers are trained to endue, but the soldiers of the Wehrmacht never trained to be starving refugees. He did not appreciate being one of the hundreds of thousands wandering about Europe, all in search of their next meal. Indeed, the sense of entitlement Nazi officers acquired during the course of war afforded him little good and even less privilege. Regardless, he knew himself to be above it all. In fact, if the refugees even suspected he served as an officer and in some way was responsible for their and Germany's seemingly hopeless state, it didn't concern him in the least.

In spite of his hunger, the first week's travel had progressed well as warm temperatures and little rain allowed restful nights, usually in a farmer's barn, concealed in the hayloft where stolen eggs supplemented his meager diet. The need to avoid British and American troops and their questions prolonged his journey beyond the ten days he'd initially anticipated. Further, he avoided urban areas—bombed out cities—and the near starvation its citizens and refugees endured. Bremen was one such city. The last two years of the war its 300,000 inhabitants had been subjected to brutal bombings by the combined

Allied air corps. With no hope of immediate relief, much of the city lay destroyed as its starving citizens struggled to survive.

It was for another reason he traveled south toward the small medieval city of Rotenberg. By the spring of 1945, everyone knew Germany had lost the war. Accordingly, the Allies withheld the artillery bombardment that would have reduced the city to another pile of ancient timber and cobblestone. As he stood at the foot of the ancient wall, next to the city's entrance, Beck was surprised to find Rotenberg just as he remembered it.

Throughout the 1930s the Nazi party promoted tourism to Bavaria and in so doing, Rotenberg, after *Kristallnacht*—the Night of Broken Glass—became one of the first German cities to systematically and quietly purge itself of Jews. In doing so, it became a model of Hitler's *Strength Through Joy* campaign. Tourists from all over the world flocked to the ancient city hoping to find the source of Hitler's near-magical success in creating a new and triumphant Germany. No one saw the truth.

In 1936 on the very spot he now stood, he'd visited with a man from New York City—a German native living and working in America. He'd been amazed by the man's lack of an accent after only five years. His stories about America seemed, at the time, outlandish and totally unbelievable. Did he return to the Fatherland or did he stay in America? What was his name again? A common name, started with an S. I remember scribbling his name on the margin of the map.

Now, having witnessed the power of the United States military and its unlimited resources, Beck frequently thought of New York City—and that man who kindly offered to take a photo of father and daughter—a photo he would give anything to hold again.

He cherished few memories, but the Bavarian vacation with his daughter, then just a fourteen-year-old girl who loved her father more than anything, meant the most. Katrin, why did you have to do it? Couldn't you have resisted them in other ways? Funny how I'm one of *them* now, another rabbit running from the wolf.

Within the thick stonewalls of Rotenberg, his memories of that vacation ebbed and flowed like the tide. On the steps of the church he sat to watch a young mother and her child. He guessed her to be Katrin's age. The fucking bastards, why'd you kill her? Were you so afraid of a twenty-one-year-old woman you had to execute her? He suppressed the thought about the grandchild he would never have and looked across the cobblestone street at the Red Cross distribution center. Motionless, he observed the bread line like an animal stalking its prey. Good, no one asking for papers.

Standing in line, he remained silent. His blank stare didn't differ from the others as they waited to receive their single loaf of bread. Only the monotonous, "Next ... Next ... Next ..." came from the mouth of the aid worker. Forty-five minutes later Beck placed a small loaf of bread in the linen sack he'd received from Otto and Trudy Bachmeier eight days earlier and looked northeast toward Hamburg.

▪ ▪ ▪ ▪ ▪

To pass the time when he walked, Beck estimated, then counted out loud the steps between landmarks. After eight hours and tens of thousands of strides, Beck—fifty kilometers from Hamburg—began his usual search for a barn in which to seek shelter. On the northern edge of Tostedt, he discovered what he'd been seeking. The stone farmhouse stood close to the barn. He walked well past the farmhouse, then doubled back using the barn to shield his approach. At the side of the barn he stood silent and listened. Good, no one's performing chores. He slipped past the door. The sun's light filtered through tree leaves to the west of the barn, barely providing the needed light for him to find his way to where the hens laid their eggs each and every day. Depositing two into his sack, he climbed up to the haymow and created his space in the corner. From the sack Beck removed what remained of the loaf and set it on his bent knee. On an upright beam he cracked open both eggs and devoured each in a single gulp. A piece of bread followed the second egg. He smiled as he unscrewed the canteen and let water pour down his throat. He then tore the remaining bread into six pieces and one after the other, placed each on his tongue; he savored its taste a long moment before swallowing. Once the final piece of bread disappeared behind his Adam's apple, he took the day's last sip of water. Lying back in the hay, he clasped both hands behind his neck and took in the remaining light while his mind tried to imagine what awaited him in Hamburg.

With any luck, only one more days' travel.

▪　▪　▪　▪　▪

It took most of the morning for Beck to replenish his provisions for the coming night—two potatoes, a small loaf of bread, two more stolen eggs, and a canteen of water. On the outskirts of Hamburg he ignored the squalor along the demolished streets. Refugees walked with no known destination, some carrying a bag, other pulling a wooden cart. All had one thing in common—hunger.

He searched for any building that might provide the assistance he sought. The swept sidewalk and conspicuous absence of debris outside a post office drew him closer. The front door, wedged open, revealed a woman, bent over, attempting to rearrange shelves behind the counter unaware of anyone studying her. A pale complexion made her appear older.

Beck cleared his throat. "I'm sorry to interrupt, can you direct me to the Ohlsdorf cemetery?"

The woman placed her right hand on her lower back and winced as she stood upright. She looked at the man standing before her, first at his dusty shoes, then his pants, and finally, she took in his worn face and unkempt whiskers. "If it's the dead you're seeking, I'd suggest you look in the street."

He ignored her lament. "I'm seeking Ohlsdorf cemetery."

She pointed to the northeast. "Cross the river as best you can. At the center of Hamburg, you'll find Hufnerstraße. Follow this north until you come to Fuhlsbüttlerstraße, follow that east. You'll find Ohlsdorf cemetery on the right."

"Thank you. Two more things if I may?" He didn't wait for a reply. "Where's the city hall and can you spare me a pencil?"

"City hall lay in ruins." She opened a drawer and handed over a useless stub of pencil. "Bombs destroyed the government offices."

Beck suppressed a smile as he shook his head in feigned sympathy. "Where is the city hall now?"

She pointed more to the west. "They moved it to the *flakturm* bunker on Feldstraße, near the center of the city."

Beck doffed his cap and said, "You've been most helpful."

The woman simply returned to rearranging her shelves.

▪　▪　▪　▪　▪

Four hours later Beck stood at the entrance to Ohlsdorf cemetery. As he crossed Fuhlsbüttlerstraße he retrieved a piece of paper from his pocket, one he had committed to memory, the one he consulted regularly. He squinted at the faded lines of a crude map drawn from Jonas Keller's description of the cemetery. *Two hundred meters east, twenty-five to the north I should find a monument of a mother and child. Oeling, that's the name.* He hastened his pace and concentrated on counting by threes with each step. At sixty-five he looked to his left. Out of habit, he looked around. Seeing no one, he wandered amongst the tombstones. His eyes darted from marker to marker east of the frozen mother and child. He walked past the granite statue and stood at the foot of Gerhard Keller's grave. Without a moment's hesitation, his eyes fixated on the marker to the west and the sod surrounding it. *Yes, Friedrich Gruen, just where that fool Keller told me you'd be.*

He forced himself not to appear interested in any one marker, as if on a Sunday stroll. Now, I must find the marker for someone born in 1893, but died soon after. Passing countless graves of fallen soldiers, all from the first war, all born in 1893 or 1894, he dropped to his knees in front of a simple, unadorned marker just beyond a fence surrounding the graves of an entire family. He removed the pencil stub and crumpled paper from his pocket, smiling as he wrote. Harold Faber, 21 July 1893. No one heard him say, "Perfect, died 15 August 1894. Harold Faber, I like it."

▪   ▪   ▪   ▪   ▪

Two hours of shuffling through the Red Cross food line gave him the time needed to solidify his plan and think through the story he had to tell. His meager allotment of bread scarcely lasted two blocks. By the time he found his way to the flakturm bunker, he'd rehearsed his newly fabricated history at least a dozen times. Outside the seven story concrete building he lingered to observe the British guards. Only when he realized no one entering the building was challenged, did he enter the concrete structure. With its anti-aircraft guns on the roof and built to withstand the Allied bombing, the monstrous structure stuck out like a lone tree on a frozen windswept plain. Not a single building stood intact within a thousand meters and the only section of cleared street lay in front of the building he'd just entered.

Beck found his way to the second floor and cursed upon discovering yet another line of refugees. Goddamned swine, why are they everywhere I go? Ninety minutes later his turn arrived.

Remember, she needs to know you don't want new identity papers. "Excuse me, how do I go about procuring replacement copies of my identity papers?"

The clerk behind the desk looked up. "Where are your papers? You should have them."

He looked unperturbed. "I know. I—I mean our regiment surrendered in the Ruhr and the Americans, they—they just recently released me—"

"Then you should have papers. I need to see your papers."

Beck exhaled slowly. "Yes, yes, yes. I know this, but on my way to Hamburg a band of marauders attacked me." He then unbuttoned his shirt and turned his neck to expose what remained of the bruising he'd suffered from the beating in the meadow camp. "They took what food I had as well as my papers."

The clerk hesitated.

"I returned to Hamburg to find my family—my wife and my son—and discovered they perished in the bombings."

The clerk withdrew a form from the desk. "I may be able to help you if you were born in Hamburg—"

"*May* be able to help?" Calm. Be calm.

"Yes, almost all of our records were destroyed by the fire bombing—"

"What am I to do?" His mind raced. "I must have identity papers."

The clerk dropped her pencil onto her papers. "As I was trying to say, the only records we have are birth records prior to 1900. If you were born after 1900, we must have records from the Wehrmacht or the Americans. This is what the British authorities now mandate."

His relief was immediate. "1893. I was born in 1893."

"Then I can help you." The clerk straightened the form in front of her. "Name, date of birth and father's name."

Father's name? Damn it. Damn it all anyway. Think, who else was buried there? After a pause the clerk failed to notice, Beck said, "Harold Faber, 21 July 1893. My father was August … August Faber."

The clerk pointed to some chairs along the wall. "Wait over there Herr Faber and I'll locate your birth records. With a birth certificate your new identity papers will be available tomorrow."

His pulse raced as three British soldiers and an officious looking man in a suit approached the clerk's desk. He tried to determine the nature of their conversation. When they didn't look his way, he returned to thinking about retrieving the documents Jonas Keller hid. I'll go after dark, the cemetery should be a perfect place to sleep for the night. Now that I think about it, I'll wait until dawn to dig up the documents, no sense risk having them stolen while I sleep.

He failed to hear the clerk.

"Herr Faber ... Herr Faber." With no response, the clerk stepped from behind her desk and touched him on the shoulder. "Herr Faber, all is in order."

He stood up, somewhat startled. "I'm sorry, I was daydreaming." He grasped what she handed over and said, "Thank you. Thank you very much."

"This birth certificate will work for now, but we still need a photograph. Follow me. Once we have your photo Herr Faber, your identity papers can be claimed tomorrow after two o'clock."

Harold Faber smiled as he followed the clerk to the photographer.

chapter 58

Rheinberg Meadow Camp
4 July 1945

PETER WIPED THE GRITTY SWEAT FROM HIS brow. What I wouldn't give for some shade. Simmering waves danced across the parched ground before the largest collection of humanity he'd ever imagined. He paused, set his suitcase down, and said, "Oh my God, I thought the first camp was bad. How can they possibly feed all these men?" Then the reality of it hit him—they can't. He resisted the urge to walk along the perimeter shouting his brother's name. To his right a sentry approached. In his best English he said, "Do you spoke German?"

"You mean, Do you *speak* German?"

Peter nodded enthusiastically. "Ja. Ja. Sprechen Sie Deutsch?"

The sentry came to a stop and reassured him that he did indeed speak a little German.

"My name is Peter Krüger. I have come to find my brother. Is it possible for me to speak with the Commandant?"

The sentry looked along the wire perimeter in both directions, then into the center of the camp. "No, but the man by the wooden building, that's Sergeant Veit." He pointed at the only other American soldier in sight. "Tell them at the gate I told you to ask for him."

"Will they assist me?"

"They should. Sergeant Veit's on the colonel's staff. He may

292

be able to assist." Before he turned to resume his patrol the sentry added, "He's fluent in German."

▪   ▪   ▪   ▪   ▪

Peter slowly walked the perimeter until he came to the gate. He couldn't take his eyes off the sea of green and grey trousers and bare chested men. Before the guard could say anything, he said, "Sprechen Sie Deutsch?"

The soldier shook his head. "Nein."

Peter tried again, this time in English. "May I converse to Sergeant Veit? Please."

The soldier looked over his shoulder and shouted to the man in front of Colonel Riley's office. "Hey Sarge! Somebody over here wants to talk to you."

▪   ▪   ▪   ▪   ▪

Sergeant Veit turned to see the guard standing next to a man holding a suitcase. "Me?" *Who the hell wants to talk to me?*

"Yeah you. He asked for you by name."

Peter set his suitcase down and mopped his brow again and waited.

Before the sergeant stood a man who looked vaguely familiar. *That voice, I've heard it before. The clothes and suitcase were British yet the man seemed Nordic.* "I'm Sergeant Veit."

Peter hesitated, then looked out over the tens of thousands of former German soldiers. "I'm looking for my brother, he's here in this camp."

You've got to be kidding me. "I'm sorry to disappoint you, but there are tens of thousands of men here. It's"—the doubtful look on his face persisted—"impossible to locate just one man."

Undaunted, Peter said, "But I've come all the way from England."

Sergeant Veit stepped toward the gate next to the guard. "Do you have papers?"

Peter reached into his pocket. "Yes. I was recently released from a prisoner-of-war camp in England." He passed the papers through the gate. "I'm looking for my brother, Hans."

He handed the papers back after only a cursory look. "Sorry. We can't be of assistance. Come back in a month, we may have more information. I would suggest you see the priest, Father Rentz, in Rheinberg. He might know what to do."

With his head down, Peter turned and began to walk south, away from Rheinberg.

Sergeant Veit ordered the soldier to open the gate. "Herr Krüger! Wait a moment, let me show you the way." When the gate closed behind him he said to the guard, "Tell the lieutenant I'll be back in a minute. This man's headed in the wrong direction." Well beyond earshot of the sentry, he said, "Peter, keep walking as if I am giving you directions." Dan raised his arm and pointed toward Rheinberg. "Hans is alive and well."

Peter stopped. "You know my brother?"

"Please keep moving."

As they walked, he told about Christmas Eve and how he and Hans had met again in the camp. The first time Dan mentioned Sermaize-les-Bains, Peter's stunned look turned to a smile. "Did he tell you about Aimée?"

Now Dan grinned. "Did he tell me about her? I mailed her a letter after I got back behind our lines. I know she got it because her father—"

"Monsieur Ferrand. You know Monsieur Ferrand?"

"And Father Feuillerat."

"Father who?"

"I can see there's much you don't know." Sergeant Veit looked at his watch. "I must be back for a staff meeting." The disappointment on Peter's face forced him to linger. "Don't worry. Continue on to Rheinberg and stop at the rectory at St. Peter's. Tell Father Rentz who you are."

"He will help me?"

"He'll know what to do. He's the one who put Hans on the train to Sermaize-les-Bains."

"Hans? In Sermaize-les-Bains?"

"Father Rentz. He'll tell you and if I'm not mistaken, he'll see to it that you're on the train tomorrow." Sergeant Veit hesitated. "Before I forget, do you speak French?"

"*Oui, assez.*" Yes, enough.

"*Bon.*" Good. "And one last thing, once you get to Sermaize-les-Bains, give your brother my regards." Before continuing, he looked in the direction of the camp. "And, there's something vital you must tell your brother. Tell him Karl Beck escaped and that he knows your brother's in Sermaize-les-Bains. But most important of all, he knows of Aimée. Don't forget. Karl Beck knows about Aimée. He'll understand."

chapter 59

Sermaize-les-Bains, France
5 July 1945

Hans awoke with a start, momentarily disoriented. For the moment, he remained in bed. *How could I have slept so hard? Last night I thought the chiming clock would keep me awake forever.* As he yawned and stretched, his toes poked beneath the bedding. *It can't be much past 8:00.* He rubbed his eyes, rolled over onto an elbow and looked out the window. *I'd say 8:30, 8:45 at the latest.* When the mantel clock chimed, he counted. *One, two, three … eight, nine … Ten!* He threw the covers back and sprang from the bed. *No, it can't be.* Reaching for his clothes on the chair, he muttered, "No one sleeps thirteen hours."

He opened the door in response to the light rap. Father Feuillerat stuck his head inside. "I thought I heard the floor squeak. As soon as you're ready, there's breakfast for you." He looked about the room and added, "Please, don't bother with the bed. Madame Dubois will see to it."

"It's no bother, besides, I'm not sure she knows the war's ended."

Father Feuillerat laughed. "We had a little visit last night before she left. Like all God's creatures, she's better after a good night's sleep. In fact, I'm not at all surprised by her idea to draw you another bath later this morning."

▪ ▪ ▪ ▪ ▪

Under normal circumstances, a simple breakfast of an egg, croissant, and coffee would have taken but a few minutes to consume, never more than an hour, but once Father Feuillerat finished asking a question, Madame Dubois would reappear from the kitchen and ask one of her own. He wondered if Father Feuillerat had told Madame Dubois anything about the 29th of August. He was certain Father Feuillerat told her about his father and André's friendship and when she said, "The first time you met Aimée was in 1940?" little doubt remained she knew all the details of their courtship during the war.

Father Feuillerat spoke up. "Now Madame Dubois—"

Hans interrupted. "Father, it's alright, I don't mind."

"You say that now my son, but after two more hours of interrogation you'll regret it."

Madame Dubois threw her head back. "Just ignore him—"

"Here it comes—"

"In Corinthians, it says, 'If any man think that he knoweth anything, he knoweth nothing.'" Madame Dubois smiled at Hans and ignored Father Feuillerat.

Before Hans could respond, Father Feuillerat winked and pushed himself from the table. "If you will excuse me, I have to finish my daily visits. I'll leave you in Madame Dubois' biblical care."

A quick hand on Hans' shoulder prevented him from standing. Father Feuillerat looked at Madame Dubois as he said to Hans, "Remember, André and Elsie are expecting you at 1:00. Aimée's due to arrive at 2:00."

"Yes sir, I'll be there."

Once the door closed, Madame Dubois sat down. "Father didn't ask me to, but I must apologize. Last night my behavior—"

Hans raised his hand. "Think nothing of it. My being here

is an intrusion and food is scarce. No, I'm the one who should apologize."

Madame Dubois twirled the ring on her finger and said, "I can see why Father thinks you're a kind man." Before he could respond, she continued, "So, you first met Aimée in 1940?"

Hans suppressed a smile. "Yes, June and I can't wait to see her again this afternoon."

"Aimée knows nothing of you being here?"

"Nothing. She knows I survived the fighting, nothing more."

Madame Dubois gathered up the dishes and placed them on the tray. "She's such a lovely young woman."

He nodded in agreement and watched her leave the room. Father was right, she is much kinder this morning. When she returned to wipe off the table, he said, "I feel just like I did before walking to her house the night André invited me to supper."

She dried her hands on her apron and sat in the chair next to Hans. "Tell me more."

Hans took a deep breath. "Before walking over I purchased a bottle of *Pouilly-Fuissé* and some flowers."

"Pouilly-Fuissé. You thought of everything."

"Yes, Madame Ferrand expected me to bring a German wine. Anyway, the instant I knocked on the door Claire opened it and there stood Aimée." He paused, closed his eyes and leaned back in his chair. "She was stunning. Her beautiful black hair such a contrast to her crisp white blouse. And all that lovely hair was tied back with a blue ribbon." He leaned forward and looked at Madame Dubois. "But you know what?"

She nodded anxiously.

"Her eyes are what captivated me."

"What kind were they?"

"Excuse me?"

"The flowers, what kind were they?"

"Irises. Lavender ones with a wonderful fragrance."

"Oh my, Pouilly-Fuissé and irises. How did you know to bring irises?"

"I didn't. In the shop I had a choice, either a bouquet of daisies—but that seemed too plain—or irises. I bought the irises, they seemed perfect."

"Ah, they were. It's no secret Aimée's mother forever stops along the road and picks the wild irises."

Hans looked around the room for a clock, then cleared his throat. Finally, he said, "If you'll excuse me, I really must be getting cleaned up. After all, there's a surprise to prepare for."

Madame Dubois kept talking. "After the last war ended love was forever in the air. And my Jean-Paul—God rest his soul—wouldn't leave me alone. My father couldn't send him away but he wanted to send me away. 'For my own good' is what Papa would say." She blushed as she said, "But this yenta—that's what Father sometimes calls me—has kept you too long."

Hans stood and bowed his head. "Thank you, Madame Dubois."

She shooed Hans out of the dining room. "I've prepared a bath and set out some clothes that should fit better than what you wore yesterday. Father set his shaving supplies out." Hans smiled when he heard her mumble, "Imagine two priests thinking they could dress him proper for a reunion with his Aimée."

▪ ▪ ▪ ▪ ▪

On his walk through Sermaize-les-Bains, Hans avoided eye contact with those he encountered and wearing the clothes Madame Dubois set out, he blended into the countryside like any other Frenchmen. The only suspicious thing about him was the package under his arm. He smiled as he envisioned Madame Dubois scurrying out to the garden and cutting the irises and wrapping them in paper while he bathed. Once in the countryside, the aroma of a recently mowed field wafted on the gentle breeze barely stirring the weeds in the road ditch. A jay perched in a tree along the road scolded as he stopped to admire the landscape. For at least the tenth time he smoothed his hair, looked down at his shoes, and assured himself all was in order.

His thoughts wandered. So much has happened since I held her last August, will she even recognize me? André reassured me she received my letter, but will she marry me? How could she possibly forgive all that I've done?

Without realizing it, Hans found himself halfway down the lane. By instinct he turned and scanned the horizon looking for the Gestapo roaring down the road, kicking up a trail of dust. He smiled at such foolishness. The instant his foot landed on the porch, the door flew open. André spilled out of the house. "Hans my boy, do come in."

Elsie brushed past her husband and stood before Hans. She extended both arms and embraced him, exchanging kisses on both cheeks, then hugged him again.

Hans stepped back, bowed politely and presented his package. "I understand you enjoy irises on your table."

Elsie smiled. "Madame Dubois has been talking, has she?"

André took Hans' arm and escorted him into the house. "What would you expect, she's still breathes, doesn't she?"

Hans paused just a moment as they passed through the living room. His eyes strayed to where he laid the dead bodies. Sitting in the kitchen Hans tried not to notice the corner of the ceiling. The floor was the same, but something had changed. Hans finally gathered his courage. "I can't tell you how wonderful it is to be back in this kitchen."

Silence.

André spoke up. "Since you were here last we painted. It needed some brightening up."

Hans eventually looked at the corner of the ceiling. "Yes, that's it, the paint"—no one noticed his eyes squeeze shut for a brief moment—"I'm sorry I left you with such a mess."

Elsie looked at her husband. "*Mess?* What mess?"

André, quick to respond, pointed to the corner of the ceiling. "It was nothing, the only thing I had to do was patch the hole."

"Do you like the color?" Elsie said.

Hans remained silent. Neither of them know, do they? God bless you Father Feuillerat, God bless you.

André nudged Hans' leg under the table.

"I'm sorry." Hans looked around the kitchen again. "Yes—er yes, I like it."

André smiled. "Good, now that's settled, we've got to get you out to the barn. Aimée will be home soon."

"Where's Claire?" Hans said.

"At work, her uncle's bakery. She knows nothing about any of this," Elsie said. "We thought about telling her, but wanted it to be a surprise for her too."

André got up from the table and went into the living room to look down the lane. "We'd better get Hans to the barn."

Elsie stood and embraced Hans. After she released him she smoothed out his shirt and held his shoulders. "Hans, you know we owe everything to you?"

Hans shrugged.

"I mean it, everything." She kissed him again on both cheeks. "Now outside with you. I promise we won't keep you waiting long."

▪ ▪ ▪ ▪ ▪

"Maman? Papa? I'm home." Aimée placed her overnight bag on the counter next to the irises in the vase, leaned over and inhaled their wonderful fragrance. Elsie entered the kitchen just as Aimée finished sighing.

"Oh Maman, these irises smell lovely. They always remind me of Hans."

"They were cut today."

She noticed the peculiar edge to her mother's voice but said nothing.

"I thought you needed some cheering up."

André joined mother and daughter and looked about. After clearing his throat he said, "A letter arrived this morning. I'm sure it's—"

"Where? Are you sure?" Her eyes darted about the room. "I don't see one. Where?" She looked at her father. "It was from Hans, wasn't it?"

André's face revealed nothing. Acting distracted he said, "I know I had it here somewhere." He got up and began to sift through the papers on the counter. "Yes, I'm sure it was …." He put the stack of papers down then held his index finger aloft. "I know, I had it with me out in the barn. I must have set in on the workbench when I grabbed the hammer to fix the gate." Before André could take a single step, the back door slammed against the wall.

Elsie moved toward the window. "Are you sure it's permissible to leave them out there. I so much wanted to see the look on her face the instant she sees him."

André touched her arm lightly. "Trust me, it'll be fine. Our Hans is an honorable man, on that you can be sure."

▪ ▪ ▪ ▪ ▪

Hans' heart pounded at the slamming of the kitchen door. He hardly had time to smooth back his hair before the barn door flung open. A solid block of sunlight slanted through the darkness. Aimée froze. Her facial features remained in the shadows of her hair, its edges teased by the sunlight. Floating dust radiated like a halo. He held out his arms when she cried, "My God, it's you."

Their embrace was complete and total. After several long impassioned kisses, Aimée lifted her feet off the ground as Hans began to spin. He stopped and kissed her again. Her arms gripped his shoulders and held him closer. As his lips moved toward her shoulder he could feel her quiver. He stroked the nape of her neck and lightly kissed her ear. As he kissed her neck again, her back arched, forcing her chest into his. Hans responded by lifting her off her feet a second time and pressing her body hard against a wooden stanchion. With both hands he caressed her face and lightly touched the tip of her nose with his lips. "God, I've longed for this day."

"Did Papa put you up to this?"

He kept kissing her neck, her back arching all the more. When he gently retracted the edge of her blouse and kissed the skin between her breasts, her breathing intensified.

"Han—"

"Shhh." Hans touched her lips with his outstretched finger, then kissed her again. "No, it was my idea."

"We'd better get back. My parents will know."

"Know what? That I love you." He held her at arms' length, knelt onto one knee and said, "Chérie, will you marry me?"

Aimée began to cry and brought his head to her chest. "Of course I'll marry you."

▪   ▪   ▪   ▪   ▪

Elsie craned her neck to look out the window. "I don't know—"

Before André could respond, she backed away from the window. "It's them, they're coming!"

Aimée bolted through the door and wrapped her arms around her papa, sobbing. "Thank you Papa, and you too, Maman. Thank you!"

Hans, right behind and all smiles, closed the door. No one noticed André place his hand on Hans' shoulder, pinch a piece of straw off the back of his shirt and slip it into his pocket. "Now, let me open a bottle of wine, just like old times. Besides, I suspect we have a wedding to plan."

chapter 60

Saint-Dizier, France
7 July 1945

PETER GRIPPED HIS SUITCASE AND STEPPED ONTO the sunlit station platform. The absence of a breeze hinted at the heat sure to follow. Outside the station, Peter saw fewer and fewer signs of war. Only the occasional hungry face reminded him of Germany, no outward signs of destruction or refugees pushing carts containing their only possessions. Unsure of his surroundings, he followed the passengers into the small terminal. After a quick glance at the clock, he stretched his back and sat down on the wooden bench.

What a night. I thought morning would never come. Yawning again, he inspected his surroundings to confirm no one expressed interest in his presence. He opened his suitcase and removed the paper wrapping containing the last of his dried cheese and bread. On the train he resisted the temptation to open the suitcase and it was only in a lonely corner of the station in Nancy did he dare steal a few bites. Hardly satisfied, he stood and walked over to study the rail map, then approached the ticket window. I hope my accent doesn't sound German. "*Excusez monsieur, quand le train suivant est à Sermaize-les-Bains?*" Excuse me sir, when is the next train to Sermaize-les-Bains?

The ticket agent continued to arrange the papers stacked before him.

Peter repeated himself.

Only after a line began to form did the agent look up and eye Peter with contempt. "There is no train to Sermaize-les-Bains."

Peter felt his pocket for the money he knew was there. "Can I hire a taxi?"

Peter's smile confused the agent and brought him leaning forward over the counter to inspect Peter further. He completed his survey at Peter's head of unkempt hair. "There's no taxi. To reach Sermaize-les-Bains you'll have to walk." The agent looked beyond Peter to the woman standing behind him. "Next."

The woman ignored the man and said to Peter, "Take rue Jeanne d'Arc to the west. There you'll see a sign indicating the way."

Peter smiled. "*Merci, madame, merci beaucoup.*" Thank you, madame, thank you very much. He stepped away from the counter and looked back at the clock. Nineteen kilometers shouldn't take more than four hours. I could be there by eleven, noon at the latest.

▪　▪　▪　▪　▪

Elsie Ferrand knocked on the door before entering her daughter's room. "Aimée, are you up?"

"*Oui*, Maman. I'm just writing a letter to Suzanne. I must tell her the wonderful news before the wedding, not after." The sound of ruffling silk brought her to her feet in an instant. "Oh Maman, it's beautiful, where did you get it?"

She held the white silk wedding dress up to her daughter's shoulders. "Yes, this should fit you perfectly. While you're bathing, I'll take in a stitch or two."

Aimée gathered the dress into her arms and squeezed it tight and twirled around on her toes. "It smells marvelous. It's simply exquisite!"

Elsie smiled. "Yes it is, isn't it? I remembered my friend's daughter, Margaux, in Robert-Espagne looked to be your size and she wore it last month at her wedding. I telephoned and asked if you could borrow it."

"The one who works at the *Mairie*? She agreed? She married Yves, does she know it's Hans I'm marrying?"

Elsie didn't stop to consider her answer. "She must. Didn't even ask if you or Claire needed it."

"All she said was 'Yes,' nothing more?"

"She needs it back by Tuesday. Her cousin's to be married the following weekend and it's promised to her as well."

Aimée ran her hand up and down the smooth panels and across the fine stitches. "Where did she ever get such beautiful material?"

"Margaux's mother said it came from a British parachute. She knew as soon as the war ended Yves would ask for her daughter's hand."

Aimée became still. "Do you think it's permissible to marry Hans even though he didn't come to the house to ask for Papa's approval?"

Elsie clasped her hands around Aimée's and guided her down to the bed. "He did ask your papa."

A smile returned to Aimée's face. "I wasn't sure—"

"Papa told me Hans asked first thing when they were together on the train. You know your papa, he said he hadn't had so much fun watching Hans stammer and squirm asking for your hand since that know-it-all Madame Fillion came to purchase eggs, then drove off with them on the top of her car. But don't worry, he said, 'It's alright, there's still Claire. When her suitor gets around to it, he'll have to come to our home, none of this train business.'"

Aimée inhaled, as if about to speak, but said nothing.

Elsie broke the silence. "Is there something you wish to ask?"

"What if I'm unable to conceive?"

Elsie put her arm around her daughter and squeezed her shoulder. "I'll tell you what your grand-mère told me on the morning of our wedding, before I took the traditional bath to wash away all the thoughts of previous loves—"

Aimée blushed. "Oh Maman, there was no one before Papa, was there?"

Elsie patted her daughter's hand. "Not like that, no. There were a few boys who would call on me, but Grand-père shooed them away."

"Because he liked Papa?"

Elsie laughed. "That's exactly what he'd say and I think he may be right."

Aimée nodded in anticipation.

"Before my bath Grand-mère said, 'Love your man like no other and he will love you in return.'"

Aimée looked confused. "That's it? That's all she said?"

"Yes, but don't you see? If you love Hans as he surely loves you and you share in each other's bodies, it will all take care of itself. Trust me, on this I am certain. You are healthy, Hans is healthy." Aimée turned crimson when her mother added, "I think the problem won't be if you can conceive, it will be how do you stop conceiving?"

"Maman!"

Elsie smiled. "Now try this dress on and while you bathe, I'll take in whatever stitches are needed."

"But Maman, I had no loves before Hans."

"Then wash away your fears and troubles. You have plenty of time before he calls to escort you to the church."

▪ ▪ ▪ ▪ ▪

Aimée called out from behind the partition. "Claire, is that you?"

"Of course it's me, who else would it be?"

"Well, I didn't expect you back so soon. The water couldn't possibly be hot by now."

"That's because Maman got it boiling while I was preparing your dress." Claire brought the copper kettle to the end of the tub. Steam flowed out the spout as the water split the bubbles. "Be careful, I can't see your feet."

Aimée eased down into the water. "Oooh, that's perfect."

Claire settled into a chair on the other side of the partition. "*Aimée?*"

Aimée raised one leg above the suds and rubbed it with a sponge. "Yes."

"Do you remember the first time Hans came to our house?"

"What about it?"

"I'm sorry I was so obnoxious."

Aimée smiled. "You weren't obnoxious."

"Well, I was and I'm sorry."

"Claire, you have nothing to be sorry about. I think we were all so taken by him." Both sisters laughed when she added, "Well maybe not Maman at first."

For several moments the only sound was that of water cascading off Aimée's back before her sister said, "How do you think he did it?"

"Did what?"

"Fooled the Gestapo. How'd he do it?"

Aimée gazed at the sponge in her hand for a long moment. "I don't know. The only thing Papa's ever said is a shot was fired in the kitchen—where he patched the hole by the ceiling—and that it was lucky it didn't hurt anyone. Beyond that, you know as much as I do."

Both remained silent, keeping their own thoughts. Finally Claire spoke up. "When—or should I say if?—I ever marry, will you be my attendant and do my hair?"

"Oh Claire, I know there'll be someone for you."

"When Hans came for supper the first time, I could see it in your eyes. I hope one day people see that in my eyes."

"They will, sooner than you think, but before that, hand me my towel."

▪ ▪ ▪ ▪ ▪

The muffled sound of conversation drifting from the kitchen

stirred Hans from a sound sleep. He dressed quickly, smoothed the bedclothes and followed the aroma of coffee.

Madame Dubois greeted him. "And how's the bridegroom this morning?"

Hans smiled. "Wonderful. Simply wonderful. Did I hear Father Feuillerat?"

"Yes, but he left to make a sick call. I've not seen him so excited since before the war. He told me to remind you to have Aimée at the church at 3:00, no later." Madame Dubois set a bowl of coffee in front of him. "Bread and jam?"

He set his coffee down and said, "Not this morning. I'm a little nervous."

Madame Dubois positioned the chair next to him closer yet and sat down. "Tell me, do you know about French wedding traditions?"

"All I know is I am to walk to Aimée's and escort her to the church."

"By 3:00," Madame Dubois added.

"Yes, by 3:00. Is there more I should know?"

Madame Dubois inched closer and adopted a serious tone. "Indeed there is. We French have a tradition—personally I think it's quite silly—called *le charivari.*"

"And what is this?" Hans inquired. "I don't know this word."

"Le charivari means racket. It's a custom, especially if the bridegroom is from another village, in which friends from this village appear on your wedding night and bang pots and pans outside your door—"

"*Friends?*"

"Yes, friends of the Ferrand family. After they do this thing, you and Aimée are expected to come out in your wedding clothes and provide snacks for these ... these—"

"Friends?"

Madame Dubois smiled then reached over and patted Hans' arm. "Believe it or not, I've heard of such plans for you and Aimée."

"Oh? They would come to the Ferrand's and do such a thing?" Hans said in disbelief.

"They surely will, but they shall be foiled."

"And how is that?"

Madame Dubois adopted a solemn tone in her voice. "Hans, I want you and Aimée to stay at my home for a few days. It's nothing fancy, but I've prepared it for your wedding night." Madame Dubois raised her hand to quell the protest. "I insist. I told Father I wished to take a few days holiday to visit my ailing sister in Nancy. No one would suspect a thing, not even Father."

Hans could see the beginning of a tear in her eyes. "Madame Dubois, I'm honored by such a gesture. How can I ever repay you?"

Madame Dubois smiled. "Allow me to tend your baby from time to time."

At the sight of Hans blushing, Madame Dubois stood abruptly. "I'm just a silly old woman for thinking such thoughts."

Hans responded by giving Madame Dubois a quick hug.

"Before I forget, Monsieur Ferrand left a message with Father that he needed to stop by to see you this morning. But I warn you, he's a prankster. And remember, not a word about my home. No one."

chapter 61

Ohlsdorf cemetery
Hamburg, Germany
7 July 1945

HAROLD FABER HELD THE OILSKIN AND LOOKED at it lovingly like a prospector admiring a solid gold nugget extracted from the mother lode after years of digging. He turned it over, back and forth, then untied the string that sealed it shut. Not a drop of moisture had found its way to the cardboard file he now held in his hand. Undoing the file's clasp, he removed three smaller file folders. SPITZENGEHEIMNIS—TOP SECRET could be read across the top of each. Before proceeding, Faber glanced over his shoulder. Satisfied no one was watching, he removed several photos from the first folder—all black and white, eight by ten inches—and poured over them. "Oh my God," he whispered, "it *is* Eisenhower." If our generals had such drivers, the war would have ended two years earlier. The photos, all taken with a telephoto lens, were of General Dwight Eisenhower and his driver in the back seat of his staff car, an American made Cadillac. Though not totally revealing, imagination was not required. One image in particular, the one the Russians must have leveraged the most, clearly shows a woman, her bare breasts exposed to the camera. A man—obviously Eisenhower—had both hands cupped around the woman's left breast, poised above it, ready to devour its proud, protruding nipple. Faber ignored the beginnings of an erection and quickly grabbed the other file. It contained two sheets of paper, each stamped SPITZENGEHEIMNIS across the front. Starting at the top, he read to himself:

Transcript of TOP SECTET (and recorded) conversation between General Dwight Eisenhower and special Russian envoy, Stanisslav Dotsenko at Supreme Headquarters Allied Expeditionary Force, Trianon Palace Hotel, Versailles, France, 2 April 1945, 1500 hours.

Faber's pulse raced, but not as fast as his thoughts. If only I could remember that man's name. Damn, it's on the tip of my tongue. With it, I'm on my way to New York City. He quickly looked in the third file only to see a small reel of tape. This must be the original recording, the one between Eisenhower and the Russian. When the tape was safely returned to its file, he resumed reading:

STANISLAV DOTSENKO: General, it is most gracious of you to receive me on such short notice.

EISENHOWER: How can I be of assistance to our Russian friends?

STANISLAV DOTSENKO: Let me be blunt General. My government, or should I say, Marshall Stalin would like your cooperation in a very sensitive manner. He wants the Allied advance to halt at the river Elbe.

EISENHOWER: This is utterly impossible. The combined British, French, and American armies are pushing east and plan to unite with your forces in Berlin.

STANISLAV DOTSENKO: Yes, Marshall Stalin realizes this, but he feels you should allow us to take Berlin. He expects the Allied forces to wait for the Russian forces at the Elbe, then halt their advance.

EISENHOWER: I see. And leave most of Europe to Marshall Stalin.

STANISLAV DOTSENKO: General, I'm here to discuss strategy, not politics.

EISENHOWER: Impossible. This is totally out of the question.

STANISLAV DOTSENKO: (sound of briefcase unlocking) We assumed that would be your response, General. But as you can see, these photographs would suggest your driver—Kay Summersby, that is her name isn't it?—drove more than just your car.

— inaudible —

As I was saying General, Marshall Stalin would greatly appreciate your cooperation in this, how should we say, this delicate matter.

— long silence —

EISENHOWER: And just what am I supposed to do? The 21st Army Group is expecting to be on the outskirts of Berlin within the week?

STANISLAV DOTSENKO: You're the general, you'll think of something. Blame it on Yalta, or Monty. Blame it on Patton for all we care. Better yet, blame it on your new President.

EISENHOWER: And what is to happen with these photos?

STANISLAV DOTSENKO: Marshall Stalin has informed me that you may have them as a reminder, but rest assured, the negatives are in a very safe place, at least for the time being.

EISENHOWER: This is blackmail, you do realize this don't you? You'll never get away with it.

STANISLAV DOTSENKO: I beg your pardon, but Marshall Stalin believes we will. Now if you will excuse me, I must prepare my cable to Moscow. Marshall Stalin doesn't like to be kept waiting.

He gripped the file and instinctively held it close. Jonas Keller's fear hinted of its significance, but this was almost beyond comprehension. Gazing at the photos a second time, the potential magnitude of the power they bestowed instantly sharpened his senses like a sound in the night, but failed to provide the method in which to harness it. For now, he only had one thought: Countries love their heroes, especially victorious ones.

Faber considered his options. In Germany this is useless to me. I must get to America. If I'm ever discovered, this could keep me hidden forever. No, not *could*. Would. His concentration broke momentarily as the corners of his mouth turned upward. But what about Sermaize-les-Bains?

He carefully replaced the files in the oilskin and cinched the flap tight. Staring off into the distance his smile widened. "Eugen Schröder. I wonder, are you still in New York City, Herr Schröder?"

I must find him …

chapter 62

Sermaize-les-Bains
7 July 1945

WHEN MADAME DUBOIS ESCORTED ANDRÉ INTO THE kitchen, Hans jumped to his feet. "Monsieur Ferrand—"

"I insist you call me André."

Hans complied. "Certainly … André."

The awkward silence ended when André said, "Madame Dubois, would you please excuse us a moment. There are some—how shall I say?—personal things to discuss with the bridegroom before he calls on our Aimée."

Madame Dubois winked at Hans before she responded. "Of course. Besides, I have some things I must get at the bakery."

André sat in the chair Hans dragged away from the table and took a deep breath. "I'm not sure where to begin … or how to say—"

"Say what, André? Is there a problem?"

"No, no, nothing of the sort. It's just that I—er, Elsie and I—well, we wonder if you have a ring for Aimée?"

André blushed along with Hans.

"No, I don't. I hope one day I can afford one."

"We thought as much." André stood and reached into his pocket. "We want you to have this. This wedding ring belonged to Aimée's grand-mère. Before she passed she insisted it go to Aimée."

315

Hans looked at André, not sure what to say.

"And"—André unwrapped a small packet—"we want you to have these photos. They are of your mother and father, taken in 1935 while on holiday."

Hans ran his fingers along the edges of the photos, staring. "André, I—I—I don't know what to say ..."

"Say nothing. We know Konrad and Greta will be missed and these photos might make you sad. This is the reason we want you to have them now, not after the wedding when all should be joyful."

Hans stood and embraced André, then kissed him on both cheeks. "Now, no more of this nonsense. There's much to do before you call on us," André said before leaving.

Madame Dubois appeared in the kitchen after the front door closed and said, "I laid your suit of clothes out. Be sure there's no holes in the pockets—you don't want to lose that ring."

▪   ▪   ▪   ▪   ▪

Satisfied with his appearance, Hans nodded and stepped away from the mirror. Before leaving the rectory, he passed his hand over his pants' front pocket. After inspecting it one last time, he slipped it back in his pocket. On the street, people smiled and waved. A group of children pointed as he crossed the intersection. He smiled at the thought of Madame Dubois telling everyone about the wedding. Each step reminded him of the second time he walked from the hotel to the Ferrand's five years earlier. The first time was only to meet the family, the second to pursue his obvious interest in Aimée. Who could have ever predicted I'd be escorting the most beautiful woman in all of France to her wedding? Who indeed? Certainly not me.

He mopped the sweat from his brow and snugged his shirt collar. At the front steps he smoothed back his hair, bent over and wiped the dust off his shoes. Before knocking, he checked the ring and rehearsed what he would say. He hadn't expected Elsie to open the door.

"Madame, may I have your permission to escort Aimée to *Notre Dame de la Nativité?*" Our Lady of the Nativity.

"Hans, don't you look handsome." Elsie stepped to the side. "Won't you please come in?"

"Handsome, indeed," André added from beyond the threshold.

Aimée appeared as the door shut. Hans hesitated before he came toward her, his smile wider than anyone there had ever seen it. When she slipped her hand into his he brought it to his lips and kissed it softly. "Aimée, you're more beautiful than ever." He gently ran the back of his fingers over the flowers adorning her hair. "Simply stunning."

Aimée beamed but said nothing.

André held his hand toward the door. "Tradition demands that you lead the way—for now—at a respectable distance, of course."

Aimée grasped Hans' extended arm as they stepped into the light. At the end of the lane, before turning towards Sermaize-les-Bains, he looked back. André, Elsie, and Claire followed. Assured they remained several paces behind, Hans leaned his head towards Aimée. "Darling, do you remember the first time we walked this road?"

She looked up. "You mean when you stole a kiss where no one could see us?"

"I didn't steal it. As I recall, you let me. It was a most precious gift."

She held his arm close. "You always know just what to say."

Hans smiled, then halted. He ignored the procession as they lingered and gently cupped Aimée's face in both hands and said, "I love you so much. You have no idea how many times I dreamt of this day."

As he was about to kiss Aimée, André blurted out, "None of that before the wedding."

Everyone laughed when Elsie jabbed her husband in the ribs. "If our Hans wants to kiss Aimée, he has every right!"

At the edge of Sermaize-les-Bains several family friends waited. When the wedding party passed, they fell in behind Claire. Hans squeezed Aimée's hand lightly. "I count over thirty. Seems we'll have quite a crowd."

André tapped Hans on the shoulder. "I'm sorry, but now that we have an official procession, I escort Aimée from here. You, I'm afraid, must go to the end. Elsie's there waiting for you."

When Hans leaned towards Aimée, André slid between them. "There'll be plenty of time for that before long." André continued to grin. "For now I must ensure Aimée comes to no harm."

▪ ▪ ▪ ▪ ▪

Aimée looked over her shoulder, blew Hans a kiss, and watched him fall in next to her mother. At the corner several more guests and well-wishers waited. The moment she saw Marjorie's arm waving vigorously, she dropped her father's elbow and the two friends shared an embrace. "I'm so glad you're here."

"And why not? Wouldn't miss it for the world."

Aimée kissed her friend on both cheeks. "Later we must visit."

Marjorie grinned. "Should I bring Madame Bissett's book? After all, it's a German translation, it may come in handy."

"Is there anything you won't say" She hugged her friend one more time before motioning everyone to join the procession. As she and her father rounded the corner, they halted. Stretched across the street a white ribbon blocked their route. Not sure what to do, she glanced at her father.

"Not to worry." André waved to summon Hans forward, removed a pair of scissors from his pocket, and handed them to his daughter. "I figured you'd need these."

"Oh Papa, I totally forgot about scissors—"

"What's the meaning of the ribbon?" Hans said as he took his position next to Aimée.

"I knew the children would be up to their mischief. It's something they do before weddings," André answered. The crowd cheered as the severed ribbon fell to the street. When Aimée handed the scissors back to her father he pocketed them and gently directed Hans to the back of the procession.

Rue de Bénard, as it crossed rue d'Andernay, was lined with several more guests. Several citizens had thrown back the shutters and were extended out the upper story windows waving at the procession as it passed. A block from Notre Dame de la Nativité, as rue de Bénard crossed rue Jean Macé, another ribbon halted their advance. On the other side of the ribbon, Yvonne and Cécile patiently waited. Both clutched a bouquet of fresh flowers. Aimée's smile widened. "Who's routing the calls this afternoon?" she said as Hans joined in cutting the ribbon.

"Ann-Julie from Couvonges," Yvonne said. "She owes us a favor."

Cécile addressed André. "The bride is beautiful, her father must be proud."

Aimée clutched her father's arm. "I'm not sure who is more handsome, Papa or Hans."

André winked. "I'll let Hans think it's him."

She looked across the street to rue du Port when someone pointed and said, "There's Father Feuillerat."

The priest waved the procession towards the church. Aimée turned and looked back at Hans and smiled to see him patting her mother's hand as they talked. She nodded her head in their direction and said, "Papa, did you ever think you'd see such a sight?"

André glanced back at his wife. "Only in my prayers, dear child, only in my prayers."

Father Feuillerat stood and smiled at each guest when they passed. At the front of the church an altar boy heaved the heavy wooden door open. André supported Aimée's hand as they stepped through the opened doorway and down into the sanctuary. A single white ribbon had been draped around each of the granite columns. Flowers adorned the end of each pew, their fragrance still in the air. She leaned into her father's shoulder. "Oh Papa, Yvonne and Cécile, they made things so beautiful."

André led the procession past the pews to the front of the church. Aimée smiled as her father kissed her on the cheek before she sat on the traditional red velvet chair beneath the silken white canopy reserved only for weddings. She turned, looking for Hans. Children scurried through the two smaller doors on either side and hopped down the three steps before finding their parents. Finally, she glimpsed her bridegroom. A tear formed when she observed the smile on her mother's face as he waited for the final guests to be seated before escorting her mother to the seat next to her father. At that moment all she could think about was those long years not knowing. *Thank you for being so kind to Maman after all she put you through.* As he finally took the seat next to her, she gently squeezed his outstretched hand.

Father Feuillerat approached the altar, genuflected and stood erect, his head bowed in prayer. It was only after complete silence filled the church that he crossed himself and turned to face his flock. He smiled and nodded at Aimée and Hans. When she saw Father Feuillerat nod at the altar boy, Aimée knew the wedding mass she'd waited so patiently for was about to begin.

▪ ▪ ▪ ▪ ▪

Hans continued to hold Aimée's hand as the Bible lessons were read. His mind wandered to the first time he'd set foot in the church almost a year ago and how surprised he was at the expansive sanctuary. He admired the smooth granite columns supporting the roof and marveled at the age of the stonewalls on either side of the columns before his eyes settled on the altar and crucifix. It's no wonder I never noticed those three stained glass panels that day. He gazed at the colorful windows. What do they depict, stations of the cross? Joan d'Arc, perhaps? He thought of his first meeting with the priest standing before him. He squeezed his eyes shut when he recalled all he'd confessed.

Aimée nudged Hans with her elbow. He lifted her hand to his lips and kissed it softly. He inclined his head into hers and whispered, "I'm sorry, I was thinking of last August."

She whispered, "I know."

chapter 63

TEN KILOMETERS NORTH OF SAINT-DIZIER—HALF THE DISTANCE to Sermaize-les-Bains—Peter turned and stepped off the road when he heard the sputtering motor. The farmer behind the wheel of the small truck doffed his cap. Several meters past, it came to a stop. Peter clutched his suitcase and ran towards the waving farmer.

"*Allo. Avez-vous besoin d'un trajet?*" Do you need a ride?

Peter hoped his accent wouldn't betray him. "Thank you, I'm on my way to Sermaize-les-Bains."

"*Escalade à bord de.*" Climb aboard.

Peter extended his hand and smiled. "My name's Peter."

"Jacques. Jacques Gallois." The farmer glanced at Peter as he shifted gears. "You have business in Sermaize-les-Bains?"

"Yes, I'm on my way to Andre Ferrand's farm."

The farmer nodded and grinned. "You've come for the wedding?"

Peter sat straight. "Wedding?"

"The oldest daughter, Aimée." He glanced at his watch and added, "This afternoon she's marrying that German soldier, the one who saved the family last August from the Gestapo." The man considered Peter's face at length. "Come to think of it, you look like the soldier I used to see from time to time."

"He's my brother."

"And they're not expecting you?"

"Oh no, not in the least." Peter could all but palpate his mounting anticipation. "I can hardly wait to see the look on Hans' face."

"How long's it been?"

"A lifetime," he said, before adding, "No, three lifetimes."

▪   ▪   ▪   ▪   ▪

When the truck came to a stop Peter stepped down and waved as Monsieur Gallois sped off in a cloud of dust. From the end of the lane, it was only natural to admire the farmhouse he'd envisioned in his daydreams. He wiped the sweat from his brow and looked around, straining to see movement within the home. Footfalls on the porch followed by a knock failed to announce his presence. *A. Ferrand*, in small script, had been painted on the door. He knocked a second time. All that could be heard was the faint tolling of church bells in the distance, nothing more. Through the window next to the door he peered inside. A bouquet of fresh iris rested on the hall table.

Stepping down off the porch he walked around the house, set his suitcase by the back door, and began walking toward the direction of the bells. I bet everyone's already at the church.

From his vantage point on rue de St-Dizier above Sermaize-les-Bains, Peter caught sight of a church steeple. He glanced at his watch when he realized the bells had stopped. The ceremony must have started already. His pace accelerated as he walked down the hill into town. I bet everybody's at the church. Just past a main boulevard, he caught a glimpse of the steeple again.

In the shade of a tree on the bank of the Saulx River across from Notre Dame de la Nativité, he smoothed his hair, adjusted his shirt, and wiped his brow. I hate to walk in looking like this. Come on Peter, don't be foolish, everyone will understand.

Stained glass windows flanked a large wooded door located in the middle of the north wall. Smaller doors were situated on each side of the church façade. The stained glass prevented him from seeing anything more than shapes. He strained to hear the faint echoes of a homily. Back at the front of the church, he considered which door to open. Discovering that both smaller doors were locked, he placed his right hand on the doorframe of the larger door in the center and gently tugged the worn wrought iron handle.

▪ ▪ ▪ ▪ ▪

André knew—as did everyone else in the parish—Father Feuillerat never allowed the door hinges to be oiled. The priest figured out long ago if the loud squeak didn't ensure parishioners would be punctual for Mass, the turning heads would. By the time all his fellow parishioners had turned their attention back to the homily, André was still focused on the back of the church. He thought he noticed a man standing along the back wall, deep in the shadows.

Elsie's nudge brought his attention back to the altar, but did nothing to remove the puzzled look on his face.

"… Yes, my friends, we have all endured a long, long struggle. Not one of us has been spared the pain and sorrow"—André noticed more than a few handkerchiefs were in use—"of that terrible day in August. But I stand here to remind you of the intense joy we all felt when the Allies liberated Sermaize-les-Bains days later. And I stand here, as your priest, to celebrate in yet another joy.

"But before we do, let me remind all of you that struggles are not new. They define the human condition for they have plagued mankind for eons." Father Feuillerat leveled his gaze on the bride and groom. "And on your walk this morning, you two encountered many white ribbons." André could feel the muscles of his face widen into a generous smile when he thought of his own wedding twenty-four years earlier. "As silly as this old tradition might seem, these ribbons symbolize the many obstacles you two will face in your married life. Cutting them together is a reminder that as one, the many struggles you shall face—and there will be struggles I assure you—can be overcome."

The priest looked about the sanctuary before focusing only on the bride. "Aimée, I've known you all your life. I still recall your Baptism and First Communion. You've matured into a fine young woman and a resourceful creature. Now you must learn to accept your husband's assistance in facing life's struggles.

"Hans, you now have Aimée ..."

André remembered the squeaky door. Realizing he hadn't heard anyone slip into the last pew, he turned again to scan the back of the church. His jaw slackened. *No, it cannot be, it's impossible.*

Elsie drew her husband's arm close and whispered. "What are you doing? This is your daughter's wedding."

André continued to stare and with a canted head and quizzical look, mouthed *Peter?*

▪   ▪   ▪   ▪   ▪

The eight foot high door was much heavier than Peter imagined it would be. His initial tug barely budged it. With a firm pull, the door opened, the loud squeak arresting his efforts in an instant. Through the narrow opening he peered inside. Past the shadows in the back of the church, colored light danced through stained glass. A shaft of sunlight enveloped Hans and Aimée. His pulse raced. Ignoring the squeak, he slowly opened the door further, then slid through with his back against the door. With equal care, he let the heavy door close. *Good, that's over.* He felt invisible in the shadows. As the priest continued his homily, he tiptoed to the last pew, sat alone along the aisle, and listened.

"... to care for and to love. Lord knows you did the impossible a year ago"—*Why is everyone looking at my brother?*—"Hans, I know your heart and I know you'll be a loving husband and provider."

Peter smiled when Aimée blushed after the priest added, "And God willing, a loving father ..." His thoughts skipped to Berlin, then to England and Dresden. He bowed his head in prayer when he remembered their mother and father. As the mass continued, he contemplated his older brother. *You're not as thin as I expected you to be.* His eyes shifted to Aimée. *Hans, you were right, she is as beautiful as a summer's day.* When he realized the couple seated behind Hans and Aimée must be Monsieur and Madame Ferrand, he thought of his own parents. *Hans, do you know of Mother and Father?* Peter then studied the young lady seated next to Madame Ferrand, her yellow dress brightened by her black hair. *Claire. Yes, that must be Claire. She's just as beautiful as her sister.*

His thoughts faltered when the man—the one who must be Monsieur Ferrand—turned to look at Hans and then back again. Peter nodded enthusiastically when he realized Monsieur Ferrand correctly deduced his identity.

With his back to the parish, the priest lifted the cup of wine toward the crucifix above the altar. Peter, unable to hear what was said, silently prayed the words he knew by heart. *Take this, all of you, and drink from it. This is the cup of my blood, the blood of the new and everlasting covenant. It will be shed for you and for all so that sins may be forgiven. Do this in memory of me.*

He listened when everyone replied, "Lord, by your cross and resurrection, you have set us free. You are the savior of the world."

At the altar railing, Hans and Aimée, leading a line of parishioners, knelt to receive the Holy Eucharist. One by one, Peter heard the priest mumble, "Corpus Christi." He briefly leaned forward behind the pew in front of him as Hans and Aimée returned to their seats. By the time it came for the last pews to come forward, Peter remained seated.

▪ ▪ ▪ ▪ ▪

Aimée and Hans stood for the Benediction. Father Feuille-rat turned to face the sanctuary and motioned everyone else to stand. He raised both arms, palms outward. When the prayer was completed, he stood before the newlyweds, motioned them to turn around and in a loud voice said, "It is my honor to be the first to introduce Monsieur and Madame Hans Krüger."

Aimée blushed when Hans kissed her again. Her father's enthusiasm incited everyone to clap along. She slipped her arm through her husband's elbow and drew it close, both smiling as they walked. She whispered the names of guests before passing their pews. Madame Dubois smiled when Hans waved as they passed.

At the last pew Aimée nearly tripped the instant Hans froze. She looked at her husband. "Hans darling, is everything alright?"

Elsie came from behind. Aimée could feel her mother's arm around her waist. "It's Peter. Papa thought he noticed him enter after the ceremony started." Aimée said nothing, instead inched closer to her husband, eyes wide. "At first I didn't believe it either," her mother added.

Aimée watched the expression on her husband's face turn from one of disbelief back to utter joy. She released his arm knowing what would follow.

"Peter!" Hans cried.

Both men, arms outstretched, embraced. They separated only to hug again and again and again.

author's note

Imagine—after five and a half years of war—the sense of impending doom felt by any German soldier in March of 1945. The Russians, driving relentlessly west toward Berlin, squeezed the Wehrmacht between the combined forces of the American, British, and French armies surging east. American General George Patton and British Field Marshal Bernard Montgomery both envisioned leading *their* troops into Berlin, victorious and forever claiming personal immortality. At the time of the Normandy invasion the preceding year, Eisenhower had declared Berlin as the "main prize." Churchill, for his part, stated, "I deem it highly important we should shake hands with the Russians as far east as possible."

Now imagine everyone's utter dismay when General Eisenhower commanded the Allies to halt their advance at the river Elbe, a tantalizing fifty miles west of Berlin. At the time Eisenhower gave three reasons for doing so: the Allies were well beyond the line of Western Occupation agreed to with the Soviets, decreased casualties, and Berlin—in his mind—was merely a political objective.

As a perpetual student of World War Two, I created the totally fictional explanation as to why Eisenhower halted the Allied advance at the Elbe. However, his driver, Kay Summersby, is not fictional. Admittedly, the extent of their relationship will, in all likelihood, never be known. Therefore, the unknown will forever be fertile ground for idle speculation.

Despite the fictional premise of *The Elbe Resolution*, all unit designations and locations, in so far as feasible, are accurate to time and place. U-357 was indeed sunk in the north Atlantic off the coast of Ireland on December 26, 1942 with eight survivors reported. The 3rd Panzer-Grenadier Division, after the Battle of the Bulge, fought to the end of the war and was ultimately captured in the Ruhr Pocket outside Iserlohn, Germany. The nineteen American-run Meadow Camps along the Rhine contained hundreds of thousands of Wehrmacht soldiers and an unknown number of civilians. The true extent of the privations these individuals suffered will never be know, nor will the exact cause and number of deaths.

As background resources, I consulted the following works:

Atkinson, Rick. *The Guns at Last Light*. New York, 2013.

Bacque, James. *Other Losses: The Shocking Truth Behind the Mass Deaths of Disarmed German Soldiers and Civilians Under General Eisenhower's Command*. New York, 1991.

Churchill, Winston. *His Complete Speeches: 1897-1963, 1943-1949, Vol. II*. New York, 1974.

Gannon, Michael. *Black May: The Epic Story of the Allies' Defeat of the German U-Boats in May 1943*. New York, 1998.

Gannon, Michael. *Operation Drumbeat: The Dramatic True Story of Germany's First U-Boat Attacks Along the American Coast in WW II*. New York, 1990.

http://www.uboatarchive.net/U-357INT.htm

Krammer, Arnold. *Prisoners of War: A Reference Handbook.* Connecticut, 2008.

Whiting, Charles. *Battle of the Ruhr Pocket.* New York, 1970.

acknowledgments

First, I thank those who willingly gave their time and provided input after reading *The Elbe Resolution*. They are—and in no particular order—Paul Veit, Linda Six, Pam Staniszewski, Norm Staniszewski, Bob Crow, Fran Crow, Meda Fulton, Sam Resnick, Dan Stutzman, Angie Atkins, and Denni Brown. Your enthusiasm, feedback, observations, and advice is truly appreciated. Rachel Rosenboom, thank you for sharing your wisdom so willingly.

Special thanks to Betsy Tice White for her continued editorial input.

Monsieur Raymond Dzieja, the former mayor of Sermaize-les-Bains, France, thank you for graciously providing me a pictorial and written history of Sermaize-les-Bains' l'eglise Notre-Dame de la Nativité—Our Lady of the Nativity.

Daniel J. Veit was an Iowa farmer and sergeant who served in the European Theater of Operations during World War II. His name is used in *The Elbe Resolution* with the blessings of his widow and brother.

And finally, I thank my wife, Gretchen, for her boundless love and companionship, her never ending encouragement, editing, reading, re-reading, re-re-reading, and honest opinions. It's been a journey worth taking with you at my side.

glossary

Battalion –Army grouping containing several hundred men.

Fräulein – German. Single girl.

Führer – German. Leader. Title Hitler gave himself.

G-2 – American military intelligence.

Geheime Staatspolizei – German secret police, commonly known as the Gestapo.

Gestapo – See above.

Glavnoye Razvedyvatel'noye Upravleniye – Russian secret police.

Gramophone – Electronic device for the playback of a recording disc, also known as a phonograph. Discs measured approximately 10 inches (25 centimeters) and at a speed of 78 rpm, allowed for approximately three minutes of music per side. Early usage of the term phonograph was reserved for cylinder recordings.

Grand-mère – French. Grandmother.

Grand-père – French. Grandfather.

Grenadier – German soldier.

Gymnasium – German school for secondary education.

Hauptmann – German rank equivalent to U.S. and British captain.

Jawohl – German. Yes or certainly.

Kilometer – Metric measurement of length. 1 kilometer = 0.62 miles.

Kriegslazarett – German. Field hospital.

Kriegsmarine – German. Navy.

Kristallnacht – Also known as Night of the Broken Glass. Anti-Semitic pogrom sparked by assassination of Ernst vom Rath, which led to the murder of nearly 1,000 Jews, the arrest of 25,000–30,000 Jews, and the destruction of 267 synagogues by the Hitler Youth, Gestapo, and SS on November 9–10, 1938.

Kübelwagen – Utility vehicle used by the German army, similar to the jeep used by the U.S. Army in World War Two. Identical to a vehicle produced in 1975 by the Volkswagen Corporation known as The Thing.

Leutnant – German rank equivalent to U.S. and British rank of 2nd lieutenant.

Luftwaffe – German air force in World War Two.

M. – French. Abbreviation for monsieur (see below). Equivalent to Mr.

Madame – French. Polite form of address for a married woman. Equivalent to Mrs.

Mademoiselle – French. Polite form of address for a young lady. Equivalent to Miss.

Mairie – French. Municipal office of the mayor or town hall.

Major – German military rank equivalent to U.S. and British major.

Maquis – French. Undergrowth. The term came to mean the French underground or armed resistance movement.

Maquisard – French. Member of the Maquis. Resistance fighter.

Matilda – English. Australian term (folklore) for bedroll or personal belongings.

Meter – Metric unit of length roughly equal to three feet.

Mme. – French. Abbreviation for Madame (see above). Equivalent to Mrs.

Monsieur – French. Polite form of address for a man. Equivalent to Mr.

Nazi – German political party led by Adolph Hitler. Active in Germany from 1919 to the end of World War Two.

NCO – Noncommissioned officer.

No Man's Land – Area between entrenched combatants in World War One.

Night of Broken Glass – Also known as Kristallnacht. Anti-Semitic pogrom sparked by assassination of Ernst vom Rath, which led to the murder of nearly 1,000 Jews, the arrest of 25,000–30,000 Jews, and the destruction of 267 synagogues by the Hitler Youth, Gestapo, and SS on November 9–10, 1938.

Obergrenadier – German rank equivalent to U.S. and British corporal.

Oberleutnant – German rank equivalent to U.S. and British 1st lieutenant.

Oberst – German rank equivalent to U.S. and British colonel.

Oberstleutnant – German rank equivalent to U.S. and British lieutenant colonel.

RAF – British Royal Air Force.

SS – German. Schutzstaffel. Originally founded as personal bodyguard corps for Hitler, the SS expanded to become the military police force of the Nazi Party. The SS ran the concentration camps and was notorious for ruthless behavior in World War Two. Also known as Waffen-SS.

Sten gun – Compact automatic weapon used by British para-troopers.

U-boat – German. Submarine.

Unteroffizier – German rank equivalent to U.S. and British rank of sergeant.

Waffen – Combat arm of the Nazi Party. Notorious for ruthless behavior in World War Two. Also know as Waffen-SS.

Wehrmacht – German. Army.

White Rose – Student resistance organization active in German during the war.

If You Loved

THE LEDGER

and

THE ELBE RESOLUTION

Don't Miss What Book Three Has In Store.

Turn the Page for a Preview …

chapter 1

New York City
Tuesday
September 15, 1953

BRIDGETTE JENKS' GAZE NEVER AVERTED UNLESS IT was for a good reason. It was imperative to scan the faces of the people as they paraded past. Each was studied—sometimes at length—until she concluded it was one she didn't recognize. In the eight years since the end of World War II, she'd never encountered the face she one day hoped to find.

As a group of New Yorkers prepared to surge across 5th Avenue, she ignored the incessant honking and edged closer to the curb to avoid being absorbed into the morning throng. Before the commuters could react to the halted traffic, she stepped down onto the street, side-stepped the rear bumper of a stopped car and quickened her pace across the wide intersection before continuing along West 34th Street.

Seventy-five feet in front of her, a cab pulled up next to the curb and a healthy appearing older gentleman emerged. He waved off the driver's attempt to give change with a curt gesture. Standing, he abruptly turned to his right and ducked as a delivery truck sputtered, then backfired—*BAM!*

"If I didn't know better, I would say that was a gun shot," said the man walking behind her to no one in particular. Several heads turned to the sound—except Bridgette who refused to be distract-ed by the noise. She remained fixated on the man twenty feet from the newspaper stand as he cut through the handful of pedestrians hailing a cab.

She wove across the crowded sidewalk to the newsstand. Her pulse raced and her breaths became shallow. Once under the canopy, she forced herself to inhale. Calmed, she pretended to be absorbed in a magazine article, and lingered.

And listened.

"So, my friend, what news do you have for me today?" she heard the man say.

"That McCarthy's something," the vendor said. "Times says he'll be investigating Commies in the UN."

"Yes, it's always something, is it not?"

"Yep. Wouldn't know one if I saw one, but to hear McCarthy talk, they're everywhere."

As the chitchat continued, Bridgette studied the features of the man. He was about fifty-five, sixty at the most. The more she inven-toried the features of his face, the more she was convinced. Yes, the angle of the nose is the same, and those high cheekbones. His gait. His gait's the same—purposeful and arrogant. It was an arrogance she remembered all too well. Not one hundred percent convinced, she edged a bit closer and looked up to the back of his hat. The hairline was precisely trimmed and minute flecks of dandruff had settled on his collar. She nodded. The height's right, too. Stepping away so as not to be noticed, Bridgette Jenks turned and flipped a page of the magazine as if she didn't have a care in the world.

The man, without looking around, paid for his newspaper. "Thanks Alfred. Perhaps I'll see you later."

"Root for them Yanks. Clinched the pennant last night, fifth in a row."

Her gaze followed as he melted into the crowd. She returned the magazine to the rack, picked up the morning edition of the

Herald Tribune, and handed the vendor a dime. "Excuse me sir, who was that man you were talking to just now?"

The vendor placed a nickel in her outstretched hand. "Him, the one with the German accent?"

chapter 2

HAROLD FABER LOOKED UP AT THE EMPIRE State Building to see the bottoms of gray clouds obscuring everything beyond the 30th floor. He hesitated in opening his umbrella, kept it closed and ducked into the newsstand just as the mist turned to rain. The vendor smiled his usual smile and said, "Think it'll quit before for the Series begins? My Yankees are chompin' at the bit to get them Dodgers."

"I've never been to a baseball match. Now boxing, that's another story."

The vendor smiled and shook his head from side to side as he took a coin from a passing pedestrian before handing off a paper. "Say, this morning, right after you left, a young lady stopped and was askin' after you."

Harold Faber forced himself to look interested in the headlines as he brought his hands together to view the next page. "Really? Any idea who she might be?"

"Nope, never seen her before. Surprised you didn't notice." He pointed and said, "She was standing right behind you. A real looker."

Faber aimlessly turned to the third page. "How old?"

"Hard to say. You know how women are these days. Thirty, maybe thirty-two."

"Did she say anything in particular?"

"Right after you left. She said, 'Excuse me sir, who was that man you were talking to just now,' or something like that."

"And what did you say?"

"I think I said, 'Him, the one with the German accent?'"

Faber diverted his eyes in the hope the vendor wouldn't see his dilated pupils.

"Didn't tell her your name. Come to think of it, I couldn't, don't even know it."

No, and you never will. "Alfred, this is very important. What *did* you tell her?"

"All I said was you worked around here somewhere. Didn't tell her where. Didn't tell her nothin'. No way."

"Now Alfred, no need to be sensitive. I'm not the least bit concerned. It's just that I dream one day I will find my wife, but I know that'll never happen." He settled his gaze onto the vendor. "What'd she look like? Would you recognize her if you saw her again?"

"You know I would. She's about five-five." Alfred raised his arm and held it out. "Came up to about your shoulder. Short curly hair. Brown. Like I said, a real looker. Beautiful eyes, brown too. Weighed maybe 'hundred and twenty, if that. Sharp, real sharp."

"Think now, was there an accent?"

"None."

"No German accent?"

"None. Not even a New York accent. Her speech was proper like, but no accent."

He tucked the folded newspaper under his arm. "Well, if you see her again, you must let me know."

"Will do. If she asks, you want me to tell her anything?"

"Uh, no. Nothing. Don't tell her anything."

▪　▪　▪　▪　▪

Harold Faber, instead of his usual strut, cautiously made his way east, along the buildings, avoiding contact with daily commuters.

Who was she? Probably nobody, but how can anyone not have an accent? Must be an American. If that's the case, it's nothing. Not convinced, he stayed to the right, frequently stopping to gaze into a storefront then steal a glance to his right, then another into the reflection of across the street.

Assured no one was following, he continued. His last conversation with Achim came to mind. The one just before he moved to New York, when he was given the address. 'Do not—I repeat—do not under any circumstances write to me unless you are absolutely certain your identity has been compromised. If you must write, address the letter to Herr Frank Müeller. Do not refer to my name and use only the code we supplied you with.'

Before he slipped down the stairs into the Lexington Ave subway, he wondered if Karl Beck would ever be totally be forgotten. At the bottom of the stairs he looked up over his shoulder one more time.

Who was she?